ALSO BY LISH MCBRIDE

Curses

THE NECROMANCER SERIES

Hold Me Closer, Necromancer
Necromancing the Stone

THE FIREBUG SERIES

Firebug
Pyromantic

RED

* IN *

TOOTH

* AND *

CLAW

RED
* IN *
# TOOTH
* AND *
# CLAW

LISH MCBRIDE

putnam

G. P. Putnam's Sons

G. P. PUTNAM'S SONS
An imprint of Penguin Random House LLC, New York

First published in the United States of America by G. P. Putnam's Sons,
an imprint of Penguin Random House LLC, 2024

G. P. Putnam's Sons is a registered trademark of Penguin Random House LLC.
The Penguin colophon is a registered trademark of Penguin Books Limited.

Visit us online at PenguinRandomHouse.com.

Library of Congress Cataloging-in-Publication Data
Names: McBride, Lish, author.
Title: Red in tooth and claw / Lish McBride.
Description: New York: G. P. Putnam's Sons, 2024. | Summary:
Now orphaned, sixteen-year-old Faolan, who has been disguised as a boy
by her grandfather for most of her life, is deemed unfit to stay on her homestead,
so the mayor hires a gunslinger to send her to the mysterious Settlement,
where ominous secrets and deadly creatures compel her to escape for survival.
Identifiers: LCCN 2024004195 (print) | LCCN 2024004196 (ebook) |
ISBN 9781984815620 (hardcover) | ISBN 9781984815637 (epub)
Subjects: CYAC: Passing (Identity)—Fiction. | Disguise—Fiction. |
Mystery and detective stories. | Fantasy. | LCGFT: Thrillers (Fiction) |
Detective and mystery fiction. | Fantasy fiction. | Novels.
Classification: LCC PZ7.M478267 Re 2024 (print) |
LCC PZ7.M478267 (ebook) | DDC [Fic]—dc23
LC record available at https://lccn.loc.gov/2024004195
LC ebook record available at https://lccn.loc.gov/2024004196

ISBN 9781984815620

1 3 5 7 9 10 8 6 4 2
1st Printing

Printed in the United States of America

LSCH

Design by Kathryn Li
Text set in TT Livret Text

To Pops, who never got to hold one of my books in his hands but is slightly responsible for this one because of all the Westerns he made me watch as a kid.

And to Gertie, who frankly deserved better.
#JusticeForGertie

Who trusted God was love indeed
And love Creation's final law—
Tho' Nature, red in tooth and claw
With ravine, shriek'd against his creed—

Who loved, who suffer'd countless ills,
Who battled for the True, the Just,
Be blown about the desert dust,
Or seal'd within the iron hills?

No more? A monster then, a dream,
A discord. Dragons of the prime,
That tare each other in their slime,
Were mellow music match'd with him.

O life as futile, then, as frail!
O for thy voice to soothe and bless!
What hope of answer, or redress?
Behind the veil, behind the veil.

—"IN MEMORIAM A. H. H."
BY ALFRED, LORD TENNYSON, 1850

CHAPTER ONE

—✳—

MY BATTERED POCKET WATCH WAS AS DEAD AS THE BODY in the coffin, but that didn't stop me from keeping it in a white-knuckled grip. After all, it was the only thing I could hold on to. I couldn't hold on to Pops. All I could do was eye my grandfather's coffin and tell him how sorry I was about the wretched farce of a funeral we'd just left. Pops *hated* funerals.

But he loved a good wake.

Funerals were for wailing. Wakes were for celebrating and toasting a life where you'd savored every bite. My people loved a good wake. Pops said that the old gods, they were much more understanding about these sorts of things. New Retienne liked the new god, and the new god liked proper funerals.

I'd never set foot in New Retienne's graveyard until today. Pops and I only came into town every three weeks for supplies—four if we could stretch it. The ramshackle church behind us blocked the bite of the winter wind some, but not completely. Far as I could tell, that was all it was good for.

"You ready, young Kelly?" the preacher asked, not unkindly,

but also like maybe he wanted away from the cold and back to his warm fire.

No. I was not ready. "Yes, sir."

He nodded, taking out his holy book. Pops didn't belong to the Shining God, like this preacher did, but I reckoned Pops wouldn't care, so I wasn't going to fuss. I ignored the preacher's warbly voice, my mind whited out with grief, as I stared over the rustling treetops.

Strange that I couldn't feel the bitter wind at all myself. But then I had my own windbreak—Eustace Clarke, the honorable mayor of New Retienne; his second-in-command, a lawyer named Finchly; and the sheriff, John Bascom. They were fencing me in, and I quashed the urge to fidget.

The mayor was an interesting-looking fella. New Retienne might have been a small town, but it had a circulating library sandwiched between Ms. Lillibet's brothel and the Crooked Donkey, our sorry excuse for a saloon. We likely wouldn't have had a library at all if Ms. Lillibet herself hadn't been fond of books. The circulating library had a natural history book on display, the illustrator indifferent at best. I'd never seen a walrus, only the fella depicted in that book, but if I'd added a waxed mustache and an overly embroidered waistcoat onto that creature, it would have been the spittin' image of our Mr. Clarke.

The mayor rested a heavy hand on my shoulder, leaning in to whisper so as not to interrupt the preacher. "He's in a better place."

I disagreed but bit my tongue.

Finchly hummed an agreement. He was a handsome older man, I suppose, but he had big, blocky teeth I didn't like the look of. Sheriff Bascom shifted at my right, smelling of cologne with a hint of old bacon fat—not quite rancid but flirtin' with the idea. All three of them loomed like scarecrows around me.

A few other townsfolk stood at the graveside along with the preacher. I recognized each of them, except for a lady standing a ways back from the group, sniffing as she brought up a lacy handkerchief to dab at her eyes. She was dressed plainly, but that only seemed to frame her beauty more strongly. She kept sending me sympathetic smiles. I kept ignoring them.

The preacher smiled at Mr. Clarke, his glasses slipping down his nose. "The Shining God takes, but he also gives. Your loved one is gone—"

"But the community comes together to support you in your time of need," Mr. Clarke said, stealing the words from the preacher's mouth.

I could almost hear Pops's snort. *Nobody can unload verbal pucky like a bureaucrat. They'll leave you knee-deep in it, Faolan, you mark my words. Best get your shovel ready.*

My grandfather had been a simple man. Didn't mean he was wrong.

And now he was dead.

They were all dead.

I didn't remember my parents much, and what I did remember, I didn't mourn. That might be on me. Some people had a knack for mourning, and despite all my practice, I didn't appear to be one of them. I did miss my grandmother. She'd hummed while she baked and said a bushel of wildflowers on the table reminded her of warm summer days in tall grass. She beat everyone at dominoes, couldn't shoot a pistol for squat, but could nail a grouse forty yards away with her eyes shut using her crossbow.

Every word from the preacher made me feel like I was filling up with sand. I wanted to bolt from the graveside like a rabbit legging it to the safety of the underbrush.

But I couldn't.

Standing graveside in a suit too big for my frame, I knew I was a pitiful representation of the Kellys. The suit itched something fierce, too, and I was sweating despite the cold. Still, I kept my chin high, wanting to do Pops proud. The mayor patted dry eyes at my side while Finchly and Bascom flanked us, stone-faced.

A tidy trap if ever I saw one.

The preacher seemed like a decent fella, but for how little he knew my Pops, he sure found a lot to say. Since I wasn't about to step foot in his church again, I had no issue with ignoring him. Pops thought life was complicated enough without adding churching on top of things, and I can't say I've strayed far from his thinking on the subject.

I could almost hear the deep singsong of his voice. *I miss the old gods, Faolan. They were distant, like mountains. Give them a bit of music and dance on feast days, and they left you well enough alone. They didn't need us nattering their ears off, and we didn't need them up in our daily business.*

Today there had been an abundance of nattering. When

4

the preacher hadn't been flapping his gums, there was music, and I use the word generously. The only good thing about it was the out-of-tune piano almost drowned out the singing. Almost.

I would have liked to play some fiddle for Pops. One of his favorite songs, like when we'd sit beside the fire in the cold months offering up a bit of song to the gods of the lands he was from. The gods that weren't welcome here. I wasn't sure they could hear a single note, but he'd loved to hear me play, and that was what mattered.

But I'd had to sell my fiddle to pay for the doctor.

Pops would have hated that most of all.

It had been a shock this morning, seeing his still frame in a wooden box. Death gave his face a softness it hadn't had in life. Made him look a stranger.

I gripped his battered pocket watch in my palm—now mine—the entire ceremony, just to remind myself of the truth.

He was gone, and I was alone.

I hadn't wanted my grandfather put to earth in the burial grounds of the new church. My grandmother had been buried on our land—I'd wanted the same for Pops, but no one had listened. I had no money, and until my grandfather's lands were settled on me, my words only had the force of my own breath. The mayor and his people spoke a different tongue, of power and wealth, and I wasn't fluent. I decided to choose my battles until I mastered their way of speaking. My grandfather wouldn't give two beans where we laid his carcass, anyhow.

"May he find solace in the arms of the Shining God," the

preacher intoned. There was a rustling as a few men came forward, the service finally done.

The ground was cold but no longer frozen, winter almost giving way to spring. I grabbed a shovel, tossing the upturned earth next to the grave onto the coffin. It thudded against the wood, and I said a silent goodbye to the best man I'd known.

I had assumed that I would do my fair share of the shoveling, but the mayor and his cronies were impatient, and before the coffin was fully covered, I was pressed into the mayor's buggy and shuffled into his stuffy parlor. Mr. Clarke and Finchly sat across from me while Bascom leaned against the wall, the air still except for the ticking of the grandfather clock in the hall.

Mrs. Clarke seemed to haunt her own home. She'd appeared in the parlor only to wordlessly place a hot mug of dandelion tea into my hand before disappearing back into her kitchen. I didn't care for the stuff, but I held on to the mug anyway. The room had a feminine touch to it, or at least the kind of feminine the mayor would accept—doilies on the small table to my left, stitched samplers on the wall—the furniture redolent with beeswax. The stiff settee I was perched on was covered in a print of large flowers.

I'd been raised better than to spit on someone's floor, but let me tell you, it was a close thing. This was a floor made to be spit on, if only because it was Mr. Clarke's.

I missed my threadbare hearth rug, the quilt my grandmother had made folded neatly in her old wooden rocking chair, the one that squeaked. I was suddenly desperate for it.

I set down my tea, harder than I meant, the noise startling in the room.

The mayor braided his fingers over his rounded belly. "Now, Mr. Kelly, we're in a bit of a pickle."

I turned my eyes on him, unblinking. He didn't like it. Most didn't. My eyes were a very pale gray, giving them a ghostly look. It bothered some folks. Don't ask me why. They're just eyes.

Mr. Clarke's tongue flicked out, lizard-like against his lips, half hidden by his abundant mustache. "The thing is, you've got little in the way of kin, and you're not of age yet yourself."

"I have nothing in the way of kin," I said, "and I'll be eighteen in a few months."

"Eight is hardly a few." The mayor's mustaches twitched as he talked. "And according to Ms. Regina, you've got an aunt. Madigan Kelly."

Ms. Regina was the local midwife. She kept track of such things. Still. "Mayor—"

"Please," he said, flashing crooked teeth. "Call me Mr. Clarke."

I could hardly see how that was any better, but I was smart enough to give him the concession. "Mr. Clarke, I don't wish to argue with Ms. Regina, but if I have an aunt, that's news to me."

Finchly clucked in sympathy. Mr. Clarke's brow knotted in concern, his mouth turning down, but I caught his eyes. They had the look of a hen sitting on her nest—roosting and pleased with herself. "Well, Mr. Kelly, then, like I said, we've got ourselves a right pickle. Wouldn't be neighborly, leaving you alone on your grandfather's land, rest his soul." Finchly and Bascom made noises of affirmation. I had yet to hear them say anything with actual meaning.

I wished I'd kept the tea in my hands so I could slam the mug down again. "Speak plainly, sir, for I've no patience left in me."

His gaze narrowed. The hen was gone, replaced by the stoat, ready to filch the eggs from the nest. "A young man such as yourself can't be left with such overwhelming responsibilities. Why, it's not suitable." He placed a hand across his chest. "How would we sleep at night?"

Just fine, by my reckoning. And I could handle enough of my grandfather's choring to get by. I'd been doing my share of the work for years.

"Now, Madigan Kelly may be only a woman, but she's of age at least." The pale hands on his belly twitched. "I'm sure we can convince her to do what's right by New Retienne. By you." He tacked on the last bit, a clear afterthought. "We need time to find her, is all."

I didn't like where this line of discussion was headed one bit. "What does that mean, 'to do what's right'?"

"Well, that's New Retienne land—that's your land. It should have one of our people on it. I'm sure your aunt's husband would be keen on our ways. Who wouldn't want to settle down on such fine acreage?"

An image of Pops winking at me as he hid the deed to our land away surfaced in my brain. I had no doubt that if my grandfather had left the deed with the bank, the mayor would have it in his sticky fingers already. Even now, Pops was looking out for me.

Mr. Clarke's expression became decidedly smug. "And if your aunt's not married or a widow, well, we have many fine, upstanding gentlemen around these parts." He shook his head, the smug expression shifting into one of almost comical sorrow. "I think we can all agree that it wouldn't be proper, leaving a young man of your tender years out on that homestead all on your own."

Ghostly fingers ran down my spine, chilling me. If the mayor dismissed my supposed aunt so easily, how would he feel about me if he knew the truth? How quickly would I be marched into the New Retienne church and down the aisle to hand all my worldly possessions over to a fine, upstanding gentleman of the mayor's choice?

I crossed my arms over my chest, grateful for my too-big suit. My voice came out soft as down feathers. "What would help you sleep at night, Mr. Clarke?"

"Normally, in a case like this," Mr. Clarke hedged, "we'd send you to a charitable neighbor."

Charity. Free labor, more like. I snorted before I could stop myself. I would spend the next eight months milking other people's goats and cows, cleaning chicken coops, digging privies, hauling wood, and doing any other unfavorable job. If I was lucky, I would get to sleep in a hayloft. To be honest, I would prefer that or sleeping under the stars, despite the chill temperatures. You sleep in someone else's house, you better trust that person an awful lot. A house could be a trap just as easily as it could be a home.

I bit my tongue. Pops always said I had a smart mouth.

Sometimes I was even smart enough to keep it shut.

Mr. Clarke sighed. "In this case, no one had room."

Ah. Now I was catching on. People in these parts didn't like the look of the Kellys—it's the red hair, I reckon. Folks get superstitious about it, like we're changelings or the spit of evil spirits. You can try to tell them it's just hair, but they won't listen.

Stubborn as mules and half as useful, some people. That's what Pops used to say.

Though I'd left it off for the funeral, usually I wore a low-crowned hat with a wide, flat brim, as it covered my hair, which I kept short. Even better, the hat shaded my eyes. Red hair made most people frown. One look at my eyes and they ran their fingers over their heart, like tracing a rainbow. It was supposed to ward off evil. It did precious little to me except tell me we wouldn't be friends. It was a handy shortcut, to be honest, and a nice way to weed out the ignorant.

And there sure was a lot of ignorant going around.

With no family forthcoming, and my looks in mind, I was officially more trouble than I was worth. "Well, I'd hate to cause my neighbors any bother. What say we tell them we tried, and we all go about our business?"

Mr. Clarke was shaking his head, those clasped hands back on his belly. "Now, Mr. Faolan, that will not do." He smiled. I wiped my sweaty palms onto my suit trousers. I didn't like that smile. It widened, like he could smell my fear and it made him happy. "As it happens, we've made other arrangements. Isn't that right, Miss Honeywell?"

The stranger from the funeral breezed in then, her dress rustling softly as she moved. Everything about her was round and soft, pretty in a dewy sort of way. She had the biggest, bluest eyes I'd ever seen, which she kept wide before batting them at the mayor, making him flush from the neck up. She smiled demurely at him, her cheeks dimpling before she turned her gaze on me.

It has always been my thinking that while words and smiles lie easily, eyes do not. For all her sweet dimples and delicate features, those big blue eyes reminded me of frozen river water, straight out of the mountain. Still, when she sat beside me on the settee and started tutting over me like a motherly hen, I will admit I wallowed in her attention for a moment. It was a weakness I could not indulge overmuch, for I knew that not a single soul in this room had my best interests at heart.

"Why, it's a pleasure to meet you, Mr. Kelly, despite the unfortunate circumstances. I'm Miss Nettie Honeywell, and I hope you don't mind, but your esteemed Mr. Clarke has told me all about your situation." Miss Honeywell placed one delicate hand over her bosom. "And my heart just went right on out to you, my lost little lamb." Tears welled in her eyes, making them appear even larger. Both the mayor and his two cronies immediately produced hankies, jabbing them at her like the first one would get a prize.

"Why, thank you. How thoughtful." She plucked Bascom's hanky and dabbed her eyes. "As soon as your beloved grandfather passed from this mortal plane, these fine gentlemen reached out and told me of your plight. I came as soon as I could."

I picked up the mug again and sipped my tea, turning my ghost eyes on the pack of vultures masquerading as upstanding citizens. My Pops hadn't been dead a week and I'd never laid eyes on Miss Honeywell before today, so she wasn't local. They must have sent a fast rider to wherever she was the instant they heard the news. The question was, what did they want?

"How kind," I murmured. See? I had manners. Rusty and ill-used, but I had them. "Did you have to travel far?"

She waved off my question. "What's a little travel to help those in need?" She folded her hands in her lap. "And you are in need, my lost lamb. But on this day of sadness, there is a blessing."

If there was a blessing, I was hard-pressed to see it.

"Miss Honeywell is from the Settlement," Mr. Clarke said when it was clear I wasn't responding anytime soon. "They're in that fort west of here, about a day's ride, up by the river. They have a place for you there."

I frowned at the mayor, sure I hadn't heard right. "I thought the fort was empty." That fort had such rotten luck, Pops thought the land itself might be cursed. The group who built it died of a pox. The next group barely survived a cold winter season, and abandoned it. For the life of me, I couldn't recollect what happened to any of the settlers after that. All this had occurred either before I was born or soon after.

Miss Honeywell smiled at me, an expression of rapture on her face. "Oh, I've heard the stories, but you'd never know it to look at the place now. Not since His Benevolence Gideon

Dillard took on the fort two years ago." She leaned in, her voice soft and earnest, like she was telling me a secret. "HisBen Dillard saw the fort and just knew it was for us—that the Shining God would look down on us in favor, and He has."

She took my rough hand in her soft one. "We've known nothing but abundance and good fortune in the Settlement, Mr. Kelly. All His Benevolence wants to do is share our good fortune with those in need, as the Shining God teaches."

It was a honey wine kind of tale, too good to be true, and I wanted none of it. I wanted my hearth, my fire, my fiddle.

She squeezed my hand. "You're found now, my little lamb."

Mr. Clarke lifted his chin, his thumbs tucked under his arms like a mayoral chicken about to flap his wings and convince everyone he could fly. "The Settlement is a fine place, a *fine place*. They will aid you in your time of need."

I looked about the room, at all the smiling faces, and could feel the trap springing shut. My stomach felt heavy with dread because I didn't think there was a thing I could do about it. "What about Pops's land? The animals?" There weren't many left except my goat, Gertie, and a handful of chickens. I'd had to sell the rest.

"The animals will go to the Settlement," Mr. Clarke said. "As for the land, we'll hold it in trust until we sort out the question of your kin." He licked his lips then, his eyes shiny. "Do you happen to know where your grandfather put the land deed, Mr. Kelly? Just in case, you understand."

I knew exactly where it was. "No, sir. Have you checked the bank?" Pops didn't care for banks. That would have been the last place he put it.

Mr. Clarke tried to hide his disappointment. "Ah, well. I'm sure it will turn up."

I was positive it wouldn't, but I smiled at him anyway.

Miss Honeywell took her leave after that—she would be going back to the Settlement today, whereas I had to tie up my affairs first. Mr. Clarke saw her to the door, leaving me in the care of his two silent cronies, Finchly and Bascom. Not wanting to sit there drinking unwanted tea, I excused myself to the privy. The mayor had an indoor one, and the hallway leading to it took me close to the front door. I snuck to the end of the hallway, stopping just short of the intersection.

Eavesdropping, I was once told by a cantankerous old biddy in town, was for naughty children who were in want of a good hiding. I'm of the mind that if you say a thing out loud, it's not my fault if I overhear it. If a body wanted to keep something secret, they should work on their cunning. I mean, how else was I supposed to find anything out?

I heard the murmur of voices but couldn't quite make out everything they were saying. Frustrated, I peeked around the corner. Mr. Clarke stood close to Miss Honeywell, his voice pitched so low I could only hear the tones. He drew two silvers out of his pocket, depositing the coins into Miss Honeywell's delicate hands. She smiled, flashing him her dimples, before he bowed over the top of her hand in farewell.

I dipped back behind the corner before either of them looked my way. That was an awful lot of coin for Mr. Clarke to be handing out, and I had to wonder not only where the money was coming from, but what it was for. The exchange rattled me, leaving me as uneasy as a pullet in a snake pit.

I decided it didn't matter. Whatever anyone else's plans might be, to my mind, the Settlement was a temporary stop on the way back to my home. That's all there was to it.

—✳—

After my trip to the privy, I was escorted to my grandfather's cabin to pack my things. It was difficult to be in the cabin without Pops there. The space was nothing as grand as the mayor's, but it was more than many had. The front door opened up into the parlor, which held a stone fireplace and two well-worn rocking chairs. A small table still held Pops's pipe and half-empty bag of tobacco, the sweet, earthy smell of the leaves making my throat tight. I could see the spot on the mantel where our clock had been, another sacrifice to Pops's doctor, leaving the oil lamp perched there looking mighty lonely.

From the parlor, there was a doorway leading into the kitchen and pantry space, as well as the small bedroom I'd lived in. Upstairs there were two bedrooms and another closet, which was where I needed to go, but I couldn't have the mayor dogging my heels the entire time.

Mr. Clarke was eyeing Pops's writing desk, no doubt wanting to get his itchy fingers on the land deed. Bascom and Finchly had stayed out on the front porch, so it was only me and Mr. Clarke in the cabin. I had the sense they were looking around, perhaps poking their heads into the barn to see what we had.

The way the mayor's hungry eyes were eating up the room, I knew leaving the land deed behind, even hidden as it was, would be a mistake. I would have to take a chance, and I reckoned a few stolen moments alone with my grandfather's desk would tempt him sorely.

"I need to go get Pops's suitcase," I said, letting my eyes drift over to the desk, my expression troubled. I dropped my voice into a ragged tone. "I'd like a moment to say goodbye, you understand."

Mr. Clarke patted my shoulder awkwardly. "Of course, son." He dipped his hand into his pocket, bringing out a fine gold pocket watch. He made a production of checking it. "You go on ahead. We have a little time yet."

I forced out a "Thank you, sir" and kept my feet heavy as I went up the stairs. As soon as I was out of sight, I hustled along, fetching a worn leather suitcase out of the closet. I tiptoed into my grandfather's room, being careful to open and close the door quietly. The tobacco, leather, and soap smell of my grandfather was still strong, the scent causing a wave of grief to hit me so soundly all I could do was close my eyes and take it. I swallowed hard, scrubbing at my face with my jacket sleeve. No time for weeping, not now.

I flung the suitcase up onto the bed and hurried over to Pops's chest of drawers. Being careful to stay quiet, I eased the top one out, sliding my hand back into the space behind the drawer, feeling for the small piece of paper I knew was back there. For a few gut-clenching moments, my fingers met only wood. And then I found it, relief washing through me.

The land deed didn't look like much, only a hair bigger than my handspan if I set my fingers wide. Small, unassuming, yet a mighty powerful scrap of paper.

If you looked at a map around New Retienne, it looked like a patchwork quilt sewed by someone who couldn't cut a straight line. New Retienne and a few smaller holdings were sprinkled in among the very few pieces of land people had managed to purchase. Mostly, folks had to lease their lands from the various tribes, depending on where the land fell. Pops told me that a few early settlers had tried to take land by force. It went poorly, and folk had learned to deal square or take themselves to other pastures. This land and its people didn't take kindly to those who didn't treat it fairly. I respected that.

My grandfather had been a stranger here when he came over by boat, my father a babe in arms, and managed a third route—he married a young widow with her own small parcel of acreage and made a go of it.

The deed in my hand was near priceless. What *wouldn't* Mr. Clarke do to get his greasy fingers on it? I undid the buckles on the leather suitcase, popping it open, then thought better of it. Suitcases were easily searched or taken. I needed to be able to keep the precious deed on my person. Pops had been a canny fella and slow to trust. There was nothing he loved more than a good hiding spot. Which was why Pops's watch had a secret compartment.

I smoothed one finger gently along the edge of the back of the silver watch, feeling for the catch. When I found it, the back lid popped open, revealing a snug carry space. I tucked the folded-up deed into it and popped it closed before stashing it away in the inside pocket of my suit jacket.

I made sure I made a racket when I came down the stairs.

Mr. Clarke was as far as could be from the desk when I reached the bottom. I nodded at him before lugging my suitcase back to my room. Since I wasn't sure when I was returning, I packed several changes of clothing, my comb, tooth powder, and a small mirror. I had my grandfather's old deerskin bullet bag, which I used to carry my hunting knife, my few spare coins, and the other kinds of odds and ends one liked to carry about their person.

I stripped out of my suit to put on clothing more suitable for daily wear—trousers, linen shirt, suspenders. I was grateful that I didn't have to wear what other young women my age had to wear in New Retienne, which seemed cumbersome to me. Keeping an ear tuned for anyone approaching, I wrapped up my grandfather's watch and wedged it into the toe of my boot, grateful for once that they were a sight too large for my feet.

When I was all packed, I was herded unceremoniously into the back of a donkey cart alongside a wicker basket carrying the three egg-laying hens we had left and my brown-haired goat, Gertie. Gertie was unsure about the endeavor as a whole, bleating at me uncertainly as she was tied to the back of the cart, and I had never felt such a kinship with a goat until that moment.

Mr. Clarke, however, appeared right pleased with the development. "Mr. Cartwright here will get you where you need going." His eyes twinkled. "You're lucky—we managed to rustle up a gunslinger for your travels." He waved a hand like a proud papa at the man sitting next to the driver. "Bandits, you know."

Bandits. Right. A keeper, more like.

The driver, Mr. Cartwright, was skinny, all rawhide and bones, with suntanned skin and fat black muttonchops on his cheeks. Broken veins traced his nose and cheeks like a map of wandering creeks. "You sit in the back. Be careful of my cargo. You damage anything, you're paying for it." He didn't look away from his donkeys as he said this.

The gunslinger was taller by inches, wider by several more, but leanly muscled. His skin was a deep brown with an undertone of bronze, the hair in his beard just starting to go a little gray, though he didn't look much over thirty. He was dressed finer than Cartwright but not fussy like Mr. Clarke. Brown trousers, sturdy leather boots, and a good black jacket that were simple, but well made and well maintained. He wore a hat like mine—wide-brimmed but in a newer style, with a higher crown. I thought it mighty fine myself and more dashing than the bowler hat on Cartwright. He ambled over to me, and his coat flared, revealing a pistol on each hip, resting in a worn leather holster.

I squinted at him. "Am I just supposed to call you Gunslinger, then?"

"Either that or Mr. Speed." He held out a hand, sizing me up.

I shook it, sizing him up as well.

He sighed, his brow furrowing. "You going to give me any trouble?"

"No, sir," I said, releasing his hand and putting mine over my heart. "You won't hear a peep out of me."

He snorted. "That's what I thought."

Mr. Clarke puffed out his chest. "Be assured, Mr. Kelly, us here in New Retienne won't rest until we find your next of kin. In the meantime, you'll be taken care of."

"I'm sure I will," I said, baring my teeth. He could call it a smile if he wanted.

And with that dubious goodbye, the cart lurched forward. The mayor and his cronies shuffled into their buggy, but I paid them no mind. My eyes were on my grandfather's cabin, the only home I'd known, as it faded into the distance.

I hadn't spent much time in New Retienne, the closest town to my grandfather's meager lands at five miles distant, and when we did, we weren't so high in the instep that we rubbed elbows with folks like the mayor. But I knew, sure as spring brings new lambs, that they'd only do as little looking as they could so as not to draw suspicion. Madigan Kelly, if she existed, would not be found.

They'd look for the land deed, but nothing else. Try as I might, I couldn't see anyone in the town sticking their scrawny necks out for me. I didn't blame the town for that choice, nor did I lose any respect for them. You have to have respect before you can lose it, and the people of New Retienne had none of mine.

I reckoned I couldn't assign much blame. It had been a long, hard winter and no one wanted an extra mouth to feed, especially not mine. Well, I didn't want them either, though no one had asked.

I shifted in the donkey cart and wished a plague upon the whole town. The cart was full of bags of potatoes or turnips.

Even if I'd wanted to sit on them, which I didn't, Cartwright would have pitched a fit. I perched on my suitcase instead, listening to the cluck of the chickens and watching Gertie trailing behind us to make sure she wasn't chewing on her lead rope.

Mr. Cartwright had an intricately carved pipe clamped in his teeth, grumbling around it at the donkeys. The only poetry about this man was that dratted pipe.

About the Settlement, I knew precious little—I'd never gone past New Retienne before. So I was keeping my eye on landmarks and marking the time by wagon. Miss Honeywell had said it was a day's ride, but a donkey cart was a lot slower than a horse and rider.

Mr. Cartwright stopped jawin' at his donkeys, and I took an opportunity to question the gunslinger. "You ever been to the Settlement?"

He grunted, "No."

He thought one-word answers were going to deter me. Pops must be cackling in his grave. I was a dog with a bone when I wanted something. "You must know something." When in doubt, flatter a little. "Surely a man such as yourself wouldn't go into a situation not knowing *something*."

He grunted again, but this one sounded amused. "I've heard a thing or two."

I waited. Nothing. "And?"

He glanced back at me. "Hearing isn't knowing."

I wasn't learning anything, but I had pried more words out of him. "It can't be a hospitable place," I ventured.

"Good enough for the likes of you," Cartwright said.

"All I'm saying is that everything else there has failed." And it sounded *charitable*, which, when used by a man such as Mr. Clarke, meant giving a pittance to make yourself feel better. I imagined rough blankets, dirt floors, watery gruel once a day.

The gunslinger grunted again, somehow making it sound dismissive. I'd never known a fella who could express so much with so little.

"They probably have rats," I said, "and beds full of fleas." No response. "Ticks the size of houses."

"You ever shut your yappin'?" Cartwright asked, his words garbled around the pipe tight in his teeth.

"Not when I got something to say," I shot back. Cartwright would be no help, I knew that, but the gunslinger knew something, I could tell. If my mental map was accurate, Settlement land was in Rover territory. I quite liked the Rovers. They had a bendy way of thinking that I appreciated, and they took care of their kin. A Rover kid never went hungry, even if their close kin were gone.

Not a single one of my neighbors in New Retienne had checked on me but the mayor, and look where that had landed me.

"Do folk at the Settlement deal with the Rovers much?" I asked in an offhand manner.

"Don't know," the gunslinger said, not in a way that ended the conversation, such as it was, but in a way that said, *Wouldn't that be interesting?*

"What about—"

Cartwright cut me off with an irritated growl. "Bite your tongue, or I'll gag you with one of my socks." He would do it, too. I could hear it in his tone. "You'll have plenty of time to find out about the Settlement when you get there, now won't you?" he said nastily, chortling around his pipe.

Eight months was a perishingly long time, and for a second, I broke out into a sweat. I took a shaky breath, calming myself. I'd get out if I needed to. I would find a way.

But I'd keep my mouth shut for the time being. The cart was slow, but Cartwright could always make me walk.

Cartwright tugged up on the reins, pulling the donkeys to a halt. "If you need a piss, now's the time."

The gunslinger kept a sharp eye on me as I climbed out of the wagon, mind working frantically. I couldn't exactly take out my piece and make water next to him and Cartwright. Couldn't hold it, either. I paused to scratch Gertie's chin as I thought.

The gunslinger put his hands on his hips. "You going to go, or you going to scratch that goat?"

"Surely both." I grimaced, holding my gut. "That dandelion tea. Runs right through a fella."

The gunslinger ran a hand over his face before looking around us. He pointed at a clump of bushes. "Go on, then. And, Faolan?"

"Yessir?"

"Don't make me shoot you this early in the trip."

I pinched the edge of my hat, giving it a little tug down, before rushing to the bushes.

We were starting to lose light and looking for a good place to stop and bed down. That's when we saw the wagon. Or what was left of it.

From where I was perched on my suitcase, I could see a small, pale hand stuck out of the back, some of the fingers nothing but bones. Acid burned the back of my throat and I swallowed hard.

The wagon had been stripped, anything useful taken. With the bodies there, it was not far from grave robbing in my mind, but again, it had been a hard winter.

The gunslinger hopped off his seat at the front to go check it out, and I followed. No matter what was in that wagon, it would be better for me to see it and know than not see it and imagine. My mind could spin horrors with little provocation.

Cartwright stayed on the cart, a shotgun in his hands. "It's not a plague, is it?" He craned his neck, straining to see. "A pox?" Sweat beaded on his forehead, and his voice squeaked. "A bear or a mountain lion?"

Mr. Speed and I ignored Cartwright as we peered into the wagon. Inside the worn canvas, bundled into blankets, were the remains of a family—a woman, a young boy, a little girl. It was the mother's hand I'd seen. The gunslinger frowned, dipping around the side and dropping down on his haunches in the long grass.

I mimicked him so I could get a good look at the last body. A man, probably the father, his flannel shirt torn at the belly, his eyes gone. A wave of sadness crashed through me, filled with echoes of my own grief. I let it flow away, back out into the world. I wouldn't cry on the roadside in front of the likes of Cartwright.

I nodded at the man. "Mountain lion?"

The gunslinger scowled down at the body before he shook his head. "Something got at him, probably drug him from the wagon, but it was after he was dead, I think. An opportunistic feeding, not a killing."

"How can you tell?"

"Very little blood around the wound. We stop bleeding after we die." He said the words absently, his mind elsewhere. He motioned to the man's face. "See the purple tint to his skin?"

I nodded.

"I think they froze to death. Happens sometimes. Folks think winter's gone, get desperate, and head out, only to get caught in a temperature drop."

Behind us, Cartwright made an impatient noise.

"We going to bury them?" I asked. Didn't seem right, leaving them as they were.

"No shovels," the gunslinger said. "But I reckon that canvas will burn just fine. Come on."

He stood up, and I helped him put the man back with his family. Cartwright fussed, but the gunslinger hushed him with a look as we dealt with the bodies. Before too long, we were on our way again. I watched the wagon burn as we clip-clopped down the road.

We should have been building camp, but none of us wanted to stay near the funeral pyre, so we kept on for a while yet.

I'd been considering sneaking away when we made camp

and heading for home on my own two feet. I put that thought aside for now. I could see, too easy, how it might be me someone found on the roadside, mouth open, eyes gone, screaming my way to the quiet fields and into the arms of whatever god would take me.

CHAPTER TWO

—✳—

THE SUN WAS RIDING LOW ON THE SECOND DAY WHEN
we made it to the Settlement. I will be honest here if nowhere
else—the sight sent a chill through my gizzards. I'd never
seen the like. The palisade walls were tall and hewn together
from entire logs, the tops carved to points, the bottoms buried within the earth.

I was a good climber, but those walls were beyond my
expertise. The palisades went on for ages, broken only in the
center by an intimidating door the size of several donkey
carts. On a few of the logs we passed I could see long furrows
cut into the wood. They reminded me of the scratches bears
left on trees in the woods sometimes.

I'd lived through lean times. I didn't expect feather pillows and silver spoons. But this place looked like it might
chew you up and spit you out if it didn't like your flavor, and
it would do worse to you if it did.

The wagon creaked across the open space, making its way
through the rutted dirt path that led up to the only entrance
in sight. The ground was still hard, half frozen, though a
spring thaw might happen soon. Around the fort was a wide

swath of dirt, and I could tell at least part of it would be tilled and turned into crops as soon as the ground allowed. Then nothing but evergreens for as far as the eye could see. Far off in the distance, I could make out the faintest trace of smoke. Not enough for a town. A cabin or two, or a camp, maybe. Off to one side, a range of hills, too short to be mountains but large enough to give the land character, cut against the sky.

When the cart got close to the gate, a dark-haired man peeked over the top. One of his ruddy cheeks was thick with chaw. I knew this because he spit a glob of it, and I watched it splatter next to me in the cart.

"Who goes?" The words came out officious and sneering, the tones of a bully.

Cartwright removed his pipe, shouting up at the gate-keeper, "Delivery."

The man looked us over. "Not sure we want any of what you got."

He must charm the little birds down from the sky, that man.

A disembodied voice floated over from another part of the palisades. "Aw, let them in, Harris, before Miss Moon grabs your ear." A man's head popped up next to Harris's. Shaggy blond hair stuck out from under a bowler cap over an equally shaggy beard. He looked like the kind of man who would laugh when you tripped.

"Shut your yap, Davens."

Their heads floated there for a minute, seemingly unattached to any sort of body as they bickered. The gates were too tall for either of them to be standing on the ground, which meant there must be something built against the interior wall, a perch or a walkway.

Finally, Davens raised a hand in a stopping motion. "Hold there, if you please."

Once I was through those gates, there would be no getting out unless I was let out. I briefly considered running for it.

The gunslinger looked at me. "Don't even think about it."

"I wasn't!" I said hotly. Not when I had no real idea where to run *to*, anyway.

A hint of smoke in the distance was hardly a sure bet. I was stubborn, but I wasn't stupid. If I ran now, I'd have to leave my things, and even if by some miracle I made it to the tree line, I could easily become like those people in the wagon. Besides, I had no weapon beyond my hunting knife. Who knew what beasts filled these woods?

I would not give Mr. Clarke the satisfaction of my death. No, I would eat the Settlement's food, sleep under their roof, and bide my time. I would leave when the time was right. Until that moment, I'd survive out of spite.

I might be a weed, but I had strong roots.

After the gate swung open and we were ushered in, I was allowed to scramble out of the cart. I stretched out the knots in my back and took a gander at my new stomping grounds. I wish I could say that the inside was welcoming and didn't match the outer trimmings of the Settlement.

That would be a crooked yarn.

Ahead of me stood a two-story building, the tallest at the Settlement. Tucked next to it was a kitchen garden, making me think that was where the kitchens were, probably along with a dining hall. The upper floor was likely for sleeping rooms. To the left of that, hugging the palisade wall, was a long, low-slung building, painted white. A belfry jutted up from it. The chapel, then. Next to the chapel, there was a good-sized barn where they would probably have stalls for horses, a few cows for milking, and a pen for the handful of goats and sheep that were wandering about the place chomping on winter grass.

I patted Gertie's side, saying softly to her, "You'll have a few friends, girl."

I bet a place like this would even have a pig or two to feed the dinner scraps to until it was time to carve them up for chops. In the middle of the yard sat a well, the kind with a crank and a bucket. Around that, the goats milled about, chewing on what grass they could find, as a few chickens scattered around them, pecking away at this and that.

I had a certain fondness for chickens, though they were often the most brainless of creatures. They could be mean and silly, but I liked them just the same. I supposed you could say I had a fondness for animals in general. Unlike humans, animals never lied. They might try to gore you with a horn or kick you in the backside, but they were honest about it.

A wildcat never pretended that it wouldn't eat you.

People lied like the sun shone.

Off to my right was another building, this one taking up an entire length of the outer wall and having the look of living quarters. There weren't many people about at this time in the afternoon. Two smaller children, perhaps nine or ten years in age, sat outside on the ground by the kitchen garden, peeling potatoes. They were dressed in what I took to be the sort of garb worn here at the Settlement, the boy in brown canvas trousers, a flannel shirt, and suspenders to keep the pants on his lanky frame. The girl wore an ankle-length dress, her hair in neat braids under a plain bonnet. Though neither of them was wearing a jacket, I was surprised to see that they had on stout boots. In winter they were necessary, but that didn't mean everyone got them.

I, myself, had boots we'd bought secondhand from the mercantile in town. They were too big, which I was grateful for now as I toed the bundle of old rags that held my grandfather's watch and my future. The boots on the children may seem like a kindness from the Settlement, but if they lost a foot to frostbite, they wouldn't be able to do their choring. So I suspect they'd been shod like they would do a workhorse, nothing more.

Despite the lingering grasp of winter, the day had been sunny and clear, and there was washing hung up on the line next to one of the buildings. A girl with neatly pinned and braided hair was taking it down, folding it into a basket. Those were the only souls I could see until I looked up. As I suspected, a narrow walkway had been built along the palisades. Davens plodded along it, rifle slung over his back. Whether they were here to discourage people from coming in or from going out would remain to be seen.

Out of one of the buildings trotted a young fella, about my age, lanky as a scarecrow, with freckles and curly brown hair. After a cursory glance at me, he focused on Cartwright. "I'm to help you unload the wagon."

Cartwright tapped his pipe against the side of his cart. "Go on, then."

"You," the boy said, nudging me. "C'mon. Drop the sacks of potatoes behind the kitchen."

Amos, as I learned he was called, released my chickens and Gertie into the yard while I emptied the wagon. When I'd finished stacking the potatoes neatly by the kitchen door, I headed back to the wagon to make my first real unpleasant discovery.

My suitcase was gone.

"Temporarily confiscated." A tall, angular woman in the same sturdy clothing as the children earlier stood by the now-empty cart. Her milky skin was wind-roughened, and a scar split her face from the corner of her mouth to past her chin, giving her lip a permanent curl to it. A tight braid was pinned to the back of her head. Her eyes were hard but not hateful. Not that I was about to trust her.

I kept my voice even, passably pleasant. "Where are my things?" I always attempted to lead with manners. It cost me nothing, and a smart mouth from the beginning would get me labeled as difficult. The fewer eyes on me, the better.

"The Settlement will provide you with clothes, food, and shelter. After we've gone through your belongings thoroughly and you've proven yourself, we'll return your things. His Benevolence prefers that everyone start their journey here on the same level."

A flash of relief cut through my boiling anger—at least I'd had the forethought to tuck my watch into my boot. But that didn't mean I wasn't as hot as a toad on a buttered skillet. I canted my head, and the light caught my eyes. I wanted to see her better, for one. Her tone was blunt, almost harsh, but her words sounded true.

So I showed her my eyes.

Like I said, my hair made people wary. My eyes gave them the shudders. They were a gray so light they were almost colorless, except for the thin darker ring at the very edge. Pops had eyes just like them, and sometimes when he looked at people a certain way, I swear their intestines turned to water.

The woman's small mouth pursed, her eyebrows shooting down. The cart driver and the gunslinger had returned as we'd been talking, and stood a little behind her. The gunslinger didn't so much as blink. He was hawkeyed, and I'm sure not a single detail of my person had escaped him. The driver was another story. Despite my spending almost two days in the back of his cart, he'd not truly seen me until now.

"The Shining God, have mercy!" He stumbled back, all the blood leaving his face. With a shaking hand, he ran his fingers over his heart, warding off evil.

I smiled at him, tight-lipped.

Fear could often shift into anger faster than a lightning flash in a thunderstorm. He shooed me back from that cart, hissing like a cat.

"I've got to get going," he growled, crawling up onto his seat. "Ghost eyes," he mumbled. "Should have charged 'em double."

The woman's frown grew. "Mr. Cartwright, I cannot in good conscience let you leave. We have a cot available to you. Night will fall soon, and it isn't safe to travel these woods then."

He gathered up his reins. "All due respect, matron, but you'd have to tie me down for me to share a roof with such a creature." He looked at me and spit on the ground.

"It isn't safe," she repeated, her gaze imparting a message to the driver I didn't understand. He hesitated, just barely, but I saw it. The gunslinger stood off to the side, eyes on the belfry, but I had the notion that he was focused on their interchange.

A familiar woman breezed in then, a knotted-up handkerchief bundle in her hands. Even though Miss Honeywell wore the same clothing—plain white blouse, long black skirt, boots, and a shawl—as the other woman, she wore it much differently. It framed her, showing off her blond ringlets and the big blue eyes she kept wide before batting them at the gunslinger, who tipped his hat at her.

She dimpled at Cartwright, taking his arm like they were old friends. "Now, Esther Moon, you've said your piece." Her tone was gently chiding, and Miss Moon bristled. "You know how menfolk are—can't tell them what to do when they've set their minds to something."

Cartwright flushed, stammering a little. Miss Honeywell handed him the bundle in her hands. "Had Cook put together a little something for you for the road."

"How kind, Miss Honeywell." The words were perfectly polite coming out of Miss Moon's mouth, yet somehow I knew instinctively that she didn't care for Miss Nettie Honeywell one bit.

I grinned wide at Cartwright, this time all teeth. Only humans interpret this kind of gesture as friendly. When a wolf smiled at you, it was a warning, and my name happened to mean "little wolf." "Thanks for the ride, mister. May the maker bless your travels."

A choked sound came from the gunslinger, but when I looked at him, his face was tipped down to the ground, his hat hiding his expression, giving nothing away.

"Keep your words," Cartwright spat, adjusting his grip on the reins.

"I'll take you up on that kindly offer, Miss Moon." The gunslinger's voice was deep, like it was coming all the way up from his boots. "I've no horse of my own, but I can probably hitch a ride with the next wagon out if that's amenable."

Miss Moon flushed as she held out her hand to shake his. "You'll be here a spell, then. Might as well call me Esther." She didn't look like an "Esther." Then, I don't think anyone likely did, even other Esthers. The gunslinger and Miss Moon shook hands, and again I couldn't put my finger on what clued me off, but I suspected that the small interaction had put the gunslinger into Miss Moon's camp while gently rebuffing Miss Honeywell. From her slight pout, Miss Honeywell hadn't missed it, either.

Miss Honeywell turned her back on us, waving at Cartwright as he snapped his reins, the donkeys lumbering toward the gate.

The gunslinger finally let go of Miss Moon's hand. "Thank you kindly, Esther." He smiled at her and tipped the edge of his hat. For a rough-and-ready gunslinger, he sure had pretty manners. "William Speed. My friends call me Will."

"Then I do hope you'll let me be so forward as to call you Will," Miss Moon said, smoothing her skirts.

Mr. Speed's grin widened. "I'd be honored."

Miss Moon turned a gimlet eye on me. "And what do your friends call you?"

If I had any friends, I wouldn't be here. I didn't want any, to be sure. I'd had enough of tying myself to others. Only ended in misery, far as I could tell. "Faolan. Mr. Kelly when you're full sick of me."

Her mouth softened, though she didn't smile. "Is that likely to be often, Mr. Kelly?"

I tried not to look at the driver and his cart, practically trotting for the exit now, although Cartwright kept turning back to look at Miss Honeywell. "No, ma'am." I'd be a polite ghost if that got me out sooner.

Miss Moon took me in from boots to crown, reaching out to pinch my arm, though not meanly. "Didn't feed you much, did they? Barely more than bones." She shook her head. "Boys need feeding."

I should have dropped my eyes, relieved. I'd passed inspection, my secret safe. Instead, my pride was pricked, and I'd squared my jaw before I realized it. "Everyone needs feeding, far as I can tell. I can work as much as anyone here, miss. Twice as hard, I reckon." I regretted it the minute it was out of my mouth. Now she'd be watching.

I cursed myself a fool. Pops had always told me my pride and temper would be my undoing.

The very corner of her lip twitched. "I reckon you will, Faolan."

The gunslinger cleared his throat. "What's 'a spell,' may I ask? A week? A month?" He tipped his hat back, offering her

36

a smile. "Not that I'm complaining about a roof over my head, mind. I'm simply unsure how frequently you see passersby."

Miss Moon spread her hands. "Could be a week, could be a month." She frowned after Cartwright, his cart kicking up dust and scattering chickens as the gates swung shut behind him. "I hope that's no problem. If it is, you better start running."

"It's no problem, miss." Will took off his hat and tried softening her up with puppy eyes. "I promise I'll make myself useful."

Miss Moon didn't melt for him like I'm certain he intended. She was too busy scowling after Mr. Cartwright. "I think that's wise, William Speed. You don't want to go out these gates after nightfall." She seemed to shake herself then, snapping back to attention. She put a comforting arm around my shoulders, and I hated how much I liked it. "Come on, let's get you settled and fed up."

I wanted to shove her hand away but couldn't bring myself to do so. Weak. I was as weak as I ever was. I followed her along like a little lost duck, the gunslinger's footsteps barely there behind me.

CHAPTER THREE

※

I WAS SEPARATED FROM THE GUNSLINGER AFTER THAT, as he was dropped off at the bunkhouse and I was given a tour. I was right in regard to the buildings I'd guessed at. The dining hall and kitchens were in the main building, with two doors leading out of the kitchen. One, I was told, led to the root cellar. The other hid a tidy little apothecary room, which Miss Moon called the Still. It was clearly her domain, where I would present myself if ever I had a cough or a cut.

"A small cut can lead to a larger infection," she warned. "I know how prideful you young folks can be, but I advise you not to hide such things from me. Come get them cleaned and bandaged. We don't have a sawbones anywhere close to call for when there's something major."

With that admonishment, she led me into the dining hall, which was filled with tables and benches and doubled as a schoolroom for the youngest children. It was noisy now, full of most of the Settlement's youngins and some adults. Someone had gone to lengths to soften the dining room. Mason jars full of local greenery sat in the middle of each table. Sunlight peered through more windows, but these were flanked by gingham curtains. A painting hung at one end of the room—someone with more enthusiasm than talent had painted the sun using cheerful yellows, burning oranges, and reds the color of fresh blood. The sun was a symbol of the followers of the Shining God, otherwise known as the Order of His Benevolent Mercy. It was the only painting in the hall.

Right now, a few of the older girls were attending to about a dozen or so ankle biters, teaching them their lessons, or helping them learn some of the smaller household tasks young-ins their age could manage.

"The second floor contains sleeping arrangements for the elders of the Settlement," Miss Moon said, leading me out of the dining hall. "With the exception of myself. I'll show you my rooms after the chapel, so you know where to go if there's trouble."

We entered the chapel, the watery winter sun casting a golden path on the planking of the floor. Miss Moon closed the doors behind us, and the light dimmed. Wooden pews marched up a carpeted aisle, the air redolent with beeswax and incense. No tallow candles for this chapel.

Two men stood at the front, a larger mural of the sun behind them, covering the entire back wall. As my eyes adjusted to the dimmer light, I caught smaller details around the chapel—a piano off to one side, a few candelabras stacked on top for later use. A fiddle case leaned against the piano, and my hopes rose a fraction. My fingers fair itched to open the case, to pluck the strings with my fingers. I shoved my hands into my pockets to avoid the temptation. The lectern in front of the men was covered in golden cloth, delicate embroidery marching down the sides of it in red and orange hues.

The two men were deep in discussion, pausing when they caught sight of Miss Moon. The younger man snatched up the notebook he'd had laid out on the lectern, like he was afraid we'd sully it with our eyes. The other man beamed a smile at us, holding his hands in front of him. "Miss Moon."

She ushered me forward, introducing me as soon as we were close enough. "Mr. Kelly, may I present to you His Benevolence Gideon Dillard, as well as Acolyte Ignatius Stuckley. His Benevolence founded the Settlement, so you have him to thank for your current situation."

"Thank you, sir," I said dutifully, though I thought her wording a mite odd. Her tone had made it sound good, even if her words lacked enthusiasm. It was a puzzle.

Gideon Dillard flashed a winsome smile as he patted her shoulder. "How kind, Miss Moon. You're in good hands here, Mr. Kelly. Miss Moon is the backbone of the Settlement."

The acolyte sniffed. "While Miss Moon is indeed in charge of your earthly self, we shall be overseeing your spiritual needs." His fingers traced the stitching on his fine gold vest.

Dillard and Stuckley appeared different in disposition— Stuckley had his nose up to us, while Dillard was all welcoming smiles—and yet they were a matched pair. Dillard was a handsome man, robust and full of the kind of charm that drew the eye. His voice had a sweet music to it, rich and rolling.

Stuckley, I could already tell, dogged his heels like a particularly pious hound dog. While Dillard was a striking man, Ignatius Stuckley was more celestial in his beauty, as if his god might reach out at any time and take him back. Pretty in a delicate sort of way, like the fine tea set in the mayor's house back in New Retienne. He wasn't made for everyday use, just special occasions, and should perhaps spend the rest of his time on a shelf.

Dillard's eyes turned solemn. "I know you've recently lost a loved one, Mr. Kelly, and while we cannot replace them in your heart, please know that not only are you welcome here, but we are all here for you in your time of need." He clasped my shoulder. "This is your home now. We are your family."

I was of a mind that family didn't need to tell you they were family, but I kept that to myself. "Thank you, Your Benevolence."

His grin returned, his eyes crinkling at the corners. "Please, call me HisBen. We'll be here all day otherwise."

I nodded. "Yes, sir."

Acolyte Stuckley cleared his throat. "I'm sure Mr. Kelly needs to be settled in. Miss Moon?" It was a clear dismissal, his chin up, though I suspected he was years younger than Miss Moon. He clutched his notebook to his chest.

"Of course," Miss Moon said, already herding me away. "Good day, Acolyte Stuckley. HisBen Dillard."

As she shepherded me up the aisle, it finally occurred to me that it was so dark in the chapel because they had most of the shutters snapped closed. The days were getting longer, but the sun still went down perishingly early, and I couldn't make sense of why anyone wouldn't make use of it. Had they simply popped into the chapel and not bothered to open the shutters, or were they trying to keep people from peering in?

The next stop on our tour proved that my initial suspicions were correct—the building that hugged the full wall of the palisade turned out to be the bunkhouse. The structure was split into two parts—girls on one side, boys on the other. I wondered where Miss Moon would stick me.

We went into the girls' side of the bunkhouse first. Inside the door, there were pegs for jackets, a space for boots, and some shelving where extra clothing, towels, and blankets lived. Parallel to the front door stood another room, separated by a calico print curtain that had been pushed to the side so I could peer in. Miss Moon had a small but serviceable room—a bed, crisply made, a quilt resting on top. A simply built wooden table held a spray of flowers, a brush, and a small blue bottle that I guessed had some sort of perfume in it.

A sampler covered in delicate plants and flowers, their names neatly stitched below, had been hung on the wall. It was well done, the stitches beautifully rendered. I wasn't any good at such things, though I enjoyed looking at them. It took a patience and an amount of care, which I found difficult. It was a peaceful room, an oasis.

"That is my room. If there's any sort of emergency at night, you can find me there," Miss Moon said, and I could hear the quiet pride in her voice. She had the same look in her eye when she ushered me past the larger space of the bunk-house where the girls slept. Rough-hewn bunk beds were nestled perpendicular to the walls, each made up with a precision that told me this was Miss Moon's domain. No wrinkled quilts or crooked pillows here. Two chests were tucked under every bottom bunk, where the residents would keep their clothing and other possessions. A potbellied stove sat in the middle, casting warmth into the space. Someone had strung a rope or two along the ceiling to hang laundry on wet days. As we turned to leave the bunkhouse, I noticed more samplers of wildflowers dotting the walls, and the occasional dolly tucked into a few of the beds.

It was a decidedly homey place and, I admit, finer than I'd been expecting. Miss Moon took me into the boys' bunkhouse next, where I was handed new clothes like I'd seen on the two youngins earlier. A ready-made flannel shirt, thick brown canvas pants, as well as a set of long underwear. I already had a good set of suspenders, and I was allowed to keep my boots, as they were in decent shape and had been oiled to keep the wet out.

"We'll set you up with another set of clothes shortly, but these will do for now. You'll sew your name into the collar. Washing is done communally, but upkeep is expected to be done by you." She eyed me carefully. "You can sew, can't you?"

I nodded, casting a quick eye over the clothes. They'd been worn before—I could see a little fraying around the cuffs and evidence that someone else's name had been stitched into the collar and then removed at some point. They were still in fine shape.

"Good. We expect you to look neat and tidy at all times. Your appearance reflects on the Settlement."

"May I keep my hat?" I was dusting off my best manners and polite tone. I wanted my things back for certain, but I also didn't want to be searched for contraband. My toe poked the bundle of rags tucked into my boot, reassuring me that my grandfather's watch was still there.

Miss Moon frowned at me. I'd taken my hat off as instructed when we'd stepped through the creaking doors and into the girls' bunkhouse earlier. We were in an alcove that acted as sort of a coatroom. I'd placed my hat neatly on top of the new getup in my hands, and Miss Moon looked from it to my hair.

There was no missing my hair, though I'd shorn it as close to my scalp as the scissors could manage. Even in the dim light of the bunkhouse, I'm sure it burned like the blazes. Esther pursed her lips—whether at the color or my poor barbering skills, I wasn't sure—and met my gaze. "I suppose you can keep your hat."

To make others feel more comfortable and so they don't burn you in your bed was implied heavily. But at least she didn't make that twice-cursed gesture that Cartwright used to ward off evil.

"Thank you, ma'am."

She led me into a long, narrow room. I was surprised to find that every building in the Settlement had at least one window. The beds and bedding were similar to the items found in the girls' bunkhouse, and were almost as neatly made. I suspected Miss Moon inspected this room regu-

44

larly as well. A few rolled-up bedrolls suggested that a few of the smaller youngins slept on the floor close to the stove.

The furniture was sturdy, lacking anything in the way of frills or ornamentation, though well-made. The center of the room held an iron-bellied woodstove, and the far end held a curtain. Someone had left it pushed aside, revealing the woodpile and more shelves full of supplies, as well as a basic washstand.

Miss Moon nodded at the washstand. "As you can see, there's a basin back there with a pitcher, soap, and towels. We expect you to stay clean." Miss Moon shooed me toward it. "Go ahead. You've missed dinner, but I'll bring you and William a plate. Hurry up now."

I pulled the curtain into place, waiting to hear her feet retreating before I stripped down, being careful of my boots. I'd jammed the rag into the toe pretty tight, but that didn't mean it wouldn't fall out at the slightest provocation.

I paused, listening, trying to see if anyone was close. I needed to take off my shirt to clean my pits, and I needed to redo my binding. The binding was going to be a problem. I only had the one now, the other tucked into the suitcase that had been confiscated, and I'd need to wash it at some point. Not now. I couldn't deal with it now. Once I'd unwrapped my chest, I did a quick swipe with the rag and redid the binding, relief washing over me as soon as it was done.

The gunslinger was already tucking into his meal when I came out from behind the curtain. I hadn't even heard him enter. He must be quiet as a tiptoeing cat. He was hunched on one of the lower bunks, a tin plate on his lap. The bed wasn't generous by any means, and he was going to have a hard time of it.

I had to stifle a smile, but he caught it.

"All of the single rooms are full. I'm to bed up with you striplings." He handed me another plate, which was covered with a cloth napkin. "With compliments from Esther."

"You're going to be crinkled up as an old apple by morning," I said, settling on the bunk across from him so we were facing each other and placing the napkin on my lap. I was greeted with the smell of beans, corn bread, and a dollop of canned peaches. Little chunks of meat swam in the beans, and I eyed them a little warily. I'm not saying I wouldn't eat rat if I wasn't hungry, but I wasn't quite that hungry *yet*.

"I'm told it's venison," Mr. Speed said with a faint smile to his voice.

"But did you believe it?" I speared the meat with a fork and shoved it into my mouth. Whatever it was, it was gamey.

The gunslinger's face remained straight, his mouth a stern line, but his eyes danced. "I thought it best to not think too hard on the matter until after I filled my belly and it was too late."

My eyes smiled at his in return, as this was a sentiment I could get behind. As I chewed, I realized I'd started to like the gunslinger. It was a wobbly feeling, new and freshly born, and I wasn't sure what to make of it. Part of me didn't want it—wanted to cut it off at the knees and bury it deep.

No good came from liking a person. The good ones left, and the bad ones stuck around too close.

But another part of me wanted to guard the feeling fiercely, wrapping my arms around it and keeping it against my skin. I didn't know which one to listen to, so I concentrated on my meal. Food had been scarce since my grandfather got sick. I'd given him the lion's share, scrimping on my own. Everything else had gone to the sawbones.

I'd grown so used to being hungry, to that hollow ache in my gut, that I didn't know what to do with the feeling of being full. I stared stupidly at my plate for a moment, my eyes smarting for no good reason.

Mr. Speed gave a sigh, wiping his mouth with the napkin. "Not fancy, but filling." He set his plate aside, his gaze casting over the room. "I have to admit, this place is finer than I thought."

I scraped my spoon along the edges of the plate, trying to get up the last of the canned peaches. "It has far exceeded my expectations." I didn't look up from my plate until I was done, setting mine aside as he had his.

Mr. Speed's watchful gaze was back on me, his elbows on his knees as he dug out his tobacco and papers to roll a cigarette. "Is that saying much?"

"No, sir," I said with a shake of my head. "My expectations were somewhere down in the dirt, so exceeding them wasn't difficult." I'd conjured a bleak picture of the Settlement. Like the full plate of food, the reality was a shock to the system. Warm, thick clothing. My own bed. Good soap, full meals. Windows letting in a wash of evening light.

And like the meal, I no longer knew how to process it. My

life, so long defined by worries and deprivation, was now fuzzy with meaning. The Settlement was a promise of care-taking, an extended hand. All I had to do was keep my head down and hand over the reins. It would be so easy.

But it put me on edge. I didn't trust a thing if I couldn't see the cost. No, my plan would remain the same. Lie low for now. Learn the way of things.

And if I saw a chance to get back home, take it.

CHAPTER FOUR

—✳—

MR. SPEED TOOK OUR PLATES OUT WITH HIS CIGARETTE,
and I was left to my own devices. I decided to go check on
Gertie to see how she was settling in. It looked like the goats
had already been herded into the barn, so I headed that way.
Miss Moon had only waved at it on our tour, barns being much
the same this world over, so I hadn't had a good look.

The barn wasn't the tallest building at the Settlement,
but it was a good size, built out of sturdy timber. I unlatched
the door and stepped in, greeted by the familiar smell of animal musk, hay, and droppings. The Settlement did have two
cows, one of them heavily pregnant. Next to their pen were
the goats, and across the aisle a few horses were stabled
along with one mule.

The goats had likely just been put away, as a young woman
was still fussing with the latch. She was a tiny thing with tan
skin, her black hair braided up around her head like many of
the other women I'd seen at the Settlement. From her size, I
would have guessed her younger, but she had a gravity to her,
a steadiness that made me think she might be around my age
or even older.

Amos, the same young fella who'd ordered me to carry some of Cartwright's delivery, stood beside her, doing nothing to help. "You shouldn't be out here by yourself, Dai. Ain't you heard? Barn's haunted. Ankle biters say so."

"Is that so?" she said absently, focusing on her task. I couldn't see much beyond the girl's profile, but there was a stiffness to her movements that told me she wasn't happy with his presence.

He smirked at her, leaning on the fencing. "That's right. Amelia said she saw a big ol'—" He cozened up to her, and I'm not sure what he would have said next, because he caught sight of me. "What are you doing here?"

"Came to check on a randy goat," I said, striding up. The girl, Dai, made a noise like a stifled cough, and Amos frowned. I barreled forward. "Ah, there you are, Gertie." I held out my hand, letting my goat nuzzle my palm. I gave her a good scratch around the ears.

"Well, you found it," Amos said. "Now scuttle off."

I ignored him, making no move to leave. Dai took the opportunity to dip away, heading for the doors.

Amos made to go after her, and I stepped back into his path like I hadn't been paying attention. He slammed into me, almost sending us sprawling. Amos grabbed me before I could fall, yanking me up by the shirt and lifting me off the floor. My hat fell to the straw, and I heard a few of the stitches pop in my new shirt collar.

If Amos was afraid of my eyes, he didn't show it. He snarled in my face. "Someone needs to teach you to step lightly, boy." He shook me. More stitches popped and one of the horses whinnied shrilly.

Hang it all, I was going to have to mend my new shirt already. I snarled back at him. "Put me down, you buffle-headed—"

He shook me hard enough to make my teeth clatter. "Or what?"

My blood boiled, and I'll admit I let my temper get the best of me. I grabbed his arms for leverage and swung my knee up into his gut. Amos huffed out a breath, dropping me in his surprise. I slammed against the hard ground, pain radiating up my backside. Still fighting for breath, Amos kicked out, hitting me in the side. I rolled, trying to get up and protect my ribs, which ached from Amos's bootheel.

He growled curses under his breath as he tackled me, his weight hitting me like a bag of grain. We scuffled, rolling around in the dirt and hay. I was fair with my fists and quick, but Amos was bigger. His knuckles slammed into my jaw, snapping my head back, the iron tang of blood filling my mouth. The next second, I was pinned under him, his face in mine.

"You stay out of my way, freak, or next time I won't be so forgiving." He spit then, the liquid hitting my face.

I didn't respond, only stared up at him, defiant even in my defeat.

He grinned, a wicked unveiling of teeth. "Good. Keep fighting. I could use the practice." His voice dropped to a taunting whisper. "And if you know what's good for you, I'd keep this little scuffle to yourself. Bad things happen to snitches around here, understand?"

"I understand." And I did. Bullies speak a universal language, and I was well-versed in it.

Amos dipped his head, like we'd come to some sort of accord, before shoving off me to stand on his own two feet. He swiped the dust off his clothing, unconcerned about me bleeding in the dirt and seething up at him. He gave me one more good kick before sauntering over to the door. "Oh, and, freak? Do lock up behind you. Wouldn't want anything coming for the goats, now, would we?"

I didn't say anything, waiting until the door had shut before rolling to my knees. Pain lanced through my ribs, and I retched, but after a few slow, careful breaths and delicate prodding, I decided they probably weren't broken. I spit blood into the dirt as I dug out my handkerchief, wiping away Amos's spittle and dabbing at my jaw.

The cloth came back bloody.

Hiding my injuries was right out, then. Not only did I need to clean up my face, but I'd need to treat my bloody lip. Miss Moon was attentive as a hawk on the hunt, and I decided my best bet would be to get ahead of this little incident. I'd concoct some piece of flimflam to explain my injuries. The last thing I needed was her watching me.

I held my handkerchief to my lip, my other hand pressing against my side, as I went to the door. Once through, I closed the big metal latch, surprised to find scratches around it. Claw marks maybe, or a tool? It was a closed fort—what critter was getting in here? What fool would try to steal a horse from inside closed gates? My aching head could make no sense of it, and I decided to leave the mystery for another day. For now, I straightened, dropping my hand and doing my best to walk like I wasn't injured while I searched for Miss Moon.

I found her in the kitchen, and I paused for a moment to marvel at the large stove squatting against the far wall. I'd seen illustrations of such things in the catalog back in New Retienne mercantile, but I'd never seen one in real life.

The rest of the kitchen was fairly standard. Cabinets held various kitchen tools and dishes, and two poor youngins were off to the side, scrubbing at dishes in a washtub. A large worktable split the middle, where Miss Moon stood with another woman as they went over kitchen business.

The cook, a short, doughy woman, was shaking her head. "Won't work. I could use some of the canned pears instead."

"I think that will be very fine. In the morning— Skies above, Faolan, what happened to your face?" Miss Moon didn't wait for an answer as she ushered me to the Still room immediately.

The cook scowled at the interruption and went back to her work.

"She looked mighty sore," I said, letting Miss Moon herd me. "Sorry about the ruckus, Miss Moon."

"Don't mind Miss Lita," Miss Moon said quietly as she shut the door behind us. "She's very focused on her work."

"Okay, miss," I said absently, my handkerchief pressed to my swelling face as I took in my surroundings while Miss Moon lit the lamp. The Still wasn't big, more of a glorified pantry, although it did have its own window. A scarred, narrow table took up most of the space. A spirit lamp, bottles, and

jars took up a portion of the surface, everything neatly organized, along with a few knives. Herbs hung from the ceiling
to dry, giving the room a pleasing aroma—clean and bright.

Miss Moon brushed my hand aside, her cool fingers adjusting my face so she could get a good gander at my injuries.
"What happened?"

"I fell," I said. Lies are best when they aren't heavily
embroidered.

Miss Moon snorted. "You expect me to believe that, Mr.
Kelly?" She took one look at my stubborn jaw and shook her
head. "I see. Let's get you cleaned up." Miss Moon moved
about the room with efficiency, first bathing my face with a
wet rag dipped in water and something astringent before
dabbing at my lip and jaw with a salve. "It's got arnica in it,
which will help with the bruising."

"Thank you, miss," I mumbled. "I'll try to not make a habit
of it."

She sighed again, shaking her head. "Now, why don't I
believe that one bit?" When I didn't respond, she heaved
another sigh. "Be careful, Mr. Kelly. HisBen doesn't tolerate
violence or tomfoolery of that sort."

I perked up a little. Surely it couldn't be that easy. "I suppose if I caused too much trouble, he'd have to ask me to
leave." It would be a joy if the only thing I had to do to get out
of the Settlement was to plant a facer on Amos.

Miss Moon finished with the salve, closing the container
and wiping her hands. "That's not how things work around
here." Her voice was stern as she turned to put the tin of
salve away. "HisBen doesn't give up as easy as that. His job

is to instruct wayward souls, Mr. Kelly. As HisBen says, 'The Shining God teaches, showering us with knowledge and kindness. All we have to do is turn our faces up to Him.'"

Before I could say anything, she continued on, her voice softer, filled with something like gratitude. "The Settlement doesn't tolerate fisticuffs."

There was relief in her tone that contrasted with her straight spine and tense shoulders. Her lips firmed, twisting the scar on her face. It was like she was simultaneously relieved a blow wasn't coming and braced for it at the same time.

Before I could think better of it, I spoke. "Pops told me you should never lay hands on anyone smaller than you, unless they done it first and gave you no choice." He'd followed that up with *Faolan, if I ever hear of a man laying a hand on you in anger, I'll gut him like a trout.* I didn't think Miss Moon would quite appreciate the sentiment. "And in my experience, women tend to be shorter than men."

Miss Moon stilled, then let out a tired little laugh. "I see someone's been carrying tales."

"Not to me, they haven't."

She crossed her arms. "Well, I'd rather you hear it from me, then. I was married once. Charming fella, until the day he wasn't. I left."

There was so much she was leaving out that it was like there were chasms between sentences. I wasn't about to say a word about it, neither.

"I had nothing." The corner of her mouth turned up as she looked around the room. "HisBen welcomed me here. Now I've got this. Now I've got you and a bunch of other little noses to wipe, scrapes to mend, and bellies to keep fed. I'm needed here."

Miss Moon glanced at the door to the Still, a strange expression on her face. Before I could figure out what it meant, she turned stern. "So just heed my words, Mr. Kelly. Mind your manners and keep your nose clean. I'd rather not see you end up in the Box, you understand?"

"The Box?"

"A place of penance." She herded me to the door. "Now shoo off to bed. I've got other matters to attend to."

I dug in my heels, curiosity getting the better of me. "What happened to your husband, Miss Moon?"

She wrapped an arm around her middle. "He cheated the wrong man at cards and found himself in the bone orchard."

"Couldn't have happened to a better man," I said, then scuttled off to the bunkhouse.

Turns out sleeping in a new place was a trial for me, though admittedly my sore ribs weren't doing me any favors. Amos, luckily, was bunked on the other side of the cabin. Luckier still was the fact that I was bunking near the gunslinger, as he had the lower bunk to the right of mine, though I was up top. Amos would be less likely to come back for another round that way. I had a feeling he was the type who liked to find a body alone before he scrapped with them.

I lay awake staring at the ceiling. People sure made a racket while they slumbered. The gunslinger snored, but it was a pleasant rumble, and I found I didn't mind. The younger boys cried out in their sleep and flopped around. Fabric rustled as people got comfortable. Until I was accustomed to the new sounds, I would have a devil of a time.

A scream woke me from deep sleep. A shriek, a sound of purest terror. I held my breath, trembling in my bunk. I wasn't sure what had awoken me at first. I'd heard—no, not exactly heard—I'd felt a scream, though that wasn't right, either. I couldn't rightly recall if the sound had been real or a remnant of dreams.

I trembled in my bunk, my breath held, my body taut. The night was quiet in a way that spoke of predators.

No night sounds. Nothing. Just eerie silence.

The banked fire and sliver of moonlight behind the clouds gave off feeble light, not even enough to really make out shapes. Eventually sounds returned. One of the children mumbled and the gunslinger snored in response. My tension eased.

But I don't think I got another wink of sleep the whole night through.

We were awake with the roosters and the dawn, and I learned the new rhythm of my days. Up, beds neatened, teeth brushed, and boots on. Shuffled to prayer. A restless night left me a trifle thickheaded, and my empty belly didn't help.

I followed Mr. Speed like a sleepy duckling as he scooted onto the pew next to Miss Moon. She smiled shyly at him, greeting us both quietly. He responded to her softly, both of them focused on their brief conversation, so I didn't bother to do anything else besides mumble good morning. The room grew quiet as HisBen took to his spot at the front with Stuckley, both of them in their ceremonial robes. HisBen's was made of a shiny gold cloth—like he'd been robed in sunshine—the cuffs, collar, and hems embroidered in oranges, reds, and white. Stuckley, who wore a similar getup, though his was white, shuffled about with thick incense that made my head even fuzzier.

HisBen smiled at us real prideful-like, as if we were a creation he himself had wrought. "It is so good to see your faces this morning. Old faces"—he turned his attention toward me and the gunslinger—"and new. Welcome, Mr. Speed. Mr. Kelly. How lucky you are to be here, to witness His benevolence firsthand." He spread his arms wide. "For are we not all lucky to be here, healthy, surrounded by such riches?"

The crowd in the chapel chorused back that they were lucky. Some, like the two guards, Davens and Harris, looked like they were just saying back what was expected.

Others, like Miss Honeywell, were more jubilant in their response. "We welcome His gifts!" She watched HisBen like every word he uttered was a shiny coin just for her.

"And the Shining God is grateful for all that you've given Him." He smiled at her, before turning back to the rest of us. "Many of you came to our gates with nowhere else to go. You have praised me, along with our God, for the gift of a new life, a new home. My children, you humble me. Know that the Shining God doesn't see it that way, and neither do I—you are the gift. To us. To our Benevolent God. Never doubt that." He spread his arms wide, the light from the windows gilding him in a pleasant glow.

To my unlearned eye, he didn't look particularly humbled. I'm of the notion that some of Pops's feelings toward the new god and his followers had rubbed off on me. It would be kind of me to put my judgments aside and give the preacher a fair shake.

Luckily, I had no interest in being fair or kind, so I was able to judge him harshly and gleefully within the confines of my own mind. HisBen Dillard was a man who had bought his own song and dance.

"Let us raise our faces to Him, thanking Him for shining down upon us and entering our hearts." Everyone raised their faces at the ceiling for a moment of silence before dropping them back down and moving along with the ritual.

Stuckley aided HisBen Dillard in the ceremony, their movements a well-worn waltz. Elegant, with precise footwork.

I preferred a country dance, myself. More lively. You could really kick your heels up at a country dance, unlike the stately waltz.

Which might have been why I fell asleep.

"Faolan," Mr. Speed hissed, his elbow jabbing me in the side. I startled, dropping my hat to the floor. It had been in my lap. I reached for it, only to be yanked back by Mr. Speed's quick reflexes. His low, quiet voice held a warning. "Leave it."

I glanced up to see if anyone else had noticed and caught Stuckley glaring at me. Well, if he wanted me awake, they should have fed and watered me first. I didn't think HisBen had caught me, but I had no doubt that Stuckley would rat me out.

After that, we were led in song by Acolyte Stuckley, with Miss Honeywell playing the piano. Stuckley's voice was reedy, and I didn't care for it. He cracked open the fiddle case after that, which surprised me, as he didn't seem the fiddling sort— and he wasn't. Stuckley played violin, and I will admit, he was good at it. Miss Honeywell joined him on the piano as she sang along with HisBen about the Shining God's love for us. I didn't know the words to the songs, but I kept an ear carefully turned to them. I would need to learn them quick-like if I wanted to blend in. The thing about passionately religious folk, I'd found, was that they expected you to be equally passionate. If you weren't, they became suspicious.

After we finished singing, we gave a last prayer of gratitude to the Shining God before finally filing out of the chapel. My stomach was growling fierce by then, my eyes fixed on the kitchen, when I caught the sound of my name. Miss Honeywell beamed at me, striding over holding a bundle of papers wrapped up in ribbon.

"I thought you could use these," she said, handing over the bundle. "So you could join us in song a little more easily."

A quick glance told me the bundle contained sheet music, the top one being among the very songs we'd sung today. "Thank you, miss."

Miss Honeywell squeezed my shoulder, her eyes bright. "I'm so glad you're here, Mr. Kelly, and I just know you'll pick these songs up quick. HisBen Dillard believes a congregation joined in song forges unbreakable bonds, so it's important, you see." She told me this very earnestly before she patted my cheek. "Now you hustle off to breakfast."

I hustled off as I was bid, the packet of papers weighing heavy in my hand. I didn't much care for the idea of forging unbreakable bonds with anyone here.

Like my previous meal, I was surprised by the generous portions. It was oats, to be sure, but they were freely dished, and I was given a pat of butter, honey, and a handful of dried berries on top of that. There was even toast.

The cook, Miss Lita, gave the young man next to me double what she'd put in my bowl. *With a smile.* "There you go, Jesse."

"Thank you, ma'am," he said, smiling wide as she added another dollop of honey to his bowl. "That's very kind of you."

"Not that you need sweeting, mind—not with such fine manners." She glared at me.

I was mighty tempted to pull a face, but I bit my tongue. It was poor thinking, getting on a cook's bad side when they controlled your vittles. Instead, I smiled at her as I got myself a cup of coffee and grabbed a seat, Jesse taking the one next to me.

I assessed Jesse from the corner of my vision as I scraped along the bowl with my last bit of toast. His bunk was below mine, so I'd be seeing him regularly. He didn't have much in the way of extra meat on him—sinewy muscle held his bones together, although he sat inches over me. His skin was a warm brown with a golden tone underneath, like he'd swallowed sunshine and it agreed with him. A very healthful aspect.

Wire spectacles perched on his nose as he read the small paperback book in his hand. He'd finish a page and then hand it over across the table to the girl who sat opposite—the same girl I'd seen the day before in the barn. She'd greeted me with a sharp nod, not mentioning the incident, so I kept my trap shut as I tried to remember her name.

She'd take the book from my bunkmate and read while he ate, and then she'd hand it back. There was a familiar rhythm to it, a well-worn ritual feeling.

She was about our age, with a delicate bone structure and fine dark eyes. Her black hair was pulled back from her tan face and plaited, revealing a pointed chin and winged brows. She appeared a dainty thing, like a firm breeze would knock her down. But something about the way she moved, the way she met the boy's eyes and smiled, told me to not trust that appearance one bit.

I drank my black coffee, wrapped in the hum of a room full of people, and listened with my ears full open. Listening to people when they were relaxed, their bellies full, was a good way to learn about the place.

I daydreamed for a spell, thinking up ways of escaping the Settlement and sneaking back to my cabin without the mayor knowing. The daydream evaporated quickly, popped by several sharp realities. The mayor would be checking on the land—that was as certain as moonrise. Miss Honeywell could tell him I'd left. Then I thought of that wagon. I'd never make it home on my own right now. Not without supplies and not until the weather warmed.

I let go of the idea for now, sipping and listening instead, catching snatches of conversation.

"I'm counting the days, Louis, you'll see. My brother will send for me, and then I'll hotfoot it out of here." This was Amos, boasting to a boy sitting across from him.

The boy, Louis, seemed dubious. "You ain't heard from your brother in months."

"It's the mail," Amos said, his voice airy. "I bet his last letter was lost, is all."

I wouldn't learn anything from Amos's thick skull, so I shut his voice out. Behind me, at the next table, two little girls whispered back and forth, just quiet enough that I only managed to hear snippets.

"—ghost in the yard. I saw—"

"No such—"

I strained, but they only got quieter. Hoping to pick up something more, I cast my gaze upon the room. Long tables lined up in two neat rows, the bench seats mostly full of all kinds of folks, more children than not. Seated in the front were the adults, taking up two whole tables. The gunslinger sat between Miss Moon and Ignatius Stuckley. I noticed that he, like me, had his jaw shut but his eyes and ears open as he drank his coffee, though he did trade a few words with Miss Moon.

He caught me staring and lifted his mug in greeting. I nodded and dropped my gaze.

The dining hall was cheery in the morning light. The

plates were tin, but the serving dishes looked fine and new. My eyes misted as a sudden yearning to see Pops's battered teakettle overwhelmed me.

Every time I'd told him to buy a new one, he'd simply shake his head. *That kettle's got history to it, Faolan. Why would I waste money on something new when ours works just fine?*

I could almost hear his voice—I missed him so much. Frustration nipped at the heels of my grief. I hadn't heard or seen anything useful. I knew I'd only just arrived, and I needed to cultivate patience. Pops always said it was the impatient hunter that went home hungry. Going off half-cocked only resulted in startled quarry, though I will admit it was my natural inclination.

Breakfast finished and dirty tin plates put neatly in bins, I was once again taken in hand by Miss Moon. She needed to place me properly, and as such she needed to assess my skills and see how the Settlement could use me best.

She watched me tackle barn work first. I mucked stalls and helped clean out the chicken coop, greeting the animals as I went. I'm handy with creatures of all sorts—Pops had taught me young how to tend the animals on our homestead. Any creature in our care had entered into an agreement with us—we nurtured them and fed them, and in turn they provided us with food and labor. To abuse an animal was to renege on that agreement on a basic level and to expose ourselves as cruel in manner. My grandfather was clear on this—it took no skill or power to mistreat those beneath us, and those who thought different were to be sneered at.

I rubbed a fist over my heart, swallowing down my grief. Thinking about Pops hurt.

I wasn't one to complain about doing things like mucking stalls or brushing down cattle. Animals are soothing company, and I was used to hard labor.

With the season being what it was, most of the Settlement's food came from stored staples, their livestock, and the land outside the Settlement's gates. The smaller children were already prepping the area for the gardens, picking up stones and such. I spent the day under Miss Moon's command— peeling potatoes, hauling wood, even helping herd the smaller children when needed.

I was helping one of the other boys, Zeke, corral the goats into their pen before the dinner bell when Miss Moon returned from checking in with the cook, Miss Lita.

"You're a dab hand with the animals," she said, stating it calmly as fact, but I responded to her anyway.

"Yes, ma'am, I am." I chased the last one, a small black-and-white goat that had tried to dodge me at the last minute as we made our way back into the enclosure. Zeke secured the gate behind me. After giving Gertie a final pat, I clambered out of the pen and into the main part of the barn.

"How are you with traps and things of that nature?" Miss Moon asked, nodding at Zeke as he left the barn.

I adjusted my hat. "I do alright, I reckon." I'd kept Pops fed when he was sick, after all.

I liked keeping my hands busy, as it left my mind free to wander, but if I was kept on this particular round of duties long, I would go mad. Trapping would also get me outside the Settlement walls, offering me the opportunity to get the lay of the land.

"Any child that can hold a paring knife can peel potatoes, miss. If I may be so bold, there seem to be plenty of small hands for that work." I said it casually, not wanting to appear too eager.

She nodded at me, her eyes trained on the bruising on my face. "We need older boys to go out into the forest," she admitted.

"I would be happy to oblige." Maybe if I played it smart, I could create a cache in the woods, lay up a few supplies for my escape.

"You'll have a partner, of course," Miss Moon said, almost as if she was following my train of thought. "To show you the trails but also for safety. There are predators in these woods. Big ones."

"I'll be careful, ma'am."

She sighed, shaking her head. "I better go check the Still's inventory. Something tells me we're going to need more salve."

CHAPTER FIVE

—✳—

THE NEXT DAY DAWNED COLD, THE SUNLIGHT SICKLY.
Otherwise, things stayed the same as the day before all the
way through breakfast, with the exception that today's prayer
had been about the selfishness of denying the Shining God's
welcome. Sleepy as I was, I stayed awake, feeling as if eyes
were on me the entire time, though I never caught anyone
looking.

I kept my trap shut as I enjoyed another full meal, sitting
next to the same folks as they passed their book back and
forth. I tried to see what they were reading and failed.

Not that I was interested, just as a way to pass the time.

After breakfast, the guard Davens met me in the boys'
bunkhouse to outfit me with a canteen, a folding knife, and a
canvas knapsack to bring back our quarry.

He watched me adjust the knapsack, a nasty grin on his
face. "Those woods are going to eat you up."

I opened my mouth to say something hotheaded, only to
be cut off by the gunslinger as he ambled into the room.

"Naw," Mr. Speed said, shaking his head. "Faolan has so
many barbs, the woods would choke on him."

Davens laughed, though he didn't seem to find it funny. "What are you doing here?"

Mr. Speed sat on his bunk, stretching out his long legs. "I'm with you for the day. Harris has to do a supply run."

Davens frowned as he dug his thumbs into the waist of his trousers. "Thought you'd want to go with him."

I pretended I wasn't listening as I finished adjusting my pack. It was curious, though, that Mr. Speed wasn't taking this opportunity to borrow a horse to go along with Harris on his ride into town. He could hand over the reins once he was there and hitch a ride wherever he pleased.

Mr. Speed crossed his boots, squinting up at Davens. "I find myself intrigued by the Settlement. Quite an interesting place you've all got here. Thought I'd stay on awhile, see if it suits me."

Davens's eyes narrowed, his mouth pinching shut. Both of them watched each other like two hawks circling the same rabbit carcass. Personally, my coins were on the gunslinger.

Davens finally shrugged one sloping shoulder. "Suit yourself."

Mr. Speed offered him a tight-lipped smile. "I usually do."

I ducked my head down, hiding a grin. I may not be sure what all of the undercurrents were to their conversation, but I had a feeling the gunslinger had won.

Once I was outfitted, Miss Moon escorted me to the gate, pointing out my partner—my bunkmate and erstwhile break-fast companion, Jesse. I ambled over to him, my eyes down, my hat tipped. When I got close enough, I stuck out my hand. "Faolan. Miss Moon says we're to be partners."

He glanced over at her, grimacing as he nudged his glasses up with one knuckle. Then he looked me up and down, quick-like. Whether disappointed in me or the situation, I couldn't tell. He sighed and took my hand, giving a firm shake. "Jesse." His voice was quiet but steady, the kind of person who wouldn't be pushed one way or the other but would make up his own mind.

Not exactly in my favor, but not the worst.

He gusted out another breath, adjusting the straw hat on his head. "Come on, then. We best hustle. We got a ways to go."

I followed along without a word. It was clear that Jesse didn't want me along, but I wasn't sure why. He didn't seem the superstitious sort. At least he didn't step away from me and he didn't drag his fingers across his heart.

I decided to hold my tongue, and managed until we were through the gates, over the flat lands, and into the forest. The other pairs had left us at the gates, scattering in all directions. Each twosome had been assigned a section of the forest, it seemed. I stayed quiet all the way until we stepped through the trees and onto a deer trail. Then, I must admit, curiosity got the best of me. It was forever my failing.

"You don't want me along," I said, my tone hushed.

His back didn't tense, and he didn't turn. "*Want* has nothing to do with it. Miss Esther's right, we're safer in pairs." He did look at me then, a backward glance. "But you've got trouble written all over you, and I don't want any part of it."

That seemed a sensible notion, and yet . . .

I should let it go. He'd given an answer of sorts. We didn't need to be bosom friends. I should just watch and learn what kind of fella he was that way, but something in me wanted to poke at him just a mite more. Pops was right. I wasn't born with a full measure of sense. That was the only explanation.

I watched my feet, my face hidden by my hat. "I can see that a big fella such as yourself would be comforted by my presence. Mountain lions will be shakin' in their fuzzy boots."

He snorted a laugh, pausing on the deer trail we'd been following. "You're smaller, easier prey. It does me good to bring a snack with me so the mountain lions will leave me alone. I can scoot home while they chew on your gristle."

My mouth wanted to smile, but I managed to keep it straight as I looked up into the treetops and assessed the light. "You may be big, but I reckon I'm faster. We'll see who ends up being the snack."

That earned me a grin, a quick flash of even teeth. We were quiet after that, but then quiet was necessary. Jesse had a rifle strapped to his back—partially as protection but mostly in case game presented an opportunity. Despite my joke about mountain lions, they didn't come down into the lower forests much, and I hadn't seen evidence of bears. I frowned. In fact, I hadn't seen much evidence of anything bigger than the deer that had blazed this trail, despite what Davens had implied.

We had to go much deeper into the woods than I would have thought, but after a few hours, the woods revealed they hid some creatures as Jesse showed me where the traps were set. By noon, the canvas sack on my back included a pheasant and a rangy hare.

We stopped for a short meal around midday, and I got a hint of why Jesse might not want company. We'd found a picturesque clearing for our use and settled in for lunch. A small brook bubbled through for us to fill our canteens, and a fallen log made a proper chair. Light cut through the treetops here, and I tipped my face up into it, my eyes closed. The cook had wrapped us up some cold pheasant, a thick slice of bread, a wedge of cheese, and two apples. A veritable feast.

While I dug into my meal, Jesse brought a leather-bound journal out of his bullet bag, along with a pencil case, and took to sketching some of the local fauna. He tucked in idly, not paying attention to what he was eating, more focused on his task.

I studied him from between my lashes as I ate my food a little too quickly. I will admit that though my mind had started to believe my hungry days were over for a spell, my body wasn't as sure. It would probably take a week or more before I stopped stuffing my cheeks like a varmint at every meal.

Jesse, on the other hand, wasn't as interested in food as he was with his sketching.

"You an artist, then?" I licked the last of the pheasant off my fingers. No one cared if you licked your fingers when you were a boy. It was one of the small joys I cherished. I didn't think I was missing nothing not wearing pretty frocks or braiding my hair. Course, I didn't know any other way, but I was dead certain that sort of life wasn't for me. Though I will admit the braids were a temptation. I liked the color of my hair, for all it caused me problems. I might like to try my hand at longer locks, given the chance.

But for now, short was better.

Jesse glanced up at me, taking in my mood. I kept licking my fingers.

"A bit." He went back to sketching.

Fine, then, I didn't want to know anyway.

Except I was fair itchin' to ask him again. I shoved a hunk of bread into my mouth to keep from saying anything.

Jesse's pencil moved easily over the paper. "You hold it in much longer, you're going to puff up like a bullfrog's throat."

I wanted to throw my bread at him. Instead, I shoved another hunk in my mouth and washed it down with my canteen. I repeated this method until my bread was gone.

Jesse looked up, blinked, and started laughing. "I don't think I've ever seen anyone out of nappies eat like that. Like you want to throw a fit, but you're too hungry to stop eating."

I was going to catch a whole mess of crickets and put them in his bed.

He just laughed and finished his food.

We were not going to be friends, Jesse and I.

We spent another hour or two out in the forest—Jesse showing me the traps, the game trails. The woods were starting to come alive slowly, green buds on the bushes and trees. Despite that, my feet were fair frozen by the time we got back to the gates.

"I don't see why we had to go so far," I groused as I stomped my feet to get warmth back into them.

"Animals don't come close to the Settlement," Jesse said, walking around a cluster of chickens. "Could be they don't like people much, but I think something's spooking them off."

"Like what?"

Jesse shrugged. "Don't know. Some of the others have seen some tracks, is all."

Any other questions I had for him disappeared as we stepped into the kitchen. We handed our sack over to the cook's helper, a skinny little lad named Simon. Miss Lita had us hauling wood before we were ordered to go scrub up and clean the muck of the day off our hands and faces.

We spent the hour before dinner in the dining hall at the tables, helping the littles with their sums or reading, depending on what they needed. Jesse's reading companion was in charge of those assignments. While not the actual teacher—apparently Miss Honeywell handled that chore—she must have helped out in the schoolhouse during the day.

She frowned at me, her brow furrowed. I felt like a fish pulled from the water, waiting to find out if I was big enough or declared a minnow and tossed back.

She crossed her arms. "Can you read?"

I nodded.

When I didn't elaborate, I expected her to get frustrated. Instead, she relaxed a fraction. "Math? Geography? Arts?" The little furrow between her brows deepened. "I know you can talk."

"Yes. Some. Does music count?" Sadly my drawing skills weren't near as good as Jesse's.

She perked up, eyes alight. "What kind of music?"

"I'm a fair hand at the fiddle." Get me near anything with strings, and I could make it sing like to make you weep, though I was best with the fiddle.

She planted her hands on her hips. "We have a small piano. I'm getting better at it, but not great." She looked at me regretfully. "You've seen the fiddle in the chapel, but I'll warn you, they only let us play praise songs." She glanced over at Miss Honeywell and Miss Lita—whose apple cheeks pushed up in a smile—before she leaned close enough to me to whisper, "We get a mess of hymns, but that's it."

From her tone, I could tell she wasn't a devotee.

"C'mon." She pinched the cloth at my shoulder and dragged me over to a little boy with a runny nose, big brown eyes, and soft brown curls that made me think of a baby lamb. "I'm Dai Lo. This little fellow has been yoked with the name Obedience Praise Jones."

I grimaced in sympathy.

Dai Lo used a handkerchief to wipe the poor mite's nose. "We call him Obie, which we can all agree is an improvement. Obie, this is . . ." She looked at me.

"Faolan."

"Fa-wyn?" Obie garbled my name, his hair sticking up like a baby bird's.

I reached out and smoothed one of the downy tufts. "Fway-lawn." I broke up the sounds until it was easier for him to say.

"Fway?"

"Good enough, chickabiddy," I said, earning me a drooly grin.

Dai Lo raked her hand through the tufts, somehow getting them to lay down smooth with one swipe. "Faolan will help you with your letters."

Obie grinned around the fist he had half shoved into his mouth and held out his other hand. I sighed, swooped him up with one arm, and went to find a slate and chalk.

The woods around me were hushed, and though I couldn't see through the dense tops of the trees, moonlight had somehow filtered in, making the tree trunks white as bone and the shadows around them like bruises. I padded along the forest, my feet making little sound. I'd forgotten my boots. I wasn't sure where I was going, but something was pulling me forward. Something like hunger, but not.

I only knew that I wanted the feeling to stop.

I climbed over fallen trees, crossed the stream, and delved out of the territory I'd spent the day traversing. I was getting closer to the foothills, the ground winding up in a slow but steady climb. The forest was quiet, hushed in a way that wild places rarely are.

Nature can be peaceful, but it is rarely truly quiet. Streams burble. Twigs snap. Bugs hum, and birds make an unholy racket. Except when a predator stalks the woods. Then it's quiet, like now, the only sound my own feet.

The hunger pulled me along until I reached a small cave opening—so small I'd have to get on my hands and knees. I *needed* to crawl through that hole. I didn't *want* to. It would be too easy to get stuck, trapped.

I dropped down onto the ground, my knees in wet, oozing mud. My stomach cramped with hunger, driving any caution from me. I placed one hand on the cave floor, expecting cold rock or sand. It wasn't cold at all. The cave was warm and wet as my fingers closed down around . . . something.

Slowly, I drew back my fist. Blood coated it all the way up to my wrist, like I was wearing a glove. Drops splattered the ground as I opened my hand. I never got to see what was in it. Something shot out of the shadowed entrance, clamped onto my arm, and dragged me into the cave.

I screamed.

Then I bolted upright in bed, my sides working like bellows. I was covered in sweat. The fire had died low, and I could just make out the room and the littles curled up on their pallets. One of them cried out in his sleep, likely the sound that had jarred me from slumber.

I collapsed back on my cot, shivering, my skin clammy.

Last year, just before Pops got sick, I had to bury my dog, Ranger. He'd been an old dog and a good one. When Ranger was a younger pup, he'd followed a scent trail into our neighbor Mrs. Leigh's croft. It was a sizable plot of land that she leased from one of the Rover clans, and I didn't know it well, Mrs. Leigh not being the friendly sort. I hadn't been properly looking where I was going, my eyes on my dog. I didn't see the hole until I fell into it.

It was a good-sized hole—deep, the sides steep enough that I couldn't climb out. Couldn't get a handhold. Then a storm came up from the east and the clouds broke and poured their bounty down upon me. The hole took on water so fast I was worried I'd drown. I shivered there like a drowned rat until nightfall, when the neighbor came across me.

I was lucky to just get a fever from it. By the time I recovered, Pops's anger had fizzled, and I didn't get the verbal hiding that I knew I deserved for not paying attention. Since then, I didn't like getting trapped, and I didn't like tight spaces.

I tried to settle back into my bunk. To calm down. I'd just clamped my eyes shut when I heard it—an eerie, rasping howl. The merest ghost of a sound, but it shook me all the same. Not a wolf. It wasn't a mountain lion, either. I'd never heard the like.

There was absolutely no chance I was going back to sleep after *that*.

I peered down from my bunk. Jesse slept uneasily below me, but the gunslinger's bed was empty. I climbed out of bed, quiet as the shadow of a mouse. Keeping my movements slow, I grabbed my boots, sliding into them only after I'd gone out the door, leaving it cracked behind me.

The grounds of the Settlement were quiet, nothing stirring during the late hour. From my place in the shadows, I could see one of the guards moving along the walkway of the palisades. The moon hid behind clouds, so I couldn't tell which guard was doing the rounds. All I could make out was his lantern as he continued his patrol.

I kept my ear cocked from the shadows, trying to hear

that strange howl again. As the minutes ticked by, I began to wonder if I'd heard it right. Maybe I'd imagined it, tight as an overwound watch from the nightmare. It could have even been the guard having fun or trying to scare the kids.

I was fair tempted to sneak from shadow to shadow, looking for another way out. The nightmare and following howl had spooked me, and I wasn't thinking straight. I wanted *out*.

Only a fool would build a palisade without an escape route. I didn't have anything with me except my grandfather's watch and the long underwear I'd slept in, but I was wily. I could figure it out.

I'd only made it to the edge of the bunkhouse before someone hissed at me.

"Surprise." William Speed pulled me around the corner of the building. Only luck kept me from screaming. "What are you doing out here, Faolan?"

I smacked his arm away. "What on earth is wrong with you? You damn near gave me palpitations."

Mr. Speed didn't seem worried. "You're not supposed to be out of your bunk."

"Why not?" I asked belligerently. "You're out of your bunk."

"That's different," he said.

"Not to me."

He grunted, annoyed. "Guards are going to catch sight of you." He peered up at the bobbing lantern light, his next few words coming out irritated. "Fools are making themselves targets up there, hauling that lantern around."

"I wanted to check on Gertie," I said, thinking quickly.

"I wanted a cigarette," he said.

I thought about calling him on that fib—he didn't smell like tobacco, and he didn't need to lurk in the shadows to do so—but then he might call me out on *my* fib, especially since I hadn't been going in the direction of the barn at all.

"You better get back to bed," Mr. Speed rumbled, "before the guard catches you."

"Yes, sir." With resignation, I let him herd me back into the bunkhouse. I was disappointed that I hadn't heard the howl again and was feeling more and more certain that I'd constructed it from dream cloth. It wasn't until I was back under my quilt that I wondered—if the gunslinger hadn't been smoking, what had he been up to, lurking out there in the dark?

CHAPTER SIX

---*---

TROUBLED, I'D TOSSED AND TURNED THE REST OF THE night. Whether it was my lack of shut-eye, the possibly imagined noise, or the mysterious actions of the gunslinger, I spent the next two days on edge. Everyone and everything seemed suspicious to me. I kept my mouth shut, worked hard, and slept like my bunk was full of burrs. On my fifth night at the Settlement, exhaustion finally caught up with me, and I slept like the dead, only waking for morning prayer when Jesse shook me.

Though I'd been managing to make a ghost of myself, my luck finally ran out, and HisBen trapped me as I was stepping outside into the yard after prayer.

"Mr. Kelly." He smiled at me. It wasn't the kind of smile that reached his eyes. It was a weak thing that died before it even left his lips. His brown eyes glowed with *something*, but it wasn't humor. His god, maybe, or his faith. Whatever it was, it made me uneasy.

"Yes, Your Benevolence." I touched the edge of my hat out of respect. With men like HisBen, I'd learned to flatter. No amount was too much. Apply it with a shovel, not a trowel, bowing and scraping the whole time, and they ate it up like it was their given right to inhale the sweetest of ambrosias.

"How are you liking our Settlement?" His eyes flicked back and forth as he watched my face. For what, I had no idea.

"It's a fair wondrous place, sir," I said, and I meant it. I'd expected a hovel. Last night there'd been custard at dinner, with canned cherries. Everyone had everything they needed. Whatever the Settlement was, I couldn't argue that it was thriving.

His grin widened as he took in his domain. "I appreciate the assessment, Mr. Kelly. You know, people mocked us when they heard our plans." He shook his head as if to say, *Those poor misbegotten fools, doubting the likes of me.* "Others had tried and failed here, you see?"

I nodded, which was all it took for him to keep going.

His hands twitched before clenching into fists. "We didn't build the palisades—they were here from an earlier attempt. People couldn't tame the land. I will admit, at first, we struggled." He leaned in close to me, like we were sharing a secret. Close enough that I could smell incense and the tang of sweat underneath. "But in the end, the doubters, the nonbelievers, were wrong. We persevered."

He straightened, his face to the sky, his eyes closed. He spoke so softly, it felt almost like he was talking to himself. "I cannot blame them for their ignorance."

HisBen blinked, coming back to himself. He shook out his clenched fists, smiling at me once again. "You see, Faolan, I had faith in my path, my God. I gave myself over to Him fully. That's the key."

"Yes, sir." It was all I could do to keep my feet rooted where they were. I wanted out of this conversation more than anything. This must be how a rabbit feels when the hawk first pins it.

He patted my arm in a fatherly gesture. "Now those naysayers, they'll know—put your faith in Him and you can accomplish anything." He gazed out, puffed up with pride, at his dispersing congregation. "You have an opportunity here, Mr. Kelly. That's what the Settlement really is—opportunity. The Shining God has extended His grace to all of us. Provided for us, for you. All He asks in return is you and your unwavering faith in exchange for His riches."

"I understand, sir." I wasn't good enough of an actor to inject awe into my voice, so I went with gravity. I could fake gravity.

"It's not too high a price, now, is it, for all the bounty we receive in return?"

It seemed mighty high to me, but as Dillard had the flushed cheeks and glowing eyes of the true believer, there was only one answer I could give to his question. "No, sir."

His grin never wavered as he checked his pocket watch. It was a fine piece, engraved silver with gold inlays. "I fear I'm keeping you overlong, Mr. Kelly. I know you have your duties." He snapped the watch shut, tucking it back into his pocket.

"I do, sir." I tapped my hat, not quite taking a full step before he patted my arm again.

"Don't be a stranger. I'm here for all of my children."

I bared my teeth at him, hoping it would pass for a smile. "That is a comfort, Your Benevolence."

He nodded, dropping his arm and stepping away, and I took the opening to hare off to the front gates.

I have found that whenever I'm particularly focused upon a goal, life will find a way to cough up an obstacle to put in my path. Today's obstacle between me, my breakfast, and eventually the forest was Miss Honeywell.

I'd been avoiding Miss Honeywell. To be fair, I'd been avoiding any of the Settlement's adults when I could, but especially Miss Honeywell.

"Mr. Kelly!" she trilled at me. Miss Honeywell's voice lived up to her name, sweet and decadent upon the ear. I'd heard her sing a few times in the chapel, and she far outshone Stuckley, a fact that I was sure bothered him to no end.

I almost kept walking. Surely, if I pretended I didn't hear— No. She would just raise her voice and draw more attention. I halted in my tracks, tipping back my hat but not taking it off. "Yes, Miss Honeywell?"

She dimpled at me. "I need a strapping young lad like yourself to haul something for me."

Why she chose me, I couldn't fathom, as I was neither strapping—at least compared to the other lads about—nor a lad at all, come to think of it. Not that she knew that. Jesse, Amos, even Zeke would have been a better choice. Several of the passing boys glared at me, obviously disliking that Miss Honeywell had singled me out instead of them. They were welcome to her.

"Of course, ma'am," I said. "I'm at your service."

This pleased her, earning me more dimples. Had I been a lad, or held romantic interests toward other women, I'm sure those dimples would have done me in. Miss Honeywell was as pretty as one of those little porcelain dolls I'd seen in the New Retienne mercantile on occasion.

But I'm not and I don't, so they had very little impact on me beyond making me wonder what she needed so badly that she felt she had to sweeten the pot.

I followed her into the stairwell at the far end of the dining hall, and we climbed up to the second floor. I hadn't been up on this floor as of yet, having no reason to. A few of the other lads hauled wood up here as part of their duties, and they seemed reluctant to part with that territory.

The hallway was dim, the only light filtering in through open doorways. I peeked into a few as we passed, and it was obvious to me that the upstairs tenants weren't subject to any kind of bunk inspection like we were. A few were a right mess. Miss Moon would have never stood for such untidiness from us. As always, the adults got to live by another standard than us younger folk.

A thick rug ran down the middle of the floor, muffling our steps. I don't think I'd ever stepped on a rug so plush. The hall ended with a final door, the grandest of the lot. The Benevolent Sun, one of the symbols of the Shining God, had been carved into it.

Miss Honeywell gave me a conspiratorial smile. "Mighty fine, isn't it? That door leads to Gideon—I mean HisBen Dillard's quarters."

Of course it did. "A fine door for a fine man," I offered. Now that we were up here, she didn't seem in all that much of a hurry to fetch whatever it was that she wanted me to haul for her.

She grinned slyly at me. "You can peek in if you want. I won't tell."

She must have thought I'd stumbled off of Cartwright's cart and hit my head twice on the way down if she thought I was going to fall for that trick. "No, thank you, ma'am."

Her grin grew. "Are you sure? He won't find out."

I waited. I'd already answered her once and didn't rightly feel like flapping my jaws for no good reason.

Miss Honeywell pouted. "You're no fun. Alright, then." She gave an airy wave of her hand, motioning for me to follow. Miss Honeywell opened the door to the left of HisBen's quarters. She paused, looking back at the door across the hall from hers. "That one belongs to Stuckley." She rolled her eyes. "I wouldn't go in there if you paid me up front."

It was obvious she wanted me to ask why not, and I almost didn't—I have an innate dislike to being pushed into anything. *Contrary like a cat,* Pops used to say. But while I wanted nothing to do with Miss Honeywell, I didn't want to make an enemy of her, either. She seemed the vengeful type.

"Oh?" I waited in the hallway, since she hadn't moved out of her own doorway yet.

"He spends a lot of time in there, our Stuckley. Ruminating on the benevolence, or so he says. I wouldn't be surprised if he was doing something less savory."

I had no idea what she meant by that, and honestly, I didn't want to think about Stuckley, savory ways or otherwise. Normally, I would keep my trap shut or offer a never-you-mind, but if I did that, I would be alienating Miss Honeywell. I had to play along a little. "Have you ever taken a peek?"

She made a big production out of looking this way and that down the hall. Once she saw no one was coming, she whispered, "I might have been a little curious, but you know he locks it?"

"No, ma'am." If I were Stuckley, I'd lock my door, too.

"I don't suppose . . ." She bit her lip.

Either she was amazingly transparent or she didn't think me clever. I honestly couldn't tell which. "Suppose what, ma'am?"

"You don't know how to pick a lock, do you, Faolan?" She gave my shoulder a little pat. "I would be so appreciative."

Now we were getting to the meat of things. As it happened, I could pick a lock or two, but I was not of a mind to share this knowledge with Miss Honeywell.

"I regret that I do not," I said, pretending that I really did regret it.

She sighed like she was up on the penny stage. "Well, it never hurts to ask. I worry he's going to lock himself in there one of these days, and then what are we going to do, chop down his door?" She fluttered her hands and finally stepped into her room. I wasn't sure if she wanted me to wait on the threshold or follow her in—it felt odd entering her domain, just the two of us. She waved me inside without looking back, so I followed her but kept my eyes open, taking everything in.

Miss Honeywell's room had a lot more to it than Miss

Moon's did, making me think Miss Honeywell had come from money before joining the Settlement. She had a bed and a vanity with a mirror. A hairbrush with an ivory handle rested on the vanity, along with several bottles of perfume and a jewelry box. Lace-edged pillows dotted the quilt. An ornate hope chest sat at the end of her bed, and one whole wall was covered with a tapestry done in bold colors—a sweet scene of a doe resting in a glade, trees and flowers all around it. I noticed a falcon in the branches of one of the trees, and I wondered what had drawn Miss Honeywell to this tapestry— the doe or the falcon?

"There's a crate under the bed, Faolan," Miss Honeywell said, her voice suddenly brisk and businesslike. "Fetch it, if you please."

I did as she said, barely straining to pick it up.

She shooed me out of the room. "On you go. We've tarried long enough. Take that to the dining hall and set it off to the side. I'll deal with it after breakfast." And with that order, she dismissed me.

Relief surged through me with every step I took. It felt like I'd escaped or gotten away with something, and I couldn't say rightly why.

I was still thinking about Miss Honeywell as I followed Jesse along our route. Mostly, I was thinking about those two silvers Mr. Clarke had given her back in New Retienne and what they might have been for. Payment for upkeep? Charitable donation? Bribe to get me out of town? I didn't rightly know.

Nothing about the situation or the Settlement itself made much sense, as far as I could see, but then, churchin' never has to me.

"Empty," Jesse huffed. He stood up from the trap, his jaw stiff.

"No need to get anxious. It's just an off day," I said. "It happens. I'm sure tomorrow will be better."

"There are worse duties than trapping," Jesse said, rubbing the back of his neck. "And there are worse partners than you. But if we keep coming back empty, we'll get reassigned." He sighed. "C'mon, then. Let's head to the next trap."

"Hey, Jesse, can I ask you something? How come you and Dai Lo don't leave the Settlement?" That's the problem with me. Sometimes questions fall right out of my mouth before I even realize I want to ask them.

"It ain't that easy, leaving." He nudged his glasses up the bridge of his nose with one knuckle. "I've been watching you, you know. Sneaking out of your bunk. Observing the guards." He glanced back at me. "I'm not going to rat you out. I've done the same thing."

"You have?"

He gave a sharp nod before waving at me to follow him along the trail. "When Dai Lo and I first got here, yeah. But there's only one way out. There's always a guard—"

"You could leg it now," I said.

That earned me a glare. "And leave Dai behind?"

I shrugged.

His lip curled. "You've got no loyalty."

"I do so," I said hotly. "To those that earned it."

He pushed a branch out of the way as he scowled at me. "Dai has earned mine. You know what would happen to her if I left?"

"What?"

"More work," he said. "Harder work. Time in the Box." Before I could ask, he moved on. "The thing is, I don't know *what* they'll do. But they won't be kind, that's for damn sure. Miss Moon, maybe, but the rest?"

I agreed with him but asked anyway. "What makes you so sure?"

Jesse lifted his straw hat so he could swipe at the sweat on his brow with his sleeve. "You know what my ma always said? Don't pay attention to words. Pay attention to what people *do*. That's how you get their measure. That's how they show you who they are."

"So what have they shown you?" I asked softly, not wanting to interrupt his chatter.

Jesse stopped, leaves crunching on the trail as he turned to me. "When I first got here, there was a girl named Ruth. Said she wasn't orphaned like the rest of us. Claimed she was at the Settlement by mistake. Said she was out of there as soon as she got a letter from her grandfather. He had money, she said, loads of it, and she just knew he'd take her in."

"You believed her?" I asked.

"I don't know," he admitted. "But a few people told me that when she first arrived, her clothes were mighty fine, and she didn't know how to do lots of chores because she'd grown up with servants." He ran a hand over the back of his neck. "She used to complain to all and sundry about the dragonfly brooch they confiscated when she first got here. Said it had real emeralds in it."

I gave a low whistle. "Bet she made a right fuss."

"She did. No one argued with her, mind. Just clucked and said 'poor grief-stricken lamb' and such." Jesse took a big breath, blowing it out his nostrils. "She kept insisting her grandfather would want her. If he didn't show up himself, he'd surely send a letter. Only she never got any mail, and he never showed. She got tired of waiting, tried to escape."

"What happened to her?" I asked.

"First time?" Jesse's expression became stony. "She spent two days in the Box. HisBen says the rules are harsh because the forest is unsafe at night."

I looked around at the forest we were currently in.

"I know," Jesse said. "I'm not saying he's wrong, but I'm not sure he's right, either. Second time, she got four days in the Box, and when she got out, they took her shoes and her pocketknife, and gave her extra prayer time with Miss Honeywell and Stuckley."

"What happened the third time?" Because somehow, I knew she'd tried again.

"She didn't come back a third time." His words fell like stones into my gut, sending a splash of a shiver up my spine.

I licked my lips. "Maybe she made it?"

"Maybe she did," Jesse said, but I could tell he didn't believe it. "Maybe a city girl who didn't know how to peel a potato made it in these woods. Maybe she was able to hide her trail so well that Davens and Harris couldn't track her. She could be back in her grandfather's fine home, sipping her tea out of a porcelain cup, every finger covered in gold rings, for all I know." He scowled at me. "But that's the thing, Faolan. *I don't know what happened to her.*"

"And you don't want to find out." My words had an edge to them, like I'd been honing them on Miss Lita's whetstone.

"No, I do not. I don't even care if that makes me a coward. I only care if it keeps me and Dai Lo alive." He gestured to the woods with one hand. "Run if you want. I can't stop you. Shoot, Faolan, I wouldn't blame you. I don't want to be here, either."

I examined him, the jut of his jaw, the set of his shoulders. I didn't think Jesse was a coward. No, sir. What he was, was clever. "You don't like the odds."

He shook his head. "I do not. Not enough to gamble my life and Dai's. I came into a little money last month when I hit my majority. Not a lot, mind, but enough to get us started." He frowned at me. "I didn't tell anyone, so if you gab, I'll know it's you."

"Understood."

He adjusted the strap of his rifle, ready to get moving again. "Dai Lo hits her majority in six weeks. The minute she does, we'll take our leave proper. Say goodbye with a handshake and a tip of the hat. Once we're both legally adults, they can't keep us here."

He started along the trail again. "Until then, I won't give them leave to find fault, which means we're not going to come back empty-handed today."

Jesse's declaration aside, our luck didn't improve as the day moved on.

"This one's empty, too," Jesse said, straightening in disgust. Jesse had leather gloves that fit, so he went about resetting the snare without leaving a scent. If it smelled like us, no critter would come near it. We were more than halfway through our rounds and, so far, had nothing to show for it.

"Maybe they'll understand," I said, though after his story earlier, I wasn't too sure about that. "They might change our route if this one is empty." I leaned against a tree, sipping from my canteen. Clouds had rolled in, cutting off a lot of the sunlight, giving the forest a hazy quality. It wasn't quite warm enough to shed my jacket, but in a few weeks it might be.

"Not sure I want to find out," Jesse grumbled.

He frowned down at me. We weren't exactly friendly, but he trusted me enough to confide in me, and a new partner wasn't a prospect I wanted to entertain. With my luck, I'd be paired with Amos.

I capped my canteen, thinking. "What if we went off route?"

Jesse knuckled his glasses back into place, his expression thoughtful. Jesse was a thinking kind of fella. He didn't rush into things. If it had just been me, I would already be tromping into the undergrowth.

"That could work." He edged off the trail, peering deeper into the woods. "Maybe if we push through, we can find another deer path or something." He brushed away a twig that was hitting his neck before looking back at me. "We don't say a word to anyone."

I pretended to lock my lips and throw the key behind me.

He snorted. "Alright. Let's see if we can find another trail."

I tucked my canteen away and followed him into the trees.

We were careful to keep track of where we were going, leaving subtle markers like piles of stones. I had a good sense of direction, but Jesse's was better.

It wasn't long before we found another animal trail. We paused to set up a spring trap—I had some extra line in the bag I carried. Jesse used my line to tie the snare. While he did that, I worked on the spring pole and the forked stake we'd need, using my folding knife to cut down the wood to meet our specifications. Once the trap was set, we packed up our gear and moved farther along the trail, of a mind to set up one more snare.

Jesse squinted at the deer path. "How far do you think we've gone?"

"Not entirely sure," I said honestly. "Why?"

"Assuming this trail keeps heading northeast, I'm pretty sure we'll end up in Rover territory. If that's the case, we'll need to double back." He eyed the canopy. "I reckon from one of the taller trees, I can take a gander and see where this trail goes."

"You want me to go up?" I asked.

"Naw," Jesse said, setting his rifle against the trunk. "Won't take me but a minute." Then he scrambled up the branches, disappearing into the tree.

I waited at the bottom, listening to the occasional scrape and crackle, and then the noises stopped. After a few minutes, I eased the pack off my shoulders. Might as well rest while I could. My eyes were closed and my head tipped back, so I was real quiet-like. Too quiet, apparently. I heard a rustle in the undergrowth close to my feet and looked down. The beady eyes of a skunk stared back at me, no more than a yard away.

Skunks were tricky eating. They were a trifle bony. Rabbit was better, and you didn't have to deal with the scent glands. They also couldn't make you stink to the skies.

Slow as I could, I reached for the rifle that Jesse had left leaning against the tree next to me. My hand was just closing around the barrel when several things happened at once.

First, Jesse fell out of the tree. In retrospect, I should have let him know about the skunk, but I didn't think of it, and I sorely regretted that. Luckily for Jesse, I broke his fall. We crashed to the earth as one, my breath knocked out of me. Jesse yelped.

Which, second, aggravated the skunk. Jesse must have spotted it, because he rolled off me and scampered away. All I could do was close my eyes and mouth as the skunk sprayed me right in the face.

I was grateful I managed that much, to be honest.

If you've ever smelled a rotten egg, you've got a good idea what a skunk's spray smells like. It's worse, though. So much worse, and I was *drenched* in it. I scrambled up, using the sleeve of my jacket to wipe my face as best I could. It wasn't like the jacket didn't already reek beyond redemption—it had received a good soaking as well.

I rinsed my face with the canteen. It wouldn't help with the stench, but it would hopefully keep the stuff out of my mouth and eyes. Despite my efforts, my eyes burned, same as my nostrils, making the former water and the latter run. I will admit that I had to lean over and retch, sadly losing any ghosts of my fine breakfast.

My canteen was empty now, so I couldn't even rinse my mouth. This day had gone wretched from the start of it. There are some mornings where I think my day would be best spent not leaving the warm nest of my quilt, and today was one of them.

I spit on the ground, attempting to clear my mouth. It didn't help.

When I'd recovered, I snagged the pack and the rifle and went after Jesse. I found my partner a few minutes later sprawled out on the ground clutching his leg. In his hasty—though understandable and, dare I say, enviable—retreat, he'd tripped on a root and crashed down, injuring his ankle.

I placed the bag and our rifle on the ground and dropped down to his level.

"Good gracious, you stink." Jesse pushed these words through gritted teeth, his eyes watering at the stench.

"The skunk and I were getting along fine before you butted in," I said, reaching for his ankle. "No one would fault me for leaving you here to be picked over by wild beasts." I began carefully unlacing his boot, then changed my mind. *Best leave it for now.* "What happened?"

Jesse choked on a laugh. "I leaned out to get a better look at a squirrel and lost my grip."

I paused, my hands on his ankle. "A squirrel?"

His ears turned red, just at the tops. "I wanted to sketch it later."

I snorted. "A fine pair we make." I pressed my hand gently against his ankle, and he grimaced. "Bad?"

He nodded, hissing air through his teeth.

"Think it's broken?"

He shrugged. "Help me up. We'll see if I can put weight on it."

It didn't take long to figure out that he couldn't, and we almost toppled back to the earth, but I got him leaned up against the trunk of a birch just in time. I took stock of us again and shook my head.

We were a right mess.

I stank something fierce, Jesse couldn't put weight on his left foot, and we were a goodly way from the Settlement. We'd also gone off trail, so it would take anyone looking for us time to find us, if they managed.

Nothing doing. We'd have to muddle through. I had Jesse lean against the tree while I found us a couple of good branches.

"What are you doing?"

"Getting us some walking sticks." I handed one to Jesse, then slung the pack and rifle onto my back. That done, I put one arm around his back and had him put one on my shoulders. We started walking.

"This is ridiculous," Jesse gritted.

"At least you're upright," I growled. "You got a better idea?" We shuffled forward a few steps.

"Yeah, to go back in time and never listen to your fool idea," Jesse said, jerking me to the side as he hobbled forward. "This is hopeless. I've seen snails move faster."

"Stop fighting me." Sweat dripped down my brow, and I couldn't do anything about it as we lurched down the trail. Moving as one involved a certain amount of joint coordination that we couldn't seem to muster. "If we ever try to do a three-legged sack race, we'll lose."

"Why are you so short?" he ground out through clenched teeth. "They don't grow people proper where you're from?"

"I'm perfectly sized, you giant." The sweat slid farther down my face, wafting the scent of skunk even stronger into my nose. I gagged. Which made him gag.

"You need to eat more," Jesse said, turning his head to the side to breathe air that didn't reek. "Or wear bigger boots, Snack."

"Now listen here, you big galoot—"

We set off bickering, our words pouring over each other's, both of us irritated and miserable.

Which is exactly how the Rover party found us.

CHAPTER SEVEN

—✦—

THE ROVER PARTY WAS SMALL—THREE SOULS ALL TOLD, plus horses and a rather rangy, rust-colored mutt. At least, three that I could see. The one in front had dark hair with curl to it, his face cleanly shaven, revealing tan skin and a firm chin. He wore thick canvas pants and a cotton shirt, the sleeves rolled up, with only a many-pocketed vest for covering.

He took one look at us and started laughing. I guess Jesse and I were a sight, and that sight was hilarious.

On the man's left was a tall woman, younger but having a similar look to her—perhaps a daughter or a niece? Her dark hair was plaited back, a floppy hat blocking her from the sun. She was dressed like the man, with exception of the vest. Instead, she wore a brown suede jacket with leather braiding that I have to admit I coveted.

Jesse tightened his arm around me, the only sign that he was worried. I'd gathered that the Settlement didn't have much to do with the local Rovers, which I considered a mistake.

The third member of their party gave me pause. He seemed younger than the woman, but I couldn't be sure. He had leaned over in his saddle to get a better look, a grin splitting his face. I froze, unable to help myself, my breath catching in my lungs. Some people are comfortable; you meet them and it's like putting on a warm sweater on a chilly night. He was the opposite—simply clapping my eyes on him made me want to fidget.

He had similar features to his companions, but his eyes were a deeper brown. Thick, dark lashes surrounded them, bringing them to your attention first. A straight nose, and even as his smile faded as he stared back at me, his lips kept some of the curve at the end, like he was always laughing at the world. One eyebrow had a slash of a scar through it, jumping his eye and snaking thinly down his cheek, the tissue lighter than the skin around it.

That eyebrow lifted at me as I continued to stare. His hair—thick, wavy, and a deep, rich brown bordering on black—went to his shoulders. I wondered if it was as soft as it appeared. It wasn't that he was handsome, because if Jesse sketched his face out on paper, I wouldn't think so. But in person? It was like there was a fishing line wrapped around me and he was a lead sinker, drawing me straight to the bottom.

He looked me right in the eyes and didn't blink.

The woman said something then, her voice a pleasant alto. I'd always liked the Rover language. It flowed like water, musical and pleasing to the ear. Most people in New Retienne refused to learn the language, but I wasn't most people. It took me a second to translate what she was saying. I was rusty, and there were a few words I didn't know.

"They reek," she said, her nose scrunching. "But I think the tall one's injured."

The laughing man wiped at his eyes, replying to her in their language. "I'm not letting them into any of the tents. What about you, Tallis?"

"I think we can maybe dunk them in the stream and keep them out of camp," Tallis said, amusement threading through his words. He had the kind of voice that you instantly wanted to hear sing. Deep, but not gravelly, smooth like the hot whisky and honey my Pops would make me drink when I was sick.

I hated how much I wanted to hear it.

Now that I'd had more time to observe him, I thought he might be a year or two older than me. I kept watching him, trying to gather all the information I could. Surely that was why I was staring at him and not for any other reason.

"I think the runt might be the worst offender. We'll have to dunk that one twice."

Or perhaps not so smooth. My cheeks burned before I could stop them, my embarrassingly adoring gaze turned into a glare. *Runt.* He best sleep light if they took us back to camp. I'd show him what a *runt* could do.

His eyes took on a speculative light as he tapped his thumb along the edge of his saddle. "Tiny, like a squirrel. Bet he chitters like one."

I sputtered. "Better a squirrel than an overgrown puppy!" As retorts go, it wasn't my best. I don't do my best thinking when I'm mad, I'll admit. I almost spit at his feet. To a Rover, that was a grave insult, but I checked myself. After all, we were at their mercy.

He leaned back and grinned. "Forget what I said. He doesn't chitter, he squeaks. Yips like a little fox."

I grunted, shifting Jesse's weight on my shoulders. He swallowed hard but didn't say a word. The older man chuckled at Tallis's comment.

"Little Fox," the woman mused. "Yes, that suits him."

"I'd like to see you make less noise, carrying as much as I am!" It was then that the realization stung me. He'd tricked me into revealing that I knew their language, because I'd unthinkingly responded in theirs when I'd cursed him.

Jesse turned his head toward me. "You speak Rover?"

No use denying. "Some." Pops had traded with Rovers as they'd passed through, and I'd soaked up as much of their language as they'd allowed. Pops and I had worked hard to build trust to make that happen. Rovers didn't share their words with just anyone.

Tricky, tricky Tallis. I'd have to watch him. I refused to be one of those people who lost all sense over a fella. I switched back to Rover. "How'd you guess?"

"You reacted." He waved a hand over his face. "To what we said."

"I see," I grated out, my shoulder hunched. Jesse wasn't putting his entire weight on me, but he was still putting a great deal, as he was bigger than me in pretty much every way. I was tired, irritated, and miserable.

I fixed my attention on the other two, since the younger man only managed to get under my skin. "I think his ankle is sprained, and I'm covered in skunk. Any help you could give would be much appreciated."

The woman, Zara, offered Jesse her horse, and the Rovers worked together to help get Jesse up on the saddle.

I stepped forward, only to be stopped by Zara.

"Not you," she said. "You stink all the way to the clouds and back, and I like my horse."

I bit my tongue because it was true, even if I didn't like it. Jesse seemed a little uncomfortable about the entire endeavor. He didn't speak Rover, and I'm sure the Settlement didn't speak highly of Rovers, either. HisBen was the type of man who pontificated on us all being one people in the heart of his god while keeping a steely side-eye on anyone different from him.

"You sure about this?" Jesse asked, watching me from the saddle.

I nodded. "They won't hurt us." Rovers took hospitality seriously. We were injured and asking for help. As long as we didn't try to hurt them or prove ourselves untrustworthy, we'd be fine. We'd owe them something in exchange, of course. They were fair, not foolish.

Zara clicked at her mare, urging her to follow, the reins loose in her fist.

The older man, Sergio, leaned from his saddle. "You follow behind." His face split in a grin. "Downwind, eh?"

I glowered at him, but he just laughed.

"Such a face," Sergio said. "It is not the worst fate, Little Fox. Tallis, have Roon keep her company, eh?"

"Yes, Uncle." Tallis dutifully gave the dog a command, and

soon his mutt was trotting alongside me, her mouth curled into a doggy smile, her tongue out.

I went to scratch her ear and she dodged. "What, like you smell so great?" I mumbled.

Tallis clucked his tongue. "I'll have you know that Roon is very clean. Besides, everyone smells better than you right now, Little Fox."

Sergio held out his hand to me, his eyebrows up. Sighing, I handed over my rifle. He passed it to Tallis, then put his palm out again. Reluctantly, I gave him my knife.

"You'll get them back," Sergio said, tucking the knife into his boot.

"I would appreciate it." Rightfully, they didn't want to risk me shooting them in the back. Like I said, fair, but not foolish.

Tallis, meanwhile, examined the rifle. "Even the rifle stinks."

"The skunk wasn't exactly stingy in his spray," I snapped, crossing my arms across my chest. "What do you want me to do?"

If I thought he was going to offer an apology, I was wrong. He didn't even look contrite.

"You know, when you get angry, your ears get red? Just the tips." He tapped a finger along the top of his ear.

"I am aware," I growled. Then I ignored him for the next two miles. He remained unbothered, keeping an eye on the landscape when he wasn't looking back at me. The horses all picked up their pace, and I knew we must be close to the camp.

Rovers are nomadic, but only after a fashion. They tend

to keep to a patch of land—a fairly large territory—though they move around on it. A camp might be in one place for a few days or a few months, depending on various conditions, like weather, grazing, gathering, or opportunities for trade.

We heard the camp before we saw it—people talking, a goat bleating, and a few souls warbling a melody as we cut through a patch of forest. I didn't make the mistake of thinking we were catching them unawares. Rovers posted sentries, though you never saw them. Tallis had sent his mutt, Roon, ahead about ten minutes ago, likely rousing the camp if the sentries didn't catch us. I wasn't sure what their methods were, but if you ever snuck up on a Rover camp, they wanted you there.

We broke through the trees, coming along a small hill. I followed the horses as they clopped easily over it, only seeing the camp when I crested the top. Rovers generally had horses and a few wagons—the wagons were mostly to carry their things when they moved, except for the healer's wagon. That would be the healer's domain alone.

Once at a camp, the other wagons might serve various functions, but the Rovers slept in big canvas tents, large enough for a whole family. The canvas itself was painted, the colors and symbols dependent on the family that owned it. Though they lived in tents, the Rovers didn't sleep rough by any means. Woven mats would make a temporary floor, and the insides could be downright cozy.

I counted at least thirty tents as I walked down the hill. The biggest tent was in the middle—that one would be set up on a platform, keeping it off the cold ground, and serving as a general gathering place for the clan. A stream bordered the camp off to the left, along with a place for them to tether the horses. Not that the horses really needed tethering. Rover horses were uncommonly well-trained, the bond between them and their riders strong. Rovers treated horses like an extension of their clan, respected and cared for like any other member. It was one of the reasons Pops held Rovers in high esteem.

A handful of children darted through the tents, laughing, as they chased one of the dogs. We went straight to the healer's wagon, which had been parked close to the stream. As we got closer, I could see the person I assumed was the healer. She sat on the steps leading into the wagon, a pipe clamped in her teeth. Her dark hair hung in a thick braid, a smattering of silver running through it. She had a strong face—a sharp blade of a nose, a full mouth, and a stubborn chin. She'd rolled up her sleeves, and an apron with many pockets covered her skirts. The woman watched us approach, and I would bet Pops's watch that she didn't miss a single detail.

"Anna," Sergio said as he slid from his horse. "This one needs your expertise." He waved at Jesse, who was precariously perched on the back of Zara's horse. Not much of a rider, our Jesse. He didn't say anything, but his lips were pinched with pain.

Anna stood, brushing off her skirt with one hand while setting her pipe on a piece of her wagon's trim. It was a cozy-looking wagon, painted with greens, golds, and blacks. I glanced up and saw Tallis watching me, so I straightened.

Sergio helped Anna load Jesse into the healer's wagon while

a swarm of young children appeared, taking the reins of the horses. The horses were patted and chattered at affectionately as the children led them out of the camp, likely to be brushed and fed. I was left standing awkwardly outside the wagon with Zara, but not for long.

Tallis reappeared, a wooden bucket full of items in one hand. He waved at Zara, who nodded before joining the others in the wagon.

"Alright, Little Fox," he said, waving me along. "To the stream with you."

I was right tired of that nickname already. "It's Faolan."

He repeated my name, letting it roll off his tongue as if tasting it. "Not bad, Little Fox. It suits you."

I gave up. There was no winning with him. Tallis caught a lad as he darted past, whispering something in his ear before the boy disappeared into one of the tents. Tallis led me past the horses, downstream from the camp. The stream curved a little here, taking us behind some trees, the camp suddenly out of sight.

He set his bucket down. "Let's get this over with. Clothes in a pile for now."

I sorely wanted to take a bath, but if I stripped, Tallis would know I wasn't a boy. I couldn't send him away, either, because I'd need help cleaning off the skunk spray. I could ask for a woman to take his place, maybe, but then I'd have to explain anyway, and all that would do was make it so two people knew my secret instead of one.

There wasn't much I could do about it, so I got on with it.

I kicked off my boots, making sure Pops's watch was still in the toe. The boots would need to be cleaned, and though I didn't trust Tallis much, Rovers weren't thieves. I set the boots to the side. "I would appreciate your care with those. My watch is in the toe."

His lip twitched. "Odd place for a watch."

I ignored him. My hat went onto the boots. Despite my resolve not to, I hesitated. I'd never stripped in front of anyone I wasn't related to.

He set down the bucket, pulling out a stoppered jug and a pile of rags. When he realized I'd stopped, he looked up. "What is it?"

My cheeks got so hot I could feel the heat all the way to my ears.

He straightened so he could peer at me. "You're red like a strawberry." He dropped his voice. "Does that mean you're ripe?"

I flexed my hands so I didn't punch him in the gut. "I'm not used to stripping for all and sundry." I didn't think it was possible, but I blushed harder.

His brow furrowed as he looked at me, perplexed. "What? Never?" He placed his hands on his hips. "Ever? What about swimming? Or when you bathe?" He tapped his fingers along his side where they rested. "Your people must stink to high heaven."

I huffed. "It's not like that." I crossed my arms. "What do you do when you swim or bathe?"

He shrugged, dropping down to unstopper the jugs. "Clothes

come off, we get in the river. It's not like anyone has something we've never seen before." He sniffed one of the jugs, grimaced, then paused and looked up, curious. "Do you?"

"What?" I dropped my arms in confusion.

"Do you have something I've never seen?" He squinted. "Scales? Feathers?"

"No." I was mystified now, not sure where he was going with this.

He nodded. "Ah, then it's simply fear. Nothing to be afraid of, Little Fox. All creatures are beautiful in their own way. I will not run screaming."

My embarrassment shifted swiftly to anger. "That's not— I'm not afraid!" I had my suspenders down and my shirt tossed in the grass before I realized what I was doing. In two seconds, I was in my drawers and chest wrap, my hands on my hips, my chin up.

Tallis eyed me for a long second before he poured the jugs into the bucket and the sharp bite of vinegar hit my nose. "Ah, no scales. My loss." He dunked a rag into the solution. "A full soak would be better, but we'll have to make do." He handed me a rag. "All over, Little Fox." He dunked another rag. "I'll get your back."

I stood there stupidly holding the rag. What had just happened?

Tallis strode behind me, slapping his cloth against the back of my neck, shocking me out of my reverie.

It was almost comical, how easily he'd maneuvered me into my skivvies. I snorted and started scrubbing my face.

We made quick work of it, Tallis soaking my hair in the

solution, which I was pretty sure was mostly apple cider vinegar. I was shivering by the time we were done.

Tallis handed me a strip of toweling to wrap myself in. "You need to let it sit a few minutes." He dunked my clothes into the bucket, keeping a rag back to scrub at my shoes while I sat there with chattering teeth. The young lad from earlier sprinted up, bringing a bundle of clothing and dropping it next to Tallis before sprinting off again.

Tallis had set my watch bundle carefully aside while he worked the vinegar into my boot with efficient strokes. "There's nothing wrong with fear, you know."

I hadn't been afraid, but arguing would only convince him otherwise.

"Fear can be very useful. It can teach you a lot about yourself, about the world." He scrubbed at the boot, his movements almost graceful.

I glared at him. "I'm not having this discussion naked except for a few strips of cloth."

He kept cleaning the boot. "You snap and growl, but I'm not going for your throat, Little Fox, nor am I going for your soft belly." He dipped the cloth back into the vinegar. "I understand. You don't like feeling vulnerable. I'd offer to take off my clothes, too, but the ground is cold and I'd rather not."

I rubbed a hand over my eyes. "Can we please stop talking about people being naked?"

He frowned. "You can swim, can't you?"

"Of course I can swim."

He glanced up from his work. "But you keep your clothes on?" He shook his head. "Your people are very strange, Little

Fox." He saw my shivering. "Sit next to me. The ground is cold, but you can cover yourself better with the toweling that way."

I sat down next to him. "We bathe, same as you, you know. But I couldn't. Not as I got older." He hadn't even blinked at my binding. I watched him out of the side of my eye. "You didn't seem too surprised."

He simply shrugged, setting one boot down and grabbing the other. "Why the mystery?"

I pushed my toes into the grass. "It was just me and my Pops. My parents died when I was little, followed by my gran. Pops didn't know much what to do with a baby girl, and he worried."

A slight furrow appeared on Tallis's brow. "Worried?"

"That if people knew, they might try to take me. What did an old coot know about raising a little girl?" I smiled—Pops had been fond of saying that last bit. "People might interfere, try to get him to remarry or take on a nursemaid or something. Pops wanted nothing to do with it. So he changed my name to Faolan, and we went with it."

I pulled the toweling tighter. "And after a while, I got used to it. Once he died, well, it wasn't safe." Being a young man on my own was complicated and made me a little fearful. Being a young *woman* on my own? In New Retienne?

"Safe?" Tallis asked softly.

"Pops left everything to me. While it wouldn't be unheard of to try to marry a fella off young, people are much more comfortable doing so with a young woman. By the point of a rifle if need be. As a young man I had a voice—not much of one, but people listened a little. As a woman? Ha! No, sir. I decided I'd rather not chance it."

Tallis set the second boot down, tossing the rag into the bucket. "You know you won't be able to keep it up forever, don't you?" He nodded to my chest wrap. "It's not just that. Your voice won't deepen. No beard."

"Someone will cotton to it eventually," I said, my teeth chattering. "But I'll keep it as long as I can."

Tallis shook his head slowly. "Your people should make you feel safe, Little Fox, not hunted. It makes me sad for you."

I didn't say anything, but I smiled a little. To be honest, I was a little sad for me, too.

CHAPTER EIGHT

---*---

AFTER MY VINEGAR BATH, I HAD TO DUNK MYSELF IN
the river. I considered walking into the bitterly cold water in
my skivvies. They didn't smell like skunk, but I figured a
rinse wouldn't hurt them none. Except I didn't have another
wrap with me, and eventually I'd have to rejoin Jesse. Despite
having not figured out my ruse as of yet, Jesse was the obser-
vant type, and he'd notice if I suddenly sprouted breasts.

No one could see us at this bend in the river. I handed
Tallis my strip of toweling. "I don't suppose you'd close your
eyes?"

He shook his head, no humor in his expression. "No, Little
Fox. The water at this time of year is very cold, and while the
river is fairly tame here, sometimes people freeze up in the
chilly waters." He flicked his chin at the river. "I'll not let you
drown just because you're afraid."

I scowled at him. "That's not going to work twice."

The edges of his lips curled, but he kept his mouth shut.

There was nothing doing. Not only would he not budge—I
could tell by the set of his shoulders—but he had a point.
It would be the height of silliness to demand he turn around

to preserve a hint of modesty if it might lead to my death. "Fine." I made fast work of my band, handing it to him before stepping out of my drawers. Then, quick as I could, I walked into the water, the round river stones making my steps wobbly.

For a second, the cold was so sharp I couldn't breathe. Air locked in my lungs, my muscles seizing. Then I dunked myself, using my hands to scrub along my scalp, grateful to not have longer hair. As soon as I felt thoroughly rinsed, I stepped out. I kept my arms wrapped around my chest, more out of cold than any desire to cover myself.

I was too freezing to care.

Tallis held the linen out, and I stepped into it. He toweled me off roughly, making soothing noises, like I was a fractious foal. When I was dry enough, he wrapped the towel around me and grabbed for the bundle the lad had brought. A clean shirt was pulled over my head, the hem falling to mid-thigh. Tallis frowned at it. "You're a tiny thing."

"Maybe you're just too big," I said, my teeth chattering so hard, I was amazed he could understand me. "You ever think of that?"

He smiled but didn't respond, pulling a warm sweater over my head next. He helped me back into my skivvies, much to my embarrassment. But I couldn't get my fingers to work right due to the cold.

Tallis didn't leer but worked with an impartial touch that I both appreciated and resented. He was doing exactly what I wanted, and it made no sense for me to be prickly just because I wasn't a tempting enough morsel to him. He helped me pull on trousers, socks, and worn leather boots that were close enough to my size. I hadn't needed help dressing since I was knee high to a grasshopper, and that Tallis of all people had to help me? Well. It was an effort not to slap away his hands, like an ungrateful lout.

As soon as I was dressed, Tallis bundled me off back to the camp. He was stopped almost constantly by people with questions, kids who wanted to show him something, and people who just wanted to say howdy.

"You're popular." I sounded sullen, which was good, because I felt sullen.

Tallis's mouth twitched with humor as he looked down at me. "My uncle's the head of this clan. My sister, Zara, and I, we help out a lot." He shrugged. "People are used to coming to us for help."

"It doesn't bother you?"

His brows crept up as he glanced at me. "They're my people. Why would it bother me?"

I didn't want to tell him I didn't know what that felt like—I'd only had one person and he was gone. So I kept my mouth shut.

Tallis herded me into a smaller family tent, where I was reunited with Zara. She shoved a cup of hot tea into my hands, and quick as that, I was huddled in a warm blanket and set onto a thick pallet by a fire. The fire rested in a wide bowl of beaten metal, like a brazier, nestled onto several large, flat rocks in the middle of the floor. With the flaps closed, it filled the tent with warmth. I sipped the drink, my mouth filling with something sweet, like honey, and the slightly floral and green taste of the tea Rovers made.

As I drank, I took in my surroundings. A second sleeping pallet, nearly twice the width of the other, was rolled up neatly, lying against the side of the tent. Two knapsacks, a horse blanket—there wasn't much. Zara had disappeared with Tallis as soon as I was settled, likely so they could gab without me listening. I sat peacefully and warmed myself, my quiet only broken by the occasional giggling child sticking their head into the opening. I was a novelty to them.

Now that I had a moment to think, I turned my mind to the bigger problem—returning to the Settlement. We could go back late, Jesse injured and me in foreign clothes, unless I wanted to bundle back into my cold, wet belongings. Which I might have to do. No matter what, trouble was coming our way. I grimaced into my empty mug. So much for keeping my head down and making no waves.

I would need a good story, that much I knew. If I told them the truth, a many-headed hydra of trouble would be the result. I tapped my fingers along the side of my mug. What could I say that accounted for our late arrival, Jesse's treated ankle, and my appearance? Beginnings of a plan began to form, but I'd need to find Jesse first and see what materials I was working with.

I left the mug by the pallet, but I kept the blanket wrapped around me as I stepped out of the tent, almost running into three women, one of whom carried a baby in a sling. They greeted me and kept moving past the brightly colored tents.

There was no uniformity of clothing here—people wore what-ever they wanted. My stomach rumbled as I smelled goat roasting over a fire while I sidestepped a young boy passing by me with a basket of fish. A boy and a girl laughed and giggled as they beat a rug, chasing each other around with the paddles. A few tents over, I could hear someone singing.

The Rover camp was happy chaos, and I couldn't help but compare it to the Settlement. My current home was a col-lection of souls with a similar purpose but nothing holding them together. The Rovers were a family made large, every-one knowing their place and purpose. As I ducked under lines of washing, stepped around the occasional dog, and dodged one little girl carrying a chicken in her apron, my heart gave a little lurch. What would it be like, to be part of something so big?

Perhaps, when I had Pops's land, I'd hire a few workers. Add some noise to my own house. But even with my abun-dant imagination, I couldn't see it.

I found the healer's wagon and knocked gently against the open door. The healer, Anna, waved me in before disappear-ing behind a bright purple curtain. The wagon was a tidy space—dried herbs hung from the rafters, and rows of jars lined the shelves on the walls like mismatched soldiers hemmed in by a carved wooden railing. A small iron cook-stove stood in one corner, a copper teakettle settled on top. The air smelled of lavender, rosemary, and a riotous blend of other dried plants along with the sharp tang of medicines. Underneath it all hovered the musky scent of incense and tobacco.

There were two cots in the wagon, both full. Jesse lay sprawled in one cot, fast asleep, his injured foot resting on a cushion. In the other cot, a man lay on his stomach, twitching in his sleep. His blanket had fallen down, revealing a heavily bandaged back, spots of blood leaking through.

Anna stepped out from behind the curtain, the cloth likely demarcating the line between the clinic space and Anna's own cot. She checked the man, tucking a blanket around him, before resting her fingers against Jesse's wrist.

He looked so vulnerable like this. For all his quietude, Jesse was a big fella, sturdy and hardy, and it was a shock to see him brought low. Had the injury been worse than we thought? It had been pure luck to land us with the Rovers. As Miss Moon had reminded me upon my arrival at the Settlement, the smallest injury left untreated could lead to larger, deadly problems.

"He going to be okay?" I had to clear my throat before I got the words out.

Anna let go of his wrist, her face impassive. "Yes. He's strong. Healthy. He'll need to stay off his ankle for at least a week, but assuming he gives it rest and doesn't reinjure it, he'll be fine in no time."

Relief flooded me, my shoulders relaxing suddenly. I had no idea I'd been tense until now. "Why's he asleep?"

She shrugged. "Gave him something for the pain. He'll wake in an hour or two." She pulled a stool from under one of the cots and took a seat. "In a hurry?"

I shoved my hands into my pockets, trying to figure out

how much to tell her, and realized with a start that Tallis had shoved Pops's watch into my pocket without me noticing. "We need to get back to the Settlement. The sooner the better."

She shook her head. "He needs rest. He won't get it there."

I frowned at her. "Nothing doing. We need to get back. We're in a heap of trouble already."

She crossed her arms. "And how are you going to get back without our cooperation, hm?" Before I could argue, the injured man next to her moaned in his sleep. She took his hand, murmuring soothing words to him. When he was settled, she returned her attention to me.

"What happened to him?" I asked, curiosity getting the better of me.

Anna held her hands out, palms up, before letting them drop. "We don't know. Something attacked him from behind. He was lucky—Tallis stumbled upon him while out riding. Chased off whatever it was. Otherwise, I don't think he would have made it."

"He didn't get a good look at it?" I asked, frowning.

"He said it was a ghost," Anna said simply. "Nothing but claws and hunger."

Spectral fingers walked up my spine. "Do you believe him?"

Anna shrugged. "Yakob isn't given to exaggeration, but whatever it was, it certainly had claws. I had to do a lot of stitching."

"Where did Tallis find him?"

"Not far from the fringes of our camp." She took out her pipe, tapping it idly against her leg. "Whatever the reason you need to go back home so soon, I have no wish to endanger my patient's life. Or yours. Tomorrow, if you promise to abide by my instructions."

"I'll do my best," I said, my expression rueful, "but I'm not in charge." And I hadn't been at the Settlement long enough to know what kind of reckoning we had coming, despite Jesse's stories. I watched the injured man twitch in his sleep, like maybe he was trying to outrun his nightmares. The healer was right. Going back to the Settlement tonight was too risky. I would just have to come up with a whopper of a tale to explain our absence.

To thank her for her care, I spent what remained of the day with Anna, helping her with whatever she needed—whether it was hauling wood for her or assisting her with her work. Jesse slept soundly, but the man in the bunk woke a few times, muttering and shrieking in garbled Rover.

"What's he saying?" I asked. I was fair fluent in Rover, but I didn't know some of the words he was using.

"He speaks of ghosts," Anna said, dipping a cloth in cool water and applying it to his forehead. "Of claws and blood and angry spirits, coming for the living."

The man's voice shifted tone, and I didn't need to know the words to understand he was begging whatever demons haunted his sleep. Some things don't need words.

I was dead tired by the time the evening meal came around. Most of the camp was in the large tent, settled around on camp chairs and pillows, talking. We feasted on a soup of cabbage and potatoes as well as an herbed bread stuffed full of spiced meat, which we washed down with red wine. Several people brought out guitars, mandolins, and a few fiddles. I tried really hard to watch them and not Tallis, who sat across the hall from me, once again the center of his own small hive of activity.

I failed and he caught my eye. He said something to the older man next to him before climbing gracefully to his feet and ambling over. I don't think I'd ever met someone as comfortable in their own skin as Tallis. It was both impressive and irritating.

He dropped onto the cushion next to me. I ignored him and sipped at the last of my wine.

"You play?"

I nodded.

His eyes narrowed on me, and it was like I could feel his stare digging beneath my skin. "You play well?"

"Fair enough." I could call the birds out of the trees with a fiddle—that's what my Pops said. When I held something with strings, everything else fell away. It was just the music and me. A calm, quiet place to just *be*. It was the best feeling, and I missed it.

Tallis stood and walked over to one of the women tuning a guitar. He whispered to her, then disappeared for a moment from the tent. In no time he reappeared, a battered case in his hands. He held it out to me.

I watched him, my hand hovering over the case.

"It won't bite you," Tallis coaxed.

I opened the case, and my heart almost stopped. Inside was a fiddle. A very fine fiddle, maybe the grandest I'd ever seen. The wood was rose-colored, the sides of the body engraved with thistles and leaves in a winding pattern. The fingerboard was embellished with a golden inlay in a floral design. I was both afraid to touch it and overwhelmed with the desire to pull it close. I glanced up at Tallis.

He grinned at me. "Go ahead, Little Fox. You owe us a song at the very least for saving you and your friend."

"And if I'm terrible?"

"Then I guess it will be a short performance, won't it?" He moved the fiddle closer to me, and I couldn't keep myself from setting aside my wine and reaching out, taking it reverently from the case. I grabbed the bow, set it in my lap for a second, and used my fingers to pluck the strings and fuss with the pegs until the pitch sounded right. Then I perched the fiddle between my chin and shoulder and drew the bow over the strings. The fiddle answered, its tone sweet and rich. Perfect. It was *perfect*.

I stood, forgetting about Tallis and the crowd around me. I closed my eyes again, drew in a careful breath, and let loose on the strings. I played Pops's favorite song, and it was like the music had been hiding in the fiddle, ready to jump out as soon as I touched it and set it free. The tune was quick, the kind of thing you danced lively to, the notes high, twittering.

In a distant part of my mind, I heard other instruments join me. Guitars and a mandolin. The thump and slap of a hand drum. The song curled around their notes, and I chased after them. The entire world held its breath for me as I played.

All of a sudden it was over, and I was standing in an oasis

of silence. I blinked, the lamplight in the tent shocking after having my eyes closed for so long. Tallis stared at me like I'd reached up, grabbed the stars, and spun them into jewelry. I'd managed to shock him.

"Again," he croaked. "Play something else. Please."

This time I started slow, the song melancholy and bitter-sweet. It was a common tune, a folk song most people around these parts knew. People started to sing, parsing out the story of loss and heartache. Tallis sang next to me, and I was right— he had a stunning singing voice. I could listen to him until the moon crashed into the sun, and it wouldn't be long enough. I closed my eyes again, putting my whole heart into the strings. It was the kind of song that ached, the kind of song that called out to the universe with want.

I couldn't help thinking the song felt like me, hollering out to the universe that I was alone.

And no one would answer back.

CHAPTER NINE

— ✳ —

I'M NOT SURE HOW LONG I PLAYED. A FEW HOURS, probably. Eventually I was trundled off to Tallis and Zara's tent, my lids drooping with sleep. Zara bundled me into a blanket, and I passed out as soon as I lay down.

The next morning my eyes were gritty. Next to my head, someone had piled my clothes—clean and mostly fresh-smelling. My boots still had a whiff to them, but nothing that wouldn't fade in a few days, a week at most, I hoped. I was alone in the tent, the sun well and truly up in the sky. I got dressed quickly, getting back into my Settlement garb. Then I sweet-talked a cup of tea off someone, and a roll stuffed with venison and potato, before wandering over to Anna's, where I found Jesse sitting up in his bunk, bright and alert.

"How are you feeling?" I leaned against the wall of the wagon, sipping my tea and acting careless. The other bunk still held the injured man, his bandage fresh, but otherwise unchanged.

"Fair to middling." Jesse rubbed a hand over his eyes and fished his glasses out of his shirt pocket. "Better than my roommate."

I stole another look at the man. "How's he doing?"

"Every time he wakes up, he screams," Jesse said. "Thrashes about. Seems to think he's still fleeing for his life from whatever got him."

"The hungry ghost," I said.

Jesse shifted uncomfortably. "You believe in ghosts?"

"I don't know," I said honestly. "I've never seen one, and I don't believe in borrowing trouble."

Jesse chuckled. "You usually have enough on your own."

I ignored his statement, mostly because it was true. "Speaking of trouble, how much are we in?"

Jesse slumped back against the wall of the wagon. "It depends on several factors."

"Are any of those factors how good of a tale we spin?"

A faint smile touched his lips. "I would think that might be the main factor, yes."

"I'm amenable." I toyed with the edge of my mug, watching him from the corner of my eye. "Are you?"

Jesse grimaced. "I'm not the best liar." He rubbed a hand over his mouth. "I've got no issue with us doing it; it just doesn't seem to be one of my talents."

"You've got to commit." I put a hand over my heart. "When you lie to someone, you have to believe it, at least for that moment. It's the most real thing in the world as it's leaving your lips." I dropped my hand. "Course it helps if you don't have much respect for the person you're fibbing to."

A slow half smile appeared, lighting up Jesse's face. "Then I don't think we'll have much of a problem, will we?"

"No, sir, we will not."

He took a final glance at the man in the cot. "Then let's get out of here. Please."

——*——

An hour later, we were deposited back at the edges of Settlement land. Zara and Tallis watched us from atop their horses, the two we borrowed tethered to their saddles. Tallis's dog, Roon, rested at their feet.

Both Tallis and Zara sat comfortably, looking for all the world as if they were born in the saddle.

Zara flicked her chin at the forest ahead of us. "Go that way and you'll soon be back with your people." Her tone said that she couldn't see why we were going back. Not that we'd been invited to stay in the Rover camp, but I'm fair certain that in Zara's mind, we would be better off on our own. I translated for Jesse.

"Don't wander off." Tallis directed this at me, which got my back up. He seemed to be implying that if we did veer off, it would be entirely my doing. He grinned. "There are more skunks out there."

I scratched my temple using my middle finger. "Got it." From the laughter dancing in Tallis's eyes, I'm certain he caught the symbolism. "Ready?" I said to Jesse.

Jesse nodded. One of the Rover kids had found him a good-sized stick to use for balance. He was still supposed to stay off the ankle, though it looked much better today.

I adjusted my pack on my back. "We appreciate your hospitality," I said, adjusting my pack before offering them my half of a Rover farewell. "Ride easy."

"Fair winds," they replied, finishing the saying.

And with that, we turned into the forest, Jesse limping, and me hoping that the Rover saying stayed true.

—✳—

"A rabbit." HisBen layered a lot of things into those two words, most of them disbelief. Stuckley smirked. We'd been met with foul winds in the form of the guard Davens, who found us at the edge of the forest. After a quick stop at the Still so Miss Moon could check Jesse's ankle, we landed directly in HisBen's sitting room.

The sitting room was small but had its own fireplace, a squat love seat, and a stuffed chair covered in so much gaudy gold embroidery it practically glowed in the light. A low wooden table shone with polish, a small writing desk overflowed with papers, and a case was full of books, most of them religious in nature. A thick hand-knotted rug was under my feet. Behind HisBen, there was another door, which I assumed led to his bedroom.

Dillard sat in his gaudy throne and turned a gimlet eye on us. Stuckley loomed behind him like an eager vulture, his face blandly beatific. Like butter wouldn't melt in his mouth, as Pops would say.

Miss Moon had escorted us and was hovering inside the door, Miss Honeywell right behind her.

"Thank you, Miss Moon, Miss Honeywell. This will do nicely." It was a dismissal if ever I heard one. Both women seemed reluctant to leave, though I suspected for very different reasons. Still, they left without argument, Miss Honeywell closing the door behind her gently. I bet she was going to try to listen at the keyhole. I would have.

Stuckley and HisBen stared at me, the clock in the sitting room loud in the silence. Oh, right. The fictitious rabbit. "I'm sure that's what I saw, Your Benevolence. Our traps were empty, and here it was—"

"You left the path for a single rabbit."

I hated when people interrupted me, but I kept my jaw shut tight and my gaze on the rug.

"Which you not only didn't get, but it means we lost two days, minimum, of work from you, and your partner was injured. Not to mention the wasted time of the guard who went to look for you." He scowled at me. "'Give thyself, and the Shining God will smile down upon you' aren't just some words in a dusty book to me, child. Your choices *took*, Faolan. They didn't give."

Behind him, a smile slowly unraveled on Stuckley's smug face. HisBen sighed. "I'm disappointed, Faolan. In you, but also in myself. You are a member of my congregation, and I've obviously failed you. Due to our failure, Jesse won't be able to work for at least a week, which means you won't be able to, either."

My gaze snapped up at that. "You're not giving us new partners?"

For the slightest second, an expression of annoyance crossed his face, but it was quickly buried under a kindly demeanor. "Do you think, Mr. Kelly, that anyone would want such a reckless partner?" He shook his head before I could answer.

Why do people always ask questions that they don't actually want you to answer? Just spit out what you want to say and be done with it.

"No one would want to take you on, and I don't blame them." He turned to Jesse. "A week of kitchen duty and helping in the classroom—anything Esther can find for you that you can do sitting, understand? Once you're well enough, I'll pray for guidance to see if you require further punishment." He said the last gravely but almost like it wasn't up to him at all. As if his god would make the decisions and Dillard was just the lowly go-between.

I had to drop my gaze to hide my grimace.

Jesse nodded at Dillard, appearing contrite. I must admit he was better at it than I was.

"You must pray for guidance," Stuckley said, his voice full of pomp and snooty righteousness. It was the kind of tone that fair begged for a bunch of fives right in the smeller. I had a mighty good rabbit punch, too.

"For forgiveness," Stuckley continued, working himself up. "Not just from our God, but for the worry and ire you caused His Benevolence here."

Forget his smeller. I'd go right for his eye. Leave him in half mourning. Actually, I was feeling mighty generous. I would go for both eyes and grant him full mourning. Two black shiners out of the goodness of my heart.

"Lots of praying," Dillard said, voicing his agreement. "To hope that greater wisdom will be granted to you, Jesse."

He was laying it on Jesse awful thick, and it got my blood up. My mouth shot off before I could think better of it. "But he didn't do anything wrong! I chased the rabbit. I scared the skunk. *Me.*"

Dillard's eyes went cold. "And *he* followed you." Dillard shook his head. "Jesse has been here longer, he's older. He knows better. You? I was going to give you privy duty, but now I'm of a mind that you need more guidance than that."

I saw Jesse's hand twitch.

"Sir?" I asked carefully.

Dillard clasped his hands together in his lap, his jovial mask back in place. "Penitence and humility are cornerstones to my faith, Mr. Kelly. We are but flawed creatures, however, and sometimes we need a reminder. I think you could benefit from a little penitence."

Next to me, I heard Jesse swallow.

—✳—

I hadn't seen every nook and cranny of the Settlement as of yet, but even if I had, I would have missed the Box since it was situated outside the palisade wall, behind the Settlement buildings. As I hadn't been to that side of the palisade, I hadn't had the privilege of inspecting the Penitent Box. I was getting that privilege now.

I suppose it could be called a shed if one was feeling particularly generous.

I was not feeling generous.

The shed walls were thick planking, letting in only a few cracks of light to illuminate the interior, such as it was. The rough-hewn floor would probably give me splinters, but at least I wouldn't have to sit on the ground. The only thing in the shed was a bucket and an embroidered scene right out of one of Dillard's sermons that hung on one of the walls. It was of a large sun, some idyllic green fields, with words wrapping neatly around the edges: *Benevolence shines down on the penitent. Hallowed be the Humble.*

I hated it.

Miss Moon ushered me into the shed, her expression blank but her words gentle. "Come on, now, Faolan. The sooner started, the sooner done."

Miss Honeywell dogged her steps, her expression concerned. She slid in front of Miss Moon, stopping to straighten my lapels, like I was her child and company was coming for dinner. "Now, Faolan, I know this all must seem too much to you, but you need to trust Gideon on this." She patted my cheek with a smile. "His Benevolence is such a wise man— we're so lucky to be here in his glory."

I honestly had no response to that, so I kept my mouth shut.

She squeezed my shoulders. "You must give yourself over to your punishment. Don't fight it but submit to wisdom greater than yours. It's the only way." She nodded once, sharply, as if she'd just imparted something wise and helpful, and not meaningless sayings. "Your boots, please."

I froze, my heart stuttering. "My boots?"

"You can't go in the Box with them, silly," she said, as though it was a great joke. "I'll also need your hat and trousers. You may keep your shirt and long underwear." She saw my expression and sobered. "Now, Faolan, think of it as less of a punishment and more as a little lesson. The Shining God gives everything you need. Your hat, your boots? Those are just things."

Things I needed to stay warm. Things I needed to live.

Her eyes went dreamy for a moment. "I had a lot of things before I came here. Before I met Gideon." She sighed happily, then narrowed her eyes as she snapped back from wherever she'd been. "And I gave them all up. We're all equal in the Shining God's eyes, Faolan. You need to remember that."

There was no arguing with her. My heart in my throat, I handed over my possessions, hoping no one checked the rags in the toes of my boots. I could not lose Pops's watch. I silently cursed myself for not hiding it earlier.

Once she had my clothes in hand, Miss Honeywell promised she'd deliver them directly to my bunk. Then she breezed away, her job apparently done.

Miss Moon's face was still blank, but the corner of her mouth was pinched. "No more dawdling, now. Into the Box."

I stepped into the shed, noting that it was small enough that I could touch the walls with my fingertips if I stood in the middle. I would hate to think of someone of Jesse's stature being locked in such a thing.

Miss Moon gripped the edge of the door. "There's a slot at the bottom that latches from the outside. Once a day someone will come and bring your rations and take your bucket. Penitents aren't allowed to speak to anyone, so if it's reported back to HisBen, your time will be extended. You won't be released early, so I don't recommend faking illness or tipping over your bucket."

I hadn't thought of tipping my bucket, but if I had, I would have instantly discarded the idea. Dillard wouldn't give one fig if I sat in my own waste.

Miss Moon's expression was flat, but her hands were clasped tightly in her skirts. "Davens and Harris are on the palisades now. They'll be keeping an eye on the Box until Lawrence and Smythe take over in a few hours."

Davens and Harris didn't care for me—they'd made their feelings very clear. Lawrence and Smythe were the more lax of the guards. Lawrence liked a good joke, and Smythe liked a good belt of whiskey.

"Do you understand?" Miss Moon's knuckles had turned white where she clasped her skirts. She was mighty afraid, though for me or for herself, I wasn't sure.

"Yes, ma'am," I said. "I understand."

She hesitated, and when she spoke, it was in a whisper. "I recommend keeping your head down, your mouth shut, and getting out of here as soon as you're able."

I tilted my head to the side, sure that she was trying to tell me something, but she shook her head and shut the door instead. "Good luck, Mr. Kelly." Either she'd said the words softly, or the door had muffled them—I wasn't sure which.

I sat down on the ground, tailor style, and leaned against the wall as my eyes adjusted to the dim light. If I was going to be stuck here, I might as well rest.

✳

A creature in the darkness howled and I startled awake, shivering. Fear licked up my spine, and I stilled, breathing heavy into the sudden quiet. I must have dozed off at some point, because moonlight lit the cracks of the shed.

Now, I was no stranger to howling. Most things that make that kind of ruckus won't bother a body unless they have to. Back at my cabin, sometimes I liked to listen to the wolves singing as I lay out under the stars. They wouldn't cause me problems beyond going after our animals if it had been a hard winter. Foxes scream sometimes in the night, and it's unsettling for sure, but not dangerous. Elk bellows . . . well, they would liquify anyone's innards if you didn't know what they were.

Still, they were part of a chorus I was used to. Eerie, but familiar.

I couldn't identify the creature I'd heard, though I'd heard the sound before. It was the raspy howl that had woken me up the first night I was there.

And it was closer.

Shivering, I pulled my shirt tighter around me, reminding myself that nothing except for a very determined bear was going to get me out of this shed. They might have the capability to shuck me like an oyster, but that wasn't what a bear did unless threatened.

None of that logic made me feel any better. I wrapped my arms around my legs, my gaze locked on the door of the shed.

Then I heard a noise. At first, I thought I was imagining it. A faint scuffing sound, like footsteps, close to the shack. Had someone come to check in on me? I wanted to call out, but I remembered Miss Moon's warning. I locked my jaw.

Featherlight taps on the wood behind me made me startle.

I leaned closer to hear what it was. My ear was pressed against the wood when something slammed into it, banging hard. I scrambled back, putting myself to the other side of the minuscule shed. My breath sawed out of me, sweat chilling on my skin.

Very faintly, I heard a snicker. Someone was out there trying hard to scare me. To get me to scream so the guards would report me. Rage pulsed through my blood as I pressed my lips shut. I tried to calm my speeding heart, breathing slowly through my nose.

Another slam against the side. Then back to the gentler tapping, the noise moving down the side of the Box, getting lower and lower, making me strain to listen.

This time, something smashed against the side, much harder than before. Like a body had been thrown against the outside wall of the shed, rattling the wood. Even prepared for it, trying to not give Amos or whoever it was the satisfaction of rattling me, I found it hard to not jump out of my skin.

I held myself tight as I heard a faint scuffle. A wet noise followed, reminding me of the way it sounded when my old dog, Ranger, ate.

It sounded like a creature outside was feeding, but on what? A scent wafted in from between the slats—the tang of iron and offal. I'd helped Pops gut deer and other things before, and it wasn't a smell you forgot. I tucked my nose into my shirt, grateful for the lingering scent of the skunk. The odor grew stronger, making my stomach twist, and I was glad no one had brought me food today and that my belly was empty.

I sat there shaking for several minutes, my arms tight around my knees, and listened. Time ticked past. My nerves wound tighter with each breath.

A loud scratching noise cut through the silence, and I jumped. The noise was very like an animal with claws had raked them down the door.

I swallowed hard, feverishly trying to come up with explanations. You could mimic the sound, surely? Nails in your fist? A rake? But why would anyone do that? Would they go to such lengths to get me to break penitence?

Dillard might be testing me, or even Stuckley, Amos, or one of the guards . . . but I'd also heard that howl. Heard an animal feeding. Smelled blood and death.

Scratch.

I covered my mouth with my hand and squeezed my eyes shut. I may have been shaking like a spring rabbit, but rabbits were quiet critters, and I was tucked deep in my burrow.

It was sniffing around the door flap. Could it smell my fear? I was certain it could.

A clawing noise, like it was digging at the door.

I wanted it to be a person. I wanted it to be Amos or Stuckley trying to make me break penitence. Anything would be better than thinking I might be next. How easy it would be, how quick, going from being Faolan to nothing but offal and a tang of iron if something with claws wanted it to be so.

Tears leaked from my wide-open eyes, for I dared not close them.

I did not want to die.

Maybe I could scare it? I didn't have anything I could

bang, and stomping wouldn't do much. The walls were thick enough that my tiny fists wouldn't make much of a ruckus. But I had to try.

I scrambled to my feet, smacking my palms hard against the door, yelling as loud as I could.

The creature roared, a sound of challenge.

I roared back, but it sounded like a mouse squeaking at a barn cat. Terror quaked through my bones as I stood there, my mind spinning for answers while fear sweat seeped from my pores.

Finally, I did the only thing I could think of.

I sang.

Which made me feel fair foolish, but what else could I do? I had very little in the way of options. My voice was pleasant enough, but more importantly, it was *loud*. I knew how to sing to the back of the room. Hoping to scare the critter away, I belted out the first song I could think of, an old folk song Pops had taught me. I sang about the harvest, my love leaving, and the turning of the seasons.

As I sang, the creature quieted.

When I hit the last note, it chirped at me. A curious kind of noise. It hadn't scratched the entire time I'd been singing. Licking my lips, I pulled up another song to mind, this time a dancing tune. I belted it out, my hands keeping rhythm on the rough wood of the wall. Again, the beast remained still.

So I picked another tune. Then another.

I sang and sang until I didn't hear the creature scratching every time I stopped. By the end, I was down to sailor shanties and pub songs—both of which were grand, but the kind prim folk frown upon due to the bawdy nature of the lyrics.

Rain came sometime in the night. The drops pattering down, gentle at first, but they were pounding at the wood after. I stopped singing then, though by that point I'd been going for a couple of hours. I heard no other sounds from the other side of the wood beyond the elemental sound of rain.

Whatever had been there was gone.

When dawn peeked through the cracks, my hands were bruised. The wood had torn into them. Faint bloody prints lined the back of the door. My throat was raw, and what little water they'd given me was long gone.

But I was alive. That's not nothing.

I fell asleep to the merry clucks of the Settlement chickens as the world woke around me.

CHAPTER TEN

—✳—

I SUCKED IN A BREATH, JACKKNIFING UP FROM MY SPOT
on the floor. Everything hurt.

One time, when I was seven, I got in a fight. We'd been in
town buying supplies. I'd waited outside the general store,
drawn into a game of marbles with a few of the local youngins. I won, but Micah Tailor didn't want to cough up my
spoils of war—specifically a fine specimen of a cat's-eye marble. He accused me of cheating—said I'd cast a spell on him
with my ghost eyes.

I may or may not have also told him his mother must be
an old cow to birth such a scrawny, wobble-legged calf.

He punched me in the mouth.

Things devolved from there. By the time someone fetched
Pops, I had a black eye, sore ribs, a split lip, and was soaked
head to toe from being dunked in the horse trough. In retrospect, telling a fella twice my size that his mother was a cow
might have been a bit foolish. I had to apologize to Mrs.
Tailor and clean the trough.

I didn't get the marble, either.

As terrible as all that felt, the next day had been worse.

Everything ached. That's how I felt now, like I'd been worked over by Micah and his cronies. My mouth tasted like old blood and my throat was all blades.

While cataloging my injuries, I realized that the insides of my thighs were sticky. A familiar ache that had nothing to do with last night tore through my abdomen. My monthlies. I hadn't yet figured out how I was going to handle such a thing at the Settlement, but I'd assumed I'd be able to figure out *something*. To be honest, I'd put off thinking about it. But being stuck in the Penitent Box severely limited my options.

The door rattled then, the slot opening. A bundled napkin, presumably full of breakfast, and a new canteen of water appeared in the breach. I snatched them up, setting the food aside and immediately twisting open the canteen so I could take a sip. The ache in my throat eased. I cocked my ear, waiting to hear a commotion of sorts. Someone exclaiming over a carcass, the blood, or the scratches on the door.

I didn't get any of that. Instead, I heard a soft huff of exasperation on the other side of the door. "I need your bucket."

I recognized that voice—Dai Lo. I wanted to talk to her, but I didn't want to add to my time. Course, if anyone had heard me caterwauling last night, I was already in here forever. Still, I didn't want to get her in trouble. I wish I could write her a note. I fetched the bucket and slid it out, but before I could pull my hand back in, Dai Lo grabbed my wrist.

"What happened to your hand?" She whispered the words so faintly I could barely hear her.

How much to tell her? Should I even tell her the truth? My gut told me that I could depend on Dai Lo. She was a solid sort, like Jesse. "An animal was sniffing around the shed last night. I was trying to frighten it away." I licked my cracked lips. "Is there . . . is there anything out there?"

"Just the Box and some overturned earth. Probably an elk or a curious coyote." She dropped my wrist and snapped her fingers, waiting for me to show her my other hand. I obliged, and she examined it quickly. "These need to be tended."

"The cuts aren't much," I said.

"Your hands are filthy, and even the smallest cut can lead to infection." Dai Lo sounded so much like Miss Moon right then, it made me smile. She held my wrist carelessly, like her mind was elsewhere. "I'll see if they will let me treat your wounds."

I shook my head, even though she couldn't see me. "You'll get in trouble."

"Not if I tell them I saw them when you grabbed your bucket." Faint exasperation lit her tone. "I can't in good conscience ignore this and let you get sick, lose a hand, or die." She paused. "Possibly in that order."

She let go of my wrist, and I almost let it go at that. It's not in my nature to trust, but I didn't see how I had any sort of choice.

"If you can gather extra rags . . ." My words trailed off.

"Extra rags?"

I racked my brains for an excuse. "For cleaning? My hands are fair dirty, true, but in cleaning, the wounds might reopen. I'm a bleeder, see." I didn't, as far as I knew, bleed more than any other body.

I was met with a charged silence. As the seconds ticked by, I licked my lips, tempted to take back what I said. "Forget it. I'm sure whatever you gather is fine."

Another irritated huff, though her words came out in a gentle sort of way. "I think I understand. Eat up. I'll be back shortly if I'm able."

And then the flap snapped close.

Now it was back to waiting.

My meal was far from inspiring—a biscuit, though at least it was fresh. Someone had smeared the insides with honey. I'm fairly certain they weren't supposed to. No meat. No fruit. The penitent weren't allowed any fripperies. The better for them to appreciate what they had, I supposed. Made me more certain that the honey had been snuck into the middle.

The biscuit was buttery and fluffy as a cloud, and despite their filthy nature, I was tempted to lick my fingers. By the time Dai Lo returned, maybe a half hour later, my breakfast was only the faintest of memories. The door creaked open, sunlight flooding into my space.

I slammed my eyes shut, unadjusted to the brightness of day. I must confess—I almost sobbed. Tight, dark places and I were the bitterest of enemies. I'd only just made it through the first night, and already my time in the shed had taken its toll. As such, Dai Lo's face took on an almost saintly countenance. More divinity than human, with light gilding her delicate features, which were arranged in a no-nonsense scowl.

"Hands." She flicked her eyes to the side, letting me know that an elder from the Settlement was with her, even if I couldn't see them. "As a penitent, I know you will do your best to be silent, even in pain."

Translation: *We are being watched, so clamp your jaw.* I nodded, mouthing the words *thank you*. Only the faintest flicker of response in her eyes told me that she understood. Dai Lo, I was beginning to comprehend, was not only smart, but leagues ahead of me in savviness.

She produced a bowl, which she filled with water from a canteen. A rag was dipped, and my hands were cleaned with ruthless efficiency. I hissed my pain through my teeth. The only sympathy I received was the occasional soft glance from Dai Lo. Once my hands were reasonably clean, she frowned. "These need salve." She turned to the side. "There should be some in the bag." Her frown morphed into a scowl, her mouth pinched and her brows drawn together. "No, no, not that. It's a brown jar. Check the other pouch."

As she scolded and directed, Dai Lo pulled a small bundle of rags from her sleeve, handing them to me. She never paused in her directions as she did, and I stood in awe of her prowess. Dai Lo passed me the rags without her chaperone taking any notice.

I took them gratefully. If we hadn't been watched, I might have kissed Dai Lo on the cheeks for such help. The rags quickly disappeared, tucked inside the legs of my long underwear.

This help would come with a price. There were too many questions in Dai Lo's eyes. But I felt oddly sure that she wasn't going to snitch on me. Dai Lo had a respect for my secrets.

The salve produced, my hands were treated and wrapped. Dai Lo was both efficient and caring in a way that left me both teary-eyed and thinking of my grandmother.

"I was forbidden to bring anything for the pain." She frowned when she was finished. "Apparently pain helps the penitent." She didn't look convinced, and truth be told, I wasn't, either. My hands ached, my throat was raw, and my guts felt like someone had scooped a shovelful of coals into them.

"I'm supposed to tell you that another night has been added to your punishment." The words held a crispness to them that told me loud and clear that Dai Lo didn't agree. "Though I told them categorically that you did not speak one word to me, there are reports of hearing you singing."

The knot in my throat bobbed as I swallowed. Damn the palisade watch all the way to the skies and back. "I sang," I whispered, cradling my bandaged hands to my chest. "To keep the creature quiet."

Dai Lo gave me the barest of nods before wrinkling her nose, which told me she didn't like what she had to say next. "Sympathy is saved for the truly penitent." She pursed her lips. Then, her movements quick, she leaned close and squeezed my wrists. "You do what you need to do to survive. No one can ask more than that." Her brown eyes flicked to the side. "No one should, at any rate."

Thank you, I mouthed again. Hoping she understood that my thanks went beyond my hands. Beyond the rags. There was something in a body seeing you, even for a second, exactly as you are, and saying, "I understand." For a breath of time, Dai Lo and I were in perfect harmony.

Moments like that must end, and ours did with her closing the door and putting me once again in the darkness.

I did my best with the rags. My undergarments, such as they were, were built for a body that I didn't have. It was better than nothing. I dozed as the light cut through the cracks, the day passing with a slow and lazy pace that I wasn't used to. By the time the night came around, I was weary but clearheaded. Creature or no creature, my goal was the same: survive. I had the strangest feeling that Dillard would be more pleased to find me dead—but assumedly contrite and obedient—than alive and unruly.

I had a decided preference. As night fell, I stared at the door. Waiting. Waiting for padded footfalls, for claws on the door. For the creature to make itself known.

But nothing came.

Nothing ever came. Not during the next day or night. Just the barest ration of food, enough water to keep me alive, and my own thoughts to keep me company.

On the fourth dawn, Miss Moon opened the door, and I fell through it, sprawling in the grass. Exhausted. Starving. My lips dry and cracked.

"Are you penitent?" she asked gently.

"Yes," I coughed, through a broken throat, my tongue scraping along my lips. And though I knew it for a lie, I also knew it for the truth. I was penitent—if that meant I could leave the shed and stumble my way back into my bunk, my belly and my mind quiet.

—✳—

I had to admit, HisBen knew what he was doing. By the time I stumbled out of the shed, I was ready to see life in the Settlement with different eyes. Miss Moon gave me water before escorting me to the boys' bunk room, which was blessedly empty, and I made quick steps over to the area behind the curtain to attempt cleaning myself up.

I pulled the curtain, shutting off the room, and the reality of the situation presented itself. Despite Dai Lo's treatment of my hands, they weren't at their best. Panic nipped through me as I tried to figure out how I was going to take off my filthy shirt with all of its buttons, not using my hands, when I couldn't ask for help.

The curtain rustled as Jesse limped in behind me. He took the clean clothing out of my battered paws and set it on the shelving. "There's no way you're managing with those mitts of yours."

After days of deprivation and fear, it was too much. Panic shot through me, and I grabbed his wrist, stopping him. He stared at me, at first confused, but his expression quickly twisted to exasperation. He carefully peeled my battered hand off his wrist. "Dai Lo told me. About the rags. We figured you must have a good reason to be hiding such things."

I stayed frozen, my eyes wide and nostrils flaring with each breath, like I was scenting the air for a predator. I couldn't help it. Four days in the Penitent Box had reduced me to animal responses.

"Land's sake, Faolan, we're not going to turn you in or nothing. I don't want to break in a new partner, and we all know you'd be miserable in the other bunkhouse. Calm down." He undid the button on my sleeve. "I'm here to help, that's all."

I started to relax, only to stiffen back up when I realized that with my hands as rough as they were, I would need Jesse's help washing. We were friends of a sort, but that didn't mean I wanted him washing me any more than he wanted me washing him.

Jesse put his hands on his hips, his discomfort obvious even in my feral state. "Look here, I don't exactly want to see you in your altogether, but we have to get you clean as a whistle, and we have to do it quickly. Dai Lo can't sneak away. I'm your only option." He looked at me intently. "I'm here to help, Faolan. That's it. Promise."

"Okay. Thank you, Jesse." My voice came out rusty and abused, but it didn't hide my gratitude. In that moment, I would have killed a body if Jesse asked me to. I was that grateful for his help.

"Alright, then, let's hurry, because if we get caught right now, HisBen will find something worse than the Box."

Jesse got my buttons undone, then poured hot water from the kettle into a bucket. He fished out the wet rag and soaped it up.

By then I was down to my skivvies, which I'd been sitting in for almost a week at this point. Jesse handed me the rag so I could get started on my face while he unwound the band.

"I don't have a spare," I warned, scrubbing quickly behind my ears. "You're just going to have to put it back on."

Jesse kept unwinding the binding. "Dai Lo got you some fresh cloth to use. I'm to sneak this filthy one to her at breakfast so she can wash it for you, since she can explain it away a lot better than you could."

Bless Dai Lo down to her organized little toes. "Jesse, don't take this the wrong way, but I think I'm a little bit in love with your girl right now. Or in awe of. I can't tell which."

He snorted. "She does have that way about her. Hurry up, now."

I washed my pits, dunking the rag back into the water frequently. Jesse helped me put on the clean chest binding, then held out clean drawers with his eyes closed so I could step into them. Nothing had ever felt so good.

"Please tell me you can manage the rags on your own," Jesse said, offering me the bundle, his eyes still firmly shut.

My hands were a mess, but I did my best. Bathing had been hard enough, although between our haste, my exhaustion, and our overriding fear of someone catching us, we'd hardly had time for the awkwardness to truly set in.

"Done," I said.

He opened his eyes and pointed at the bucket. "Before you put on new clothes, dunk your head. We can make quick work of your hair, since it's so short."

"Can't it wait?" I asked, but I was already doing as he said.

"You stink, Faolan, and your hair is greasy. We don't want to give HisBen any reason to pick on you today."

I dunked my head. Jesse's strong fingers scrubbed my scalp, before rinsing my hair over the bucket using the last of the water from the kettle. He handed me some toweling to dry my hair while he swiped at my feet, then slipped a clean sock on each one. In a second I was in my trousers and a new shirt, getting buttoned up.

"You're not mad?" I asked, watching his face. As I'd been washing, it hit me how much I'd already come to rely on Jesse. He'd become my friend at some point—reluctantly, but my friend nonetheless—and I didn't want to hurt him.

Jesse grunted, finishing off the last button. "Am I happy? No. Do I understand? Not entirely." He shook his head as I pulled my suspenders up. "Will I want you to explain more when you have time? Yes." He grabbed my boots off the floor. "Faolan, I haven't known you long, but I know you're a practical type. You've created this fiction for a reason, and I have to have faith that it will be a good one."

"It is," I said simply.

"Then we let it rest for now." He eyed me carefully as he helped me get my boots on. "You okay?"

"Fit as a fiddle," I mumbled, wincing as my split lip reopened. Jesse left the boots for a moment to hand me a canteen, and I drank deeply from it.

He wheezed a laugh. "Not like any fiddle I ever seen."

I carefully slid my foot into the last boot, relaxing when

my toes hit the familiar bundle of rags. Pops's watch remained hidden. That would have to be enough for now.

While Jesse did up my boots, I ran a comb through my hair. Then we hustled out of the bunk and headed straight to services, barely sliding into the pew on time.

"Sacrifice," HisBen said, his voice floating all the way up to the rafters. "Sometimes we must give of ourselves for the good of the few."

I let HisBen's baritone lull me. In my exhaustion, I was grateful for the little comforts. Warm pews, a friend at my side, the light on my face. Maybe this was how HisBen got people to enjoy his churching.

Spiritually fulfilled, I was herded straight from there to feed my earthly body at breakfast. Getting to stuff my cheeks with honey-sweetened oats dappled with dried berries after HisBen's long sermon drew a correlation between the two for me. Listen to HisBen's words, get food.

Perhaps I was weak, but I'd happily sign up for preaching if I knew it came with a filling meal, at least for a little while.

After breakfast, we went to our assigned roles. Jesse was still on rest, and the other trackers were paired up. None of them wanted or needed a third wheel, let alone a half-starved one. I had the whiff of pariah about me, I reckoned.

I couldn't say I blamed them. As long as I was under Dillard's jaundiced eye, I would be alone.

I was standing in the courtyard with my bag over my shoulder, wondering what to do with myself, when Miss Moon waved at me from across the courtyard, the gunslinger in tow. Mr. Speed was garbed in Settlement gear now, clean-shaven and clear-eyed, a rifle over his shoulder. I didn't think he ever missed much, to be honest. As I watched, he reached out, touching her shoulder, and she smiled at him.

Both of them took advantage of the sunlight to get a good gander at me. I had the feeling that neither liked what they saw, but Miss Moon put a good face on it. "Will has offered to take Jesse's place today." Though she wore her usual calm expression, her eyes lit up when she looked at the gunslinger, like maybe he not only hung the moon but framed it with stars while he was at it. Couldn't say I blamed her. William Speed was a handsome enough fella and, even when not compared to the slim pickings of the Settlement, cut a dashing figure.

"You're feeding me, Esther, so it stands to reason that I should be doing my part." He kept his face impartial as he silently assessed me, but I felt like the runt of the litter wriggling from someone's fingertips while they decided if I was worth the feed. Then he turned to her and smiled. "I'm not too good at sitting on my hands anyway."

We all smiled at each other and pretended like butter wouldn't melt in our mouths. Miss Moon clasped her hands in front of her. "Faolan knows the route." Her temporarily sunny disposition faltered a little. "You *will* stay on it today, yes? And be careful?"

I touched the tip of my hat in a respectful motion. My eyes felt gritty, my body ached from sleeping on the cold ground, and my split lip throbbed. I wasn't saying I'd never stray off the path again, but I certainly wasn't doing so *today*. "Wouldn't dream of doing anything else."

Sunny Miss Moon was back, eyes alight at both of us like we'd performed an unexpected but utterly delightful trick. The gunslinger and I stared at each other, and I felt we both got each other's measure, before we turned as one and grinned back at her.

Moments later, both Mr. Speed and I walked to the gate, our features grim. I wasn't sure what he had in mind, but I was dead certain it wasn't just a neighborly notion of helping out.

The gunslinger refrained from saying his piece until we were passing into the tree line. Then he stopped, digging one hand into his pocket. He pulled out a handkerchief and a tin of salve. "You look like someone dragged you through a hedgerow backward and then tossed you back in for good measure."

I grunted, taking the cloth from him and pressing it to my lip. He pried the tin open. The salve had a strong smell— lavender and comfrey, most likely.

"As soon as you get the bleeding to stop, you put this on, you hear?"

Until now, Mr. Speed, like me, had kept to himself. Not in an unfriendly way, but he didn't go out of his way to dip his toe into my area of the Settlement's business. Suddenly showing up to my aid, garbed as he was, and offering help, made me suspicious.

"Nice clothes."

The corner of his mouth twitched. "Mine needed a good washing."

I scoffed and regretted it, as it made the throbbing in my lip worse. "You're not a very good liar, Mr. Speed."

That earned me a quick flash of teeth. "Will, please. I'm actually an excellent liar." He dipped his head down. "Let me see your lip."

I showed him, and he nodded, offering the salve, so the bleeding must have stopped. He frowned at my hands. "Those don't look good, either."

"They've been treated." I slicked some of the salve onto my mouth, feeling the balm of it almost instantly. My shoulders relaxed in relief.

"Well, they could use some salve, too, I reckon." He shook his head. "You going to tell me what you did to get four days in the Box?"

As I rubbed the salve into my hands, I carefully weighed my response. My first instinct was to not say a word. My allegiance wasn't so cheap that it could be bought with a hanky and some salve. I was halfway to a glib answer when I thought of that empty courtyard this morning, no one meeting my eye. I thought of my time in the Penitent Box. And I thought of sitting alone in the dark, listening to something feed.

It was possible that I had been going about this all wrong.

Maybe I didn't need to keep my head down completely. Perhaps I needed to build a few alliances.

I didn't need to regurgitate every little detail for Will, but would it hurt to give him something? Taking Jesse and Dai Lo into my confidences had only helped. I wasn't going to suddenly become best friends with every soul in the Settlement, but Will seemed like a good person to cultivate. After all, he wasn't part of the Settlement. He was an outsider here, like me. And unlike me, they couldn't shove him in a box.

I'd been pondering it too long, if Will's amusement was any sort of indication. He would be critical of anything I told him now, but that was okay. As far as he was concerned, I was a careful and quiet sort. I could practically hear Pops guffaw at that.

As I closed the lid and handed the balm over to Will, I gave him an edited version of Jesse's and my adventures. We started walking along the path as we talked, and it was clear from the looks he was throwing me that Will knew I was leaving some things out. He didn't need to know about the Rovers, and I was reluctant to mention them if I didn't have to. It wasn't that I assumed he wouldn't treat fair with them, but that I knew in my bones that HisBen wouldn't. Will didn't push, though. He didn't hide his skepticism, either. I respected him for that.

We stopped at the first trap, which had been triggered but was empty. I carefully reset it.

"Seems like a heavy-handed punishment, don't you think?" Will asked. "Four days in the shed for going off trail?"

"Woods like these? Easy to get lost, I guess. They need to set an example."

Will snorted. "Faolan, you're small, not young, and despite occasional lapses, you've got a brain in that head somewhere." He flicked the lid of my hat. "Anyone with a lick of sense can see you're comfortable in these woods. They weren't worried about you getting lost."

I frowned at him. "Even experienced woodsmen can get turned around sometimes."

He bent down so our gazes met. "That's a stern talking-to and kitchen duty. Maybe digging privies. Not four days in a *box*."

"I may have argued a little." I straightened, resettling my pack. "And I got an added day for making noise."

He shook his head, laughing. "You forget that I spent quite some time in the wagon with you, and in your bunkhouse. You don't rattle. You keep your counsel." He grabbed my wrist and held up my bedraggled hands. "And a few days sitting quietly in a shed wouldn't make you try to dig your way out. Tell me about the Box."

Again, I hesitated, searching his face. On the one hand, I was afraid he would laugh and tell me I was inventing things out of whole cloth. On the other . . . on the other, I was afraid he would take me seriously. I didn't want what happened the first night in the Box to be real.

My head hurt, and out of pure exhaustion, I opened my mouth and let the entire thing spill out.

The gunslinger frowned as he listened. "Could have been an animal."

"It could have been," I said, but my tone said I didn't put much faith into my words.

"None of the livestock got out, and no one has said a word about anyone missing." Will adjusted his hat before propping his hands on his hips. He stared at me thoughtfully. "But you still think something happened."

"I do," I admitted.

He dropped his chin to his chest, his fingers tapping along his belt. When he looked up, his gaze was steely. "I want to see where you went off trail."

I'd just spent four days in a box for this very reason, *and* promised Miss Moon, and he wanted me to hare off the first chance I got to do it again? Only a complete fool would even entertain the notion. But perhaps I was foolish. Or perhaps the Penitent Box hadn't made me the least bit penitent.

As Pops would say, I was born contrary. Because I didn't pause for more than a moment. "Follow me."

CHAPTER ELEVEN

—✳—

WE CHECKED THE TRAPS ALONG THE WAY, GETTING US two scraggly hares for our trouble. I'd thought it might be difficult to find where we'd gone off path, but I was able to track us easy enough. I led him to where I'd befriended the skunk.

"It's like a stampede went through here."

I dropped my pack on the ground, deciding this was as good a place as any to have lunch. My stomach was still mad at me for several days' deprivation, so I eagerly dug into my pack for the hand pies the cook had made. I handed one over to Will.

"There was a skunk," I said, biting into the pie. Rabbit and potato. Not my favorite, but I'd eat every crumb. "I'd like to see you act delicate in such a situation."

He grinned at me. "How bad did it get you?"

I made a face.

"You puke?"

"Worse than the time I got into Pops's whiskey."

He chuckled, tucking into his own pie. "You didn't come back smelling to high heaven, though."

I paused midbite. So easily caught out, I was. Here I thought myself so clever, and it didn't take him a moment to narrow in on my lie. This was the problem with getting too comfortable with a person. You let your guard down and things slipped out. "Must have been one of them non-stinking skunks."

Will didn't argue—he just waited. When I didn't offer up anything else, he waited some more.

After his pie was gone, he sipped at his canteen. "Can't help but notice that we're awfully close to Rover land."

"Is that so?" I calmly sipped my own canteen. He kept watching me. Normally, this wasn't a tactic that worked with me. I had perfected the facade of the sort of person who had no worries and was secure in the path of honesty and plain-speaking. As if I weren't fibbing up a storm. But I squirmed under Will's assessment.

And I'm ashamed to say, I broke. I pointed off through the trees. "That way. Not far."

He nodded, unsurprised. Blame a brain dulled by hunger—but I'd known from the get-go that Will didn't miss a trick, and I'd forgotten. Well, as Pops would say, no use caterwauling after the horses have left the barn. It just wastes time and spooks the horses.

"They help you out?"

"Course. Washed me up and took a look at Jesse's ankle." I narrowed my eyes. Will didn't seem like the type to be wary of Rovers, but you never can tell. People can be prejudiced about the strangest things.

Will simply nodded again, absently, like my response was

expected. Tallis might have irritated me some, but his people were a good sort, and I didn't want to bring anything down upon them for simply helping us out. Will tapped his fingers mindlessly along his canteen before closing it back up and stowing it. "Take me to where you met them?"

I sighed and scrambled up, brushing off the seat of my trousers as I led him deeper into the forest.

It didn't take long to find the spot—I was moving much more quickly now that I wasn't trying to support a limping Jesse. Will put his hands on his hips, squinted, and took in the landscape. As he turned away from me, a small green leaf floated down past my face. I tipped my head up.

Up about fifteen feet, hidden by the branches, crouched Tallis. His lips were moving slowly, mouthing a word at me. Confusion was clear on my face, because he tried again. I still had no idea what he wanted.

He scowled at me, and looked at Will. He flicked his chin at the gunslinger, a questioning expression on his face. Ah. He wanted to know if Will was trustworthy. I won't lie—I was tempted to leave Tallis in that tree. Nothing good would come from me talking to him. But Rovers didn't just hang out in trees for fun. He'd been waiting for me, I thought, but I had no idea why.

"Will, how do you feel about Rovers?" I very carefully didn't look back up.

The gunslinger frowned at me. "I treat Rovers just like any other person—I'm cautious until I get their measure."

I shouldered out of my pack. "Good, because we're about to be joined by one, so please don't reach for your pistol."

With my free hand, I waved Tallis down. Will looked up, surprised, as Tallis nimbly made his way down from the tree.

Will peered into the branches. "I've grown too used to city living. Didn't once think to look up." He sighed. "Lucky for us, he's friendly." His gaze narrowed. "He *is* friendly, right?"

"He is." I settled my pack against a tree. "Tallis, this is Will. Will, Tallis."

To my surprise, Will got the formal greeting. Tallis held out his hands, showing his palms. Then he clasped them together in the middle of his chest, right under his throat.

As greetings go, the Rover one was straightforward. Palms to show that they were empty and that Tallis meant no harm. Then crossed over his chest to show that Tallis would take his share of the responsibility for Will's health while we were here, protecting us from any outside threat while we were meeting.

Will did the same without my prompting, though he hesitated a little, more like he was trying to remember how something went than actual reluctance.

"You speak Rover?" I asked Will.

"A sprinkling," Will said.

"If it's easier, we can speak like this," Tallis said in my own native tongue, albeit with an accent.

I scowled at him. "You had that trick up your sleeve this whole time?"

He grinned.

I wanted to stomp my foot, but I didn't because I had dignity. "Why didn't you say anything?"

His grin widened. "You didn't ask."

I threw my hands up and huffed.

The smirk fell from Tallis's face as fast as lightning as he grabbed my hands. I tried to yank them back, but he tightened his grip. He made a chuffing sound, the Rover version of the motherly tongue cluck. "What happened, Little Fox?"

My scowl darkened.

He let out a frustrated breath. "What happened, *Faolan*?"

Like I was being ornery because I didn't want his pet name? "Nothing." I attempted to yank my hands away again, but failed.

He held them for another heartbeat, then let them go. "That's not *nothing*." He glowered at Will. "What happened to her?"

Will was watching our back-and-forth attentively, and I realized for a second I'd forgotten he was there. I felt my cheeks flush as I shoved my hands into my pockets.

"She had to spend four days in the Penitent Box," Will said dryly, though not amused. His tone was cutting, but the blade of it wasn't directed at us.

I whipped around to look at him. He'd said *she* . . . and he didn't look surprised. I pointed a finger at him. "You knew!"

Will shrugged. "Figured it out when you kept making excuses to use the bathroom by yourself."

I dropped my hand, confused. "Why didn't you say anything?"

He snorted. "Why would I?"

Tallis's brows knit as he stared at the gunslinger. "How can a box be penitent?"

Will barked a laugh. "I think the real question is, can Faolan even *be* penitent?"

Tallis didn't smile at the joke, his face thunderous. "What is this box, and how did it hurt her?"

Will's humor drained out of him as he quickly explained the Settlement's brand of punishment. For my part, I pinched my mouth shut and didn't offer a word.

By the end of it, Tallis's arms were crossed, the scar on his face white from how tense his jaw was. "I don't think you should go back to this place, Little Fox. It's not a good place."

My hands balled into fists in my pockets even though it hurt. "Who are you to tell me what to do?"

Tallis looked like I'd slapped him. "I don't need to be one of your people to be concerned for you." He bit the words out carefully.

"I thank you for your concern, but I don't need it. I can take care of myself." It was all I could do to not laugh in his face. It was all well and good to say, *This is a bad place for you*, and another to offer an actual solution. Where was I to go instead, I ask you?

Will rubbed a palm against his jaw. "What Faolan isn't saying is there's nowhere to go. No kin. No people."

Tallis had his mouth open like he was going to say something, but Will's words snapped his jaws shut.

I whipped around, glaring at Will. He had no right to spill my truths. "I have a cabin. I don't need no one else."

"And if you go to that cabin right now," Will said patiently, "what happens?"

I had the sudden overwhelming urge to claw at both of them and run. I swallowed it down. I felt exhausted and beat, like an old, overwashed cotton shirt on a drying line, so thin you could almost see through it. I looked away, my eyes smarting.

Will continued grimly. "I'll tell you what will happen. The mayor of New Retienne and his lawyers will send me to wrangle you and drag you back here. If not me, someone else. Maybe someone meaner, understand? They want time, Faolan, and they don't want you underfoot." He kept talking, his honesty almost brutal. "And I understood that if you showed up in New Retienne as *Miss* Kelly, things would go from bad to worse."

My blood boiled. The forest around us was silent except for a small trapped animal I could hear panting.

It took a second for me to realize that I was hearing myself. *I* was the trapped animal. Tallis muttered something before gently grabbing my wrist, pulling me somewhere. Will stopped him with a hand, but Tallis snarled something at him. Whatever he said, it didn't filter into my ears. It felt like I was standing on the top of a hill, a fierce wind whipping past, blocking all sound and buffeting my body.

When I finally snapped out of it, I was sitting on a downed log, my head between my knees, Will nowhere in sight. Tallis's hand gripped the back of my neck, his touch light. He wasn't making words, just the kind of soothing noises he would use on his horse.

"Not your horse," I grumbled.

"Certainly not," he said easily, but didn't move his hand. "Neev is wise and a good listener—prudent, even."

I grunted at him.

"You, I think, would leap into a burning tent carrying a thimbleful of water."

I slapped his hand out of the way and sat up, ready to tear into him. His smile was serene, his eyes practically twinkling. I realized that he'd very neatly brought me back to myself.

His smile faded. "Is what Will said true?"

"That I don't have any people?" I said it like it didn't hurt, my hands braced on my legs, my back straight. "It's not that big of a deal, I don't know why—"

Tallis put his hand over mine. "It is. To me, it is. I can't even imagine—the very idea, Little Fox . . ." He thought for a moment, his attention elsewhere. "It's annoying sometimes, my little cousins always after me for one thing or another. Sometimes I wish for nothing but a moment's peace . . . but to be alone?" His lashes made dark half-moons as he stared down at our hands. "I cannot fathom it."

He sounded shook down to his bones, which irritated me. "Didn't ask for your pity," I snapped.

"No, you didn't, and you don't have it, anyway." He glanced off to the woods. "Let's go back to your friend. I have news."

I stood, squaring my shoulders. He reached out, tweaking my chin. This time when I tried to slap his hand away, he sidestepped easily.

"You'll keep what's yours if you want to, Little Fox. I don't doubt that for a second."

I pushed my toes against the rag bundle in my boot, reassuring myself that it was still there. A short walk led us back to the gunslinger. He was leaning against a tree, arms crossed, like he had all the time in the world.

"Feel better?"

I brushed off his question, asking him my own—one that had been lurking around in my brain. "Why are you still here? At the Settlement. You're sticking around for a reason."

I thought Will would argue or try to dodge, but instead he fished something out of his pocket, handing over a sepia-toned photograph. I took it, Tallis leaning over to see as well. In the picture sat a young woman, maybe a year or two younger than me. She sat primly in an ornate chair before a fireplace. Her hair was up, a small hat pinned to the updo, her folded hands resting in the lap of her gown. Diamonds dangled from her ears, a matching necklace around her neck.

She wasn't beautiful, but she had a fierce look about her that I liked. "Who's this?"

"Mary Ellen," Will said, his voice sad. "After her parents passed away, she was supposed to go to her aunt's house. Never showed." He took the picture back from me, looking it over. I had the sense he'd done that many times before now. "She was a steady kind of person, Mary Ellen. Bright."

"You knew her?" Tallis asked.

Will nodded. "Her mother was a friend of mine. I followed her trail to the Settlement, but she's not there."

"What did Miss Moon say? Or HisBen?" I asked.

Will folded his arms over his chest. "I didn't ask."

"Something made you uneasy," Tallis murmured.

Will nodded. "I got hired to escort Faolan, and I thought, *Here's a good a way as any to get my foot in the door without raising their hackles.* Only, the whole thing stinks. The mayor paid me handsomely to make sure Faolan made it to the Settlement, just like he paid Miss Honeywell to get Faolan there."

"The two silver coins," I murmured, my mind serving up the image of Mr. Clarke putting those coins into Miss Honeywell's palm.

Will dipped his head. "Yes. Lots of money exchanging hands. Then I get here, and there's no sign of Mary Ellen. I have no idea what's going on, but what I do know, I don't like." Will rubbed a hand on the back of his neck, his expression weary. "And I got to thinking about Mary Ellen's no-good cousin, Luke."

"What's wrong with Luke?" Tallis asked.

"Luke likes to bet on cards," Will said. "But he's terrible at playing them. He owes people a lot of money. Mary Ellen's parents were wealthy, her aunt is sickly, and I can't help but wonder if Luke was looking for a payday." He eyed me. "I'm wondering if the Settlement is the kind of place you send someone if you want them out of the way."

We stood quietly for a moment, all of us thinking about this. I wasn't sure what to make of it, but I suspected Will was onto something. "The real question is, where is Mary Ellen if she's not here?"

"I don't know," Will said, "and I'm not leaving until I find out."

"This might be a good time to tell you why I was looking for Faolan." Tallis cleared his throat. "There's a body, and I think it's one of yours."

CHAPTER TWELVE

—✳—

TALLIS'S NEWS NATURALLY BROUGHT FOLLOW-UP questions—ones he wasn't willing to answer. He wanted to show us instead. We followed him, ducking under trees and pushing aside dense undergrowth. There was no deer path here. Just forest. Like the prey knew to steer clear of this section. I shivered, focusing on Tallis's back, all the while mentally marking the way we came so we could find our way to the trail when we were done.

Tallis finally stopped at an old tree, its trunk gnarled and massive. If all three of us held hands, we could circle it but only just. I didn't see a body. I also didn't see Tallis's horse.

Will glanced at me with a question in his eyes. I shrugged.

Tallis stopped walking about a foot from the base, tilting his head back, and we joined him, mimicking his stance.

A pale hand dangled down, stark against the deep brown of the bark. I was grateful I couldn't see the face.

Thick branches stretched out from the trunk, twisted by time and nature. Spring continued to wrest control from Winter's grip, buds already unfurling along the branches. If I'd looked up even a week from now, I wouldn't be able to see very far. But for now, I had a clear view of the body tangled up in the base of one of the branches.

Will let out a low whistle.

"Big cats do this sometimes." Tallis didn't bother hushing his words like some would. "Stash a kill for later."

"What makes you think he's one of our people?" Will asked.

"Weird boots." Tallis shrugged. "And since he isn't one of ours, it seemed a good guess."

I couldn't see his boots from here, so Tallis must have crawled into that tree at some point, or maybe looked from horseback?

"One of us is going to have to go up there," Will said. "Get him down."

I dropped my pack. "Someone needs to boost me up."

Tallis immediately made a stirrup with his hands, thankfully not arguing. Since he knew I wasn't a boy, well, I guess I'd been preparing myself for the list of things I shouldn't be doing. My people had strange ideas about what a body should or shouldn't do based on how we were born, and not on who we were as a person. Rovers didn't seem to care about that sort of thing as much.

He boosted me up until I could catch the lowest branch with my battered hands. Then he grabbed the bottoms of my boots, giving me another shove. I clambered up onto the branch, climbing closer to the trunk of the tree.

Closer to the body.

Up here, there was no mistaking the smell. We were lucky it wasn't summer. The cold had kept the body from rotting too badly. But something had obviously been gnawing at it. Animals start with the soft bits first—the eyes or the belly. This man's torso had been ravaged. The trunk under him was stained a dark reddish brown. His head—though I was guessing from his clothes and the tight cropping of his hair—was nearest to me, his face turned toward the trunk.

I maneuvered closer, inches from him. I couldn't see an easy way to get him out of the tree. Push him out? Lower him? Pushing him seemed . . . rude. He wouldn't know—he was long dead. But I would, and it didn't feel right to just pitch him like old garbage.

"Can someone toss me up a rope?" I asked. "There's one in the bag."

Will dug through the bag, quickly locating the thin rope we used for snares and tossing it up to me. He had to do it twice before I could grab it, and I only got it then because it stuck on one of the lower branches. Rope in hand, I turned back to the body.

I didn't want to touch it. For a brief, odd moment, it wasn't a stranger tangled there but Pops, facedown in the barn where I'd found him. I swallowed hard, blinked, and the stranger was back. My hand shook as I reached out, so I paused. Took a breath. Let it out slow-like, waiting for the shaking to stop.

I'd touched dead things before. You don't grow up the way I did and not get used to handling the shells of things once alive. I've plucked chickens, helped slaughter a hog, and buried my own dog when he passed. Death and I were old friends, in a way.

But this . . . this one struck me different, and I couldn't say why. But I did what I always did—brushed the thoughts to the side for later and got to work.

It was difficult, getting the rope around the body, twisted up on itself as it was, while I balanced on a branch. I wasn't in the best shape for such an endeavor, either. Four days in the Box had left me exhausted and abused. I wouldn't be able to wrap up the body or hog-tie him or anything that would make it easier. The best I could manage was to get the rope under his shoulders. I eased the body up, trying to not think about how cold it was. How stiff. How it should have been heavier.

Once I had the rope secured under his armpits, I knotted it. Then I strung the loose end up and over the branch. I pulled on the rope, pleased to see the body lift away from the branch. Keeping one hand on the rope, I used the other to nudge the body away from the tree.

Which caused it to spin, twisting as it dangled, so that now we were face-to—what was left of his face.

His nose was gone, as were his lips, revealing yellowed teeth gripped into an almost rictus grin. Holes where eyes should be. A scream built up and trapped itself in my throat, like even it didn't want to get closer to the dead man. I squeaked and lost hold of the rope for a second. The body slipped down a few feet before I grabbed it again.

I likely wouldn't have been able to recognize him if it wasn't for his fat black muttonchops.

Mr. Cartwright. The driver who'd brought me to the Settlement. Dead, chewed up, and left as a feast to the crows.

I wondered, briefly, what had happened to his donkeys. I hoped they got away from whatever had eaten Cartwright. Those beasts deserved a happy ending. Not that anything deserved being eaten and stuffed into a tree like leftovers, but I couldn't say I would mourn Cartwright much. I wouldn't spit on his grave, either. I'd thought I'd seen the last of his backside when he left, and discovering him here was unwelcome.

I carefully lowered the body down. As soon as it hit the ground, I poked my head out where they could see it better. "It's Cartwright."

Tallis's expression didn't change, but Will took off his hat and slapped it against his thigh with a curse. "I hope his donkeys are okay."

Tallis dropped to his haunches, examining the body in the sunlight. "So I was right. He's one of yours?"

I eased down until I was dangling from the branch before I dropped to the ground. "Not exactly."

"He was paid to take Faolan and myself to the Settlement." Will replaced his hat, staring down at the remains of Mr. Cartwright. "Which means we've got a problem."

I snorted, dusting my hands on my pants. I wanted to wash them something awful. "More than one, I reckon."

"We need to report this," Will said. "But I want to leave Tallis out of it."

"Thank you," he said, with that odd mix of amusement and gravity I was beginning to associate with Tallis. "My uncle doesn't care to deal with your people much."

"Not my people," I said automatically, then thought of Jesse and Dai Lo. Miss Moon. Heck, even little Obie. "Or at least, not most of them. Does Zara like them, then?"

"She harbors an almost violent dislike of the Settlement," Tallis said cheerfully.

"Which means we need to move Cartwright." Will grimaced. "We can't have found him *here*."

Because *here* was way out of our territory, and the last time got me three days in the Box. Dillard wouldn't care that Will was with me—somehow it would be my fault. It was also too close to Rover land. I didn't exactly want to hand over a reason for Dillard to turn aggressive against Tallis's people on a gilded platter.

I nodded. "We move him to our territory."

Will scratched thoughtfully at his chin. "Can't be directly on it. Otherwise you would have found him before now. He's been dead awhile."

I considered this. "We're going to have to put him up another tree, aren't we?"

Will nodded ruefully. "Or at least right at the bottom of one—say we fetched him down. I'll tell Dillard that I went off path to water the lilies or something."

That decided, we then had to figure out how to carry the body. Tallis suggested trussing him up against a long limb. That way two of us could carry him along. We made quick work of it before going back to the spot we'd met Tallis.

He let out a long, sharp whistle. To my surprise, a few seconds later his horse came trotting up, almost like a dog. Tallis grinned at me. "She didn't like the area around the body. Balked." He scratched under her chin affectionately. "So I let her wander."

If I had done that, the horse would have never come back.

Tallis swung up onto her back and, as soon as he was seated, put his palms against his chest and back out. The official Rover farewell.

"Thanks," I said, mimicking his gesture, though I wasn't sure why I was thanking him. This seemed a right mess, and though he didn't cause it, he'd pulled me into it. I didn't blame him, but that didn't mean I wanted to thank him.

"Anytime," Tallis said. "Things are always interesting around you, Little Fox."

I scowled at him.

Will tipped his hat. "We appreciate your help, Tallis. Give my thanks to your people."

Tallis nodded sharply and turned his horse, galloping off toward his own lands.

"Come on," Will said with a sigh. "Let's get Cartwright back to the trail and extricate ourselves from this predicament."

I wanted nothing more.

It was decided that Will would go and fetch someone from the Settlement. Dillard wouldn't take me seriously, or I might end up being grilled by several people and take hours to get back to Will. Which is how I ended up standing sentry over Cartwright's corpse.

We'd untied him from the branch we'd used to carry him, leaving him at the base of a large tree, his back to me. I sat about ten feet away, my eyes on that back. I felt weird, like if I looked away even for a second, he might rise up and come at me.

I knew he wouldn't. It wasn't like I'd ever seen a creature cheat the underworld and come back. I wasn't even sure I believed in ghosts, though I couldn't help thinking about the man in Anna's wagon. *Hungry ghost.* But fear is a mindless beast and doesn't listen to reason.

I've never been very good at sitting idle. It wasn't long before I was on my feet, stepping closer to Cartwright's body.

Some kind of animal had taken him down from behind. Now that he was in the full sunlight and my shock was passing, I could see that his neck had been crushed. I'm surprised his head was still attached, to be honest.

I carefully rolled him onto his back. If there was a big cat about, one interested in me as a food source, I wanted to know. Generally, big cats avoided humans. There's easier, tastier prey out there, but it had been a hard winter and it was possible one had gotten desperate.

I found a twig and used it to prod some flaps of torn clothing away from Cartwright's torso and was rewarded with the discovery of puncture wounds. The spacing and number told me that the paw was a big one. I couldn't recall a local cat that grew that big.

Once I'd seen all there was to see, I used my boot to nudge Cartwright back into place. I sat down, keeping my ears open for the noises that would let me know someone was coming up on me. The forest was relatively still, except for birdcalls and the skittering of creatures through last fall's leaves. I unlaced my boot, which took several minutes because of my hands. I tapped the heel until the bundle fell out and landed lightly in my waiting palm.

Too lightly. My boots were heavy on their own, but surely I would have noticed if the weight of one of them had changed—

My heart froze and dipped, sinking like a pebble in a pond. My gut clenched. Though I knew what I would find, I unwrapped the rags anyway.

Nothing.

I found nothing.

Pops's watch was gone.

I officially had nothing to my name but my boots and my hat. Everything else on my skin belonged to the Settlement. Even my wretched carcass belonged to the Settlement right now.

I will admit that, for the second time today, I cried. Great, racking sobs, splitting my lip back open. I didn't care.

What was there to care about anymore?

Nothing. There was nothing.

After a few minutes, I wiped my face with a handkerchief. If anyone came soon, there would be no hiding my tears. Pops always said I resembled a frostbitten tomato when I cried—all red and splotchy. They would think I was feeling tenderhearted for Cartwright, I'm sure. Let them think that.

With clumsy fingers, I replaced my boot, slowly doing up the laces. I paused as a thought occurred to me.

If someone had stolen my watch, it was unlikely they'd

had a chance to pawn it or give it to anyone. Unless it was one of the guards who took it with them on the supply run. If my boots had been by my bunk while I was in the Box, anyone could have searched them. Amos, maybe, or one of the curious youngins. Which meant it could still be in the Settlement somewhere.

The snapping of twigs and murmur of voices told me someone was approaching. I arranged my features into a stoic mask, one that said that I was doing my duty as a good person and representative of the Settlement and that was it.

Stuckley came crashing through the underbrush like he was made up of an entire herd of cattle. Even if he wasn't, I would've guessed that he'd spent little time in the forest by the wild look in his eyes as he whipped his head back and forth, obviously believing that he could be attacked at any moment. He made a strangled noise.

"Acolyte Stuckley, becalm yourself," I snapped, still short-tempered due to the loss of my watch. "You're being loud enough to wake the dead, and we got one right here." Well, so much for presenting myself with the decorum befitting the Settlement.

Stuckley straightened, wiping shaking fingers down his waistcoat. "I don't know what you're saying, Mr. Kelly. I'm perfectly at home out here in the Shining God's domain. Godly men have nothing to fear." A bead of sweat dripped from his hairline, and he swiped it away.

"Even if they were, with the amount of ruckus you were making, you've scared away anything dangerous." Will moved quietly to stand next to him, his face grave, but I caught a twinkle of amusement in his eyes.

Dillard stepped out from the trees, moving confidently on surprisingly silent feet. I'd assumed he'd be like Stuckley, more city mouse than country mouse. I'd never seen either of them do any work, and their hands were as soft as a babe's. But Dillard moved gracefully, like he walked through the woods every day. He spotted Cartwright. "Poor man. At least he's with the Shining God now."

Cartwright probably found that very comforting.

They examined the body, mostly in silence. Will had obviously told them the circumstances before they arrived, for both HisBen and Stuckley looked up and examined the tree.

"You found him here?" Dillard's expression was shuttered, his hands behind his back.

"Yes." Will pointed up at the lower branch of the tree we'd picked as Cartwright's resting place. It wasn't as large or as impressive as the real tree, but it would do the job. "Faolan scrambled up and helped me attach the rope and bring the poor man down."

Stuckley twitched. "What do you think did it? Coyotes? B-b-bears?"

Dillard sighed, turning to face him. "Ignatius, coyotes are not known to climb trees. And while a bear can do so, they aren't in the habit of stashing their food like this." He shook his head. "More likely a cougar, hungry from a long winter."

All the blood left Stuckley's face, and he quickly blessed himself. I was tempted to tell him that his god would have also created the cougar and might see fit to answer the cougar's prayers before his, but I remembered the Penitent Box and kept my mouth shut.

"Surprised you didn't find him sooner," Dillard said to me, "what with him being so close to your route."

I was loath to remind him of my earlier transgression but couldn't see a way around it. "Besides the other day, Jesse and I stay on the path. Unless the breeze was going the right way, we wouldn't have smelled him. Even if it was, the cold has kept his scent to a minimum." As I said this, Ignatius turned a sickly green. I wondered if he'd cast up his accounts all over Cartwright.

I'd sorely like to see that.

"If I hadn't had to respond to a call of nature," Will said delicately, "he might have stayed up there for months."

Dillard put his hands on his hips and shook his head. "Poor man. Esther did warn him. The woods can be dangerous at night." He snapped his fingers at Ignatius. "The shroud, please."

Ignatius fumbled with the small pack that he carried, pulling out a folded length of cloth and summoning me to help unfold it. Cartwright was placed inside and then wrapped up in a neat bundle. Under HisBen's order, Ignatius got one end of the cloth and I got the other. I wasn't as tall as Ignatius, who was built as if someone had pulled him like taffy when he was a baby. As such, the going was awkward. At least now that Cartwright was covered, Stuckley's nerves had settled. I was half worried that he would have kept dropping his end otherwise.

We walked our awkward bundle through the Settlement

gates, the guards eyeing me with suspicion. I ignored them, though their glares made my back itch. We carted the body into the kitchen and through the door leading to the cellar. Much to Stuckley's horror, we dropped Cartwright twice while getting him down the stairs.

"Be careful, Mr. Kelly," he snapped. "A man has died. I would expect you to be more diligent in your duties."

I hadn't been the one to drop him. "Yes, sir."

"Right," Stuckley said, sniffing. "Let's get this finished."

The cellar had a wooden ceiling from the floor above, but under my boots was nothing but packed earth covered in loose boards. They made a floor of sorts, but nothing was nailed down or put together in a permanent fashion. The walls had no pretense, just packed dirt with cobbled-together shelving units to hold pickled vegetables, jam jars filled with preserved fruit, and old barrels off in the corner holding root vegetables and other things that needed storing. It was a long and low room, the ceiling a scant inch above Will's head.

Someone had set up a sort of makeshift table down there, which was where we placed our bundle.

"He'll keep here until morning," Will said.

Much like the turnips he'd brought along with me to the Settlement.

I was on the stairs, sneaking back to the boys' bunkhouse, when Dillard's hand dropped onto my shoulder. I didn't flinch, but it was a near thing.

"Mr. Kelly, I'm certain that the Shining God guided today's discovery. He wanted Cartwright found and put to rest."

He seemed to be waiting for something and agreeing seemed safe enough. "Yes, sir."

"Far be it from me to argue with His wisdom. As such, I can see no one better to prepare him for his return to our creator."

I hesitated. When HisBen said *prepare him* . . . did he mean prepare the body? Something must have shown on my face because he continued on, answering my question.

"Ignatius and I will, of course, tend to him spiritually, but we'll need to build a coffin for him to rest in." He looked to Will. "Did he ever mention kin we could notify?"

Will shook his head.

Dillard sighed. "Well, we can talk to any other merchants that stop at the Settlement. If you wouldn't mind, Mr. Speed, perhaps you could send a letter with the next group to notify your employers? They hired him, I assume?"

"They did." From Will's tone, he obviously thought it a fool's errand, but one we'd have to try.

"Even so, we're looking at months of waiting for an answer. The weather is turning warmer, and we can't keep him down here for long. So tomorrow Faolan will build the coffin. Then he can set about digging the grave." That heavy hand on my shoulder squeezed as Dillard smiled down at me. "Seems only fitting that you be the one to put him in the ground."

I had to give it to HisBen—it took skill to disguise a punishment as a reward. I had no desire to build a coffin, but if I argued, I'd go back into the Box. I was certain of that.

"It would be my honor, Your Benevolence." I sidestepped

away from him, appearing to be turning so I could bow. I just wanted his hand off me. "I'll start first thing tomorrow after breakfast."

"I'm sure you'll do a fine job, Mr. Kelly." A smile unfurled on his face, but there was nothing good in it.

CHAPTER THIRTEEN

✳

AFTER DINNER THAT EVENING I HAD TO HELP DAI LO with the youngins. Little Obie had taken a shine to me. From what I could guess, Obie had been rolling in things all day, and now it was my job to try and mop the fella up.

This was fine by me, as it was a mindless task, and I had a lot to think about—namely, where my watch might be. Miss Honeywell had been the one to walk off with my things in the first place, but I couldn't see why she'd want it. Same with HisBen. He already had a fine timepiece. The only way I could see either of them wanting it was if they knew I'd hidden my land deed inside, which I deemed unlikely.

Davens or Harris could have swiped it, or even other youngins or Amos, but I had to start somewhere. The thing was, most of the adults, like me, were busy. Hands always full of tasks. Miss Honeywell and Stuckley, however—well . . . beyond churchin', I never really saw them do much. It didn't seem to Stuckley's taste—too plain in ornament for that popinjay. While they both had time to take the watch, I still couldn't for the life of me figure out *why*. To them it was just a broken timepiece.

The only time I could sneak into their rooms was during service, which was mandatory unless you were deathly ill. I'd have to trick Miss Moon, and that seemed unlikely . . .

But I *could* be given another task by HisBen Dillard.

With Obie clean, I settled the boy on my lap, attempting to read to him from a little handsewn booklet painted by one of the older kids. It was a cute thing about baby animals. Obie liked to trace them with his fingers and make whatever noise they made.

"Baaa, Fway." Obie still couldn't say my name properly. "Sheep goes baaaa."

"Yes," I said absently, my mind working on my own problems. "The sheep does go baaa."

"I like sheep. They fluffy *and* stinky," Obie said, a note of respect in his voice.

"They sure are," I said, though I was only half listening. By the time we'd hit the page with the donkey on it, I realized that I already had an excuse.

HisBen had given me a job that needed doing fast. Would building a coffin get me out of services? Only one way to find out.

To get out of a service, I needed to get permission from Stuckley or HisBen Dillard himself. With Obie tucked up onto my hip, I grabbed one of the lanterns from a table and climbed the stairs that led to the adult quarters. Obie quieted, leaning against me as I walked down the silent hallway, swallowing my apprehension. The silence here felt unearthly, like we'd stepped into a less pleasant reality. My lantern cast strange shadows on the wall as I set it on the ground in front of HisBen's door and rapped a knuckle against the wood politely.

"Sir? It's Faolan, sir."

No answer. Obie curled against me, his thumb in his mouth. He didn't like being upstairs, either.

"Not supposed to go up here, Fway," he whispered in that overly loud way most youngins managed.

"No," I said quietly, "you're not. But you're with me, so it's okay, as long as you keep to your best manners, you hear?"

Obie stuck his thumb back into his mouth and nodded. I tried knocking on HisBen's door again. Where could he be? I realized I rarely saw him in the evenings, and I'd assumed he'd retired to his rooms to work on his sermons or what have you, but if he was here, he was ignoring me. I leaned my ear against the door, straining for sound, but I could only hear Obie's breathing.

One of the doors opened behind me and I whirled around. Miss Honeywell stood in her doorway backlit by the soft glow of candles. "Mr. Kelly, is there something you need? Or an emergency perhaps?" Her hands were clasped at her waist, her face serene.

I dipped my head. "Good evening, Miss Honeywell. I was looking for His Benevolence, ma'am."

One eyebrow skated up toward the skies. "Obviously, Mr. Kelly."

"It's just—he'd tasked me with making Cartwright's coffin, ma'am." I shifted my weight, acting unsure. Miss Honeywell was a bit like HisBen in that, with her, it was best you shoveled it on thick, though what you shoveled changed. HisBen wanted praise and accolades. Miss Honeywell, in my humblest of opinions, craved respect and deference. I treated Miss Honeywell with the kind of respect one gives a rattlesnake. Move quietly and try to avoid it altogether.

"Did you need more instruction, Mr. Kelly?"

I shifted Obie on my hip, and he clutched me more tightly. "Only, I was thinking it was one of those things that should get done sooner rather than later." No one wanted a corpse in the cold cellar for long.

Her head tilted, a sparkle appearing her eyes. "You're hoping to skip services tomorrow morning?"

"If that's okay, ma'am." I lowered my eyes, letting my uneasiness show. She'd think it was for the task, not because I didn't want to be there.

Her grin was sly. "I understand. Young man like you needs a little time to himself." She patted my cheek, and I was careful not to jerk back or wince. I didn't like her touching me. "Don't you fret about His Benevolence. I'll handle Gideon. You just go right to building tomorrow."

"Thank you, Miss Honeywell," I said.

She shooed me off. "You're welcome. Now get."

I got, moving as fast as I could away from that hallway without actually running.

—✳—

I crawled from my bunk before dawn broke, when the sky was lighter but night hadn't quite given up the stage yet. I wanted to get some of the building done before services started so that when everyone came stumbling out of the church, I had something to show them. I picked up my boots, trying to let the others sleep. Amos's bunk was already empty. It wasn't like him to get up early.

I peered closer to his bunk, wondering if he'd even gone to sleep. His bed was neatly made, his boots gone. Maybe he was in the Box? Something to worry about later. For now, I would just hope I didn't run into him skulking about the place.

Tools were kept in the barn, in one of the corners, along with the wood I would be using. A sleepy Gertie bleated at me, and I gave her a quick pat.

I gathered up what I needed to get going—bringing out the sawhorses, planks, and so on, setting them up outside the barn. The day was chilly, but bright and clear. A good day to work on a coffin—if there was such a thing. I was trying hard not to think of Pops. My toes went automatically forward, searching for my bundle of rags, only to remember they weren't there anymore. I took a steadying breath. Nothing to do but move along.

By the time I was all set up and ready, people were heading into the chapel, Miss Moon herding a few of the younger girls at the rear. I trotted over, my expression solemn. People didn't like you whistling or smiling when you built a coffin. Gave the wrong impression, I suppose.

"Mr. Kelly," Miss Moon said. "Are you not joining us today?"

"No, ma'am," I said, digging my thumbs into my waistband. "I'm getting started on Cartwright's coffin. Only, I need to take measurements."

Miss Moon looked torn for a second, frowning at me as she shooed the youngins ahead to the chapel. After a moment's thought, she handed me her ring of keys, showing me the one I needed. "I don't think I need to remind you that Miss Lita runs a tight ship in that kitchen and in that cold cellar. People will know exactly who to come to if anything goes missing."

If anyone else had said this to me, I'd have taken it as an insult. But Miss Moon? I could tell from her expression and her carefully placed words that it was a warning. She didn't want to see me back in that box, or worse. Miss Moon wasn't all smiles, like Miss Honeywell or HisBen Dillard. But she was the one living in the girls' bunkhouse. She was the one wiping youngins' noses and making sure everyone had what they needed.

Miss Moon, I decided, was a good apple. "Not a single thing will be out of place," I told her, letting her know that I understood her warning. "I need to get measurements, ma'am, honest."

Miss Moon nodded, though she still looked a mite worried. I tipped my hat and trotted over to the main building, ducking into the kitchen. I had the keys in my hand, pretending for all the world like I was on my errand, but really, I was listening.

At this point, everyone should have been at the chapel, but there were stragglers, always. Sure enough, I heard rapid footsteps thumping down the stairs, the tread heavy. One of the guards, by my guess. The women would have been lighter, and Stuckley and Dillard were already in the chapel.

Once the front door shut, I palmed the key ring, stopping it from making any sound. Keeping my ears open, I ran as softly as I could across the dining hall and up the stairs. Then I was left with a decision. Miss Honeywell's room first or Stuckley's?

Miss Honeywell's. She'd carried off my clothes, and I didn't think it would take me that long to search. Wasting no time, I let myself in, searching quickly—in the hope chest, under the bed, careful not to disturb her stuff. I didn't want Miss Honeywell to know someone had been in here.

I sat back on my heels, frustrated. Nothing. I didn't entirely buy it. Miss Honeywell seemed the type who delighted in secrets. She would want to have something hidden away, even a silly little thing like penny candy or a letter from a sweetheart. A treat just for her. Which meant I was missing something. I took a few seconds to step along the floor, looking for loose boards. There had to be—

I froze. Footsteps coming my way.

My heart thudded in my chest as I cast my eyes around for possible hiding places. No time. I dove under the bed, even though that was a foolish place to hide. Better than being out in the open. I rolled as far under the frame as I could, holding my breath as my pulse thundered in my ears. The footsteps ran past the door, going into the room across the hall. Stuckley. He must have forgotten something.

I lay under the bed, controlling my breathing. He had no reason to come in here. He had *no good reason*.

But my heart was still jackrabbiting in my chest.

It was hard to hear over the thunder-skip of my heart in my ears, so it took me a moment to realize that Stuckley had shut his door again and was leaving.

"You forgot your prayer book, Ignatius." Stuckley said the words in a strange falsetto before making a disgusted noise. "Like the Shining God cares. I swear, that woman . . ." His bootsteps on the stairs covered up the rest of his grumbling.

I stayed frozen, my eyes wide, my pulse finally slowing.

It took me a few seconds to realize I was staring at a handful of papers tucked into the mattress. They looked like they were torn from a notebook. Symbols covered the paper—strange and peculiar-looking. They gave me an odd, shivery feeling in my innards. The longer I stared at them, the more uncomfortable I felt.

I wish I knew what they meant.

But they weren't Pops's watch, and time was wasting. I rolled out from under her bed, leaving the strange scribblings behind.

I'd been away from my post too long—I could feel it—but I couldn't abandon my search now. Stuckley's room was *right there*. I blew out a breath and flicked through the keys, trying them one by one. There were at least a dozen keys on Miss Moon's ring.

And not a single one of them fit.

I frowned at Stuckley's door. What was he hiding in there?

Whatever it was, I wouldn't find out today. My time had run out. I stuffed the keys into my pocket, my hand on them to keep them from jingling as I crept down the steps and headed down into the cold cellar to get Cartwright's measurements.

CHAPTER FOURTEEN

—✳—

I WAS IN A FOUL MOOD BY THE TIME PEOPLE FILTERED out of the chapel and we all headed to break our fast.

I ducked into the boys' bunkhouse to wash my hands and took a moment to wipe a cool cloth against my face. If I walked into the dining hall angry, people would notice. HisBen would get all kinds of smug, feeling like he'd pulled one over on me. I couldn't stomach it.

When I sat down at the table and tucked into my food, I was placid as a pond with no ducks, at least on the outside. On the inside, well, it was all frothy white rapids.

"I can't believe you found a body," Dai Lo said, shoving her spoon forcefully into her oats. From the downward curve of her mouth and furrowed brow, she looked more indignant than upset.

"I'm sorry?" I ladled a generous dollop of honey onto my oats and took a second helping of toast.

Her eyebrows furrowed. "I wonder if I could think of an excuse."

"For what?" I mumbled.

"Don't talk with your mouth full," Dai Lo chastened.

I shrugged. "Then don't try to talk to me during breakfast."

Jesse chuckled into his coffee.

She shook her head. "You're like a locust."

Now it was my turn to be indignant. "I'm hungry!"

Jesse refilled my coffee from the pitcher at the table. "Don't get between a growing boy and his meal. That's what my ma always said."

I felt a great welling of affection for Jesse then, for not slipping up, even in conversation, about me.

Dai Lo made a scoffing noise. "Girls grow, too. We get just as hungry. That doesn't mean we attack our plates like rabid wolverines."

Jesse laughed again, nudging me with his elbow. "Don't mind her. She's just mad she didn't get to see the body. Dai Lo wants to train as a healer."

She turned her glare to her toast. "Getting to see a body *is* a form of study. How else am I supposed to learn? It's not ghoulish. It's science."

I mopped up my oatmeal with my toast. "I'm all for science." Besides, I owed Dai Lo. Not just for keeping my secret, but because she helped me when I was in the Box, even though she could have gotten in trouble for it. A person who sticks their neck out for you was the kind of person you should take pains to keep around. I also liked Dai Lo. She didn't waste time bellyaching if she could do something instead.

"I'm building the coffin." My stomach was finally full, so I sipped my coffee, luxuriating in the warmth. My hands were still rough, though they'd been healing much faster due to Dai Lo's and Will's care.

"I can volunteer to help, I think." Jesse propped his elbows on the table, the steam from his coffee temporarily fogging up his spectacles. "I'm sure I can talk them into it. Tell them I need to be humbler or something."

He took off his spectacles so he could wipe the lenses with a handkerchief. His eyes were all for Dai Lo, and for once, they were speculative. Usually when Jesse looked at her, it was with his whole heart. They were the kind of couple that were made from one piece, you could tell; they fit so neat together. "It's going to be harder to figure out a way to get you in. You know how they are with this stuff."

Dai Lo sighed. "Ah yes. The 'a woman's place' argument."

I'd been drinking when she said it, unfortunately, and I snorted some of my coffee and ended up choking. Jesse had to smack my back a few times, which, in my opinion, only makes it worse, but people like to feel like they're helping.

"Can you offer to help prep the body?" I asked. Cartwright would need to be washed, and I doubted the Settlement would leave him in his rags. They wouldn't want such a presentation for their almighty.

Dai Lo shook her head. "Only elders allowed." She filled up my coffee for me, to save my hands extra movements. They might be feeling better, but they weren't fully healed. Finishing Cartwright's coffin was going to be a treat.

"Maybe . . ." Jesse frowned, slipping his glasses back into place. "What if you offered to embroider a shroud or something? A project the youngins could do with you."

Dai Lo thought this over, her mouth pursed. She shook her head. "Shrouds don't need specific measurements or anything.

There wouldn't be a reason to get me in there." Her shoulders slumped. "There's no chance. I can't think of anything that will let me look at him for more than a few seconds, if at all."

The room filled with clatter as everyone started to get up and put their dishes away. I laid my hand on Dai Lo's wrist. "I'll think of a plan. I promise." I felt I owed her something, and though I couldn't much fathom it, this was what she wanted. I only needed to figure out how.

She watched me for a heartbeat, then nodded. Promise accepted. Now I just had to not break it.

Jesse was allowed to assist when I needed someone to hold a board, but it was made clear that the actual construction was to be on me. Which stymied Jesse for a minute. But only a minute.

How did he talk them into it? He told them he'd do his best to create a sketch of what Cartwright had looked like based on his remains and what I could remember from my travels to the Settlement. They could share it with the traders who came through and find Cartwright's people. Jesse would sketch while I took new measurements—I claimed that I'd lost the slip with the ones from this morning—and then we would be escorted to the yard to do the actual building.

They wanted to keep an eye on me, I reckoned.

I'd dallied while I took the measurements, allowing Jesse time to document not just what was left of Cartwright's face but his body and wounds as best he could. That way, if I failed to get Dai Lo in, at least she had something. But even with all my dallying, we couldn't stay in the cellar forever.

Once we were back outside, I got to marking the wood with a stubby pencil, measuring twice before I even thought about sawing into the planking. Jesse took a seat on the grass to the side, resting his ankle, while I measured planks to cut. As far as I was concerned, it was no different than building a crate, and I'd done that before.

This was just a crate for a person instead of, say, apples.

A *dead* person.

I shuddered.

I didn't want to think about it anymore, deciding talking to Jesse would get my mind off it a bit. "Why's there a lock on the cellar, anyway?" I readjusted my hat to block out the sun a mite more. The weather was definitely shifting into spring.

"We have visitors often enough, and a lot of supplies are stored there."

I looked at him. "Who's going to steal a turnip? Let alone enough turnips to justify a lock?"

"Someone that's very hungry." He didn't even glance up from his sketch. He was adding in details from memory.

"Who all has the key, then?" I marked the last plank with my stub of a pencil. "Or who has access to it, besides Miss Moon?"

"The cook, Miss Lita." He paused, thoughtful. "HisBen, of course. He has a key to everything."

"And they keep the keys on them?"

Jesse stopped sketching. "You're not thinking of stealing a key ring. Did you *enjoy* the Penitent Box?"

"Not stealing," I said, placing the first plank up onto the two sawhorses I'd dragged into the yard. "Borrowing." I was good at borrowing. If only Miss Lita hadn't locked the cellar door behind us this last time.

He snorted. "You can call it whatever. The result would be the same." He shook his head. "I can't see any of them leaving their keys about where you can grab them. They all take them back to their rooms at night, I reckon."

I went to work sawing at the wood. Sometimes if you got your hands busy, it left your mind alone to work out something thorny. I was halfway through the fifth plank when it hit me. "I've been coming at this all wrong. We're making it too complicated." I smiled at Jesse. "I don't suppose you've gotten any better at spinning tales?"

Jesse just looked at me.

"Fine, fine—let me do the talking, then, and do exactly as I say."

Jesse didn't seem particularly comfortable with that, but he didn't argue, either.

I found Miss Moon taking inventory in one of the small storage sheds.

"You wrote the measurements down wrong?" she asked.

I held my hat in my hands and did my wretched best at looking mournful. She frowned at me, one hand suspended over the beeswax candles she'd been counting for inventory. "First you lost them; now you wrote them down wrong?"

"I'm not sure? They don't look quite right." I screwed my

face up. "I've never had to measure someone . . . like that." Which was a bit of a truth. I'd never had to measure someone mauled to bits. "My hand got a little shaky, and I can't tell if two of the numbers are threes or eights."

I turned big eyes on her then, like a scared pup. "I'd never used a measuring tape before. If I don't get this right, I might be back in the Box . . ." I will admit that I was both laying it on a little thick and putting a lot of weight on my assessment that Miss Moon didn't agree with the Penitent Box as a good punishment. It helped that I truly was afraid of going back in there.

She hesitated, her hand still hovering by the candles. I twisted my hands around my hat brim, drawing her attention to their sad and sorry state. I wanted to remind her of the reality of the Box. People had a way of putting unpleasant things out of their thoughts.

The corners of her mouth curved in sympathy, pulling at the network of scars there. Miss Moon was a plain woman, in some respects, but I suspected she was a good one, despite the Settlement. I preferred good to pretty any day.

She tucked her notebook into her apron and fetched out her key ring. "I can give you five minutes to check your numbers. That's it."

I grinned at her and placed my hat back onto my head. "That's all I need."

I made a production out of rechecking with the fancy measuring tape the Settlement had. The small, flat disc contained a strip with measured increments on it that I could stretch out and see exactly what length I'd need to cut the wood so I could build properly. Pops and I had eyed a similar one to this at the local mercantile, but it had been out of our budget range. The one at the mercantile was seventeen dollars, and it wasn't half as nice as this one. That one didn't even have any numbers on it. The little disc in my hand was almost two months' wages for most folk.

My work ostensibly done, we went to leave the cellar. Miss Moon had her keys out again, ready to lock the turnips and Cartwright up tight, when Jesse hustled into the entryway.

"Miss Moon?" His voice held a thread of concern, which caused her to immediately turn to him.

"Jesse?"

"I'm not sure how, ma'am, but a few of the goats got loose. I'm usually good at wrangling them, but what with my ankle . . ."

Her eyes widened. "Goodness!" She hitched up her skirts, the lock forgotten. "Show me at once."

"I'll help," I offered, hurrying them along. "No time to lose!" I didn't want her remembering to lock the door. "Goats can cause all kinds of trouble."

That wasn't even a fib. Goats could cause a *heap* of trouble.

We spilled out into the yard, and indeed, a few goats were loose. Actually, three goats were loose, including Gertie. Miss Moon took off, clucking at the big-bellied brown-and-white one.

I clapped my hat onto my head. "I thought you made the goat thing up."

The big gray was already going for the hanging laundry. Gertie had her head through the slats surrounding the kitchen garden, attempting to nibble at the small shoots already popping up. The big-bellied goat seemed content to annoy the chickens.

Jesse shook his head. "You wanted a proper distraction to keep her from worrying about the doors. Well, the goats qualify, since they occasionally get out on their own. So no one would think it odd."

"Jesse, you're brilliant."

He gave a wide smile that made me laugh.

Now we just had to hope that nobody else needed the cellar today and that door was left unlocked.

It took us a good half hour to round the goats up and return them to their pen. At which point Miss Moon went back to her inventory, and I went back to cutting wood. I was grateful that Dillard didn't want me to make a traditional coffin—those are six-sided and more difficult than what I was doing. A basic box was quicker. I might have felt bad about it if Cartwright hadn't spit at the ground in front of me last time I saw him. As far as I was concerned, he was lucky to be getting the box.

I put my back into it and got the basic build done by supper. I'd need to sand it down and make sure the construction was neat and tidy in the morning. It may only be a box that was going into the ground, but it needed to meet Dillard's standards, or I would find myself in a very *different* box.

Supper came and went, followed by the usual evening rituals. The youngins in my cabin needed help with their baths, so I was tasked with hauling and heating water, as well as aiding some of the smaller ones, making sure they scrubbed behind their ears. I cleaned myself up behind the curtain, pleased that the older youths were allowed a smidgen of privacy.

Amos's bunk remained blessedly empty, for which I was grateful.

The gunslinger read to us from a dog-eared paperback. Some wild adventure tale about battling giant snow beasts up north. The tales were supposed to be true, but I'd never seen anything so fantastical in my life. I bit my tongue, though, because the little ones loved the story. Didn't see the harm in letting them believe that such things still roamed the land. Maybe it would make them grow up cautious, and there were plenty of things out there that could snap them up in one bite.

Just ask Cartwright.

It was difficult to stay awake when everyone else started dozing off. So difficult, in fact, that I didn't manage it at all. I was deep in a dream about a cave in the forest when a hand covered my mouth.

My eyes flew open. Jesse's face hovered over me in the dim light of the stars coming in through the window. As soon as I relaxed, he removed his hand. I slipped silently out of bed, grabbed my boots, and followed him to the door. We didn't make much sound, but anything we did was likely covered by Will's snores.

As soon as we were outside, we took a second to put on our boots. We didn't lace them. Didn't want to be caught out in the open, so that would have to wait. We sneaked across the frosted grass, moving carefully until we were outside the kitchen door. When we got close enough, Dai Lo detached herself from the shadows, her face alight.

I snorted softly. "I'm surprised you waited." She was *that* excited.

She pinched me. "I said I would. I don't break my oaths so cavalierly."

"Never said you did," I mumbled. We crept into the kitchen until we were in front of the cellar door. Hoping that Miss Moon hadn't come back after the fact, I grabbed the handle and depressed the lever. We all breathed a sigh of relief when the door opened with only a faint squeak. I ushered them in and, with a final glance around, followed them, closing the door behind me.

We were instantly cocooned in darkness. I felt my way down the stairs, the air growing noticeably colder as I descended, the smell of earth, vegetables, and the faint hint of decay teasing my nostrils. A soft click followed by a spark let me see the outlines of shelves, jars, and barrels. Jesse stood below me, using a beat-up metal lighter to light a candle that Dai Lo had brought with her in the pocket of her nightgown.

The candle lit, the room grew slightly more into focus. It didn't give off much light on its own, but we didn't dare more.

Jesse flicked his lighter shut and stored it before shouldering out of his jacket. "You're going to freeze to death."

Dai Lo stuck the candle into a small tin holder with a loop for her finger that she grabbed from one of the cellar shelves. "I'm fine. It will get in the way, and I didn't want to make extra noise by getting my coat. Miss Moon has the ears of a bat." She moved toward the table where Cartwright was laid out, paused, then swung around to go up on her tiptoes and kiss Jesse on the cheek. "But thank you."

He put his jacket back on but didn't like it. He wanted to care for her, which was sweet, but to my eyes, it was far sweeter still that he included listening to what she wanted as part of that care. Some folks will do what they think is right by you, no matter that you're hollerin' that it's not. Dai Lo knew her mind, spoke it, and Jesse listened.

For a faint, fragile moment, I was jealous. I snapped that moment clean in two. Wouldn't do me no good, thinking that way. Maybe I didn't have what they had, and that dug in my craw, but I was sure glad that Jesse and Dai Lo *did*.

Dai Lo pulled back the sheet covering Cartwright and raised the candle above, taking him in with focused attention. I'd already seen the show, so I got myself comfortable as I took in the long, low room around us. As I looked around, I realized the room was in itself a sort of coffin. Only a thin layer of wood between us and packed earth.

Only a thin layer between us and the worms.

A shiver worked its way up my spine, and I hoped Dai Lo hurried up. We couldn't spend the night in here. By my guess, we'd already been down here twenty minutes.

Another ten or so passed, with Dai Lo using a pencil to push Cartwright's tattered clothing to the side so she could examine his wounds. They were making her frown. She dug a small strip of wood out of her pocket, unfolding it into a neat little ruler. As she was rattling off the measurements to Jesse, who was in turn recording them in his sketchbook, I thought I heard a sound.

Nothing loud. Just the hint of movement.

I held up my hand, grabbing Jesse's attention. He touched Dai Lo's shoulder, and we froze for several long moments. I was starting to think I'd conjured the sound when I heard a floorboard above my head creak. Someone was in the kitchen.

I stared at my compatriots. We couldn't go up the stairs, and if they decided they wanted into the cellar, we had about a second before someone joined us.

Dai Lo jerked the sheet back into place and snuffed out the candle.

CHAPTER FIFTEEN

※

OUR OPTIONS, SUCH AS THEY WERE, HAD BEEN LIMITED,
which was how I found myself hunched behind a barrel and
hoping whoever our visitor was, they weren't in mind for a
late-night turnip. The barrels were only about a foot or so
from the wall—just far enough to keep the moisture from the
dirt wall from getting in.

I'm not a big person, so I was easily cramped behind it.
Dai Lo sat next to me, probably wishing she'd taken Jesse's
jacket. If anyone peeked, she would be the most visible in the
bright white of her nightgown. Jesse's stature meant he didn't
fit in our hiding spot at all. He'd had to shift himself sideways,
his head practically dangling out of Dai Lo's lap and into mine.
His eyes were clamped shut, and I wondered if he was hoping
that if he couldn't see the intruder, they couldn't see him.

And I knew all this because whoever was stepping down
the cellar stairs had brought a light with them.

Candlelight flickered as they came down the steps, making the boards creak. A fairly big person, then—not one of the
youngins sneaking around on a dare. We held our breaths,
not wanting any sound to betray us.

The footsteps moved across the boards now, heading toward Cartwright. I heard a soft murmuring, a soothing tone, cajoling. The kind of voice you used when trying to get a body to go along with your way of thinking.

"We can't just take it," a man said in a whisper so low, I couldn't quite make out everything he was saying or who he was, either. A man's voice, but beyond that, I wasn't sure. His next whisper was sharp—a command, surely. "No . . . something else . . ."

A bone-chilling growl made my fingers go cold, my insides feeling liquid with fear.

Animal musk filled my nostrils as I breathed in as slow and quiet as I could.

The growl was low, the kind of noise you felt rather than heard. My blood iced in my veins, and despite the frigid air, I broke out in a sweat.

The person hissed something. ". . . carrion. Fresh, I promise . . ."

A low snarl. Dai Lo's hand grabbed mine, and I gripped tight. Whatever was out there was going to scent us. Scent us and then eat us up for supper, just like it had Cartwright.

This cellar was a coffin alright—mine. Ours.

Because I had not a shred of doubt that whatever had ended Cartwright's life was snarling a few feet away from us.

"They'll know," the man argued, his words so low it took me a second to make sense of them. ". . . may be ours . . ." and then more words that I missed, followed by ". . . you'll feed."

The creature stopped snarling and chuffed. I couldn't hear

the next exchange at all, but a few more seconds passed, and then blessedly, the footsteps retreated.

The stairs creaked.

The click of the door shutting.

Darkness.

Dai Lo's sweaty hand in mine, both of us shivering in terror. I assumed Jesse was as well because he was a smart fella, and smart people would be terrified right now. We didn't move or make a sound.

I counted off seconds in my head.

Then minutes.

Fifteen went by before I shifted, the other two following my lead, straightening up. Jesse's lighter flicked. Blessed light. The room looked the same as it had before. Cartwright still stretched out on the table, the sheet over him outlining him like a shroud. And yet, somehow, the entire room had changed, and I wanted nothing more than to run out of it.

The next morning, after HisBen's ruminations on sacrificing for those in need, I was just exiting the chapel when I heard a shout by the barn. One of the older boys, Ernest, had gone to feed and water the animals before breakfast. As I watched, he came barreling out of the doors, barely making it to the side of the barn before casting up his accounts.

I was running to the barn before the puke hit the ground.

Dai Lo beat me by a hair, so we opened the barn door together. The smell hit me before my eyes could adjust to the lower light. Along with the usual hay, manure, and animal musk was an overpowering stench of death—coppery blood, offal, and fear.

I put my arm up to cover my mouth and followed Dai Lo deeper into the barn. A quick glance told me the horses and cows were fine. I could hear the grunting of the pigs, along with the scuffing sounds of animals moving around.

But the goats.

The goats were a different matter. Nothing moved in the goat pen. Nothing made noise. There was so much destruction, so much gore and half-dried, sticky blood, that it took my eyes a moment to make sense of it. It was like an angry giant had smashed its hand into the goat pen, breaking and tearing until there was nothing left.

"Oh," Dai Lo said softly. "Oh no." Tears streaked down her face and her breath hitched.

I climbed into what was left of the goat enclosure, my boots making soft thuds in the dirt as I stepped gingerly around the mess, the sounds echoing in my empty heart.

I found Gertie by the water trough.

Her eyes were glassy and fixed, like a doll's. She was a bloody mess, broken and torn. I picked her up anyway, holding her in my lap. My fingers shook as I traced her cheek, before putting mine against hers, the hair rough against my skin. "Oh, girl. My sweet Gertie girl."

I didn't sob or keen, though my eyes watered enough. It hurt too much, like a really bad burn. The kind you felt later. The pain longer, more lingering, when it arrived.

Dai Lo put a hand on my shoulder. She didn't say anything. I took her hand, holding it while I held Gertie.

A shadow fell over us, and I looked up to see HisBen, his face held in mournful lines. "A tragedy. Someone must have been careless with the gates. Coyotes can sneak in so easily— all it takes is an inattentive moment." He cast his gaze over the destruction. "For something so little to cause such a mess—I'll have a word with the guards about the gates."

I couldn't imagine a single coyote doing all this. My mouth opened to howl at him—I know not what—maybe about the creature we heard last night, or to say I didn't care about his perishing gates.

Dai Lo's fingers clawed into my shoulder, and I clamped my jaw shut.

HisBen rested a hand on the back of my neck. "Mourn lightly, Mr. Kelly. The Shining God takes us all in His arms, no matter how big or small. Your Gertie is with Him now. Take comfort in that."

I found little comfort in his words.

In fact, I found exactly none.

I buried Gertie. I have no recollection of what they did with the other goats, but I buried my old friend, feeling a lot like I was burying my own heart. The rest of the day blurred, and I went to bed early.

The next day found me digging another hole, this one outside the palisades around the back of the Settlement. Not my favorite pastime, but I was glad to be on my own. I'd put aside Gertie's death, wrapping the thought up and burying it deep, so I could focus on the night of her death. Who had visited Cartwright's corpse? What had been with him? Were the stranger and the creature responsible for Gertie's death? There were several men about the Settlement, many I didn't know well, like the guards.

By midday, I had no answers, but I was dizzy with exhaustion. My sleep had been poor, and I'd barely touched the last few meals. Compounded grief had about killed my appetite. I hadn't been in the best shape to begin with. If I hadn't managed to talk Miss Moon into lending me some gloves, I would have reopened the wounds on my hands by now.

"You look like something the cat brought in," Will said.

I tossed another shovelful of dirt onto the pile before taking a moment to rest.

"And the cat was more mad than hungry," Will added. He shook his head and handed me a canteen. "Thought you could use some water and a meal."

I set the shovel down along the side of the hole and climbed out. I'd been working since an hour after breakfast and was about halfway through. Dillard wanted it deep, something about discouraging scavengers. Without help, it would take me all day.

I pulled off my gloves, dropping them to the ground, and took the canteen. I drained half the water before taking a breath. Will produced another canteen. I traded with a question on my face, but he just smiled. The second canteen held coffee, still hot. Will was a god among men.

"Take a load off. I come bearing other gifts."

I sat on the ground as Will delivered my lunch to me. Cartwright's grave was not only behind the Settlement, but close to the Penitent Box. I'd had to stare at it all morning while I was digging. I wondered if that was why HisBen had chosen this spot.

Will unloaded my lunch—cold chicken, an apple, a hunk of goat cheese, and even a few oatmeal cookies. He'd apparently brought enough for two, setting out his own lunch on a napkin.

Will rubbed his hands together. "Say what you want about this place, but the food is plentiful."

"Not what I imagined," I said, biting into the apple.

"Yeah," he said, almost to himself. "Not what I imagined, either." He didn't seem pleased by it but didn't expand on it further.

"You'll find her," I said, wanting to comfort him. "Mary Ellen, I mean."

He nodded at me, grateful for my empty reassurance.

We ate in silence for a moment. As soon as I'd bit into the apple, I was suddenly ravenous. "I must have been more focused than I thought. I didn't even see you walk up." Cartwright's grave was close to the tree line, several paces away from the Settlement wall. I should have been able to see Will coming from a ways off, as he would have had to walk along the line of the wall to get to where I'd been digging.

The side of his mouth kicked up. "I found a sneaky way."

He had my full attention now, and he laughed.

"Yeah, thought you might like that. Thing about these places? Stuff happens—emergencies and the like. Sometimes you need a bolt-hole or some way to sneak people out during an attack." He tipped his head. "The Settlement has a hidden escape route."

I finished the last bite of my chicken as I contemplated this. "Should you be sharing this knowledge with me? After all, you don't want me haring off." Bitterness crept into my tone at the end. Not aimed at the gunslinger, but at the people who would hire him. Okay, a little bit at the gunslinger, too.

He bit into his own apple, and when he spoke, his voice was soft. "Thought about it. Decided you needed a way out. Just in case."

"Why's that?" I asked, breaking my cookie in half.

He looked back at the Settlement. "After Gertie—I know there's something very wrong here, and you seem all caught up in it." He let out a frustrated noise, biting into his apple again. He tapped his chest. "I can feel it. Here. I just don't know quite what it is yet. I don't have enough pieces."

We ate silently for a while, both of us lost in our own thoughts. I was trying to decide whether to tell him about Cartwright's visitors. As I turned the notion around in my head, I couldn't see any reason not to. Will wouldn't turn any of us in for snooping.

Before I thought better of it, I told him about the man, the beast, and my missing watch, though I didn't say a word about the deed hidden inside. I figured Will might be able to help me find it.

Food now gone, he sipped at the last of the coffee, considering this new information. "Odd. Very, very odd. People do make pets of wild creatures sometimes. Knew a fella who had a pet wolf once. The way it stared at you . . ." He shook himself.

"Do you think a wolf killed Ger—" I swallowed hard. "The goats?"

Will's brow furrowed. "I don't know what did that. Animals kill to eat. Whatever happened in that barn, I don't think food had much to do with it."

"Man, then. What about Davens, or Amos—"

"I don't think it was Amos."

"Why not?" My tone held a challenge to it. I would have *loved* for it to be Amos.

"His family came for him," Will said, surprising me. "While you were in the Box." He frowned thoughtfully at me while he sipped his coffee. "Thought you knew."

I shook my head slowly. "I thought for sure he was making all that up. Couldn't for the life of me understand why anyone would want Amos."

"Me, either," Will admitted before returning to the more important topic. "You have no idea what kind of animal was in the cellar?"

"No, sir."

Will's gaze skated along the trees as he thought, taking in the area around us. I was knotted up tight, waiting to see if he'd dismiss what I'd said. He hadn't been there. Hadn't felt the fear of the moment. He might decide I was fibbing or making too much of a thing. The more he thought, the more I relaxed.

Will capped the canteen in his hand, tossing it aside.

"Whatever it is, someone is bringing it into the Settlement." He leaned back onto his elbows, turning his face up to the sun. After a long moment, he tipped his chin at my morning's work. "How many bodies you think are buried out here? And how many of them died like Cartwright?"

CHAPTER SIXTEEN

—✳—

THE GUNSLINGER'S WORDS STAYED WITH ME, CHASING themselves around and around in my head until I was fair sick of them. They stuck with me while I ate, whispered in my ear when I tried to sleep, and downright shouted when I attended Cartwright's sham of a funeral.

The thing was, I couldn't rightly figure what I could do to discover the answer to Will's question. I couldn't exactly walk up and ask Miss Moon or Miss Lita, and there was no way that I could figure to casually work the question into conversation. *Pass the oatmeal. Oh, and by the way, how many dead are outside these walls?*

Not exactly subtle, and I'd drawn enough attention my way. The only people I could ask were Jesse and Dai Lo, and that presented its own problems. The only time I'd seen them both together was at meals, when we'd be overheard. Since Jesse and I hadn't been cleared to hunt again yet, we were never alone together, either. Every time I tried to have a private conversation with either of them about what we'd seen in the cellar, or about deaths at the Settlement, we were interrupted or given more chores. All we could do was share nervous glances over the table, and I was sure I wasn't the only one with an uneasy gut, jumping at the slightest noise.

A week passed before I was able to broach the subject. The weather had turned nasty. Icy rain dumped in buckets and wind slammed into the Settlement, sneaking through the cracks, biting at you just when you'd finally got warm. Everyone was fair miserable, the youngins especially.

Tonight we were piled in the dining area. The littles were down at one end, listening to a story the gunslinger was spinning about beanstalks and finding magic treasure. Miss Moon sat next to him, rapt, a contented smile on her face while she braided one of the little girls' hair. Will paused and said something to her and she laughed. Will stared at her for a second, frozen, the moment dragging out.

"Then what happened?" one of the younger boys bellowed.

Will startled, flushing before diving back into the story.

I sat at one of the tables, mending one of my shirts. Wasn't sure how I'd torn this one. Pops always said I was unreasonably hard on my clothes. For a second, my grief was so sharp I could have cut glass with it, and my hand shook, making me drop the needle.

Jesse didn't notice—he was sketching, all his attention on his drawing. Dai Lo, however, seemed to have more than the normal set of eyes. I could have sworn she was focused on her work, but she reached over and picked up my needle, handing it to me without once glancing my way.

"It's no use talking any more about it," Dai Lo said, returning to the conversation we'd been having while everyone was distracted by the story. The room had a faint chatter to it—

kids fidgeting, the gunslinger talking, the murmur of other adult voices. Enough so that no one would be able to hear us unless they were right on top of us. "We don't have enough information to speculate on what we heard in the cellar. We'll just have to keep our eyes and ears open, that's all."

"And avoid the haunted cellar," Jesse said.

"It couldn't have been a ghost," I argued, not for the first time. "I smelled an animal, and ghosts don't have a scent."

"How do you know?" Jesse asked, finally looking up from his drawing. "You ever seen a ghost before?"

"No," I said, irritated. "But I'm fairly certain they don't smell."

"As I said, we don't have enough information," Dai Lo repeated with a tone of finality. She was embroidering a hand-kerchief, her tidy stitches making delicate purple flowers blossom along the cloth.

"That's very pretty," I said, admiring her work. "Wouldn't have thought embroidery to be your thing."

That earned me a set of raised ebony brows. "Why not?"

I didn't have a good answer, so I shrugged.

A smile tugged at her lips. "I like pretty things, and embroidery is soothing. Lets you think while it keeps your hands busy." The smile grew. "Besides, you'd want a doctor with good stitching skills, wouldn't you?"

"Not sure I want a doctor at all," I grumbled.

She laughed softly.

I stuck my needle into my shirt, keeping it in place. How to ease into it? "How long you two been here, at the Settlement?"

Jesse looked up from his sketching briefly, his pencil still moving. "Four, maybe five months?"

Dai Lo's needle flashed in the light. "In a week, it will be five."

This surprised me. There was an ease to them being here, being with each other, that made me think they'd been here longer. Some of what I'd been thinking must have shown on my face.

"Jesse and I came to the Settlement together." She tied off the thread she'd been using, switching out the purple for an emerald-green color. "We were at a more temporary situation before that."

Not the answer I was hoping for. I wasn't sure if they'd have the information I needed.

"People don't come here as frequent as you may think," Jesse said. He stopped drawing, taking a moment to assess it as he tapped the side of his pencil against the page. "Between us and you, I think we've only had two others come in. One of the youngins, Felicity, and an older boy, Alfred."

I remembered seeing Felicity. She was one of the really young ones toddling about the place. I hadn't met an Alfred, and I should have. The boys' bunkhouse wasn't *that* big. I cast my gaze around the room. "Which one's Alfred?"

"He's gone." Dai Lo's needle was flashing again, the movement almost hypnotizing.

"Family came to get him." Jesse pulled out his eraser, removing a troublesome line.

A small crease formed between Dai Lo's brows. "No, he ran away, didn't he?"

Now they both stopped to stare at each other. Some sort of wordless communication flowed back and forth between them.

"I was told family came to get him," Jesse said slowly.

"Maybe someone got confused, or the information became garbled. Like a game of messenger." Even though she'd offered the excuse, Dai Lo didn't seem convinced of it herself.

I was beginning to wonder if poor Alfred had really left, or if he was out there in a hole, much like Cartwright. Which even to me seemed like a bit of a leap. Then I had another thought. "Did either of you see Amos get picked up by his family?"

Jesse shook his head. "I was laid up with my ankle."

Dai Lo pursed her lips. "I didn't see him leave. He was just here, then he wasn't." The crease between her brows was back.

Cold dread slushed through my veins. "So how do we know he left?"

"Of course he left. He's not here, is he?" Jesse closed his sketchbook. "What's this about?"

I told them what Will had told me, about Mary Ellen, about all of it, hoping maybe they'd be able to conjure up an idea where I'd had none. My hope was half repaid.

Dai Lo carefully finished up the vine twining around her purple flowers. "Let me make sure I'm correct. You're trying to figure out if something is going on—something to do with unexplained deaths, like Cartwright's." She examined the room, making sure no one had sidled up to us in the last few minutes. "Perhaps something to do with what we heard in the cellar."

"Yes." I caught Miss Moon's gaze on me, and I quickly

picked up my mending again before she came over and found something to keep me busy. The Settlement subscribed to the belief that idle hands lent to mischief.

Dai Lo ran a finger over her embroidery, checking her stitching. "What you need to do is get up on the walkways."

I carefully moved my own needle, trying to keep my stitches neat. Try as I might, I couldn't see where she was going with this. "You mean up along the palisades?"

She dipped her head in a nod. "Up high, you can see irregularities."

I waited, but she didn't continue. She looked up at me, exasperated. "In the soil. The greenery."

I glanced at Jesse, but he looked as confused as I was. Well, at least I wasn't ignorant alone.

Dai Lo sighed. "When you dig a hole and then close it up, you're going to see differences in the grass, right? Even if you keep the sod together and replace it?"

Now it was my turn to nod.

"That would leave irregularities in the soil. Plus, you've added fertilizer."

"We did?" Jesse asked.

She smiled at him fondly. "Not the nicest thought to some, but I find it very comforting. When we die, we return to the soil. We enrich it. Grass will grow differently where a body has been buried." She turned sharp eyes on me. "And I would be willing to bet those other bodies didn't get a nice box, like Cartwright."

"Don't you think it's weird that no one is asking questions or talking about any of these deaths?"

"Why would they?" Jesse said. "If they've been told that the person left? It's what we all want, isn't it? To have someone whisk us away from here?"

She flattened her neatly embroidered handkerchief onto the table. She'd done a fine job of it, turning the necessary scrap of cloth into something beautiful. "Faolan, what happened to you when you talked back?"

Since she knew full well what had happened to me, she was obviously driving at something. "I got the Box."

She traced along the vine with the tip of her finger. "Yes, the Penitent Box. And what happened if you spoke there?"

I played along. "More time in the Box."

"Would you willingly go back there?" Dai Lo asked, not looking at me.

"No," I said softly. "I would not."

She folded up the cloth and pulled out a fresh one, before digging into her sewing basket. "You're almost grown, and you're strong-willed. Can you imagine going into that box when you're five or six?"

My stomach knotted. "No."

Dai Lo pulled out a neat bundle of golden thread, the color of summer sunshine. She put it back into the basket, rummaging until she came back with a smaller bundle of red. "This place doesn't encourage curiosity. It teaches obedience. You question, you end up in the Box. So the youngins won't question."

"Maybe," I said, finishing up my mending and carefully tying off the thread.

Jesse reopened his sketchbook, his pencil once again gliding over the page. "All of that's well and good, but how are we going to get up onto the palisades?"

I checked my handiwork, only to realize in my distraction that I'd sewn one part of the sleeve to the main part of the shirt. I sighed. "Dai Lo, you have a seam ripper?" She handed me the small metal tool with a smirk. I took it with the requisite chagrin.

"We don't need to get up there." I tore out my work with a few well-placed jerks of the seam ripper. "*You* need to get up there."

Jesse was wary now. "How do you mean?"

"I try to go? Dillard will be on me in a second. Dai Lo has no reason to be up there." I tipped my chin at Jesse's notebook. "But you, the budding artist? Who just wants a chance to sketch the Settlement in all of its glory, to better understand the work of His Benevolence?"

"That's laying it on a little thick," Jesse murmured.

I took up my needle again. "Lay it on as thick as you deem fit. Out of all of us, you would be the least remarked upon for going up. And unlike me, you'd be able to come back with something we could all see." I reached over and tapped his journal. "You'll not only see a bird's-eye view of the land outside of the palisades, but you'll be able to draw it so that we can see it, too."

Dai Lo kept stitching, this handkerchief earning a red leaf border. "As plans go, it's not the worst."

Jesse huffed. "Well, excuse me if 'not the worst' isn't exactly a ringing endorsement. What if I end up in the Box?"

Dai Lo shrugged. "Be clever, and you won't."

He frowned at her, but she just laughed. "I have faith in your wits, my sweet."

Jesse tilted his face down, but the tips of his ears were scarlet. He nudged his glasses back up with his knuckle, grumbling as he did, but I could tell he was basking in her affection all the same.

I was getting used to the pang of jealousy that dug into me. How nice it must be, to have a person just for you. Someone who looked at you with the faith that Jesse and Dai Lo did. To know that in the darkness, their hand would always find yours.

I had empty pockets and no one to call my own.

But at least I had friends. That wasn't nothing.

CHAPTER SEVENTEEN

— ✳ —

AS IF BLESSING OUR ENTERPRISE, THE NEXT DAY dawned dry, if stubbornly cloudy. It had warmed up some, and more things were going green and unfurling. Change barreled through the world, but I was comforted that some things, like the sharp ammonia smell of chicken droppings, remained constant.

While Jesse was jaunting along the palisade walkway, I was shoveling out the chicken coop. Chickens, at least, are sociable things, happy to peck at your boots as you work. I'd kept a hunk of biscuit from breakfast in my pocket, crumbling it onto the ground for them. It still felt extravagant, to be somewhere that had food aplenty and burned beeswax candles like they weren't precious.

I wondered where the money came from. As far as I could tell, we didn't produce much that we didn't either use ourselves or trade for other supplies. It was a conundrum for sure.

I finished shoveling the last of the manure and leftover bedding for the chickens. The Settlement used a mix of wood shavings, dried leaves, and hay, which needed to be replaced regularly. Other dried flowers or herbs were mixed in, mostly to drive away pests.

All of it went into the wheelbarrow so I could take it over to the compost by the kitchens. The Settlement had built clever bins for the compost to cut down on the smell and the rats. I wheeled the results of my labor over to them to mix in with the kitchen scraps and whatever else had been tossed in there.

After I was done, I gathered up the wheelbarrow handles to make my way back over to the coop—I had to put out fresh nesting material—only to pause. No one was about. Will had told me about the hidden door, though I hadn't been able to find it for myself yet. I studied the yard, but everyone was temporarily busy elsewhere. The problem was, it wouldn't stay empty for long.

I trundled the wheelbarrow back over near the barn, quietly parking it close by. I didn't try to sneak. People notice sneaking. The best way to do this, I figured, was to brazen it out.

Hands in my pockets, I strode over to the other side of the main building, to the corner where I should find the hidden door. I tipped my head up to see where the guards were along the walkway. It was easy to forget they were there if they were quiet. But only one man, Lawrence, was on duty currently, and he was standing next to Jesse, probably jawing away and driving Jesse to distraction. Obnoxious for him but dead useful for me.

The area I needed was tucked away and under shadow, so

it took me several minutes of feeling along the wood to find the catch, but I *did* find it. One of the wooden pegs didn't line up with the others, and if you leaned on it, a section of the wall clicked open a sliver. I yanked the peg back into place, filled with triumph.

"Mr. Kelly!"

I stepped away quickly at the shout, alarm sizzling along my veins. I turned to see HisBen Dillard and his ever-present lapdog, Stuckley, coming toward me. Dillard's eyebrows arched in what was somehow both an expression of surprise but also reproof.

"HisBen. Acolyte Stuckley." I touched the tip of my hat in respect. Funny how you didn't have to feel any of the actual respect to do so.

HisBen cast his gaze, rather exaggeratedly, in my opinion, around the area I was in. "Am I wrong, or were you on chicken duty today, Mr. Kelly?" I'm not sure why he phrased it that way. It was obvious that he thought he was never wrong, but doubly so right now.

I had no good reason to be here, and HisBen knew it. From his smirk, Ignatius knew it, too. My mouth opened and I prayed that something smart actually came out of it. "I was looking for Jesse."

HisBen's dramatic eyebrows swooped down. "And you thought he might be here?" The *in this empty corner for no reason* was implied. Heavily.

"He likes quiet places, you know, to draw." Okay, why was I looking for Jesse? Think, Faolan. *Think.* "For tomorrow."

HisBen frowned at me.

"To see if we're back on duty," I said quickly. "I thought of it when I was going to gather new bedding for the chickens. Wanted to check in with him before I forgot."

"You could have asked him at dinner." Stuckley's words almost dripped with condescension as he stuck his nose in the air. He only had a snub of a nose, so there wasn't much punch to the motion. Despite his looks, Stuckley sometimes reminded me of a baby deer, fresh from its mother. All spindly legs, big eyes, and an awful lot of quivering, but markedly less adorable.

When in doubt, lay it on thick. I edged my hat back and gave Stuckley my full ghost eyes. "You know, sir, you're right. I hared off without thinking it through. Pops always said I didn't have the sense they gave a goose." My Pops absolutely never said that to me. "I'll get back to work. Thank you for your wisdom, Acolyte Stuckley."

His mouth twisted, and I could tell he still wanted to argue with me, but in agreeing with him, I'd made it impossible.

HisBen stared behind me for a second before snapping back to me. "I'll save you the trouble. You will be going back out tomorrow, but not with Jesse. I'd like you to take Ignatius instead."

All the blood left Ignatius's face and his mouth hung open like a fish going after a fly. "Sir?"

"Acolyte Stuckley needs to see all the roles here at the Settlement."

Acolyte Stuckley looked like he absolutely wanted nothing

in this world *less* than learning all the roles in the Settlement. I can't say there wasn't a fair portion of me absolutely gleeful over Stuckley's discomfort. He was a bootlicker, and I'd never been overly fond of them.

But Dillard sending me instead of Jesse as escort rang all kinds of warning bells in my head like a three-alarm fire. "Of course, sir, I couldn't be more pleased than to escort him, but if you wanted a real depth of knowledge, why not send Jesse or one of the boys who have been here longer?"

Dillard's expression was contemplative, but it didn't reach his eyes. Those glittered with a strange emotion I couldn't quite identify. "You're right, but I don't want to tear anyone else away from their duties, and I'd rather not send Jesse out until he gets a pass from Miss Moon. I want to make sure he's fully on the mend." He smiled, and it was both charming and self-effacing, the look of a truly god-touched and humble man. "My people are precious to me, and I'd hate to see him injured." He fanned out his hands. "That leaves you."

Jesse was fine and we both knew it, but what kind of monster would argue to send out a recently injured friend instead of them? Dillard had neatly boxed me into a corner, and I couldn't say one word against him. So I bared my teeth and tipped my hat. "In that case, I would be honored."

By the time I turned my grin on Ignatius, it had gained a feral edge. You could slice a finger on my smile and get a disease that would eat you from the inside out. I didn't think it was possible, but Stuckley lost even more color. "Tomorrow, then, sir. I cannot wait to show you the ropes." My fingers left the brim of my hat. "Now, if you'll excuse me, gentlemen, I need to see about some chickens."

I hightailed it out of there, and for the life of me, I couldn't tell who had won the round.

—*—

When I told the gunslinger the news, he didn't care for it, either.

He was sprawled on his bunk, his boots on the floor, and his stockinged feet crossed at the end. He had a hole in his sock, right along the big toe.

"You should ask Miss Moon to take care of that," I said.

Will wiggled his toe. "You think I can't sew up my own stocking?"

"I think it would give you an excuse to talk to her," I said.

He grunted. "I can handle my own affairs, Faolan Kelly." He pursed his lips, looking speculative. "I might just do that, though."

He put his arms behind his head, returning to the subject at hand. "I don't like it. You're the newest person here by months. If he truly wanted to send Ignatius out to learn, why you?" His gaze sharpened on me. "What did you do to draw his attention?"

I lifted a shoulder and dropped it. "Just being my regular charming self."

Jesse snorted. He sat sketching at one end of his bunk while I sat tailor-style at the other, chewing a hole through my lip as I tried to figure out what Dillard wanted from me. Did he want me hurt? Dead? That didn't seem likely. Unless he'd found the deed? Remove me and get my lands?

A bit penny opera by my thinking.

Or was I going at this wrong? Was Ignatius a spy, trying to catch me up on a mistake? Maybe Dillard was punishing Ignatius, not me. There were too many variables and not enough facts.

With that in mind, I poked Jesse. "How did your sketch turn out?"

He ambled over to his trunk, fishing his journal out quickly. After flipping through several pages, he held it open with his thumb, shoving it out for me and Will to see.

Even in the short time he'd had, Jesse had done a fair sketch of the land behind the Settlement. His talent was evident in every stroke of the pencil and the shading he'd managed using his precious pastel pencils. I quickly made out the Penitent Box, the tree line, and the fresh grave I'd dug for Cartwright. But what caught my eye was the patches of color, the varying shades of green that made up the grass and clover of the immediate area.

Patches of deep green overlapped bright green or pale yellow, kept short by grazing livestock. The grass was bouncing back into vibrancy nicely after winter. I could trace out what we guessed would be several graves, showing it to Will. But I only counted five, maybe six. In a place as big as the Settlement, that wasn't outrageous, and I said as much.

Will traced his finger along one of the lines, frowning. "I wonder, though. How do we know that each of these means one body?"

Jesse drew back, horrified, but I thought that would be the smart way to go about it. "I think the better question might be, how many got lost in the woods? How many ran away, never to be found? Or tried to go on to the next town, like Cartwright?"

Will's brow furrowed, his mouth turning down. He didn't like what I was saying, but he also saw the sense in it. "Easy way to rid yourself of someone causing trouble." He speared me with his gaze. "And face it, Faolan, trouble follows you around like a faithful hound."

The truth of his words made my stomach drop, but I put my chin up, draping the bravado around me like a winter quilt. "Kellys aren't that easy to get rid of. Don't you worry about me, William Speed."

I figured I could worry enough for the lot of us.

CHAPTER EIGHTEEN

—✳—

A SOUND FLOATED ALONG THE AIR, MAKING MY HEAD snap up. My heart pounded a wild beat in my chest. I was in the forest, my bare feet planted into a pile of cold, wet leaves moldering away from winter. I stepped away quickly, stumbling to a harder, beaten path. I shivered. I'd gone to bed in my shirt and drawers.

I'd grown uncomfortable, and taking a risk, I'd slipped out of my breast wrap before bed. I shouldn't have done it. If anything had happened in the night . . . but it was getting harder and harder to hide. With access to regular meals, I was starting to fill back out, gaining the weight I'd lost while Pops was dying.

Soon I might not be able to conceal who I was. Should anyone find me now, it wouldn't matter. My secret would be out, and if I was lucky, I'd be shuffled off to the girls' bunk.

At best.

At worst? HisBen Dillard didn't seem the type to find what I was doing as understandable or amusing. No, there would be a reckoning. A chilled breeze came through, flirting with the hem of my shirt, icing me to the bone. I shivered harder this time.

The sound came again, a sort of desperate wail. It was terrifying, the kind of sound that made every hair on your body
stand on end. Made your skin prickle and your teeth chatter.

And yet.

There was something so unbearably sad to it. Something
desolate. Whatever it was, it called to me, making me step
forward, move toward the noise without thinking about it.
Before I knew it, I was running, dipping through the woods,
moving under branches and skirting bushes. The ground bit
into my feet, but I didn't really feel it.

All that mattered was that sound.

Branches tore at my clothing, scratched my bare legs. It
didn't matter. Nothing mattered. I just needed to reach that
sound. That wail. My heart was breaking and I—

"Faolan."

I screamed, the sound tearing out of me, my knees shaking. My heart felt like it was going to burst. Hands gripped
my shoulders. I smacked them away, clawing at the fingers.
Trapped. I was trapped and—

"Faolan!"

This time I came fully awake. I was barefoot, my body
quaking from the fear and adrenaline. The forest was gone—
I was on a hilltop. Stars glittered coldly above me while the
wind whipped through the tall grass. Nothing howled. The
voice calling me had disappeared and I felt hollowed out,
scraped clean by a dull spoon.

Bereft.

First Pops, then Gertie, and now this. The slow burn of
my grief hit a flash point, and I shattered.

I wept, and the hands gripping me pulled me into an embrace. Held me while I cried, sobs racking my entire frame. I couldn't remember *ever* crying quite like this. I cried for Pops and Gertie. I cried for the sad, lonely sound that had called me from my bed.

And I cried for me most of all.

I came back to myself in degrees. Warm arms wrapped me tight. I was being rocked, a low, comforting voice singing to me in Rover. The smell of leather, tobacco, and spice, undercut with the faintest tang of sweat and horses, met my nostrils.

It was a comforting smell. And for once, I didn't push away. I let myself be rocked, crooned, soothed like a baby. A hand cradled my skull, fingers sifting gently through my hair, occasionally stopping to rub my scalp. I'd never felt so cosseted in my life.

I looked up into Tallis's face.

"Hullo, Little Fox." He grinned, the scar pulling tight, but worry etched lines around his eyes.

And how quickly he ruined the moment.

I replied in Rover. "You said you wouldn't call me that anymore."

He hummed. "Maybe on special occasions, yeah?"

"How is this special?"

Now the grin fully reached his eyes. "Not every day I catch a half-naked stranger roaming about."

I smiled back, and I realized how relieved I was that it was Tallis who'd found me. How happy—how safe—I felt with him here. Without thinking, I reached for him, my fingers shaking as I touched his jaw. For a second, we stared at each other, and my courage tried to scrabble away, but I wouldn't let it. At the end of the day, I was a Kelly, and Kellys weren't cowards. I grabbed my fleeing courage, yanked it back, stood on my toes, and kissed Tallis on the corner of the mouth. I'd been aiming for the center, but it turned out I didn't have as good a hold on my courage as I'd thought.

His face inched close to mine, his warm breath feathering across my lips in ways that made me feel like I was made of bubbles.

"What was that for, Little Fox?"

It was on the tip of my tongue to say, *I don't rightly know*, but I did know, and lying felt like a cheat. "For being here," I said. "For being you."

I realized he was swaying with me now, one arm banded at the small of my back. The other hand loosened its grip on the back of my head, sliding down, fingers ghosting along my neck. Tracing my cheek, my jaw. The bubbles had returned and tingled under my skin.

"You've had a shock, I think, a big one. This conversation we're having, it might have to wait."

"What conversation?" I asked.

"This one," Tallis said, touching lightly along my ear. "I'd like to have it—mind, when things are calmer. When you're more yourself."

My body was warm against his, and I realized he wore only a jacket, trousers, and boots. No shirt. Combined, we nearly had a full outfit—I almost giggled. Except nothing felt the least bit funny.

"I think I'm more myself now than I've even been," I said

honestly, "and if we wait till things are calm, I'll likely be dead." I ran my fingers over the warm skin where his neck met his shoulder. "I've been told rather reliably that trouble follows me around."

Another brush along my chin. I sucked in a breath. His eyes were dark, intent. Focused as his thumb glided along my lower lip. More bubbles in my belly went straight to my head. My lungs stopped working proper.

"Can't say I blame it." He moved closer. "Breathe, Faolan."

I sucked in a breath, and it was the worst idea—those scents hitting the back of my throat. Leather. Tobacco. Tallis.

He'd stopped swaying. We were both stock still, the only movement the faint sweep of his thumb.

And then he dropped it away from my lip.

A frustrated huff left me. The corner of his mouth hitched up, but he didn't put his thumb back. Instead, he very carefully, very gently, put his mouth on mine.

The faintest hint of heat. Warm breath on my lips, his face so close, I'd barely have to lean. Another graze of heat. Slower. Longer.

I had the strangest notion that this is how he'd approach a wild horse—endless patience as he got them used to the feel of him, doing all he could to keep them from bolting. I trembled, but not out of fear. I pressed my hand against his chest, right over his heart. Steadying. But I didn't push away.

He kissed me like there was nowhere else he'd rather be. No rush. Almost coaxing.

Turned out that there was nowhere else I wanted to be, either. I'd never been kissed before. Never much had the opportunity nor the inclination. I fumbled, trying to match his movement. There was a knack to it, and I wasn't sure I was getting it. Not much skill on my end, but an embarrassing amount of enthusiasm.

He leaned back, his thumb replacing his lips.

I growled.

He met it with a soft laugh. "Easy, Little Fox." He tipped his forehead against mine. "It's not a fight. Follow, okay? And we'll both win."

I wasn't sure how to take that, and any response I had died when he nipped my lower lip between his teeth, tugged, then traced lightly along my top lip with the tip of his tongue.

I gasped and then—I thought we'd been kissing before, but maybe I'd been wrong. Because this.

This.

I wasn't sure what this was.

I just knew all the bubbles inside me burst at once into a sort of shivery heat. I will admit that I melted.

I was not proud of myself, but there you have it.

When Tallis stopped kissing me, I had all of the internal integrity of a cloth doll. He looked decidedly smug. I wanted to be mad, but . . . he should be smug. He'd earned it.

A lopsided smile lit his face. "Well, Little Fox. Aren't you full of surprises?"

I stuttered out a breath. "I'm full of a lot of things."

His fingers brushed the side of my face before he released me. "As delightful as this is, we should probably go." He glanced up at the sky, watching the stars. "Then again, the grass is soft, we're alone—"

I shivered again, this time from the cold.

He sighed. "And if you stay here, you'll probably lose bits to frostbite." His eyes met mine, and they twinkled. "And I think I like your bits, Little Fox."

I glowered at him. "A kiss in no way guarantees you any bits."

He chuckled and I felt it in my *toes*. "Guarantees are boring. But earnings?" He nuzzled along my chin, stopping right behind my ear and *oh*. "I'd like to earn your bits, I think."

I opened my mouth to argue and . . . I had nothing.

I guess I wanted him to earn my bits, too. I shivered again, and he sighed, letting me go so he could shoulder his way out of his jacket.

"I'm always dressing you. You need to take better care of yourself." He herded me into his jacket, and I was suddenly swamped in warmth that smelled like him. He quickly did up the buttons.

"I can dress myself." I frowned. This time when I shivered, it was from fear. "Tallis, I don't know how I got here."

He fumbled the last button. "What do you mean?" Then he carefully threaded the stubborn final button through the proper hole. If he was cold, standing there in only his trousers and boots, he didn't show it.

I snuggled deeper into the jacket. Ostensibly for warmth, I will admit to myself that I was mostly hunting for his scent again. I'd never thought myself a particularly biddable or easy person, but apparently one kiss and I toppled like a wobbly house of cards in a windstorm. "Last I remember, I was in bed, and I put the pillow over my head because Will was snoring something fierce. Then there was a noise—like a wail? A sound. It was so sad, and I was chasing it, and then . . ." I looked up at him. "Then you were here."

He put his hands on his hips and frowned at the ground. "You don't remember leaving?"

I shook my head. Cold swept through me as I looked up at the sky. Along one of the edges, the faintest of graying could be seen. Was I imagining it? I didn't think I was. Dawn would be here soon, and not only was I *not* in my bed as I was supposed to be, but I was in my drawers in a Rover coat with nothing to bind my peaches. If I went back now, like this, and someone caught me . . . "Tallis." I didn't know how to finish my statement, but my fear must have shown on my face.

He rubbed a hand over the nape of his neck. "I'm not entirely sure you should return to such a place, but if you leave your Settlement, it should at the very least be with the clothes on your back." He grabbed my hand, laced his fingers in mine, and pulled me close. A quick kiss this time, a hard pressing of lips. "But I'm giving serious consideration to sneaking into that cursed place, tossing you onto the back of my horse, and making for the camp."

And I was tempted to take him up on it, which, frankly, was terrifying.

"I'll get my horse." He kept my hand but tipped his head back and let out a sharp, short whistle.

"What are you doing here, anyway?" I couldn't imagine him out here, running around the hills in the middle of the night.

Tallis hummed again, head tilted so he could watch for his

horse, his hand warm in mine. "We've been very careful about sending out regular patrols since Yakob was attacked."

Fear crept into me, claws digging in. "You found him close to here, didn't you?"

Tallis nodded slowly. "Which makes it very interesting to discover you out here. We have a . . . system. Something that lets us know when someone wanders into our lands. And you, Little Fox, tripped it." He lifted our joined hands, examining my fingers, his expression thoughtful. "Yes, very interesting indeed."

He shook off his thoughts, planting a quick kiss on my hand. "I volunteered to come check it out." He grinned. "I'm very glad I did. My sister was supposed to take tonight, but she was with her betrothed, so . . ." He shrugged. "I offered to go."

"Your sister is betrothed?"

Hoofs thudded along the grass as his horse, Neev, cantered toward us, stopping close enough to snuffle his hair. He laughed. "Yes. Somehow she caught the eye of Anna. My uncle is very proud—a healer in the family. Quite a feat. We've been holding our breaths, hoping that my sister doesn't mess it up."

My eyebrows pinched together. "Why would you think that? Zara's very beautiful."

He scoffed. "Handsome, yes, and doesn't she know it? She's a handful, my sister. Lots of spirit." He said it like a compliment. "It's good, yes? But takes a certain handler. Anna seems capable, but . . ." He lifted a hand, palm up, and dropped it. "If she can handle it, then a very good match, I think."

"You think Anna will calm Zara, then?" My voice must have expressed how unsure I was about the question. I didn't like the idea of anyone tamping down Zara's spirit.

He hugged his horse's face to his. "Why would we want that? When you suffocate fire, it goes out. Anna will help build it—guide it—or the match won't work." He examined me carefully. "Is that the way of your people, then? Putting the fire out?"

"My people?" I wasn't sure what my people would do. But the Settlement? "If HisBen Dillard had his way, I think he'd prefer cold ashes."

Tallis didn't like my response, but a quick look at the sky stalled any rebuttal.

His horse didn't have a saddle, only a bridle. I guessed he'd been in a hurry to see what had triggered the alarms. He made a stirrup out of his hands. "Before you chatter at me, my horse is tall, you are not, and time is wasting."

I sighed, put a hand on his shoulder, and stepped into his hand. He boosted me up easily onto the horse's back. I tightened my legs and held out a hand. He took it, leaped, and swung up behind me.

Neev's muscles bunched beneath me as she sprung forward. We tore down the hill, our bodies hunched low, Tallis a hot line at my back. I should have been scared. It was dark. The horse left the hills, tearing through the trees. If we didn't get back in time, I'd end up in the Box for sure.

But I wasn't afraid. We were moving so fast we were flying, the night air flowing beside us as we cut through the trees. Tallis behind me, steady and sure. I laughed, feeling better than I had in a long, long time. The sound bounced along the trees, and behind me, more feeling than sound, Tallis laughed with me.

The black of the sky had shifted to mostly gray by the time we made it to the edge of the woods at the Settlement. Soon the roosters would ruckus and people would rise. I tried to see where the guards were, but I couldn't make out anybody along the palisades.

Tallis hummed again, a warning sound. "I really don't like leaving you here, Faolan. This is a bad place."

"I know," I said. "But I have to go."

He sighed. Kissed me, stopped, thought better of it, and kissed me again. "If that's what you want."

"For now," I said.

He grasped my waist and lifted, helping me down from his horse's back. "Soft feet, Little Fox."

"I just wish I could see the guard."

He grinned, a quick flash of teeth in the dark. "Don't worry about that."

Then he leaned down, grabbed my chin, and kissed me a final time. Before I could respond, he clucked at his horse and she took off, belting along the tree line. Invisible to the guards, but the sound would carry. And their attention would be focused all along Tallis's path.

So with quiet feet, I ran along through the shadows. Across the grass. Through the hidden door. All the way back to the bunkhouse.

It was only then, my back to the door, my breath sawing in and out of my chest, that I realized that I still had Tallis's jacket on.

Jesse's eyes met mine in the dark, and I raised a single finger to my lips. I stood there listening to the stove pop as embers collapsed. I went over and edged the stove door open, feeding it another log. Now if anyone woke up, I had an excuse to be up and about, even if I'd have a hard time explaining the jacket. A few of the more restless youngins shifted in their bunks. Jesse watched me with careful eyes but didn't say a word. Finally, he rolled over and buried his face into his pillow. I knew better than to think I would get away with it completely—he'd have the story out of me soon enough, and he knew it. Until then, he was going back to sleep.

The jacket was a problem. Unlike Pops's watch, it wasn't easy to hide. The soft leather was obviously not Settlement issue, so I couldn't wear it. My bunk could be searched at any time, so I couldn't hide it under the mattress or with my things. That left me with precious little in the way of options.

I closed the stove door and resettled blankets onto one of the smaller boys who'd tossed them off during the night and listened for anyone who might decide to peek in on us. I didn't think I'd been seen, but I couldn't guarantee I hadn't, either.

When my heart was no longer thumping along like a jackrabbit going full tilt away from a pack of hounds, I moved as softly as I could over to the gunslinger's bunk. He was snuffling in his sleep, a quiet snoring sort of noise. His pistols weren't with him, but that didn't mean he wasn't armed. Didn't see how I had much of a choice, however.

I put my hand over his mouth, hoping it wasn't the last thing I did on this earth.

His eyes flashed open, the blanket rustled, and the next thing I knew there was the cold bite of a blade against my jugular. I fought the urge to swallow. He blinked again, his brows furrowing. His lips moved against my hand, but he didn't make a sound.

I held a finger to my lips, then removed my other hand from his mouth.

He put away the knife. "I almost slit you from neck to gizzard." His words were barely a whisper in the quiet cabin.

"I'm sorry," I murmured, shouldering out of Tallis's jacket. "Can you hide this for me? I'll explain later."

I folded up the soft leather jacket, handing the bundle off to the gunslinger. I could trust him to stash it somewhere smart, and they were much less likely to search his things. After all, he was a guest here, and an adult.

As soon as he took it, I climbed into my bunk, nestling under the covers. Miss Moon would be in soon to rouse us. As I curled up, exhausted but my blood singing with triumph at getting away with it, it struck me that I had two more problems. First, I would need to rewrap my chest before Miss Moon called us from our beds. A hassle, but no big deal.

The second problem I wasn't sure how to fix—now that they were warming up, my feet were beginning to hurt. I'd run who knew how far on bare feet. My feet were tough, but they were used to boots, and they ached dully now. The warmer they got, the worse they were going to hurt.

And I couldn't think of a single way to explain my injuries, which meant I was going to have to put my socks and boots on and march about the forest after breakfast, dragging Stuckley around behind me.

I was going to be miserable, no two ways about it.

CHAPTER NINETEEN

─✳─

IT WAS THE GUNSLINGER WHO CAME TO MY RESCUE.
Miss Moon had come and gone, shuffling us out of our warm
bunks and into the cold morning. I dressed quickly, trying to
slip my socks on before anyone saw my feet. I'd almost managed, but I'd lost my balance after hastily pulling on my
trousers, and Will caught sight of my injuries.

He put a big hand on my shoulder. "What did you do to
your feet?"

I didn't answer him at first, glancing around the room to
see if anyone had heard him. Everyone else was half asleep
and too busy putting on their own clothes to pay us much
mind. Two of the littles blinked sleepily at their shirts, not
realizing they'd put them on inside out, and that was why
their buttons were suddenly not behaving.

We were as good as alone as we could be in a room full of
people. I quietly sketched out as best I could waking up in a
field last night, skimming past some of the more private details.

"You need to get them bandaged," Will said.

I made a frustrated noise. "You think I don't know that?"

I tucked my shirt into my trousers and settled my braces over my shoulders. "I'm supposed to take Stuckley out after breakfast. How am I going to find time to sneak off and get my feet looked at? More importantly, what could I possibly tell them to explain the injuries?"

There was no way I was going to lay out this whole mess to HisBen or any of his people. At best, I would be considered a liar and put in the Box. At worst, I would be a liar, accused of escaping the Settlement and possibly leaving the secret door open to let the Rovers or someone else in, thus endangering the whole Settlement, *and* ending up in the Box. Either way you cut it, I would be spending many days of my life in the Box.

Will, having come to the same conclusion as myself, frowned absently at my feet. He let out an irritated sigh. "Head on to prayer. I'll think of something by breakfast."

"Faith." HisBen's fingers gripped the lectern as he stared out at us. "Goes hand in hand with trust. Sometimes in this world, they can be hard to come by. Faith in the Shining God's wisdom. Trust in his path."

He searched the room with his gaze, and it might have been my imagination, but I thought he lingered on Stuckley, who stood next to him, his face pale. I didn't think Stuckley was looking forward to today any more than I was. "We all falter and stumble on our way. That's why we go together. So there are hands to catch us when we fall, and feet to guide us back to our path."

I think HisBen's words were meant as comfort, but they didn't comfort me. When the sermon was over, we all stood and marched over to the mess hall for our repast. Watery light filtered into the Settlement, the clouds heavy with spring rain. The dark green of the tree line marched deep into the hills, contrasting nicely with the gray mist eddying skyward. I tipped my face up into the light for a moment before plodding along behind everyone else.

Walking, even with socks and boots on, felt not unlike stepping onto a path of broken glass. It was a good thing that I was used to hiding things, keeping my face bland and mask-like as I stepped into line for my ration of vittles. Today we had a warm corn porridge, dappled with ham and fried onions. I breathed in the delicious scent. Underneath the smell of salted ham and fried onion, I caught a hint of butter and cheese.

I opened my eyes with a contented sigh, catching Miss Lita's happy face. Everyone liked to have their work appreciated. The cook's smile faltered as our gazes met, and it had the effect of a crashing domino against my own smile.

Why does a body have to ruin good things for no reason? Still, I nodded at her friendly-like before moving on to grab a tin mug and filling it with coffee.

Dai Lo and Jesse were already at the table when I sat down, their communal book in Dai Lo's hands. "After breakfast, you're going to meet me in the Still." She didn't look up from her book at all. Her words were soft enough that only Jesse or I could hear her.

I dug into my breakfast. "And how are we going to manage that?"

"Will said he'd handle the cook and Miss Moon. Matilda's on kitchen duty. We'll owe her a favor, but she'll keep her mouth shut. Jesse will delay HisBen and Stuckley." She handed the book over to Jesse with a fond expression on her face.

He gave her an equally lovestruck look back.

"Save your sugar," I grumbled. "Breakfast doesn't need sweetening."

"Neither does Dai Lo," Jesse said amicably. "She's sweet enough."

She rolled her eyes, but I could tell she liked his sugar talk from the way she lit up.

I scraped up another bite with my spoon. "It's a good plan, but risky. You could end up in the Box, same as me."

Dai Lo jabbed her spoon at me. "Then don't get us caught."

Jesse snorted a laugh.

Dai Lo must have seen my argument building, because her face twisted into a fierce expression. "You keep that trap shut, Faolan Kelly, unless you got something sensible to say. From Will's account, your feet are a mess. You know what happens when you don't take care of your feet?" She set her spoon into her bowl. "Infection. You know how close the skin is to the bones in your feet?"

She held up fingers, pinching a small amount of air. "Your feet get infected, your bones can get infected. Fever. Death. Or you might lose the foot."

She picked up her spoon but kept her eyes on me. "So, with that nugget of information in mind, you still feel like flapping your gums?"

"No, ma'am, I do not," I said, cleaning my bowl.

"That's the first sensible thing I think I've ever heard you say," Jesse mused as he turned the page of his book.

I jabbed him with my elbow. "I'm plenty sensible when my own carcass is involved."

Jesse handed the book back to Dai Lo, leveling me with a stare. "All evidence so far points to the contrary, so I suggest you quit before you get too far behind."

The only time I opened my mouth for the rest of the meal was to drink my coffee. They were right. When you didn't have much of a leg to stand on, it made sense to sit down and rethink your life choices.

Dai Lo got us into the kitchens by offering to carry in the dish trays. Miss Lita praised Dai Lo for being so thoughtful, while keeping a baleful eye on me. I attempted to look humble and chastened. Miss Lita sniffed, turning away from us as we picked up trays already laden with dirty dishes.

I followed Dai Lo as she made her way to the kitchen.

"What was that?" Dai Lo hissed as she pushed open the swinging half door using her back.

"What was what?"

"That face you made at Miss Lita."

"I was trying to look humble."

Dai Lo scoffed. "You looked constipated. If you're not careful, she'll break out the prunes just for you."

I glared at her, but she grinned cheekily as she carried her tray over to the dish tub. Matilda stood next to it, pouring hot water from the kettle into the tub. Matilda was about four years younger than me, by my guess, and thin, with a pale complexion and blond ringlets. If she hadn't been scowling, she would have looked like a little doll. She gusted a breath at our stack.

Dai Lo set the tray down on the large wooden worktable. "I told you it was a bad idea."

I glanced at her as I set my own tray down, a question in my eyes.

"Matilda tried to duck laundry duty."

Matilda grimaced, holding out her hands. They were reddened and chapped. "Of course I did. I'm practically bleeding." She sighed. "It's difficult to embroider when your hands are a mess."

From her expression, this was upsetting. I wasn't good at embroidery myself—I lacked patience. But I understood not being able to do a thing you loved. I felt the same way about the fiddle. "You ask Miss Moon for balm?"

Matilda scrunched up her nose in disgust. "His *Benevolence* told her I didn't need it. That it would help me learn humility." She crossed her arms. "I'm not sure how cracked hands help with that, but what do I know?"

"You should talk to Mr. Speed," I said gently. "He's got a tin. He'll see you right."

She eyed me warily before glancing at Dai Lo. "Will the gunslinger tattle?"

Dai Lo shook her head. "No. And we won't, either."

She didn't look convinced.

"Especially since we're hoping you won't tattle on us." Dai Lo leveled her with a meaningful stare.

Interest lit up Matilda's face. "Yeah?"

Dai Lo nodded. "We need a few uninterrupted minutes in the Still."

Matilda cast a quick glance at the kitchen doors. "Hurry and be quiet. Anyone comes in, I'll make lots of noise and try to distract them away from the Still."

"Thank you," Dai Lo said, already moving to the door.

I touched my fingers to where the brim of my hat would normally be. "We owe you one."

Matilda dipped her chin, taking her due, before turning back to the dishes.

We hurried into the small room, careful not to bump into the scarred, narrow table that took up most of the space. Light shone through a high, skinny window, illuminating the vials and bottles of things on the shelves. The smell of various dried herbs filled the tight space.

Dai Lo became a careful mouse, pattering around on silent feet as she pulled out one of the two stools that had been tucked under the table, waving at me to sit on it as she shut the door. She left it open a crack so we could hear the kitchen better, but no one would be able to glance into the room and see us. While she was doing that, I quickly shucked off my boots and socks, holding them in my lap.

She gently assessed my feet, concern etched on her features. "These need a good soaking, but we don't have time." After a quick search, Dai Lo found the bottle she wanted, as well as a tin and some rags. My feet were wiped down swiftly with an astringent that stung something awful, but I clamped down my teeth so I didn't make a peep.

Next came salve—I wasn't sure what Miss Moon put in hers. It could be anything from honey to comfrey to a passel of herbs I'd never heard of, as my healing knowledge was spotty at best. Dai Lo smoothed some of it onto the poor, battered soles of my feet before wrapping them up in strips of clean linen. That done, my socks were replaced. I put on my own boots, grateful once more that they were a mite big. That meant the bandages would fit. While I wrangled with all of that, Dai Lo neatly tidied up the table until it looked exactly as it had when we'd entered.

If the doctoring didn't work out for her, Dai Lo would have an excellent career in burgling.

I was half done tying up my second boot when there was a sudden ruckus as Matilda slammed pots and pans together. We froze.

Someone was in the kitchen.

I left my boot untied and hopped off the stool. I am ashamed to say that no plan came to me after that. I became the still deer in the woods, straining for sounds of the hunter.

Dai Lo had no such problems, for which I will be forever grateful. She shoved me behind the door a split second before it opened. I was neatly trapped, but also hidden, in that space between the wall and the door. Unfortunately, that left Dai Lo in plain sight.

"Dai Lo?" Miss Moon's voice held a note of surprise. "I didn't think we were working in here today. Matilda, quietly please." The banging stopped. "Aren't you supposed to be heading over to help with the children's lessons?" Her earlier surprise was gone, replaced by confusion.

"Yes, ma'am." Dai Lo had to be nervous, but I couldn't hear it in her voice. She was still waters, even as lies flowed easily through her teeth. "I helped to bring the dishes in after breakfast. Then I remembered little Issac had a rash, and I thought I'd check to see if you had any of that unguent left . . ."

"We should," Miss Moon said. I heard shuffling, like she was moving Dai Lo out the door. "But you don't want to do that out in the main hall. Why don't you bring Issac in here?" Miss Moon's hand wrapped around the edge of the door, just enough that I could see her fingers. Everything in me bunched up tight, my pulse hammering.

"You know, ma'am, maybe you should come look at it first. I'm not even sure it's a rash, and I'd hate to drag him all the way in here for nothing. It would disrupt the little ones . . ."

The hand on the door relaxed.

"That's a good idea. Let's go. Daylight's wasting." She started to close the door and I eased a fraction. Then, very softly, so that I almost didn't hear it, she spoke. "That should give you two minutes to hare off, Mr. Kelly, and I recommend you use that time wisely."

Before I could even consider responding, she shut the door.

I did as Miss Moon bade, hightailing it out into the main courtyard of the Settlement, ready to gather my pack and go on my ill-fated journey. I couldn't shake the heady feeling that no good would come from this adventure, but short of injuring myself more, I could see no way out of it.

All I had to do was make it through today and come back in one piece. Then I'd find more time to look for my watch.

I waded through loose chickens and a few errant youngins on my way through the courtyard. As I approached, Stuckley was already waiting. He'd lost his watery uncertainty and replaced it with condescending arrogance. I didn't know a nose could stick that high. It was a wonder a birdie didn't perch on it. `

I preferred him scared, and not just out of spite. A body that walks into the woods that arrogant is a body that lacks respect for nature. And while nature encompassed an unspeakable depth of beauty, it also had teeth and claws. Stuckley lacked respect.

The gunslinger handed me my pack when I entered the courtyard, and for a moment I hoped that meant he'd weaseled his way into our expedition, such as it was, but my hopes were soon dashed.

"I mended the strap for you." Will's voice was a gentle rebuke, though it didn't sting me. There'd been nothing wrong with the strap, and we both knew it.

"Thank you, sir. I am in your debt." I shouldered my way into the pack. Stuckley carried nothing, though his belt held a small pouch and a sheath for a field knife. Stuckley with a blade made my shoulders itch. I didn't believe he had much skill with it. The leather holding it looked new and stiff.

We assessed each other, both of us certain of our superiority, and again I wondered at the *why* of this little expedition.

HisBen approached us, all smiles, a folded piece of rough

paper in one hand and a canteen in the other. Miss Honeywell drifted behind him, her face also wreathed in smiles to see Stuckley on his way. Both were treating the farewell like this was a big deal for Stuckley, though I couldn't fathom why. HisBen clapped one hand on Stuckley's back, while Miss Honeywell had her arms crossed, almost like she was holding herself.

Dillard handed the canteen to Stuckley. "Acolyte," he admonished gently. "You mustn't forget your canteen. As Mr. Kelly will no doubt tell you, it's of the utmost necessity."

Stuckley flushed red, and as his eyes flicked to me, there was a flash of malice. "Thank you, Your Benevolence. I'm sure Mr. Kelly would have mentioned it eventually." He spat my name like it was the bitterest of poisons.

Dillard appeared not to notice, his smile never slipping. "Mr. Kelly." He handed me the paper with a flourish. "For you."

I opened up the folded paper. A map of the area with a route sketched out stared back at me. The path wasn't the one I usually traveled with Jesse but led to a different area entirely. This one went farther into the foothills. "Your Benevolence?"

"Since your route hasn't been producing much lately, I took the liberty of making you a new one."

While arguing with HisBen seemed a poor idea, I couldn't see my way around it. "Sir? We've no traps on this trail, and the traps on our old one—"

He flapped his hands, like he was wafting away my objections. "Already taken care of. Someone will check them today." His hands settled into a steeple. "This way, Acolyte Stuckley can see the process from the beginning. Show him how to assess the best places to set a trap and how to go about it."

HisBen's logic was faultless, I'll give him that. Couldn't shake the idea that it was a heaping layer of dung, either. I did the only thing I could. I thanked him and let him go on his way. I waved Stuckley before me, heading toward the gate, the gunslinger keeping pace.

"Where you off to today, Will?"

Stuckley sniffed at my usage of the gunslinger's first name without an honorific.

"I offered to take your route," Will said. Then softly, just for my ears, "Leave a path. I'll follow if I can."

I chose my words carefully so as to respond to both comments. "That is mighty kind you, sir, and I appreciate it, I do."

With that, all that was left was to tip my hat to him as we stepped out past the gates. He went one way. Acolyte Stuckley and I went the other.

CHAPTER TWENTY

—✳—

ACOLYTE STUCKLEY SURPASSED EVERY EXPECTATION I had within the first ten minutes. He wasn't just useless in the woods, he was a danger to both of us. Twice I'd had to keep him from grabbing on to stinging nettles. If he tried a third time, I wasn't stopping him. Though I knew he had no interest, I attempted to tell him about the fauna, only to be snarled at. He didn't need lecturing from an upstart country rat such as myself, so I quit trying.

From then on, I spent all my energy attempting to keep him on the deer path. He didn't watch where he was stepping and almost broke his foot in a burrow. He needed constant breaks to "bask in our Benevolent creator's gifts."

Really, he was just winded and didn't want to ask for a breather. I used the breaks to mark the path for Will—leaving piles of stones or anything that would catch his eye.

We made slow progress, and as Stuckley complained about everything from his boots to the weather—it was "too dry"— to the bugs, it was a fair wonder that my ears didn't bleed to death.

After the first hour, I was ready to find a ravine to push him into, and I'm certain he was entertaining similar thoughts about me. Though I made no conscious decision to do so, I began to ignore him.

I didn't even peek back to check on him. I knew exactly where he was by the sheer amount of hullabaloo he generated.

Which meant that by the time I realized something was dreadfully wrong, it was too late. Sometimes I wished I could kick my own behind for my thoughtlessness.

Stuckley grew quieter as we progressed. Quiet from a man such as Stuckley always spelled trouble. I was so grateful for the lack of noise that I didn't question it, nearly jumping out of my skin when Stuckley grabbed my shoulder.

I yanked away from him instinctively, spinning in place.

"I want to see the map." He stood close to me now, pale as a sheet, and sweating. His eyes were so bright, I wondered if he might be feverish. He moved erratically, as if he was watching something that I couldn't see.

"You don't look well, Acolyte Stuckley."

"I didn't ask for your impertinence, Mr. Kelly!" He snapped the words, teeth biting the air. His chin was up, shoulders back—a captain laying down a command for a lowly foot soldier.

I didn't want to give him the map but, once again, couldn't see a way around denying his request. Attempting to compromise, I unfolded the map so he could see it. Instinct told me to keep the map in my possession.

Stuckley growled and snapped it from my fingers. Then he stared at it for a long time. Too long. I began to wonder if he knew how to read a map. His eyes flitted over the page, like he was tracing a snake in the brush.

He licked his lips, mumbling, sweat dripping from his brow. He swiped at it absently with his shirtsleeve. "You're taking me in the wrong direction." His words were so soft, I had to lean in to hear them. "A trick or a trap?"

"Pardon?" I hadn't left the marked trail, though I'd been sorely tempted. To be honest, I wasn't entirely sure whether Stuckley was talking to me, himself, or ghosts. His pupils were big as saucers.

His face lit in exultant wonder. "A test." Stuckley crushed the map in his hands as he suddenly clutched it to him. "I will not fail."

Then he turned on his heel and darted into the trees.

"What test? Who's testing you?" I shouted the words after him but got no response. Cursing, I stood there trying to decide what to do.

I will admit that, for a moment, I considered letting him go and retracing my steps. If Stuckley was bent on dying in these woods, who was I to stop him? From what I'd seen this morning, his odds were not good. Stuckley was a critter out of his habitat.

Ultimately it was the idea of coming back without Stuckley that got my feet moving. I wondered if that was HisBen's plan all along, though I wasn't so prideful to think that he'd throw away his fawning creature just to rid himself of me. With the toe of my boot, I drew an arrow pointing into the forest to

258

alert the gunslinger before I took off through the trees, following the crashing sounds of Acolyte Stuckley.

I'll give him his due—Stuckley may make as much noise as a herd of startled sheep, but he had the agility and speed of one of the deer that often dotted the plains. My hesitation had cost me. He was far ahead of me now. I had to follow him by sound and trail sign—bruised vegetation, snapped branches, and the like. Normally I wouldn't rely on such things, as they could be from larger animals, but with the knowledge that Stuckley had gone this way, and all the ruckus, it was enough to give me some confidence.

I drew up when I hit the entrance to a boarded-up cave, or possibly a mine. I wasn't sure. It had been long abandoned, the boards nailed to the front weathered by both time and the elements. Someone or something had been in recently—a few of the boards were broken, leaving a hole. An old mine or cave to us might be a new burrow to something else.

Pops had always said strange things lived in the hills, in the earth. I did not want to test his supposition. I especially didn't want to do so *now*.

Stuckley was a coward, and I couldn't see him plunging headfirst into an unknown cave. I spent a few precious seconds looking for signs that he'd hared off to the sides, heading deeper into the woods.

I did not find them.

Stuckley had gone into the cave. Which meant I had to follow. My pack didn't contain a lantern, though I had a flint and steel kit for emergencies, but making a torch took time and materials.

I had neither.

I cursed myself twice the fool as I plunged into the darkness after him.

—✳—

I didn't expect my erstwhile partner to get far. The light from outside didn't penetrate deeply into the cave, and after a few feet, I could barely see my hand in front of my face. Now that I was inside, I was leaning more toward cave than mine. The ground had been smoothed a little by erosion, but the sides were jagged against my fingers. If I wasn't heedful, my hand would be sliced to ribbons. So I kept my touch gentle as I traced one hand alongside, being careful not to lose my connection with the wall completely.

Caves were dangerous things, and it was easy to get lost or disoriented in them. When I was deep enough that the entrance was a mere pinprick of light in the velvety darkness, I paused, straining my ears. For several heartbeats, I breathed in the musty air of the cave, smelling rot and something unpleasant, but hearing nothing beyond my own labored wheezing.

I held my breath, listening again. An odd shuffling noise drifted to me, but I couldn't tell where it had originated. Sound went funny in caves.

"Stuckley?" My voice echoed around me, but no one responded. The shuffling continued.

I moved deeper into the cave.

I crept forward farther, refusing to leave that pinprick of light behind. When the cave turned, I paused. I had a decision to make. Continue forward in the darkness or abandon Stuckley to his fate.

I did not hanker after any more time in the Penitent Box, but as terrible as it had been, I'd survived it. I didn't feel so confident of my chances blundering about in an abandoned cave without a whisper of light.

Stuckley was on his own.

I'd turned around, taking my first step of retreat, when light flared deeper in the cave behind me. I squinted, my eyes long adjusted to the almost complete darkness of the cavern. I blinked rapidly, a trick Pops had taught me to adjust my eyes quickly. The light in the cave flickered.

Firelight. Perhaps Stuckley had lit a torch.

I'd turned back into the cave and taken two steps before I wondered how he'd managed such a thing. He'd had no torch or lantern, either. Just his knife, canteen, and that small pouch. He didn't even have any food. I carried our lunches on my back.

What had he found in the cave that he could light?

I sped up my steps, curiosity and a growing panic urging me forward. The cave was large enough as far as I could tell, but it held much in common with the Box. With the pit I'd fallen into as a child. With that nightmare I'd had, my hand coming back bloody and—

Fear made me sweat, causing my eyes to burn if I didn't wipe it away. My breath came in shallow pants. If I wasn't careful, I'd hare off in a panic before I ever found Stuckley.

When I was closer to the light, I called his name again. "Acolyte Stuckley?" Only my echo answered. "Ignatius?"

A whisper of sound then, slithering along the rocks. I wondered why he didn't answer. Was he being bratty, or could he not answer my summons? He'd looked feverish before he ran off. Maybe he'd fallen down or collapsed into a swoon?

I was practically trotting now, my hand barely touching the wall. I wanted to find Stuckley and get out.

The cavern veered left and I followed it, pelting toward that light. It had become a symbol of freedom, a symbol of the end.

Then something grabbed me from behind and jerked me to a stop.

The telltale chill of steel bit into my throat, while another arm pinned me tight against a bony chest.

Stuckley let out a cackle of triumph. "You thought to test me. *He* thought to test me. But I won, didn't I? I *won*."

I had not the faintest inkling of what he was bleating about, but I knew better than to argue with a man who held a blade to my throat. "Yes," I wheezed. "You won."

"I can feel His light." Stuckley crouched, whispering in my ear. "This cave. This cave is *full* of it." He started babbling then, taken up in some kind of frenzy. The knife's blade slipped down to my collarbone, his grip loose. The sharp edge pointed away from me for just a moment, an opportunity that I would exploit. I tucked my chin to my chest, then flung my head back at Stuckley's. Pain shot through me as I connected. I'd hit him hard, but he didn't lose his grip.

He'd turned his face away at the last minute, so I missed his nose.

"God's light!" Stuckley cursed, flinging me away from him.

I hit the cave wall, my forehead cracking against the jagged surface.

Fireworks exploded against my eyelids, their light fading into darkness.

—✳—

I woke trussed up like a hog ready for slaughter. My hands and feet were bound, my skull splitting, and my face sticky with my own blood. Light from a small fire lit up the open area where I was lying, causing my headache to sharpen. Stuckley was nowhere to be seen. I used my bound hands to wipe the blood from my eyes, only to be momentarily overwhelmed once I could see clearly.

Symbols covered the cave walls, shimmery and weird. They reminded me of the drawings I'd seen scribbled on the sheets underneath Miss Honeywell's bed. Close, but not exact. Had she been trying for these and failed, or were these symbols a corruption of the ones she had?

I didn't know rightly how to explain it, only I had the passing thought that I'd never truly seen evil until this moment.

I struggled against my bonds, pushing at the rough weave of the rope. Stuckley's knots were surprisingly solid. I hadn't thought him capable of anything so competent, but then today seemed to be a day of surprises where he was concerned.

My struggling must have drawn his attention, because suddenly I saw Stuckley's boots, inches from my face. He dropped down into a squat, peering at me. Sweat sheened his face, his eyes wild but joyous.

Ecstasy. Stuckley was communing with his god.

I'd thought I was afraid before, but that was only a shadow to the fear slicing through me now. I'd be damned twice to the quiet fields if I was going to let someone like Ignatius Stuckley make this wretched cave my tomb.

I took my fear and folded it up, tucking it away neatly into a box. It would do no good to let it run rampant. I pulled on a layer of false calm instead, steadying my heartbeat. When I felt more settled, I cleared my throat. "Acolyte Stuckley, there seems to have been a mistake."

He grinned at me then, white teeth floating in the dim light. There were far too many teeth in that smile. Whatever gripped him, he was still in the middle of it. "There's no mistake. Not anymore. Now everything is right."

He shook his head, giving a good-natured chuckle as he picked up his canteen from the cave floor. "I doubted, you see? Didn't trust in his plan. But now? Oh, *now*." He sighed happily. "Now I believe."

He twinkled down at me in the darkness. "And that's all thanks to you." He frowned, setting the canteen on the ground. "This won't work. I need you upright." He spent a few minutes wrestling me up against the cave wall, my bound hands and feet in front of me. Stuckley uncapped his canteen then, holding it to my lips.

When I didn't oblige, he clamped his fingers onto my nose, blocking off my air. I struggled, twisting this way and that, holding my breath. In the end, it was for naught. My need for air betrayed me, and I gasped. The acolyte was ready, pouring water down my throat. A foul taste flooded my mouth, musty and rotting. I coughed, spluttering, causing Stuckley to curse.

All I'd achieved was slowing him down. He began praying, mumbling the words in a continuous flow, alternating between pinching my nose and half drowning me with his canteen. I kept gagging, spitting as much of the liquid up as I could, but some made it down my throat.

I cannot say how long this went on, only that it felt like a pocket of eternity. Finally, the canteen lay empty on the ground next to me. "Do you see now? Do you see God's hand?" Stuckley grabbed my chin and waved his free hand at the cave walls.

Whatever Acolyte Stuckley was seeing, it was for his eyes alone. I only saw the same jagged walls, the same wretched symbols, and the dying fire.

I tried to lie anyway. "Yes," I whispered. "I see it."

But it did me no good. Stuckley stared at me, his gaze darting back and forth as if he was searching my face for a divine answer.

He didn't find it.

"You don't see!" His cry was anguished, like he was genuinely upset that I wasn't sharing his vision. He plunged his fist into my hair, yanking it back so my face was upturned. Pain stabbed through me so violently, I almost vomited his water back up. "The book, I've read the book. The words whisper to me in the darkness. Old words from old gods, revealed in the light of the Shining One."

My harsh breaths filled the air as Stuckley raved. What was in that canteen? Had he poisoned us both?

"It's your eyes," Stuckley said, his fierce expression gilded by firelight. "Those wretched eyes." He searched the cave floor with one hand, the other keeping my hair in his grip. When he raised his hand up, his field knife glinted in the darkness. "I'll fix it. You will accept His gift. You will see God's benevolence."

The tip of the knife edged along my skin, tracing right under the eye, though not cutting yet.

Stuckley planned on taking them. A twisted gift for his twisted faith. If I survived such a surgery, it would be a miracle.

Well, if I was going to die, I would do it fighting.

I knitted the fingers of my bound hands together and punched Stuckley in the throat.

He choked, his grip on my hair disappearing as he instinctively cradled his neck. Using the wall as leverage, I rocked forward, tackling him awkwardly to the cave floor. The knife clattered out of his hand, skipping across the ground into the shadows.

The movement sharpened the pain in my head, and Stuckley took advantage of my distraction, bucking me off. I flopped back against the cave floor, vomiting up water. I felt like someone had reached inside me and pulled all my insides out. From the sounds of it, Stuckley wasn't faring any better.

I didn't have much time, and if I didn't do something soon, I truly would die in this cave.

I blinked hard, trying to clear my vision. I was staring at the jagged cave wall. The rope Stuckley had bound me in wasn't thick—more glorified twine than anything. It wouldn't stand up to the jagged wall, at least that was what I was hoping.

I wormed closer, then placed my bound hands against one of the juts of rock, sawing against it like a serrated blade. It was messy work, tearing into my flesh as often as the rope. I didn't care. I went at it like a wild thing, my teeth gritted against the pain.

The rope slid free just as I heard Stuckley pushing himself up from the floor. My time had run out. I twisted onto my stomach, breathing through the sharp edges slicing through my head, and crawled in the direction of the knife.

There! On the other side of the fire. I crawled with everything I had, my palm meeting the cool wood of the handle just as Stuckley's hand gripped my ankle.

He yanked me to him, and I didn't fight, turning onto my back. And as Stuckley reared up over me, his face a snarl, his throat already turning purple, I did the only thing I could.

I plunged the field knife into the heart of Acolyte Stuckley, and I twisted the blade.

CHAPTER TWENTY-ONE

—✳—

I HAD NEVER KILLED A BODY BEFORE.

Never occurred to me that I would.

From the expression on his face, it hadn't occurred to Stuckley, either.

He looked surprised.

He fell forward then, and I tried to roll away. His blood flowed over my shirt, hot and sticky. I threw up again at the feel of it, dry heaving onto the cave floor, which made my aching head even worse.

For being so skinny, Stuckley was heavy on my back. I crawled blindly away, but he seemed to come with me, a twitching, moaning weight.

Desperate, I rolled to the side. He managed to stay attached, his dying hands clutching at my clothes.

The cavern floor, so smooth and solid beneath me, suddenly gave way, and we both tumbled in, the cave swallowing us whole.

I hit the ground hard, pain clawing at my side. My ribs, probably breaking. I'd been managing to stay conscious through a mix of stubbornness and fear, but that pain proved too much, even for me, and I passed out again.

Blessedly.

When I woke up, Stuckley was dead, his body already cooling against mine. I had a passing thought that Dai Lo would be jealous—here I was, another corpse on my hands, and she'd never get to look at it.

I started laughing, and it hurt.

Something growled in the darkness.

I froze.

There are moments in life when you're so afraid that you go over the edge of fear and into an entirely different feeling. A body can only take so much.

I'd been cracked in the head, tied up, and my wrists were a ragged mess. At least one of my ribs felt broken, I'd killed a man, and was currently trapped under his corpse. I should have been terrified of that rasping growl so strange to my ears, but frankly, I was fed up.

"Don't you growl at me," I snapped. "I didn't interrupt your nap. He did." I rolled Stuckley off me, shoving away his body, moving it toward the growling sound. "So if you're mad, you get mad at him."

My energy spent, I flopped back down onto the cold floor of the cave. Everything hurt. "Now let me die in peace."

I became insensible for a spell, and I do not know how long it lasted. Hours would be my guess. Lights danced in front of my eyes, soft blues and purples. Giddy things, drunkenly swirling about. I drifted in and out of consciousness to strange sounds I'd never heard before. I knew I was dying, and I opened my arms to the old gods, hoping to see my grandparents again.

At one point I awoke and started crying, overwhelmed with feelings that didn't seem my own. Loneliness. Such soul-wrecking loneliness. I cried for that feeling, and when that didn't seem enough, I began to sing lullabies and comfort songs.

Singing hurt. Oh, how it hurt. My entire body a chorus of pain. But I did it anyway. I sang with all my heart, saying it wasn't alone. Whatever it was, it wasn't alone.

I grew warm then, like something had curled up against my side. I reached over and my fingers met the softest fur.

This was it.

I was finally dying, seeing things in this world that weren't there. Hearing sounds that couldn't be, feeling things that didn't exist.

Still, fear refused to find me. Instead, I found great comfort. I curled up against the warmth, sighed, and went into a natural sleep.

To my great surprise, I woke up. To my greater surprise, I woke up to a lantern dangling above me in the darkness. The light from it lovingly traced the gunslinger's face. He was a handsome man, truth be told, and I could see what Miss Moon saw in him.

Right now, he looked as if he'd seen a ghost.

I grinned at him. "You should ask those lawyers for a raise," I slurred. "As this is above and beyond your call of duty."

The gunslinger swore. "Saints alive, Faolan, I thought you were dead."

"Me too," I said. "And I'm still not sure I'm not."

"You certainly have that look about you. I've been searching for you for hours. Missed one of your trail signs and had to double back." He shook his head slightly and gave a low whistle. "I can't tell whether you're the unluckiest person I've ever met or the luckiest. Can you stand?"

"I'm not certain." I spent the next several minutes attempting to sit up. It went marginally well, as I didn't have anything left to throw up, though the act of heaving made pain flash through my ribs and skull. Eventually I ended up leaning against the cave wall.

The gunslinger held his lantern higher. "That Stuckley?"

"Yup."

"Can he stand?"

"No, sir, he cannot." I laughed then, and it had a hysterical edge to it, until the pain made me stop.

The gunslinger eyed me in the dim light. "All that blood yours?"

"Some of it's mine, some of it's Stuckley's. I'm not sure how much of either. Am I going to need to climb out of here, because I'm not sure if I'm able . . ." My words petered out as something moved in the darkness. Steps padded forward, hesitant. Wary.

I saw his feet first. Large, ghostly white paws. Another step revealed chest and face as he moved into the small puddle of light. A large catlike creature came toward me. Lithe and powerful. Purplish rosettes on slick white fur. Whiskers. A lean face. Eyes a deep, cool blue.

I'd never seen the like.

"What is that?" The gunslinger breathed.

"I don't rightly know," I said, but I held my fingers out. My hand was shaky, but it wasn't from fear. I had a bone-deep conviction that this creature wouldn't hurt me. He sniffed my fingers, hot air wafting over them.

"That what killed Cartwright?" he asked.

I looked into the cat's face. Glanced at his paws. "No. He's too small."

"He doesn't look small to me," Will said, and I quietly agreed. "Looks bigger than a cougar from here, anyway."

"I don't think," I said slowly, "that he's done growing, whatever he is." Now that I'd had a good look at him, the cat had that gangly, slightly awkward look of a juvenile.

"He going to let me take you out of your hole?" Will asked.

The cat chuffed over my fingers and sneezed.

"Only one way to find out," I said.

After a little trial and error, Will managed to pull me up with a rope. He'd made a loop, lowered it, and I put it over my head and under my arms. It hurt like you wouldn't believe, being pulled like that after what I'd been through, but I survived. Will landed me like a fish onto the edge of the hole, and I panted there, every inch of me in agony. A second later, there was a scrambling noise, and then a thud as the cat landed next to me.

Will didn't move. Barely breathed. The cat turned his head toward Will, scenting him like he did me. The cat made a sound then, almost a chirp.

"He's a friend," I said. "You leave him be, now." To my surprise, the cat returned to my side.

Will handed me the lantern. "I'm going to have to carry you out of here. You hold on to the light."

"My pack," I said. "Grab my pack."

Will took a few seconds to locate my pack. He slung it over his shoulder, then tried to pick me up, the pack sliding back down and getting in the way. "I might have to make two trips."

I wanted out of the cave badly and said as such. To my surprise, the cat padded over, clamped his teeth over part of the bag, picked it up, and trotted off with it. He stopped a few feet away, looking back, waiting.

"I'm beginning to wonder if I hit my head or something," Will said.

"Well, wonder outside. I *have* hit my head, and I want free of this wretched tomb."

Will scooped me up. "What about Stuckley?"

"My concern for Stuckley fled at the same time he decided to truss me up and take out my eyes."

Will shuddered but didn't say anything.

Getting back out seemed to be much faster than getting in, though Will paused a few feet from the entrance. We waited until our eyes were comfortable again with the light before attempting the tricky business that was getting through the jagged wooden covering of the cave. Will ended up kicking a few more of the boards away.

Once we were through, he sat me down gently on the dirt. The light was fading fast, night coming on quickly. I'd been in that cave most of the day. It felt like longer.

Will used his field knife to cut away at the bindings on my ankles. That done, he handed me his canteen. I rinsed my mouth and spat before taking a sizable drink.

He watched me carefully. "You should see yourself. You looked bad in the cave. Out here"—he resettled his hat back on his head—"you're a sight, and not a good one, for all that I'm pleased you're alive." He shook his head. "We need to get you some medical attention. Esther—"

"I can't go back to the Settlement, not like this." To be honest, I wasn't sure I was going to go anywhere. The gunslinger was a robust man, but he couldn't carry me forever.

"You need a healer." He sighed, gaze traveling along the trees. He rubbed an arm over his face. "You want me to take you to the Rovers, don't you?"

Now, that idea had some merit to it. "I do." I took another long sip of the canteen. Had water ever tasted so sweet?

Will tipped his head up at the sky. "Night's coming on and the Rover camp is in the other direction, past the Settlement. I can carry you, but I'm not sure I can carry you that far."

"I'm open to other suggestions, but you can't take me back to the Settlement like this. You know it, and I know it." I was no longer worried about the Penitent Box. If I came back like this, Stuckley's blood all over my person?

It was finally, truly sinking in. I'd killed a man. My fingers started to shake. I didn't even know I was crying until Will handed me his handkerchief.

He cursed. "Don't do that. Please don't do that."

"I'm sorry," I said, wiping at my face.

Will set his hands on his hips. "It's gruesome. Looks like you're crying blood."

That surprised a laugh out of me, and it made my ribs hurt. "I thought you were telling me not to cry over Stuckley."

"You can cry over whoever you wish, once we get you washed up so you don't look like the quiet fields done spit you up for tasting bad." He adjusted his hat. "Well, I reckon dithering over it isn't going to make this any less difficult."

The gunslinger dropped down, making it easier for me to climb up onto his back, though *easier* was a misleading term. I'd used up most of my energy leaving the cave, and my entire body had gone from a chorus of pain to doing the melody in rounds, the screaming from every muscle and bruised bone overlapping the other.

He slung his own pack, which he'd left at the opening of the cave, onto his front, the creature padding alongside us, my bag clutched between pointed teeth. It didn't move like any cat I'd seen before. All cats move like shadows, lithe and soft-footed. This creature moved like the shadow's own shadow. I couldn't hear it over our footsteps.

It was a long trek, and whenever Will needed a break, I'd try to walk a bit. I didn't make much progress that way, and Will was concerned I'd injure myself more, but I'm a stubborn thing and insisted. On one of the breaks, Will had me try a few bites of a roll from his pack, tossing a rangy hare from one of the Settlement's snares to the cat.

The large feline sniffed at it before lying on his belly, the hare between his paws as he tore it apart easily. My meal didn't go as well. I took three bites before I sicked it all up in the grass. Will took the roll away. "No more until you see a healer."

I will admit that I lost track of things shortly after that, since I passed out once the gunslinger got me up on his back again.

When I regained consciousness, it was to the sound of a pitched verbal battle.

Squinting against the light of several lanterns, it took me a few moments to parse out the different voices—Will's angry voice, followed by Sergio's. The Rover's tone like nothing I'd ever heard from him before. I'd never heard him yell.

Tallis's voice entered the fray, like a hound harrying game, and I wasn't sure whose side he'd taken. I wasn't getting words yet, just tone.

Finally, the words filtered in.

"She looks half dead, Uncle!" Tallis bit out.

"Looks?" the gunslinger snarled. "She is half dead. She needs a healer."

"We cannot let her into camp," Sergio spit. "She stinks of dark workings."

They continued verbally circling each other. I started to pass out again, but a rough tongue on my cheek startled me awake. The cat thing was trying to keep me conscious. I blinked at him but couldn't actually see him until he moved and his eyes reflected the lantern light.

My trembling fingers met slick fur, but I still couldn't see what I was touching. Just the long grass of the hillside behind us. The twinkling stars. How hard had I hit my head?

As the men argued, I heard a set of soft footsteps. I leaned my head back to see Zara, the healer's leather satchel in her arms, Anna herself at her side.

Anna dropped down on her haunches to get a closer look. That was when the creature decided to make himself known. Where there had been seemingly empty space was suddenly filled with a pissed-off feline. He growled, a strange mix of hiss and scream. The sound drew shivers up my spine, as did the sight of the sharp teeth in his jaws.

Anna froze, and suddenly the group was silent.

I was hit with a strange wave of emotions that felt distinctly different from my own, and I knew the growl for what it had been—a warning. I was wounded and the creature didn't like strangers approaching me. The cat creature knew I was okay with the gunslinger, but Tallis and his people were new to him.

I touched his shoulder tentatively. "It's okay. They're here to help."

The cat turned those bright blue eyes on me and chirped a question.

"It's okay," I repeated. I slowly reached out and touched Anna's coat sleeve. "Friends."

The cat relaxed into a more settled position, doing this odd snarl-talking, almost like he was complaining, reminding me of when Pops would grumble about something. Like the cat didn't agree with my choices but would go along with my fool-headed notion.

Anna let out a slow breath. "Oh, child. What have you done?"

I settled a weary hand on the cat's back. "Same as I ever done. Survived." I tilted my chin back so I could see her better. "Are you going to help, or was this a fool's errand?" I coughed, my ribs squeezing in pain. When she didn't move, I patted the cat carefully, my fingers still not quite working right. "He won't hurt you."

Anna studied us for a long moment before she seemed to shrug and reached for her bag. "It is in your best interest that he does not."

Zara grasped her shoulder, speaking softly in their language, but not soft enough. "Are you sure about this, my heart?"

Anna began digging through her bag. "It's this or let her die. I don't want that on my conscience."

Her hands were chilly but careful as she examined me in the light of the lantern. After a few moments, she settled back on her haunches. "This is no good. I need my wagon."

The men had been silent, but now Sergio broke in. "She cannot come into our camp, not like that."

"You can't leave her here to die, either, Uncle." Fury coated Tallis's words.

Anna, ever practical, sliced through the beginnings of their argument. "Then you will bring my wagon to me. Quickly, if you please."

CHAPTER TWENTY-TWO

—✳︎—

ANNA DID EVERYTHING SHE COULD TO KEEP ME AWAKE as Zara fetched her wagon. Sergio stayed, keeping an eye on all of us. The gunslinger sat at my feet, almost as beat as I was. Well, I reckon what with him playing pack mule to my carcass, he was plumb exhausted. Tallis hovered at my feet like a fretful ghost, not wanting to get in Anna's way.

Anna appeared to find this both funny and annoying. "If you're going to hover, be useful. I need water from the river. Go on, then."

Time seemed to be passing for me in jerky stops and starts. Next thing I knew, someone was picking me up. I mumbled about being sorry, feeling like an awful lot of people were carrying my weight about today.

This was met by irritation from Tallis. "Everyone needs to be taken care of sometimes, Little Fox, from the babe in arms to the elder. You think you're above us mere mortals?"

"I take care of myself," I said hotly. The cave cat growl-talked next to us in complaint.

"You're doing a poor job," Tallis snapped, then gentled his

voice to the cave cat. "I don't want to hear it. Someone has to tell her these things."

I was trundled into Anna's wagon and laid on one of the cots. After depositing me, Tallis stepped out and fetched the bucket of water. Zara immediately transferred some of it to the kettle and set it on the stove. The embers had been stoked already, the air inside the wagon much warmer than the outside. Everyone was shooed away except for Zara, who started helping the healer divest me of my clothing, or what was left of it.

Once they were done with that, Anna poked and prodded me in the way of healers everywhere, while Zara poured the steaming water into a bowl filled with herbs. The pungent smell filled the wagon. Zara dipped a rag into the water and began the tedious task of washing the blood from me.

Anna tutted at me. "You want the truth, or you want the pretty version?"

"Truth," I gritted out.

"You're a mess," Anna said succinctly. "Your wrists and ankles are horribly abraded. If we're lucky, you won't get an infection, but you don't seem terribly lucky. You have a concussion—a nasty one. Your ribs are likely cracked, or at the very least heavily bruised." She turned and started plucking various bottles from their shelves. "The good news is, if you wake up tomorrow without a fever, you'll probably live."

"And if I have a fever?"

She smiled at me, tight-lipped. "Then you better send all your good words to the skies and hope I'm as good as I think I am."

They cleaned me up as best they could, applying salve to my abrasions and a cool cloth to my head. My wounds were bandaged, and I was redressed in someone's long cotton shirt.

Anna poured a foul potion down my gullet. "You'll need to keep that in your belly," she said firmly, "and not sick it up all over my nice wagon."

I managed.

Blankets were then wrapped around me, and I was allowed to drift off at last. Once I was settled, the cat crawled into the cot with me. It was a tight fit, but somehow he succeeded, and it brought me comfort.

Throughout the night, I was prodded awake. Sometimes I was fed a little broth, others cold water. The wakings began to blur together. Images coming and going. Voices from the darkness, speaking softly to me. Cajoling. At some point, I swear I heard Tallis alternating between a quiet pleading and irritated, angry statements, but I couldn't make sense of things.

I remember most his hand in mine and the warm heat of the cat along my side.

When I woke up, it was to rain pattering along the top of the wagon. The sleepy gray afternoon light seeped in through the cracked door. My eyes felt gummy, my body heavy with exhaustion. Tallis was sprawled in a chair next to my cot. His sleeping body was relaxed, but even in the dim light, I could see the bruising under his eyes, and the scratchy beginnings of a beard across his cheeks. It made his scar stand out more.

I must have made some sound, because he blinked awake,

staring at me for several moments before suddenly straightening in his chair. "You're awake." There was an unmistakable note of surprise in his voice.

"Same as every morning so far," I said, my voice sounding scratchy to my own ears.

He scoffed, levering himself out of his chair, rising with an easy grace I envied. He fit an arm around my shoulders and helped me sit before fetching me a cup of water that had been resting on a nearby folding table, pressing the cup to my lips.

"I'm not a babe," I grumbled. "I can do this myself."

"You go right ahead and fight me for this cup, Little Fox. We'll see who's the victor, hm?"

Irritated, I raised my hands to bat him away and discovered that I had all the strength of a newly birthed kitten.

Tallis smirked, keeping his hold on the cup. "You've had a fever for three nights." His smirk faltered, and he swallowed hard. The sudden gravity of his expression weighted my belly. With shaking fingers, Tallis smoothed my short hair back. "We weren't sure you were going to make it."

His fingers continued to smooth and pet my hair, a faint smile returning to his face. "You look like a baby bird. Little tufts of flame feathers." He pressed his hand against my skull, then released. "They won't stay down."

I glowered at him and snatched the cup from his hands, though it took all my meager resources to do it. "Little Fox, baby bird. I'm not an animal."

Again that derisive scoffing noise. "You're half wild. Animals have better manners."

I emptied the cup down my throat, welcoming the cool water. I wasn't going to win this argument, because he was right. I was a wild thing, more animal than person sometimes. I hadn't fit back in New Retienne, a different beast than the others around me. Meanwhile, Tallis seemed elemental— patient as the woods, smooth as water.

It was irritating.

He took the cup back from my loose grip, hooking my chin with a finger so he knew he had my attention. "I like you wild. It wasn't a criticism."

This, by far, was the most unsettling thing about Tallis. His hawkeyed ability to peer inside me, my feelings the easy rabbit in open grass. All he had to do was swoop down and snatch them up for his consumption. It was a vulnerable feeling.

Something scratched at the door and Tallis got up and opened it. The creature from the cave padded in, chin up, eyes bright. He chirped, and I was met with a rush of relief.

"Yeah," I said. "I'm sitting up, and apparently it's a minor miracle."

The creature grumble-growled at me, the sound having the unmistakable tone of a lecture to it.

I snorted. "It's not like I got sick on purpose."

He sat, chin up, long tail lashing. He certainly could pack a lot of attitude into his posture.

"Can you understand him?" Tallis asked, curious.

I opened my mouth to argue, *Of course not. He's an animal*, when I realized that I sort of could understand the creature. "Of a kind," I admitted slowly. I tapped my sternum.

"I get a sense of things. More emotions than thought?" I peered at the cat. I truly had never seen anything like him. "What is he?"

Tallis tipped his head to the side. "I don't know. None of us know. My uncle says you reached into the place of dreams and pulled him out."

"What does that mean?"

Tallis stroked his fingers along my arm, above the bandages on my wrist. It seemed he was doing it as much to comfort himself as me. Like maybe if he stopped, I would disappear. "When Uncle Sergio was younger, he used to travel far. Sailed to strange lands. Saw many things. He said that on one island, he saw someone do evil workings. The man punched a hole in the world and brought something out."

The hairs on my arms rose up as I listened, and Tallis paused to readjust my blanket. "Uncle wasn't sure how the man did it, but there was a lot of blood and screaming. Strange writings covered the ground and even the man." His voice grew soft. "What he remembers most is the smell. Blood and death and something wrong. That was how you smelled when Will brought you to us."

I swallowed hard. "Did the man survive?"

Tallis shook his head slowly. "Whatever he brought out, it ate him."

My stomach pitched and the cave cat trilled a soothing sound at me. "Did it—" I licked my lips. "Did it look like the cat?"

"No," Tallis admitted.

I stared longingly at the empty cup in Tallis's hand. "Whatever he is, he hasn't tried to eat me yet."

"No, he hasn't," Tallis said as he fetched a pitcher of water and refilled my cup. "In fact, he seems keen on doing the opposite. He's been a useful sort of thing. He's brought you a pheasant and two rabbits." Tallis pressed the cup into my hands. "He obviously thinks you need fattening."

"He would be correct," I said, sipping this water more slowly. I grew more alert with every mouthful, the scene around me sharpening. Tallis moved with his usual grace, but there was a weight to each movement that spoke of exhaustion. He seemed stiff, like his muscles had been bunched too long. He wore the signs of someone who had been sitting vigil. I knew the signs well from when I sat with Pops.

The similarities made the reality of my situation hit me then.

I'd almost died.

I gulped more water.

I suddenly noticed how quiet it was. Tallis's people were a noisy bunch when they went about their daily comings and goings. When I'd stayed with them before, it was a pleasant chorus of people talking, laughter, children hollering, horses, and snatches of song. Constant. A homey sort of sound, like the lifeblood of a people.

With the exception of Tallis and the cave creature, I couldn't hear a blessed thing. "We're not in your camp."

Tallis had his back to me, but I was watching and saw him stiffen—just for a breath—then he relaxed. "You're not allowed among my people." He sighed, hooking the chair with his foot and bringing it closer before he sat. He settled in, resting his elbows on his knees. "My uncle is afraid that you are dangerous. At least he doesn't think you're the cause of all this anymore."

"What?" I stared at him, shocked.

Tallis shrugged. "When you showed up outside our camp the other night in the same area we'd found Yakob, he grew suspicious. Now he's thinking you're more prey than predator."

I set the empty cup in my lap. "Does he think the cave cat hurt Yakob?"

"Paws are too small. Claw marks wouldn't match up."

I nodded, regretting it. I was sore still. "I've never been seen as dangerous before."

That earned me a ghost of a smile. He jerked his chin toward the cat. "I suspect you'll be considered such to most people as long as you have Chirp."

The cat raised its head and made a noise at Tallis that did sound like the cheerful sound of a cricket or a bird.

"Chirp?"

Tallis rolled his shoulders. "Had to call him something. You've been unconscious for three days. He's been my most stalwart companion." He leaned over and scratched Chirp's chin. The beast made another noise, a trilling sort of rumble. His version of a purr, I reckoned. He certainly seemed smitten with Tallis.

Part of what Tallis said filtered into my brain. "You've been here the whole time?" I couldn't quite wrap my head around it. Why sit with me for three days instead of being with his people? Guilt? Duty? *Guard* duty? Was Tallis here to make sure I didn't scamper at the first opportunity? Fear seeped through me, and though I kept my face blank, Chirp still seemed to know. He turned his blue eyes on me and snapped his teeth.

"He told you," Tallis said, his voice amused, even if his expression was serious when he gazed at me. "I wonder what you were thinking to get that response."

I hedged a little. "I was wondering why you were here, like I said."

Tallis glanced at Chirp before turning his attention back to me. When he finally spoke, his voice was rough. "You almost died, Faolan. Where else would I be?"

I wasn't sure what to say to that. Of the categories I'd come up with, that answer didn't quite fit. I frowned at Tallis, trying to figure him out.

He made a frustrated noise. "I'm going to go tell Anna you're awake. While I'm gone, I want you to think on something." He stood abruptly, sliding the chair back. Then he leaned until only an inch or two separated our faces. "If I'd almost died, would you have sat in the chair?"

And then he left.

Chirp made a series of clicking, growling noises.

"It's a fine thing," I grumbled, "getting lectured as soon as one crawls back from near death. I haven't even had any coffee yet."

Chirp wasn't very sympathetic of my plight, flicking his tail in irritation.

I slumped against the wall, my meager energy spent. Would I have sat vigil for three days for Tallis? Except it wasn't the same. Tallis didn't *need* me to sit for him. He had his people. I didn't have people. All I had was a weird cave cat and my own battered carcass.

I frowned. That wasn't entirely true, now was it? In a way, I had the gunslinger. Sure, he'd been sent by the people trying to take what was mine, but he'd also carried me on his back for quite a distance. He'd pulled me out of the cave. He'd done a lot, really.

There was also Jesse and Dai Lo. They would sit vigil for me, if only to harangue me over whatever fool thing I'd done in the first place.

I reckoned I did have people, after a fashion.

Tallis didn't need me worrying my hands by his sick bed.

But I would be there all the same, and I think he knew that. I found that thought worrisome, though I couldn't put my finger on why, exactly. I found it funny to no end that I wasn't scared of a cave cat from who-knows-where, but this . . . this gave me the shivers.

Voices and footsteps interrupted my thoughts as Anna came into the wagon, followed by Will.

Anna immediately took up my wrists, holding them, and then used her thumbs to edge my eyelids up so she could peer into my eyes in an unsettling manner. She huffed. "You're alive. Isn't that a surprise." She spoke in my language, though her accent was heavy. I suspected this was for Will's benefit. Like many Rovers, she probably knew our tongue better than we knew hers. They generally picked it up to make trading easier.

I scowled at her. "As a healer, maybe you should show *less* surprise."

She snorted. "I'm a healer, not a god. You were burning up and speaking nonsense. I didn't think you were long for this world."

Will leaned against the opposite wall, his arms crossed. "You did give us a scare. Several of them."

"I'm surprised you're still here."

Now it was his turn to snort. "While I might be interested in what's going on at the Settlement, I'm not going to let you out of my sight. Besides, I wasn't sure going back was a good idea." He must have seen me start filling up with questions, because he shook his head. "Oh, no, all that's going to keep. After Anna takes a gander at your sorry hide, and we stuff your gullet, then we'll chatter all you want."

"You will chatter exactly as long as I let you," Anna said. "She needs rest."

"I've been resting for three days!" I protested.

Anna deftly ran her fingers under my jaw, pressing the tissue. "Fighting a fever isn't resting." She straightened. "You'll do as I say if you know what's good for you." Her eyes wandered over to Chirp. "Though I'm not certain you know what *is* good for you."

Will laughed. I was starting to wonder if it would be better to go back to being unconscious.

After Anna declared me fit enough, she helped me wash and get dressed. Someone had managed to clean my boots and trousers. My shirt hadn't made it, and my hat was somewhere back in the cave. I was given someone else's worn cotton shirt and a thick, soft sweater that had seen better days but kept me warm enough. I missed my hat, as I felt weirdly vulnerable without it, but I missed Pops's watch more. I could replace a hat.

I was basically carried out of the wagon, despite being on my own wobbly feet. Anna thought fresh air would do me good. I was wrapped in a blanket and deposited before the fire. Day was fading into dusk, the air holding only the faintest bite of cold.

Tallis handed me a bowl filled with a soup of rabbit meat and root vegetables, along with a flat round of griddle bread, which I used to mop it up.

I ate every bite, and then I was given another helping. I ate every bite of that, too.

With my belly full, we began to rehash the situation, Will, Tallis, Anna, and I, though Zara joined us shortly after I finished my meal. My reality was coming into focus, and I wasn't sure I liked the picture.

I couldn't go home because of the mayor and his men. I wasn't sure I could get back into the Settlement, and Tallis's people weren't letting me within their camp. My options were very limited. In fact, it appeared I had no options.

I huddled into the blanket. "I have to go back to the Settlement."

"Over my dead body." Tallis folded his arms.

Will shook his head.

Zara's lip curled. "Why?"

Anna finally ended it with "I didn't pull you from the jaws of the serpent of death just to let you throw yourself back into them."

"What's my other option?" I said softly. "I have the clothes on my back, half of which aren't even mine. I have my pack, I think. How long will I survive out here on my own? I can't go home." I speared Tallis with a gaze. "Your people won't take me in. Otherwise we'd be in their camp right now."

Tallis looked away, a muscle in his jaw ticking.

It was Zara who answered from where she was sprawled by the fire. "Uncle is scared. Perhaps for good reason, perhaps not." She waved a hand at Chirp, who was curled against me, watching the fire. "Maybe if you told us how you got him, hm? Knowledge is how you chase away fear."

Uneasiness moved through me with heavy feet. "I found him in the cave. That's where he came from."

Zara's eyebrows winged up gracefully. "There are no creatures like him around here. Never have been. I think you know that."

"Speak," Anna said bluntly. "And tell us what happened."

I thought about what Tallis had told me. Beyond the quiet fields, where we went when we died, and the realm of whatever gods one believed in, it hadn't occurred to me that there could *be* other worlds. I curled deeper into my blanket. "Well, I didn't do any magic. I don't know any."

Will jabbed at the fire with a stick, resetting some of the logs. "You did something. Otherwise, we wouldn't have your new friend here."

Chirp bumped his head against my shoulder, and I sighed. I told them everything I remembered about that day. The canteen and its weird taste. Stuckley and his ranting. The cave walls. Symbols covering them, rife with evil. Strange sights, unfamiliar sounds. Did I believe it was another world? I wasn't sure. But they were right. I'd never seen anything like Chirp.

"You share space with him," Tallis's words were soft but not gentle. They were like the tide, calm if you gave yourself over to it, hard if you fought.

"That's not true, I—"

Tallis carried on, unrelenting. "You can communicate. I've watched you. And he has other tricks."

"What?" I asked, examining my companion warily. "Can he fetch or something?"

"Ask him to hide," Tallis said.

I felt silly, but everyone was watching, and I couldn't see a way around it. "Fine. Chirp. Hide."

The cat disappeared.

I startled, then froze because I could still feel the warm, solid weight of his body next to mine. Slowly, I reached out, uncurling my fingers and dropping them down until they met the soft touch of fur. Chirp was still there. I just couldn't see him. Only empty grass.

"Stop," I said, my voice wavering.

Chirp reappeared, my hand resting on his back. He trilled at me.

I whistled low. "That's some trick."

"I think," Will said, still fussing with the fire, "that maybe you should tell us again what happened in that cave."

CHAPTER TWENTY-THREE

—✳—

BETWEEN THE FEVER AND MY BATTERED HEAD, I WAS surprised that I remembered as much as I did. I coughed up whatever details I could manage. Stuckley's weird behavior. The strange liquid in his canteen. The symbols. His death.

Anna shoved a cup of hot tea into my hands as I talked. The meal had given me a small amount of energy, but I'd spent it by the end. I was weary again and ready to return to the cot.

"Mushroom tea, maybe," Anna said. "In the canteen. Some mushrooms make you see things that aren't there."

"Sounds like he set up some kind of ritual," Zara said. "Or someone had. All you had to do was stumble into it and make your offering."

"My offering?" I asked.

"Some of the old gods liked death and blood," Tallis said, his arms crossed over his chest. "None that we followed, but others welcomed them."

Stuckley had been my offering.

Will ran a palm over the stubble on his cheek. "Can't say

I thought Stuckley had that kind of . . . initiative. Or follow-through. Usually needs a bit of hand-holding, our Stuckley."

I was in agreement with Will and said as much. "I don't think he really knew what was doing. He might have set it up, but I don't think he understood."

"Like giving a child a lighter and not explaining fire," Tallis said.

No one argued with him. Our campfire crackled as we all stared thoughtfully into its depths.

"I hadn't known such a thing like this was possible," I said.

"You can't go back there." Tallis offered the words softly, though his eyes were hard.

"I really don't have a choice." I smoothed my hand over Chirp absently.

"Someone gave Stuckley that lighter," Tallis said, "and sent him to burn. They handed you over as the intended sacrifice. You were meant to die in that cave."

I nodded stubbornly because he wasn't wrong, but he wasn't exactly offering up any options, either. "I was." My brain, sluggish as it was after everything, finally chugged along to the next logical stop. "If Stuckley was doing anything, it was HisBen's orders."

Zara had been watching the stars come out, but she turned her face toward me to speak. "All the more reason not to return, yes?"

"All the more reason *to* return," I said. "If HisBen wants something, he's going to keep going after it. He'll send someone else to that cave to die. He'll send someone else to that cave to get their own Chirp." Besides, I still needed to find my watch. If I had my land, then there would be somewhere to *go*. The mayor could come for me all he wanted.

Tallis grunted and Anna nodded, but Zara kept looking at the stars. Will continued watching the flames, his face thoughtful. The gunslinger had a good mind, he'd proved as much to me during the time I'd known him. I waited him out until he was ready to share.

"I think HisBen has his own one of these things, and I think you heard it when you took Dai Lo and Jesse to see Cartwright. And something went after those goats."

I remembered Gertie and swallowed hard. I also remembered something feeding outside the Box, the wet sounds it had made. Had that been HisBen's cave cat?

"Chirp hasn't so much as taken a swipe at us." Tallis stood and stretched. The movement seemed to go on too long. I realized I was staring, and he knew it. I scowled at him. There was a faint smile on his face when he sauntered over to gather up my dishes. "He lectures if he's unhappy, but he doesn't attack. Whatever's going on with HisBen's cave creature I don't think is natural."

"A rough hand can make any dog mean," Will said.

"Whatever you and Stuckley did," Anna said, "he has made worse."

"All the more reason to go back," I told her.

"All the more reason to stay away, Little Fox," Tallis snapped. "The fox stays alive by being cunning. Not by jumping into the hunter's sack."

I stiffened, ready to spit venom, only to be cut off by the

swift chop of Anna's hand through the air. "Enough, children. We will sleep on it. My patient must rest, and our minds need time with the problem. Nothing will get solved tonight."

I was bundled back into the cot in the wagon, arguing the whole time that I'd just got up and there was no way I could sleep.

I was out as soon as Anna pulled the blanket over my chin.

This time I woke up with the birds as they made a ruckus over the morning and their breakfasts. Someone had thoughtfully left out a bowl and a pitcher of water, along with some tooth powder. My body protested the movements, as I was still sore and battered, but I needed the refreshing. Anna had attached a small sticking plaster to the cut on my face. I hadn't noticed it yesterday. I'd been more out of it than I'd thought.

After I got my boots on, I took Chirp outside. We both needed to make water, and he apparently needed to chase after some birds. Those chores handled, I hobbled back to camp, Chirp at my heels, some kind of grouse hanging from his jaws.

The gunslinger was already up, his borrowed blanket neatly folded. He was fussing with a brew bag and a billycan to make coffee. He'd left the skillet out from roasting the beans, and Tallis was now utilizing it to cook some sausage.

Tallis was stealing glances at me as I settled by the fire. He still seemed irritated with me but also like he needed to see that I was okay. I decided it could all wait until coffee.

We sat in silence for the short spell needed for the contents of the billycan to boil, and I was soon rewarded with a steaming mug. Tallis nudged a small ceramic pot with honey my way, and I added a dab to my coffee. As irritated as he was, I still got treats. I used my mug to hide my smile, but from the scowl on his face, I think I failed.

After the coffee had been doled out, I was given a sausage wrapped in the leftover griddle bread from yesterday.

Will didn't talk until after he'd swallowed the last bite. "I have an idea. Not a plan, really." He huffed a laugh. "Not enough of it to be considered a plan."

"I'm all ears." I'd inhaled my own breakfast, barely taking time to chew, and was handed another bread-wrapped sausage.

When I hesitated, Tallis's expression softened. "Since you seemed better, Anna and Zara went back to camp to check in. They're eating breakfast there. Eat, Little Fox. Slowly this time. It's not going to run away."

Now it was Will's turn to hide a smile behind his mug. The gunslinger enjoyed me getting chided for some reason. Chirp noisily crunched through his own breakfast, nosing aside bothersome feathers.

"I thought if there was nowhere for you to go, we'd create a middle ground."

I chewed slowly, trying to make sense of Will's statement. "How so?"

"It's probably not safe for either of us to go back—Dillard sent you to your death and, more likely than not, thinks that was accomplished. Best to let him keep thinking that. Probably assumes I've scampered off to the next job. If I do show up, days later, even with a plausible story, I'll have his attention." He grimaced. "Not a particularly healthy thing to have, Dillard's attention."

No, it was not. I nodded, though it pained me a little, sore as I was.

"I say we make camp. I don't have much supplies, but I might be able to barter a few things away from Tallis and his crew, or at least borrow."

Tallis didn't say anything, but he didn't argue, either.

"We find a spot close enough to keep an eye on the Settlement during the day. Then at night, we sneak in that back door. Figure out what's going on. Warn the folk that need warning."

"Or get them out," I said.

Will rubbed a hand over the stubble on his jaw. "Not sure we have the resources to get everyone out."

We didn't even have enough resources for the two of us. The idea of leaving anyone to HisBen's tender mercies sent lead into my guts. A flash of memory from the cave hit me. Stuckley screaming. His warm blood on my hands.

I had to swallow past the taste of fear in my mouth. I washed it away with the last of my coffee. Fear wouldn't do me any good, anyway.

When Zara and Anna came back to take another gander at my bedraggled carcass, Will and Tallis set off for the Rover camp. It did not escape my notice that they all thought I needed a nanny. Considering how creaky my movements were, I didn't have much ground to argue. That didn't mean I didn't argue, mind, just that those arguments were weak as day-old kittens.

After breakfast I was feeling more myself and said as much, but Anna ignored every word, instead checking my wounds and watching the way I moved. Finally, she grunted in what I took for grudging approval.

"You need to keep those clean," she said, gesturing to my scabbed-over wounds. "I'll make sure Will has the supplies to replace the plasters if needs must." She dug a battered tin out of her bag. "And I'll leave you some tea."

I eyed the tin speculatively. Anna was a healer and would not do anything to harm her patients, but I was awful curious about what was in it, nonetheless.

She saw my expression and snorted. "It's for the pain, and to aid healing. My own blend—black willow bark, boneset, and a few other odds and ends. Drink it about every four hours or so."

"As you say, ma'am, thank you." Even I knew better than to argue with Anna. From the smirk on Zara's face, she knew I was fighting my own tongue. I opened the tin, and the sharp smell of the willow bark hit my nose. The fainter scent of boneset—grassy and mild—lurked in the background, but what boneset lacks in olfactory power, it makes up for in looks. It dries to be a vivid green.

Chirp sniffed the tin and sneezed. I jerked it away from him, and the movement made my muscles scream in protest, but I didn't need Chirp slobber on my tea, thank you very much. "Watch it, cat." I sealed up the tin again and set it aside.

Next, Anna handed me a stoppered clay pot, small enough to fit in the palm of my hand. Something inside smelled like chamomile with a bit of a floral overlay. "Arnica, but what else?"

"Yarrow," Anna said bluntly. "They will help with the bruising." She took the jar back, gesturing for me to raise my shirt. "I'll apply some now, but later, you'll either have to take the pain or have *someone* help you with the areas you can't reach, like your back." Her tone was matter-of-fact, warming some of the salve on her hands as I lifted my shirt and sweater, but I couldn't stop the flush rising to my cheeks. Not because of what the healer was doing—neither her nor Zara was interested in my battered carcass in any way beyond healing. But because the minute she'd said *someone* I'd thought Tallis, and . . .

I blushed harder. "I'm sure Tallis has better things to do."

"She never said who that *someone* had to be." Zara's grin was sly. "I wonder what's making you turn so red. What are you thinking of over there, *Little Fox*?"

I did not miss her emphasis on the nickname Tallis had chosen for me, but I didn't rise to it. "It's hot out," I muttered. We were all wearing sweaters. I was fibbing and they knew it, but beyond a soft laugh, Zara didn't say anything.

After a stern lecture to watch my ribs and take better care of my sorry hide, I was ordered to rest by the fire. I wish I could say that I was restless and annoyed at the practice, but the reality was that I dozed for a bit, curled around Chirp, a blanket wrapped around me.

When I woke, Tallis and Will had returned, both of them on horseback. Roon, Tallis's dog, trotted alongside, his tongue out. Tallis rode his horse, Neev, and had taken the time to wash and shave. His saddlebags were packed full, and two bedrolls and a roll of canvas were lashed behind the saddle. He had a small camp guitar secured to his back. I guess he was planning on staying awhile.

Roon approached Chirp warily, hackles raised and his step light, but he didn't make a sound.

Chirp whickered at him, his tone one of disdain that all felines seem to muster as easily as drawing breath. He sat down and began cleaning his paw. Roon, for his part, seemed to find this funny. His tongue lolled out and he gave one sharp bark. When Chirp continued to ignore him, Roon came over to sniff the big cave cat, and I decided they were doing well.

Will was on an Appaloosa—a white horse with gray spots, and she was a beaut. The gunslinger knew his way around a horse. His own bags were stuffed full, a bedroll and canvas tied tight.

"Now, I know for a fact that nothing we have would be worth that fine animal or those supplies." I frowned at him as he dismounted.

Will grunted, amused. "You don't even know what the supplies are."

"We had nothing," I said dryly. "And I know what nothing is worth."

Tallis slid to the ground, clucking at Neev to follow him. "But I have things to trade, and you have something I want in return." His eyes were filled with laughter as he slowly raised one brow.

My mouth went completely arid, like its own minuscule

desert. That's when Neev turned and I saw the hard case tethered to the back of the rolls. Tallis had brought the fiddle.

Seeing my expression shift from a heavy cocktail of embarrassment and want to an entirely different kind of want made Tallis laugh. "I would like you to play with me, Little Fox." His tone was innocent, but his eyes held a mischievous glint. He patted the top of his guitar, sliding from my language into his. "I don't know your word—play together?"

"*Accompany,*" I said, my cheeks hot, damn the skies. Pale as I was, when I flushed no one could miss it. I was as red as a strawberry in summer. "You want me to accompany you on the fiddle." To overcompensate for my hot cheeks, my tone was cold, like I hated the idea. No one bought it for a second.

Anna stood, dusting off her skirts as Zara gathered up their things. Zara went to speak quietly to her brother, concern furrowing her brow. Anna took that time to go over her medicines and instructions with Will as well, not trusting me to pass along the information without conveniently leaving out any rules. Irritating, but also fair enough.

Before they retired back to camp, Anna glowered at me. "Stay alive. I've put a lot of work into you. Don't waste it."

"Thank you," I said. "I will do my best."

Zara gave me a hug. A quick thing, over before I realized it was happening. "I also wish you not to die." Her mouth twitched.

I was beginning to see where Tallis got his sense of humor.

"I wasn't planning on it," I said wryly.

She grew suddenly serious. "Take care, Little Fox. What

you're doing will be very dangerous." The sly gleam came back into her eyes. "And if you hurt my brother, or get him killed, I will curse your ghost."

As farewells went, it was the kind you couldn't really top, so I just nodded.

CHAPTER TWENTY-FOUR

※

A PROBLEM QUICKLY PRESENTED ITSELF IN REGARD TO our transportation, namely that there were two horses and three people. Tallis solved this by swinging me up behind him over my protests. He clucked his tongue, and the horses moved forward at a steady walk, Chirp and Roon trotting alongside.

"I'll ride behind Will," I huffed, making my ribs twinge.

"He's a much bigger man," Tallis said mildly. "You will not fit, Little Fox."

I didn't think Will was *that* much bigger, though he was a fair-sized man, and I said so.

Tallis ignored me. Will started whistling, ignoring us both.

I knew better than to huff again, but I wanted to. Badly. "Then I'll walk."

"No," both men said in unison.

I distinctly disliked being outvoted. I sulked at this. It wasn't that I minded being pressed against Tallis's back. In fact, the problem was that I didn't mind enough. He was warm and he smelled good. I liked it too much, and it was making me uncomfortable. I considered sliding down off the horse.

Tallis, as was his way of things, seemed to read my mind. "If you slide off this horse and try to walk, we'll tie you to the saddle. It'll be far less comfortable, and you'll be more unhappy."

"That's not fair!" I said hotly.

Tallis shrugged.

"You're bullies," I grumbled and thought about dismounting anyway, despite their protests and their logic.

"Faolan, I sat and watched you almost die for three days. If you don't have the good sense to ride on my nice horse while you are injured, then, yes, I will be a bully, and I won't lose a wink of sleep over it." For all that Tallis's tone was mild, there was a hidden steel to his words.

My jaw snapped shut.

Will went back to whistling.

I wasn't used to anyone saying such things about me, not since Pops, and even then, he wasn't much for words.

I kept my trap shut and let the conversation drop like a feather, floating slowly away.

We stuck to the trees, letting the horses pick their way along a game path, the undergrowth thick along our sides. I dozed for a while, the rocking of the horse making me sleepy, and the knowledge that Tallis wouldn't let me fall making me feel safe.

I hadn't been able to hand over my safety like that to

another person for what felt like years. That kind of security was something you didn't notice or realize you even had until it was gone. Suddenly you're adrift, a leaf tossing through white water rapids. Small, lost, and achingly fragile.

I realized that just as suddenly, that had been reversed. I'd been plucked out of the rapids. Gone from having no one to having someone. *Someones.* Jesse. Dai Lo. Will. Tallis. Chirp. Even Miss Moon, in her fashion. And when you had that feeling back, you held on with an iron grip.

That was why I was going back. Why I *needed* to go back. Jesse and Dai Lo had rescued me. I wasn't about to let them drown, not when I could help it. They saved me first. Now it was my turn.

From down along the forest floor, I heard Chirp make a soft trilling noise. He understood. Somehow, he knew why I needed to go back, without me saying words at all. I wondered how much of what I thought or felt was filtering down to him. And how much of that he comprehended.

Tallis led us to a small clearing that wasn't entirely natural. Someone had used it as a place to camp before. Large trees surrounded us, along with the bushes and plant life around the forest floor. Wind and time had moved most of the leaf litter from last fall to the edges of the clearing. It would be difficult for anyone to approach without us hearing.

The clearing itself was mostly moss, but the rocks had been moved and used to make a circle around a pit for a campfire.

Tallis helped me slide down from Neev before he followed suit. "We'll dig the pit down a little deeper. If we keep the fire small, there won't be much light."

"How close are we to the Settlement?" Will asked, gracefully sliding from the saddle to the ground. "They'll see the smoke, surely?"

Tallis shrugged. "We're on Rover land, and this spot is used often enough that they likely won't pay much attention to the smoke. I might be willing to skip the fire if it was only about food, but we'll need it to make Faolan's tea, and to ward off the chill. Temperature still drops drastically at night, and we won't do anyone a lick of good if we're half frozen."

I was given the task of gathering kindling so we could start the fire. It was time for my tea, and they didn't want me to do anything on the strenuous side. I had the feeling I was only allowed to go out of sight to gather because I had both Roon and Chirp with me. Roon was marking our territory in the time-honored way of canines, darting from tree to tree, but Chirp padded along at my side, curious. After I had a small handful of sticks, he seemed to understand my mission, and starting digging about more.

He pawed at a fallen branch, giving a little trill.

"That's too big, at least for now." He seemed to droop, and I hated to see him downcast. "We'll mark it for later, when we need bigger wood. I bet Tallis has a hatchet in all of his gear. This branch would make good logs."

Chirp preened then, scooting along happily to the next find. It was a silly thing to take joy in, this gathering of supplies, but the cave cat made me laugh nonetheless. As did Roon, whenever he pounced onto a pile of leaves or brush. Such joy in this world was fleeting, and I'd learned to gather it to myself when I could.

By the time I made it back to the campsite, Tallis and Will had used ropes to secure a length of the canvas to tree branches, creating a makeshift roof. The other length was stretched along the ground, held down by a handful of fist-sized stones.

"It won't keep the wind off," Will said, double-checking the knots. "But it will keep us dry."

"In this case, I'd prefer to see what was coming than hang more canvas." Tallis took my armful of twigs, smiling at Chirp and taking the one he had in his mouth. He turned to Roon. "What did you bring, eh? How have you earned your supper?"

The dog tilted his head and huffed at him. It was a look that gave the sense that Roon was saying, *I kept these two out of trouble. Surely you don't expect me to do that* and *carry wood.* It made me smile.

"It's good to see you smile," Tallis said, setting up the sticks into a cone structure.

"Don't reckon either of us have had much to smile about as of late," Will said, bringing over the small bundle that held his steel, flint, and a bundle of dried moss that he'd gathered at some point. "'Course, I suppose we should both be grinning like fools over the fact that we're still breathing."

"I reckon you're right, gunslinger." It was frankly a miracle that I still held the breath of life in my chest. "Let's hope that our luck holds."

"I would like our luck to be a little better," Tallis grumbled. "Before you lose a limb."

"I'm good at staying in one piece," I said softly, sitting tailor-fashion on the ground. I was tired from gathering wood, which was a sad commentary on things, for me to be worn out so easily.

Tallis grunted but didn't say anything. He let Will get working on the fire while he finished taking care of the horses. As the fire caught, Tallis brought me the fiddle case.

I looked up at him, my brow furrowed. "Now?"

"Yes, now."

I took the fiddle case, not bothering to hide my confusion as I figured out why Tallis was so fixed on me fiddling. I would not put on false modesty and say I wasn't any good, but now was hardly the time. Yet, Tallis did things for a reason. I just couldn't figure out what that reason might be.

Tallis sat next to me on the ground with his guitar. "What I'm going to show you—both of you—must be kept between yourselves. No one else. Not even your friends."

I examined both Tallis and Will, who appeared as lost as I was. "Alright," I finally said.

"You have my word." Will sounded serious as he tended our small fire.

"Have you ever wondered how a Rover's sentry system works?" Tallis moved his fingers easily on the guitar strings, checking the sound as he waited for our answer.

"Of course." I should follow his example and tune the fiddle, but I wanted all of my attention on this. It had been killing me for *ages*, trying to sort out how Rovers always knew you were entering their camps.

"We use music." Tallis adjusted one of the strings, his deft fingers moving over them again afterward to pluck out the notes he wanted. More notes but not more words. "A Rover trick."

"There must be more to it than *that*," I said, irritated when he didn't continue his explanation.

"You have no patience, Little Fox."

"I have pounds of patience," I said. "Have I punched you yet? No, I have not. If you knew how often I've thought about it, you would applaud my patience."

He gave a soft laugh. "Peace, Little Fox, peace. Yes, there's more to it than that. There's the song itself, but there's also the musician." He tapped his thumb against the body of the guitar. "I could teach this song to everyone at the Settlement, but it probably wouldn't do a thing for them."

"But you think it will work for Faolan?" Will asked.

Tallis nodded slowly. "Yes, I do."

"Why?" Sometimes simple questions were the best.

"Because I've heard you play," Tallis said, resettling his guitar more comfortably in his hold. "I'll play through. You listen."

Tallis started playing then, slowly the first time through. The song didn't sound like anything I'd heard before. It didn't seem to have any words. To be honest, it reminded me more of birdsong than something a human would call forth.

He sped up for the second run-through, and this time I could hear the song's . . . message? That's what it sounded like to me. A clear message. Maybe that's why it reminded me so much of birdsong. The notes were beautiful—but an unspoken warning, though I could feel the words in my very bones. *This is our nest, and you are not welcome. This is our nest and not for you.*

It was both as simple as that and more complicated.

Tallis paused after the second round. "Do you hear it?"

I nodded. "Yeah, I think I do."

"Stick to the song, okay?" He frowned at me. "This isn't the kind of thing you add flourishes to. Understand?"

I was fair certain I did. Any deviation on my part might change the message, and that wasn't what we wanted.

I readied my fiddle and closed my eyes, waiting for Tallis to start playing again. I let him run through the melody on his own for one round. The second time, I joined him, my fingers moving to strings of their own accord. I didn't think, letting my mind go quiet, letting the music flow through me.

It was short, Tallis's song, so we played through a few times. Playing the song felt different. It was difficult to explain, but it was like a little bit of me went out with the notes. Musicians always put a little of ourselves into our music, but not like this. Never like this.

Suddenly the tune was over, our little glade eerily quiet. I popped my eyes open to find Chirp sitting right next to me, staring me down. He was purring.

"He likes the music," Tallis said.

Chirp started growl-talking then, and it sounded like a complaint. I brought my fiddle back up, picking my way through the notes again, my eyes on Chirp. Tallis followed my lead this time, joining in after a few notes.

Chirp began to hum, more feeling than sound. I felt it in my chest, a vibration. It reminded me of the noise crystal makes when you strike it. It resonated. This time when we finished the song there was a *whomp*, like a giant had let out a gust of breath. The feeling nipped pleasantly along my skin.

Tallis stood, setting his guitar down on the ground. He walked into the trees, Will on his heels. I nestled my fiddle back in its case before taking a moment to scratch Chirp's head and croon at him. When I caught up to them, Tallis and Will were staring at their feet.

Tallis glanced at Will. "You can feel it?"

Will adjusted his hat. "Yup. Tingly feet." He took a large step forward. "No tingly feet."

Tallis turned to me then, dropping onto his haunches so he could look Chirp in the eye. "What did you do, hm?"

Chirp sniffed, not deigning to respond.

I frowned. "Is it bad? Whatever he did?"

Tallis turned his gaze on me, the usual laughter in his eyes missing. A solemn Tallis was a powerful thing. I crossed my arms so I didn't give in to the strange compulsion to run my fingers along the lines of his face.

The corner of his lip kicked up, like he knew full well what I was thinking. "No, I don't think it's bad. But Will's never felt our warning system before, and now he can. Our sentry shouldn't be this far out."

He gave Chirp a scratch, then stood. "Normally it only goes as far as the music travels. When Rovers set up camp, we send our musicians out to the edges to play. The song goes out, casting our magic like a net. As far as it touches, that's where our sentries are."

I gave a low whistle. No wonder it was impossible to sneak up on a Rover camp. Invisible sentries. It hit me then, how much Tallis must trust us. This was a big secret he was letting us in on, and something we could use against his entire people.

"So it's . . . good?" Will asked.

Tallis frowned. "I think so? It seems more powerful. Chirp appears quite pleased with himself." He scratched the cave cat's head. "Aren't you full of surprises?"

Chirp huffed in a very smug manner.

Will clapped his hands together once. "Alright, perimeter is handled. Camp set up. I suggest we get some grub into us and nap if we can. It's going to be a long night."

I thought for sure I wouldn't be tired, but after I drank my tea and ate a quick meal, I felt my eyelids drooping. I took off my boots, crawling into my bedroll. Chirp curled up next to me. Will slept on the other side of Chirp, his hat over his eyes, and Tallis and Roon had my back. Between that and the perimeter magic, I felt safer than I had in months. I dug a hand into Chirp's short fur, feeling his steady heartbeat. I was asleep between one breath and the next.

When I woke up, it was dusk. I'll admit that I felt better for the sleep. Warmth blanketed me on both sides, and I realized that Chirp had stretched out against me, and at some point, Tallis had rolled over so his front was along my back. One hand rested on my hip in a very familiar fashion. I could feel it like a hot coal, even through my trousers. Judging by their steady breathing, they were still asleep.

I would have happily dozed back off if Will hadn't appeared above me with a mug of my tea.

I sighed and tried to crawl out from between Chirp and Tallis, both of them grumbling in their sleep as I did. I took the mug from Will and sat down by the small fire he'd built. He had a pot nestled into the coals. I peeked under the lid, and it took a minute for me to figure out what I was seeing. It was a soup blend the Rovers liked to travel with—they would bundle up rice, dried corn, peppers, and seasonings. If you had a potato or a few vegetables to throw in, or maybe some meat, great, but if not, it was a filling meal on its own.

Will had chopped in a potato or two, it looked like, and something else. I sniffed, trying to figure it out.

"Dried fish," Will said. "Tallis packed some into the stores we had. Thought a warm meal before we went off to do something boneheaded was wise."

"As possible last meals go," I said, "it's not bad." The joke didn't even coax a hint of a smile out of Will. He was unshakably grim this evening. He waved at my mug of tea, and I drank it dutifully. I was feeling better from the rest and the food, but I still felt a little on the delicate side, as if I were dandelion fluff bracing against a stiff breeze.

Tallis was up shortly after and we ate our meal, speaking little, and of nothing of consequence. As night began to fall around us, we got ready. I checked my clothes, looking for anything light-colored or shiny that might attract attention. Tallis did the same to the saddles while Will eyed me with a frown.

"I'm worried about your face," Will said.

"Me too," I said evenly.

Will ignored me. "I know you go outside, and yet, you're pale as a ghost."

I shrugged. As a rule, redheads didn't tan well. In my case, the sun just turned me red, then I peeled, and I was back to ghostly.

"We could cover her face with soot," Tallis suggested.

I shook my head. "If I get caught in the building with a soot-covered face, there is no way I can talk my way out of that."

"I don't see any way you could talk your way out of the situation if you get caught. There's no excuse for you showing up there in the middle of the night."

"Oh, that's easy," I said. "I'm a ghost. I died on the trails, and I'm here to haunt them."

"Shall we powder you in flour, then, like they do for ghosts in plays?" Tallis said, his mouth curving. "And does that mean we'll have to be floured as well? Otherwise, what, we're just escorting your spirit about the Settlement?"

Will snorted. "I bet even as a ghost, you could use an escort."

I wanted to argue, but I had a gut-deep feeling he might be right. "I'll just keep a hat on, my chin tucked, and hope for the best."

CHAPTER TWENTY-FIVE

—✳—

WE RODE THE HORSES UNTIL WE COULD SEE THE EDGE of the forest from our saddles. The horses would remain here, tethered loosely to the branches. Tallis wanted to give them the idea to stay put, while giving them the option to hoof it if things went wrong.

There was a high possibility that things would go wrong. I had argued that I should go in by myself. A single, smaller person was easier to overlook. Will shook his head and Tallis stared at me with amusement. They were coming with me, whether I wanted them to or not.

We took our time picking our way to the edge of the clearing. It's difficult to step quietly in the forest. Dead leaves and twigs crackle and snap. Undergrowth can be thick. Since the canopy of the forest was substantial, we weren't getting much in the way of moonlight, and we didn't dare use lanterns.

There was no way we weren't going to make some sort of ruckus. The best we could do was move slowly and attempt to mimic one of the forest critters out for a nose-about. I wasn't sure how well the sound would carry all the way to the Settlement palisades, anyhow.

As soon as we were close to the edge of the forest, we stopped, waiting for the guards to pass. Minutes ticked by and there were no lanterns. No movement. Just darkness and stars.

"Maybe they finally listened to me," Will whispered. "Those lanterns made them targets. Anyone with good aim or an ounce of luck could take them out."

It was as good an explanation as any. It made sense. Perhaps they'd listened to Will. But I couldn't shake the uneasy feeling that had come over me. From the expressions on Tallis's and Will's faces, I didn't think they were buying it, either.

But we still needed to go in.

Tallis sat back on his haunches, putting a hand on Roon. "Stay here. Guard the horses."

Roon dutifully trotted off, stopping when he got close to Neev. He settled in by her feet, ears up, eyes watchful.

I put a hand on my cave cat. "I need you to hide, Chirp." There was no way he wouldn't follow us—we'd accepted that—but things would go smoother if he pulled that disappearing trick he did so well.

Chirp tipped his head, staring at me.

I waved a hand over myself. "Hide." Nothing. I put my hands on my shirt. "Camouflage."

Chirp stood on his back feet, put his paws on my shirt, and licked my face. His tongue was as scratchy as any other cat's and it hurt. I also got the feeling he thought I was being funny. I didn't know why he'd done it so easily before and now didn't seem to know what we wanted.

When covering my eyes didn't work, I tried thinking at him. I imagined him in front of me, then imagined him vanishing. He made a sad sound, and I realized he thought I was telling him to go away. So I pictured him popping in and out, here, then not.

Finally he got it, disappearing in front of me. My shoulders drooped in relief. "Yes, good fella. *Hide.*"

I felt him brush up against me, but I couldn't see him. I dug my fingers down until I could feel his fur.

"That's the strangest thing I've ever seen," Will said.

"Strange is good," Tallis said. "Especially when it keeps you alive. Let's go."

There were still no lights up along the walkway, and we hadn't seen any shifting shadows, so we decided to duck low and run as fast as we could. It wasn't silent by any means, but it wasn't loud, either.

We made it to the hidden door, Will insisting on going first. He opened it slowly, and the hinges made very little sound. He held a hand out to us as he peeked through. We stood still, listening.

I heard . . . nothing. No restless farm animals. No one walking around after dark.

That uneasy feeling deepened. Chirp leaned against me, still hidden, but I had the sense that he was leaning into me for comfort. That his expression was as uneasy as ours.

Will waved us in, and we followed him on ghost feet, closing the door quietly behind us.

We had decided to go to the boys' bunkhouse first. It was more familiar territory, and we wouldn't have to worry about

Miss Moon catching us. I just had to hold on to the hope that my friends were sleeping soundly and safely in their beds.

We kept our steps light, but in the watery light of the poorest excuse for a moon, it was difficult to see, and I stepped on something that made a large *crack*. It echoed in the courtyard, the sound bouncing off the walls.

I felt Tallis's hand on my shin, and I realized he'd squatted down. He pulled gently, trying to get me to lift my boot. I complied, watching as he picked something up off the ground. The twig I'd stepped on.

Only as he brought it close to my face, it didn't look like a twig.

"Is that . . . ?" I whispered.

"A bone," he said, his voice low and soft. "Chicken, I think."

It was an odd place for it, that bone. What we didn't give to the pigs or other livestock, we buried outside with the compost. For our crops, yes, but also to keep vermin from coming into the Settlement.

Still, it was just one bone. Lots of ways to drop just one bone in a strange place. The youngins were always sticking food into their pockets. Made wash day a real hoot.

Tallis dropped the bone and we continued on, keeping close to the buildings.

It was so quiet. The night wasn't usually. Lots of critters came out at night, making all kinds of noises. Owls hooted and screeched. Raccoons . . . well, they could make quite the ruckus when they were fighting over a morsel or getting amorous.

The bunkhouse had always been full of Will's snoring and youngins talking in their sleep. The quiet was getting to me, making me jumpy. I chose to stop paying attention to it, to make my jabbering mind hush up. I focused on Will's back, the warm brush of Chirp's fur at my side, and the sound of Tallis's soft breathing behind me.

We finally made it to the boys' bunkhouse, the trickle of moonlight making shadows where there normally weren't any, giving the building a mean and hungry look.

Will paused. "The door looks open."

Everyone, even the smallest youngin, knew better than to leave the door open, especially at night. I suddenly grew very worried about what we were going to find.

We approached the bunkhouse door same as we had to get into the Settlement—Will taking point, with Tallis and me dropping back to keep an eye out. Will tried peeking through the opening gap in the door. I couldn't see much from where I was standing. The fire must be well and truly banked, because I couldn't see any rosy glow.

Will pushed the door open wider and stepped in. I moved to follow as Chirp made a low, distressed sound. I put a hand on him, offering solace, though I didn't know for what as we followed after Will.

The smell hit me first. Iron, offal, and something slightly sweet, but not like candy sweet. Like fruit gone bad. Rotten. I put my arm over my mouth to block it, dread and grief hitting me as my mind conjured up poor Gertie, her eyes fixed. I shoved the feelings aside for now. I needed to be ready for whatever we were going to find.

We passed the cubbies. Last time I'd walked through this entryway, just before I'd gone out on that ill-fated hike with Stuckley, the cubbies had been neat as pin. Miss Moon would countenance nothing less. Clothes folded. Dirty boots scraped at the door and left lined up right inside. Orderly.

The cubbies didn't look like that now. Clothing was everywhere. A boot here and there, knocked every which way on the floor. Not enough boots. Not nearly enough.

I wanted to turn tail right then and scoot my carcass back out into the eerie night. Only Pops's voice in my head kept me moving. *A Kelly doesn't run, and we surely step into the jaws of death with our chins high and our backs straight.*

If I had been alone, I'm not sure Pops's words, strong as they were, would have helped.

As I wasn't alone, I stepped forward as Pops would have wanted. Chin up. Step sure. Ready to meet whatever the bunkhouse hid in its inky depths.

Will stepped in first and froze. I moved around him so I could see.

Before Pops got sick, we'd hitch up the mule and cart and head on over to Wallhalla Springs, which was the next town over, for their spring fair. It was a good time to trade seeds and gossip, pick up new tools, cloth, and livestock. It was always fun, and if we had a little extra, Pops would get me something special. When I was eight, he got me my own little carving knife so I could whittle by the fire with him. It hooked on to my belt, and I felt very fine with it on. A grown-up, like Pops.

That same year, one of the farmers got full as a goat on

blackberry moonshine. I'm not sure what set him off—I only saw the outcome. I'd never seen a grown man pitch a fit before, not like that, and he was a big fella, too. He was tossing jars from the jam seller, and pots from the potter, and when he wasn't tossing, he was throwing fists. Took five people to put him on the ground before the potter could hog-tie him with some of his twine.

In that moment, I'd been impressed by the devastation one man could wreak so quickly. Jam was splattered everywhere, the seller crying as she picked up her broken jars. The potter spitting on the ground in front of the farmer and cussing a blue streak.

The bunkhouse looked like a whole passel of drunken farmers had been turned loose inside it. Bunks were splintered, bedding strewn about. Blankets shredded. Deep gouges in the walls.

And over a lot of it, splattered on torn shirts and broken furniture, was blood.

Blood and . . . other bodily things.

Chirp made a distressed noise. I looked down at my feet and caught a flash of something, I wasn't sure what, but before I could stop myself, I leaned down and pulled it from the wreckage.

It was a finger.

Just . . . a finger. I dropped it, wiping my hand desperately on my trousers, trying to get the feeling of that cold, bony finger off of my skin.

I swallowed hard and wished I hadn't. My stomach rolled, and I found a corner to be sick in.

Tallis must have followed, because I felt his hand on my back, comforting me the same way I'd done for Chirp only moments before.

"At least it wasn't a small finger," Tallis said.

I must have been in shock, because it took me several moments to understand what he meant.

That didn't mean the youngins were safe, but whatever had happened to them, we didn't know for sure that it was bad. Though there's whole mountains and valleys of land between good and bad.

I didn't think I could feel worse, but then cold slithered through my belly.

Jesse's bunk. I needed to check Jesse's bunk.

I ran over to where we'd slept, examining it to see if there were any clues. It looked just like the others, shredded and splintered. No blood, though. Not here.

My bunk was worse than Jesse's. Over the destruction was the sharp ammonia scent of urine. Will dug under his mattress, pulling out Tallis's jacket and handing it to him. Somehow it had avoided destruction.

"Thank you," he said, shrugging into it.

I nodded, eyes scanning the room. "Someone died here, didn't they?"

Tallis ran a hand over his face. "Yes, probably. If they didn't die here, they started dying here and crawled somewhere nearby."

"No one in here now," Will said, his voice pitched low. "We should move along."

I didn't need to be told twice. I turned on my heel and

headed for the door. Only Tallis's hand on my back kept me from barreling out into the courtyard.

"Slowly, Little Fox."

He was right. I couldn't thunder out of here, no matter how much I wanted to. We had no idea whether or not the person who had done this was still at the Settlement or where they might currently be.

I was afraid to go see what the girls' bunkhouse was like.

We all were.

CHAPTER TWENTY-SIX

—✳—

I CAN'T SAY WE MOVED ANY QUIETER OR FASTER TO THE girls' bunkhouse because we'd already been moving with the stealth of house mice, but we plowed onward with more purpose now, our imaginations conjuring the most terrible of evil spirits.

Chirp stayed close to my side, bumping against me as we continued on. Tallis reached out and took my hand. I clasped it back, like it was an anchor. As if I'd been doing it my whole life.

The door to the girls' bunkhouse was in ruins.

"No beast did this." Will was eyeing it critically. "There are claw marks. But no cat, even your cave cat there, could manage this destruction." He pointed to some of the deeper grooves. "Someone took an ax to this door."

My heart was lodged in my gullet as we stepped over the threshold. Tallis and I bypassed Miss Moon's closed door and moved swiftly into the main room, while Will splintered off, whispering her name, his movements frantic.

The room was nothing like the boys' bunkhouse. It was

like whatever was driving the attackers, whatever rage had guided their hands, had been expended at the door.

No blood.

The only thing torn up was a little rag doll.

For reasons I couldn't explain, the girls' bunkhouse was more chilling than the boys'. Perhaps because we'd expected blood and in contrast we found this empty room, and that dropped dismembered doll felt eerie. Prophetic.

And it made me wonder. "Which room was first, you think?"

Tallis turned troubled eyes on me. "I don't know."

Will rejoined us, toeing the doll's remnants with his boot. "Could be this room was first, and when they found it empty, they turned the fury on the boys' bunkhouse." He turned solemn eyes on me. "Esther isn't here."

"Or it could be that, by the time it made it through the door, the creature discovered it was already full and took them elsewhere." Tallis reached out, touching one of the crisply made beds.

Will propped his hands on his hips, his chin on his chest. "I don't want to think that."

I was still staring at that crisp bed. "I want to see Miss Moon's room."

"She's not there," Will said, a catch in his voice.

Miss Moon's delicate, feminine room broke my heart. It had been desecrated. The small luxuries, the tiny fripperies that she'd allowed herself, which had helped me really see that big-hearted part of her, were gone. Her vase broken, the flower petals scattered across the floor. Her stitchwork in tatters.

Her quilt torn and, like Jesse's bunk, befouled, the stench muted by the scent of Miss Moon's lavender water that had been dumped onto the floorboards.

She'd allowed herself so few soft things, and now they were gone.

But there was no blood, and for that I was grateful.

We avoided the barn—if the animals were still alive, we didn't want them to make noise and draw attention. If they weren't alive, we couldn't help them, and I didn't want to face a repeat of the goat pen. I didn't want to see those silly chickens reduced to feathers and bones, despite my love of one in the stewpot. That was for survival. A body needed to eat. What we'd seen so far was carnage, and that was something entirely different.

So we passed the barn, heading for the back door of the kitchen. It was on our way there that we finally discovered what had happened to the guards that had been on the palisades tonight. Davens and Harris were several yards apart, sprawled on the ground in inelegant heaps. They reminded me of eggs I'd once dropped onto the floor of our old kitchen, causing Pops to toss sharp words at me about taking more care with delicate things.

I'd never considered Davens or Harris delicate. Quite the opposite. Seeing them like this, you saw how easily breakable even large men could be.

Will nudged Davens onto his back with his boot. His throat had been torn out, his chest mauled. His once-white shirt was black in the moonlight from blood. I hadn't particularly liked Davens, and I'd actively disliked Harris, but I felt no satisfaction in their violent deaths.

We left them there for now, as there was nothing to be done.

Will let us into the kitchen. Though there was no damage, someone had been through here. I could see part of a bloody handprint on the cook's table, like someone had paused there to steady themselves.

"Miss Lita's going to have someone's hide when she sees what they did to her table," Will said, staring at the bloody handprint.

Without a word, we moved on to the dining room, where we realized that Miss Lita wasn't going to have anyone's hide ever again. There was an ax in her back, her eyes wide and staring in death, her mouth open.

Tallis stepped forward and closed her eyes, murmuring soft words only she could hear. He stood then, taking a moment to free the ax from where it was buried in her back. I winced at the sounds it made, and I had to look away until he was done. I agreed he should take it—not only might it do us good, but I didn't want to leave a weapon behind us where anyone could grab it.

I made a silent promise to Miss Lita that we would come back and do right by her—if we were still upright and breathing when the night was done.

Right now I didn't have a whole lot of faith in that.

Tallis handed me the ax. I blinked at him. "Don't you want it?"

He shook his head. "I have a good knife, Little Fox. Don't worry about me. I'm more concerned about your own teeth and claws. A fox cannot live by their wits alone."

"The wits help, though."

His smile was the barest flick of the lips. "So will the ax."

I couldn't argue with him there.

We moved on, searching the main building, finding a body here or there, gutted like fish and left to meet their maker like an animal. Dying where they fell, with no gesture of comfort. No covered eyes, no dropped flowers—nothing to ease their way from this world to the next. It made my fingers itch for Tallis's fiddle.

There were no bodies in HisBen's room, but there were other surprises there. I'd never been into his inner sanctum, as he called it. Just his sitting room, before he put me in the Penitent Box.

What the sitting room had whispered, his bedroom shouted. Moonlight crept in through a large window framed by velvet draperies. Thick carpet on the floor. Soft sheets and embroidered bed hangings. An intricately carved hope chest sat at the end of the bed, the kind people pass on for generations. A crystal decanter squatted next to a lantern on the bedside table, and when I sniffed, the caramel scent of whiskey hit my nose.

I was more interested in the brass lantern. It wasn't as finely made as everything else in the room, though it was of sturdy construction. It was the *kind* of lantern it was that caught my attention.

"What is it?" Tallis whispered.

"It's a blackout lantern," I said, showing him the little brass peg attached to the door that you could use to adjust the amount of light that it threw off. It was the sort a thief used, not a holy man, though Pops would say they were one and the same.

I sniffed the lantern and grimaced as the pungent odor of camphor hit my nose. "Burning fluid."

"You be careful of that," Will said from the other side of the room. "That's dangerous stuff."

He wasn't wrong. Burning fluid, otherwise known as camphene, was a cheap fuel often used for lamps. The mixture of turpentine, alcohol, and camphor was extremely volatile. Camphene lamps could explode. We had enough problems right now. We did not need a fire, on top of everything else.

I surveyed the room. There was no visible violence here. The room was untouched, as if Dillard had wandered out for a moment and could be back at any time.

It was Will who opened the hope chest, and his eyes went wide. Chirp reappeared, distracted out of his hiding trick by his curiosity over what was inside. His nostrils flared as he scented the air. He made a despondent noise.

Tallis and I leaned over the chest, trying not to block what light there was streaming in through the window.

Pops had liked to tell stories. I loved the yarns about animals the best—cunning foxes tricking farmers, brave mice going on adventures, and clever cats pretending to be wealthy merchants. One of his favorites was about a long-ago creature, one that had died out before he was born, called a dragon. A big thing it was, with wings, and scales, and fire it could shoot out its nose to best warriors that came after its hoard. Any dragon worth its salt had a hoard, whether it be books and other fine things or coins or jewels.

Turns out Dillard was a dragon, though a human one, and the hope chest contained his hoard. Will started bringing things up into the light so we could see better. A pearl necklace. Diamond cuff links. An emerald dragonfly brooch. A set of fine pistols in a leather holster. Gold timepieces. A ruby hatpin. Silver sugar tongs. Delicate snuffboxes. Unfathomable wealth.

Will set the pistols aside with the satisfied expression of a body reunited with old friends. When he dug out a silver locket, the name *Mary Ellen* etched in delicate letters, his eyes welled up. I reached out and grasped his shoulder. He swallowed hard and nodded. With her locket in HisBen's hope chest and herself missing, we'd have to count her among the dead and mourn later.

"At least you know." I squeezed his shoulder, trying to comfort in a situation that gave none.

One object in particular caught my eye, and I gasped before I plunged my hand into the hope chest. When I pulled my hand up into the light, I braced myself for disappointment. I opened my fingers, revealing Pops's watch. I clutched it, my teeth clenched against the sob that wanted to break free. Out of all the things to cry over tonight, a recovered watch was such a tiny thing, but a few tears escaped, and I quickly wiped them away with my wrist.

When I clicked open the hidden compartment, the land deed was still there. The relief was almost heady.

Tallis pulled out the next object I recognized—the finely carved ivory pipe I'd last seen clenched between Cartwright's teeth.

Will shook his head. "What has Dillard been up to all these years?"

"No good," Tallis said immediately. "You don't get something like this by doing good things." He poked at the treasure indifferently, as if it held no meaning for him.

"We're still missing a lot of people," I said. There had been no sign of Miss Moon, Miss Honeywell, HisBen, or the children. We only had a few places left to check—the food cellar, the barn, and the chapel.

We decided on the cellar next.

But we waited a moment for Will to put his pistols on first. Tallis grabbed the blackout lantern. I held the ax to one side, with Chirp flanking my other. I might be hoping for the best, but I will forever be the kind of soul who prepares for the worst.

There was no way we were going to be able to head into the cellar without bringing our own light, so it was a very good thing Tallis had the blackout lantern.

Will dug out one of his precious matches, using it to light the lamp with care. "Don't go swinging this about, you understand? I'd like to live to see the dawn, thank you very kindly."

Tallis's look was so solemn that I somehow knew he was teasing Will, if only a little.

Since Tallis had the lamp, he got to go first.

"Stay to the side, if you're able," Will said. "I need a clear line of sight."

We didn't have Miss Moon's keys, which I thought might be a problem, but it turned out it didn't matter. The cellar door was closed but not locked. I ordered Chirp to hide and once again we stepped into the unknown.

The cellar looked exactly as it had the last time I'd stepped foot in here. The only difference was Cartwright's body wasn't laid out for burial. We made it quietly down the steps, though the space appeared to be empty. I heard the pad of Chirp's paws on the wooden planking as he went to examine the barrels I'd hidden behind last time.

I didn't think he'd go looking if there wasn't something drawing his notice. I caught Will's attention, motioning at him to be ready. He put his hands on the butts of his pistols.

I adjusted the ax in my hands, just in case, and stepped closer to the barrels. I leaned over the top and looked, my heart rabbiting in my chest.

Someone screamed.

I screamed.

She screamed again.

Which made me scream again.

Which caused Chirp to growl and another someone to yelp.

Then Chirp stopped hiding and both of them screamed.

It was a mess.

That was about when my brain boarded the train, and I realized that I was screaming at Dai Lo. Sitting behind her, his glasses askew, sat Jesse. Both of them looked like their eyes were going to fall right out of their skulls.

"Chirp, hush."

The cave cat growl-talked back at me argumentatively.

"They're friends." I lowered the ax. Chirp settled, but the ruff of fur around his neck was still puffed out.

I huffed the last of the fear out of me. "Aw, for goodness' sake, Dai Lo, you about scared me to death."

"Faolan!" she wheezed, her hand over her heart. "What is that? *What is that?*"

Jesse stared at Chirp, his hands absently patting his pockets like he was trying to find his pencil and his notebook. The need to sketch Chirp must have been overwhelming for him.

At that moment relief hit my chest so hard I almost had to sit down. They were alive. They were okay. "I have never in my life been so happy to see two people."

Tallis snorted. "I nursed you back to health."

"Your healer did that."

"I helped," he said patiently.

"I pulled you out of a cave," Will said, crossing his arms. "And carried you, actually *carried you*, all the way to safety."

He did have a point, at least partially. "And I am very grateful," I said diplomatically. "But seeing as I didn't think either of you might have been mauled to death, my statement stands."

Dai Lo gave an irritated growl of her own. "Faolan! I asked you a very important question! I don't think it was too much to ask!" She put her hand out, palm up, at Chirp. "What. Is. That?!" She followed it with "And who is that?"

I smiled. "This is Chirp, and that's Tallis." My smile fell as I realized I had no idea how to explain Chirp. I turned helplessly to Tallis.

He sighed. "Faolan screwed up a ritual Stuckley was trying to do and accidentally reached into a different world and pulled out Chirp. We don't know what he is. We've been calling him a cave cat." He scratched Chirp between the shoulder blades. "He has the best tricks."

I nodded. "He does. Chirp, *hide*."

Chirp blinked out of existence. Jesse fell back, hands frantically searching for his notebook. Dai Lo leaned forward and squinted. "Is he gone?"

"No," I said, reaching out and scratching his head. "You can touch him if you want. He's still here."

Dai Lo held her hand out, and Jesse hissed, "Dai! Don't do that! What if he bites your hand off?"

She looked calmly up at me. "Is he going to bite my hand off?"

"No." I gave him a friendly pat. "He could, I think, but you'd have to give him a good reason."

She slowly and gently patted his fur. Chirp reappeared, startling her a little, though she kept her hand in place. She ran her fingers over him reverently. "He's beautiful."

Chirp preened.

She hesitated, her fingers nestled in his fur. "Is this what we heard? The last time we were all in here?"

"My money's on that," I said. "But I don't think that one's like Chirp."

"From the claw marks," Will said, "I'd say the one you heard was bigger, for starters."

"I've also never seen Chirp try to eat anyone," Tallis said dryly.

Dai Lo straightened suddenly, lurching around Chirp to wrap her arms around me and squeeze tight. "We thought you were dead."

"Owwwwww," I whined.

"She's not dead," Tallis explained, his wide grin pulled lopsided by the scar on his cheek. "But she wasn't far off. Be gentle."

Dai Lo dropped her arms so fast you'd think I'd burned her. "Oh no, are you injured? What hurts?" She didn't wait for my response but examined me to assess for herself.

"Hey, Faolan," Jesse said, giving up on his notebook. "We're overjoyed to see you, as you can tell."

He reached out with one hand and squeezed my shoulder tight. "We thought—well, we weren't sure what to think. You and Stuckley didn't come back. We were worried, of course we were worried, but at first, we just figured you'd gotten lost."

Dai Lo shook her head as she ran sure hands over my ribs. "Don't know what HisBen was thinking, sending him out with you."

"He was thinking I should go die in a nice cave," I said, wincing when Dai Lo found a delicate spot. "I'm okay, Dai Lo, honest I am."

She scowled at me.

I sighed. "I *will* be okay. Ask Will. Ask Tallis. I've been seen by a competent healer."

She turned her attention to Will, who nodded, then moved on to Tallis. Her sharp eyes examined him quickly. "Who?"

"Anna, one of my people. She's the best healer I've ever met, on my word."

Dai Lo's expression stayed flinty. "And I should take your word because . . ."

Before Tallis could respond, knowledge seemed to reorganize in Dai Lo's head and her expression cleared. "You're the one who helped Jesse when he injured his ankle." She looked at me. "And the one who . . ."

I could feel my ears go hot. "Brought me back, yes, with the feet. I mean, with my feet. We know he has his feet."

Tallis tipped his head to the side to see me better, his expression amused.

"I have an ax," I said, brandishing it at him. "So don't tempt me." I dropped my arm to my side, letting the head of the ax touch the floor, the weight of the evening coming back to me. So many bodies.

"What happened?" I asked.

Dai Lo's brow furrowed, and she tipped her face up to Jesse, who looked equally troubled.

"We're not sure," he said.

Dai Lo took his hand. "We came down here to talk."

"You were still missing," Jesse said. "And things around here . . ." He rubbed a hand over the back of his head. "I couldn't explain it. Tense. Weird. It didn't feel right, you know?"

"Always trust your gut," Will said. "What did it feel like, then?"

"There's a certain kind of tension," Dai Lo said slowly, as if she was searching for the right combination of words. "A certain feeling when you're worried about someone. When you're waiting for them to come home. It didn't feel like that. It felt like an incoming storm, when you smell ozone and the air feels crackly."

"You know how it is, though," Jesse said. "Eyes on you all the time. We had to try and find a place to talk it over."

I sometimes wondered if Jesse knew how much he revealed of himself when he looked at Dai Lo like that. I'd heard the phrase *heart in his eyes* before and thought it grand and all—who doesn't want someone to gaze at you with their whole heart? Grand, if you're on the receiving end, but on the giving end, you leave yourself open. Vulnerable.

Soft.

I hadn't been able to be soft in a long time. Jesse may not know how much he revealed, but Dai Lo did, and she mirrored it back to him, like they were two lightning bugs flashing their admiration.

She turned to me. "We were trying to decide what to do. You were gone. HisBen said they were looking for you, but . . ." She scrunched up her nose. "We didn't believe it."

"With how things were going," Jesse said, his voice full of the fear and apprehension they must have been feeling, "we were wondering if we should try to look for you ourselves and hightail it out of here."

"The air felt dangerous," Dai Lo said with a nod. "Tonight, we were meeting up to try and decide what we were going to do, what our options were."

"We weren't down here long when we heard . . ." Jesse swallowed hard. "Screaming."

"Crashing, like someone was fighting in the kitchen," Dai Lo said.

"Yelling," Jesse said, "and then—"

"It went so quiet," Dai Lo finished. "We were scared to leave here and see what had happened, so we waited. When we heard your footsteps, we hid and blew out our candle."

"From what we've seen," Will said, his face grim, "that likely saved your lives." He gave them a quick sketch of what we'd witnessed since we got back to the Settlement. Even glossing over the details, it was a devastating picture.

And it would only get worse.

Everyone was silent when Will stopped talking, our grief thick, our fear a weight. We couldn't linger in it. Later, if we lived, we could mourn as we saw fit. For now, we could only go on.

As usual, Tallis's thoughts seemed to dovetail with mine. "The real question is, what do we do now?"

CHAPTER TWENTY-SEVEN

---*---

NO ONE SERIOUSLY CONSIDERED LEAVING. AS MUCH AS
I wanted to send my friends off, as their lives were precious
to me, I knew better than to say it. One look at Dai Lo's defiant chin and the solid support in Jesse's eyes, and the words
died on my lips.

My suggesting they leave would only make them argue. I
had to accept, if only silently, that my life was as precious to
them as theirs to me. Same as Will's. Same as Tallis's.

And we couldn't abandon the youngins or Miss Moon, not
if they needed us.

I didn't at any time consider that Dillard needed saving. If
I'd had any doubt of his complicity in the manner, that hope
chest would have writ it large and the blackout lantern in
Tallis's fist would have underlined it. Miss Honeywell . . . I
wasn't sure about Miss Honeywell, but I wasn't as worried
about her as I was Miss Moon.

Which meant the only real decision was where to go next—
the barn or the chapel.

We chose the barn. Not because we thought HisBen was

there, but because we figured that was the last place he would be. But I was hoping we might find some survivors there.

Maybe we were walking into a slaughter, or we'd upset the animals, but we couldn't avoid it forever, and if HisBen hadn't heard me and Dai Lo screaming, then I didn't think he'd hear the farm animals. I also thought, if the critters were still alive, we should take the chance to set them free. There was a good possibility we weren't coming out of that chapel. The only person in our group that I knew for certain could do any actual fighting was Will. The rest of us had more guts and gumption than skill.

We would face our doom together anyway.

But we'd do our best to take care of the innocents before we did.

The barn had two doors—one that faced the chapel and one that faced the front gate. We picked the door that faced the gate. As we snuck up, I gave Jesse my ax. I'm not sure why I did. It left me without a weapon besides Chirp and my fists, and it made Tallis frown, though he held his tongue. He knew that I needed my friends to have their own weapon.

I also had the feeling that the weapons that would serve me best were Chirp, my friends, and my wits. None of them had let me down yet. I had to hope they wouldn't let me down now.

We paused outside the barn so I could tell Chirp to hide again. As soon as I did, Tallis stepped up to open the door. It creaked as he opened it. There was nothing we could do about that. Will went in first, with Jesse and Tallis bringing up the rear. Dai Lo needed to be behind Will. If we ran into anyone who needed help, she was the best option, as she knew her way around a wound.

I stepped into the barn, the heady scent of hay, earth, and animal hitting my nose. I didn't smell any blood, and something in my stomach unclenched. Animals didn't greet us. I suspected that, though they couldn't see Chirp, they could still sense a predator and were keeping to themselves.

We spread out, checking the stalls, and it wasn't long before Tallis gave a soft whistle.

I made it over first and almost sobbed in relief. There was Miss Moon, her hair in a messy night braid, her face dirty and smeared in blood, shoeless and in her nightdress.

All around her, shaking and crying silently, were the youngins.

She let out an uneven breath. "Mr. Kelly?"

"I told you," I said absently, counting all the little faces in my mind, "it's only Mr. Kelly when I cause trouble. Otherwise, I prefer Faolan." *Matilda. Ernest. Cora.* I matched up names to faces as I counted. *They're all here.* Every single one. They were scared, yes. They were terrified, and rightfully so. Banged up some. One little boy was cradling his arm like it was broken. The boys seemed the worse for wear out of the two—some of them would be scarred for the rest of their lives.

But they were alive. They would need care, soon. But they were *alive*.

We all piled into the stalls, Jesse patting backs and murmuring gentle words, Dai Lo checking wounds and giving her own brand of solace. Tallis, despite being a stranger and a

Rover to boot, moved among them with a quiet ease, settling the little ones like they were fractious animals. Before long he had one little girl on his hip as he smoothed a young boy's hair.

Will ambled into the stall last, his eyes on Miss Moon. He hunkered down, one knee on the floor, and, without a word, opened his arms.

Miss Moon sobbed once, a startling sound, and hurled herself into his embrace. She'd been holding herself together through it all, for the children, and now that he was here, she could let go. Words tumbled from her, though I couldn't make much sense of them. Something about the children, about one of the children.

It hurt something in me to see her broken like that, reduced to racking sobs, not because she was weak or because I thought less of her, but because, like me, Miss Moon had had such few soft things in her life. Tonight had taken most of them away. All that was left was the children, who were arguably the most important, but also still in danger.

People should get to be soft sometimes. A body should have someone else's arms to hold them, to catch them every time they needed to fall apart.

Will rested a hand on her hair and let her weep. The kids started to hiccup and sob, but if we let them start wailing, we'd never get out of here.

Will shushed them sweetly. "Now, now, none of that. We're going to go on an adventure, you hear? You need to be brave, just a little longer. You think you can do that?"

He was met with a chorus of sniffles and nods. They would listen to Will. He'd earned their trust. "Good. I knew I could count on you—all of you. Now we just need to get your leader here ready. You ready, Esther?"

Miss Moon collected herself, sniffling and wiping her eyes. She took a shuddering breath and let it out, squaring her shoulders. "Yes," she said, her voice cracking. She sucked in another breath, returning to herself more fully. *"Yes."*

Will offered her the smallest of smiles, brushing a thumb over her cheek. "I knew you would be. Do you know where the hidden door is?"

She shook her head.

Will explained it to her, going over it and the mechanism carefully.

"What about—" she started.

He shook his head. "The only thing you need to worry about is the youngins. Get them out. We'll handle the rest."

I grinned at her. "You know me, Miss Moon. I can cause a whole mess of trouble."

Her expression turned serious. "I can have faith in that. That's something I can take to the bank, every time."

"Once you're out," Tallis said softly, "we have our horses picketed at the edge of the woods, not far from our camp. When you get there, take one of the older children—the steadiest one you've got. Put them on the big bay—her name is Neev. You tell that child to carry a message to the Rovers. Let them know that we need help. The children are going to need a healer."

345

"We don't know where the Rover camp is," Miss Moon said.

Tallis shook his head. "Neev knows. Just tell her to go home and pat her rump. Not hard, mind. A light tap."

Miss Moon nodded in understanding.

"Good," Tallis said. "Neev will get them there. All you'll need to do is take the little ones to our campsite. Get the fire going. My people will find you from there."

"Okay," Miss Moon said. "Okay."

She stood then, Will following suit, before shaking out her nightdress. She was once again the Miss Moon I knew.

She surprised me by reaching out and tracing the bruises on my face with light fingers. "Why do I feel like I failed you, Faolan?"

I lifted my chin. "No, ma'am, you did not. You kept their bodies and souls together. I cannot tell you how much finding you has meant to me, to us. You just keep it up."

A rueful smile hit her lips, and I realized she was kind of pretty when she smiled. It lit her up. "You were my charge, too, Faolan. You were my charge, and I don't think I did enough to keep *your* body and soul together."

"You did what you could," I said adamantly. "And if you want to do more, you get these youngins out safe and sound."

She drew herself to her full height and stared me square in the eye. "We will talk more after this." She took in our group. "All of us. You will do me the courtesy of doing everything you can to make that happen."

"Yes, ma'am," I said, tipping my hat, meaning every word.

If we died tonight, it wouldn't be from lack of trying.

The fierce expression on her face withered as she took my hand. "And, Faolan, I didn't quite succeed. We're missing one of the children. That's what I was trying to tell you when you first came in."

"What?" That couldn't be. I counted again and swore. She was right. We were missing one. "Which one?"

"Obie," Miss Moon said softly. "I couldn't find Obie."

The youngins didn't want to leave the animals, but we couldn't risk it. I had to promise them that we would get the animals when we left.

If we didn't leave . . .

Well.

The youngins were paired up, olders with littles, to help make sure everyone made it okay. Tallis went over the directions to the horses again, making sure Miss Moon understood.

We watched them trail away, a silent line of terrified faces, all doing their best to be brave. While they disappeared around the building, we crept to the chapel. There was no back door to the building. There would be no sneaking in. I buried my hand in Chirp's fur, trying to soothe us both. He bumped me with his shoulder.

"Do we have a plan?" Jesse asked, the ax in his hands.

"No plan," I said. "Just stay alive."

Our group approached the chapel. The night was quiet again, hushed, like everything was holding its breath. The whitewashed chapel shone, even with the dim light of the moon, like the beacon it was meant to be. We walked past the bell, the one HisBen liked to ring to call us in, and I wondered what happened to chapel bells when chapels fell. Did they go to new churches? Did the other churching folks think the bells would bring bad luck?

I guess I'd never know.

We stood in front of the tall door, weapons in hand, our faces grim. I took a deep breath, let it out, and nodded. "When you're ready, gunslinger."

Will shoved at the doors, but they didn't open. He shoved hard, and they budged, but only a little. "Something's blocking the doors."

"Put your backs into it, I guess," I said as we all stepped up to set our weight against the doors. They creaked open slowly, the church spilling butter-yellow light onto us. With all that light, it wasn't long until we saw what was blocking the doors.

It was His Benevolence Gideon Dillard, belly down, his robes ripped, his eyes closed, and his skin pale.

We'd shoved him to the side when we opened the door, smearing blood across the floor.

His blood.

CHAPTER TWENTY-EIGHT

———✳———

DAI LO HUNCHED OVER DILLARD, CHECKING ON HIM IN the flickering candlelight. I heard Will hiss a curse, but I ignored whatever was making him ornery, as he could no doubt handle whatever it was without me. I helped Dai Lo roll Dillard over more gently than he deserved.

Blood trickled from his mouth, drawing a stark line across his waxy pale skin. He shivered, baring his bloody teeth at us in a grimace as his eyes blinked open. Dai Lo studied his wounds, her face grave.

It looked bad to me, but then, I wasn't a healer. Blood soaked the front of his robe. It was so saturated, I couldn't much tell where, exactly, he was bleeding from. So I asked what I thought might be a fairly boneheaded question. "Is it bad?"

"He's been stabbed at least three times."

It wasn't the answer I'd expected. I'd assumed he'd been mauled like the others. "Can you do anything for him?"

Dai Lo looked at the blood on the floor with a frown. "Maybe if I had Miss Moon with me and we were in the Still. Even then . . ." She pointed at the blood dripping from his mouth.

"The blade nicked his lungs, and he's lost so much blood. If he doesn't choke on it, he'll likely die of blood loss."

Dillard's eyes started to roll back in his head.

Oh, no you don't. I smacked his cheek, not as hard as I could, but enough to sting.

He swam back to consciousness, staring at me. "Mr. Kelly? Am I dead?"

"You'll meet your maker soon enough, I reckon." I gave him a little shake. "What did you do? Unburden yourself while you have the chance."

He coughed, blood speckling his cheeks. "When we first got here—" He wheezed, struggling over the words. "Went wrong. Bad crops. Sickness, taking healthy workers. No money for tools. Couldn't—couldn't fail." He coughed again, a wet, nasty sound. "Promised we wouldn't. We'd be protected by the hand . . . hand of our God." He struggled for breath. "Couldn't let my people d-down."

More like he couldn't admit he'd been wrong, but I didn't argue. "So how'd you fix it?"

He shivered again, harder this time. "Sought help. Other holy men. No one—no one could help. Said . . . called it . . . fool's errand." He sucked in another breath, coughing. "Finally found someone. Gave . . . book." His eyes closed briefly as he tried to swallow. "Said ritual would bring power. Riches. The book . . . so full of strange words. Didn't—didn't understand it all."

Anger filled me. The Settlement hadn't worked, so instead of leading his people to safety, Dillard had delved into something he didn't understand.

His eyes squeezed shut. "Did ritual. No riches. That thing— that thing came through. Learned—" Another coughing fit. More blood. He wasn't going to last much longer. "I could make it do what I wanted. They can smell—" He paused to suck in a few rattling breaths. "Riches. Gold. Gems. Seek them out. Take them. Send Davens, Harris, to trade them. Supplies. Settlement pro—" He tried again. "Prospers."

He forced the cat to find riches, stole them, and then traded them for what he needed. He made the Settlement work through stolen goods and blood.

"Why all the killing?" I asked. "They don't need to kill like that." I still hadn't seen Chirp show any interest in mauling people.

"Didn't . . . didn't want to do my bidding." The blood dripped slower now from his lips. "Had to keep—had to try new ritual. Bind it. Bind it more. Feed it. Keep it . . . keep it in my power."

It took a few seconds for me to piece together his meaning, but in the end I understood. The cat hadn't wanted to do what he demanded. It kept fighting him. Dillard didn't know what else to do, so he'd started sacrificing bigger and bigger things to bind it, and to feed it. He started listing names— Mary Ellen. Ruby. A few more that I didn't know. Amos. That's what I'd heard when I was in the Box. Amos had probably come out there to taunt me, to try to get me to make noise so I'd get more time in the Box, only to end up being dinner.

And the goats. My silly Gertie. So very many dead.

The amount of blood Dillard had spilled to get what he'd wanted. "Why them?" I spit out. "Why not the others?"

Dillard shuddered, coughing up more blood. "Got paid to . . . to get them out of the way."

I thought of Mary Ellen with that rich, no-good cousin. Will was right. He'd probably paid HisBen to whisk her away and get rid of her so he could inherit. Then Dillard had fed her to the cat—it was all so awful I felt sick.

Dillard was a weak man, too mean and rigid to admit he'd been wrong about something, and he'd dragged probably dozens of people to the afterlife for his trifling ambitions. I didn't want to look at him anymore, but I had one more question. "How do we send them back?"

He didn't answer, his breath a faint, knocking rattle.

I slapped his cheek. "Dillard! How do we send them back?"

Dillard's eyes were closed. Dai Lo shook her head. "I think that's all you're going to get."

"Figures he'd be stingy to the end." I straightened, washing my hands of the disgrace that was Gideon Dillard.

I wiped my bloody palms on my trousers and turned to see what had made Will curse a few minutes ago.

The chapel, like much of the Settlement, had gone through a major transformation since I'd been here last. Pews were overturned. The air was thick with incense, making me cough, but it was the walls, *the walls*, that really caught my eye.

Bright symbols covered every surface, their lines wavering with power, the sequence repeating over and over from ceiling to floor. I couldn't tell, but I think they'd been done in charcoal. Dozens of candles, stuck in candelabras that were set along the ground, in the pews, and even on the piano next to a fiddle case, gave off a dim glow over it all. Not even the back wall of the chapel had been spared from destruction. Symbols marched across the mural, covering the sun, as if the focus of their faith was no different from any other surface in this chapel.

Up at the front, Miss Honeywell stepped out from behind the lectern. She watched us with bright eyes, her face euphoric. Her hair was down and tangled, her grin wide and feral, and her right hand held a large knife that I recognized from the kitchens. Her left hand was wrapped in bloody cloth and was holding a hollow-eyed little boy pinned against her.

Obie. Little Obie, his face still streaked from earlier tears, stared at us blankly. Drugged. He'd been drugged.

A sudden movement as something shimmered into place, certain death coming toward us.

A huge cave cat hurtled in our direction, bigger than mine, filled out in a way that Chirp wasn't. Same slick white coat and purple rosettes, but the eyes were pumpkin orange, mouth agape. Large white teeth gleamed in the low light.

Right for me. I was going to die.

Something crashed into the cave cat, tumbling to the ground. I couldn't see what hit it, but I knew—Chirp.

HisBen's cave cat rolled to its feet, snarling. Miss Honeywell reached down and grabbed a tether. In my fear, I'd missed that the cave cat had one tied to his neck. Miss Honeywell somehow managed to secure it, keeping Obie in front of her the whole time.

Will was watching her, hands hovering over his pistols.

He wouldn't be able to shoot her, not with Obie in front of her like that.

I'd seen a face like hers before. Stuckley. She reminded me of Ignatius Stuckley, right before he tried to stick a knife in me.

"Mr. Kelly," she said, her voice an eerie singsong, "and the gunslinger." She giggled. "I told Gideon you weren't dead, but did he listen to me?"

She sneered now, staring at Dillard's body. "No. He *never* listened to me!" She spit on the ground. "If only he'd listened!" Her eyes were fire now, lit from within by fury and fanaticism. Her hand tightened on the knife. "*I* had potential. *I* was ready. What better vessel for the benevolence than me, but he chose *Stuckley*?!"

"Well, at least we won't have trouble getting her to talk," Will muttered, his gaze never leaving her.

She was snarling now, swinging the knife around. My heart rate picked up every time she swung it close to Obie. "How was Stuckley better than me? How was he more benevolent because he was a man? I was *made* for this." She swayed where she stood, her face serene again. "Who is more benevolent than I?"

Out of the corner of my eye, I saw Dai Lo pressing what was left of HisBen's robes to his side, trying to stop the bleeding. He must not be dead yet. From the amount of blood, I didn't think it would be long. Jesse hovered behind her, ax in hand, while Tallis stood behind me. I wasn't sure where Chirp had gone.

I kept my gaze fixed on Miss Honeywell, as if staring at her would keep her from doing anything rash. At the same time, I was trying to get a sense of the other cave cat. It had a beat-down look to it. Sick, maybe.

Right now, Miss Honeywell was the threat that most needed my attention. We needed to get Obie away from her. I held my hands out, trying to look nonthreatening. "You're right, Miss Honeywell."

Her attention whipped to me, but it was like she was struggling to focus. She kept blinking. "How's that?"

"I was there," I said, tipping my head toward one of the walls. "When Stuckley tried to do this. He wasn't a good vessel. He wasn't ready for the gift your god had for him."

"I know. You know." She hissed at Dillard. "Why didn't *he* know?"

"He wasn't a good vessel, either," I said. "He was flawed."

"Yes," she said. "*Yes!* Looks like your smart mouth is good for something after all." She licked her lips. "He kept losing control."

I nodded solemnly. "That's why I want to help you, Miss Honeywell."

She looked suspicious now, her grip on Obie tightening. I heard Jesse suck in a breath. Will and Tallis were both breathing steady next to me, not moving. Just ready to jump in when I needed them.

"How can you help me?" Her eyes narrowed. "Why would you help me?"

"Because you're right, Miss Honeywell. Everything you

said about Stuckley. About Dillard. Overlooking you. It wasn't right."

"It wasn't," she said, but she wasn't entirely with me yet, still suspicious. "I had to sneak looks at Dillard's book. Make my own copies."

"As to how"—I looked side to side, licking my lips, like I was anxious to reveal a big secret—"well, I've done this." I waved a hand at the symbols, the cave cat beside her. "With Stuckley. Only he failed." I leaned forward and dropped my voice so she'd have to lean in a little to hear me. I wanted her to feel like we were in this together, on the same team. "That creature, the one you have up there?"

She glanced at it.

"I have my own."

She blinked at me before throwing back her head with a laugh. Gone was the girlish giggle. This was a full-throated belly laugh. "You? Please." She shook her head. "I'm no fool, Mr. Kelly."

I kept my face stubborn. "Chirp?" I tried to send him a picture in my mind, an image of him but fading in this time, not just popping out of nowhere. I didn't want him to startle Miss Honeywell. Not with that blade in her hand. Even though I didn't have a command to get him to reappear, he seemed to understand. He faded in slowly, starting at his nose, the colors flowing back like water until he was at my side.

Miss Honeywell gasped. She stared at Chirp, her eyes wide. "How?" she spluttered.

"Stuckley failed," I said simply. "*I* didn't."

She swayed some more, her arm almost absently around Obie. "Failed?"

"Failed," I said firmly. "There's a trick to it. See, they think they got the ritual right, but they don't."

Her head whipped back like I'd hit her.

Before she could pull together an argument, I plowed ahead. I waved a hand at the other cave cat. "Look at 'em. There's something not right with that one. Not all there. Sick. Not like Chirp here." I tried to send more thoughts along to Chirp to get him to show off a little, but he kept his attention glued on Miss Honeywell. She was our prey. *That* he understood.

She seemed almost convinced but needed another push in the right direction. I frantically tried to think of a reason, but my mind was suddenly blank.

"You're far from a perfect vessel," Miss Honeywell mumbled. "Those eyes. Your hair."

"Like I said, there's a trick." For the life of me, I couldn't think of what that might be.

"You need a better offering," Tallis said, his body posture loose and easy. Like they were two old biddies chatting over tea. "That boy? Too small."

She frowned down at Obie.

I had to jump in quick—I didn't want her to think Obie was *useless*, because who knew what she would do with him then? "He needs more training, is all. For now, why don't we trade?"

Before I could offer up myself, Tallis jumped back in again. "Me."

357

"You?" She sneered. "You're a *Rover*."

As if he wouldn't know that.

She eyed him suspiciously. "Why would you offer yourself up for him?"

Tallis shrugged one shoulder. "It's not for him. It's for Faolan. Why do you think she brought me?"

Miss Honeywell blinked hard at him. *"She?"*

Tallis's expression blanked, trying hard not to show a reaction to her question. It was too late, though.

"Mister Faolan, huh?" She gave another eerie cackle. "Did Gideon get anything right about you?"

"No, ma'am."

She sneered at Dillard again, her eyes wild. "How could I have been so wrong about him?" She seemed to be talking to herself now, momentarily forgetting we were there. "I let him shame me. To get closer to the light of our God. I gave him *everything*. And he's *nothing*."

We were losing her. I had to bring her back to us, get Obie free. "Forget Dillard," I said, leaving his title off on purpose. "You don't need him. You need me. Let Obie go." I put my hand on Tallis's shoulder. "Take the gift I brought. For you. All for you. Then I'll show you how the ritual *should* go."

Her grip loosened on Obie as she considered this. She needed another nudge.

Jesse cleared his throat. "Ms. Honeywell? Why don't I bring you this Rover, huh? Take Obie off your hands?"

She melted into a beatific expression, her fondness for Jesse not diminished, even being full to the gullet with whatever potions she'd taken. "Such good manners, Jesse."

"Yes, ma'am." He kept the ax loose by his side, not bringing it to her attention, as he clasped Tallis's arm and drew him up along the wall of the chapel, coming up the opposite side from where the cave cat was.

As they got close, Miss Honeywell focused on Jesse, her grip loosening on Obie. A bud of hope blossomed in my chest. Maybe this would work out the way we wanted.

Just as they got close enough to make the trade, Miss Honeywell pulled back, holding the little boy against her. "No. Wait." Her eyes darted between us, her brow furrowed. "Not yet." She pointed the knife blade at me. "Do the ritual first. Show me your trick. We'll make the exchange when it's time for the sacrifice."

The bud withered and died, the petals of hope falling down my chest and crumbling to dust. Blast it all.

And now I had to think of a trick. I had no idea how I'd finished the ritual beyond stabbing Stuckley, and that wasn't really a trick that would work twice. What else had I done? What did I have to work with? *Think, Faolan!* I was a Kelly. A Kelly should be able to skip circles around the likes of Miss Nettie Honeywell.

I caught sight of the piano. Now, my piano playing was only a hair above disrespectful. It wouldn't do me any favors here. But on top of the piano was a fiddle.

"Music," I drawled, adopting a confident swagger. "That's what the ritual needs."

Miss Honeywell's face twisted in confusion, so I plowed ahead, not letting her think about it too hard. "That's how I got Chirp here. I added music to the ritual."

"I heard you were a fair fiddle player," she admitted grudgingly.

I stiffened. Miss Honeywell always was good at getting my back up. "Fair? *Fair?* Why, Miss Honeywell, I can coax a song so pretty from those strings as could make a wood thrush die of envy."

"So prideful," Miss Honeywell said, clucking her tongue, and for a second, she sounded like her old self.

I shrugged. "Ain't pride if it's true, is it?" I didn't wait for the answer. "Tallis, can you play the piano?" I'd played with Tallis before. That would work best, especially since I didn't like him so close to Ms. Honeywell and that knife.

He grimaced, shaking his head.

"I can play," Dai Lo said. "Well enough, anyway." She tilted her head up at Will. "Can you take over for me here? Put pressure on the wound?"

Will nodded, taking her place but keeping an eye on Nettie.

I moved slowly to the piano, not wanting to startle Miss Honeywell and her knife hand.

"Hurry up," Miss Honeywell snapped. "We don't have all night."

I wondered if the night part mattered, if she was ashamed to have the sunlight touch her ritual, like it was the eye of her all-seeing god, and she didn't want him to know what she was up to.

Dai Lo met me at the piano. She perched on the seat, blood-stained hands holding steadily over the keys as she stretched her fingers some and played a few notes. I freed the fiddle from the case, taking a second to tune it. When Miss Honeywell gave an impatient snort, I glared at her. "You want to go into the ritual with an off-key instrument? Do you know what that will summon?"

She dipped her chin, reluctantly pulling together her patience.

I settled my fiddle into position and thought furiously about what I should play. I could make something up, shooting for a song that sounded mystical and eerie. A song that sounded like it could reach out and tear a hole in the worlds.

I reckoned it would be a bit hard for Dai Lo to follow on that.

I remembered the cave. What had I sung to Chirp? Surely I'd called to him then as much as he'd been calling to me. Had it mattered *what* I'd been singing, or just that I'd been singing at all? I couldn't remember what I'd sung. What I could remember was the soul-wrenching loneliness that I now realized had been Chirp's.

I watched Dillard's cave cat for a moment and wondered what it was feeling. That same loneliness, stuck in a strange world? No—or not quite. Maybe at first. I had to remember that the cave cat had been stuck with Dillard. A pushy, domineering fella bent on his own righteousness. The cat wasn't straining at its tether, trying to take a bite out of us. No, with Dillard unconscious, probably bleeding to death, it was acting like Chirp now, only a sick and tired version.

What song would I want to hear if I was the cave cat? That thought called a tune to my fingertips, and I felt my lips curve up at the ends. It was an old Rover song, a lover's song, about homecoming and forgiveness. Miss Honeywell was going to hate it.

Perfect.

"You know 'Raina's Lament'?" I whispered to Dai Lo.

She frowned, her nose wrinkled. "I don't think so."

Oh, well. "I'll start it. See if you can jump in."

I closed my eyes and let the music take me, pairing my voice with the sweet notes of the fiddle. *"There once was a woman named Raina, and a fierce beauty was she. Full of pride and the hope of her people, for her fate, she took to the sea."*

The lament was a bittersweet tune, full of longing and regret, though it had a surprisingly happy ending. Raina had been lost from her people, ending up in a battle, doing things she regretted and felt ashamed of.

"Finally home, no longer to roam, she sailed back into town. But with bloodied hands and a heavy heart, she'd known that she let them down." When Raina went home to her love, she'd felt she didn't deserve them, with such blood-covered hands. Her love welcomed her, forgave her, and they built a new life together. In true Rover fashion, there was a second ditty telling of their marriage and adventures that was actually quite bawdy. It was one of my favorites.

About halfway through the song, Dai Lo joined me. Then from behind me, from the other side of the chapel, Tallis's voice floated out over the pews, blending seamlessly with the music, three parts becoming one. My heart rejoiced. Gone was the heavy sadness of the day, the death, the grief. The fear. The music washed them from me, much like Raina's love had done for her.

It was a momentary respite, like I'd been swimming through a rough river and temporarily found a log to rest my weight on. Any second, the river would snatch it away from me, but for this moment I could breathe. The music flowed out from us, comforting, welcoming listeners with open arms.

I felt Dillard die, because much like Stuckley, it triggered whatever strange ritual they'd been conducting.

I finished the song and opened my eyes.

It was different than it had been in the cave because the church was lit up with candles. I could see what was happening this time. There, at the front of the chapel, where the sun mural had been, was a ragged hole.

It was as if a cave mouth had appeared from nowhere, leading to a mysterious and unknowable place. I couldn't see much through it, but I could smell something wet and marshy and hear strange calls from unknown birds. Or at least, I thought they were birds.

Miss Honeywell shrieked in triumph. "Mine. Mine!" She danced in place, yanking Obie about like he was a rag doll. Her face glowed in the candlelight, her expression the same as when we'd sung praise songs in this very chapel. Beatific. Ecstatic.

Distracted.

"Now!" I shouted, and though we'd discussed no plan—how could we?—everyone moved at once, jumping in whatever manner they saw fit. They were of such like minds in this, however, that even if we'd had time to orchestrate something, I don't think we could have moved more smoothly.

Jesse leapt forward, dropping the ax and snatching Obie away as Tallis kicked the blade out of Miss Honeywell's hand. The knife spun across the floor, landing close to the tethered cave cat. Both Tallis and Jesse kept moving, using what speed they had to split away from Miss Honeywell. She hovered, unsure who to follow first, her weapon or her sacrifice?

She went for her weapon.

Chirp beat her there, standing over the knife, snarling in such a way that I was reminded that at heart he was a fearsome thing when he wanted to be.

Miss Honeywell froze, hovering between the two snarling cave cats. She focused on the tethered one, her face dreamy and unconcerned. "The ritual is done now. You're mine," she crooned, leaning forward, her good hand outstretched.

The cave cat roared, bucking against the tether, and Miss Honeywell jerked away, suddenly wary. As she stepped back, a shot rang out, the staccato sound echoing in the acoustics of the chapel. Red bloomed on her shoulder, reminding me of a red poppy, the petals unfurling for the sun.

Miss Honeywell staggered back, hand going to her shoulder.

I dropped my fiddle as Dai Lo darted up from the piano. She ran to Jesse, probably to check Obie over and see if he needed help. Dai Lo was a healer, and that was always her first impulse.

I was not. I had no interest in healing Miss Nettie Honeywell. I leapt over the pews, heading for Chirp.

Tallis beat me, scooping the ax up and running to the tethered cave cat.

My heart skipped a beat, fear making me shout. But this was Tallis, and I should have trusted him.

The ax came down, splitting the tether easily. "Go!" He

pointed at the ragged hole, the cave growing hazier by the second. I had no idea how long the ritual would last. I needed to make my move while I could.

Leaping over the last pew, I slammed into Miss Honeywell with all my force. She fell back, mouth a wide O as she moved from our world and into the other, falling into the ragged hole in the wall. She hit the cave floor with a thud, crying out as the landing jarred her wound.

Will stepped forward, pistol ready, steadily advancing. Jesse stood to the side, blocking Dai Lo and Obie from harm. The cave cat lurched like it was going to move to the cave and then hesitated, before sitting on its haunches. Chirp made a low, sad noise.

Will kept advancing. "As I see it, you've got two choices, Nettie Honeywell. I can fire this pistol again. This time, I can promise you I won't miss." He was about ten feet away now, so close to that other world. "Or you can turn around, you can run, and you can try your hand at life in the land you so desperately wanted to reach."

"But . . ." The hand that pressed to her wounded shoulder shook. She took in the cave around her before looking over her shoulder into the darkness. Eerie bird calls split the air, sounding gut-chilling for all that they were far off. "I don't belong here. This isn't . . ." She sniffled. "I'll be alone."

"You'll be facing the exact same fate you wished upon Chirp here." I jutted my chin out stubbornly and she flinched. "I can't think of anything more just."

She wilted, the fight going out of her. Then she straightened up to her full height.

"Fine, but you just remember this, Faolan Kelly. I don't sink easy. I will rise up. My faith has not deserted me." Her eyes flashed with either confidence or a mighty fine bravado. I don't know that it mattered which one it was.

"To my mind, you deserted your faith," Will said. "But as far as I see it, that's a never-you-mind. Get on, now. You've made your choice."

"You'll see," she said, her voice fierce, her eyes hard. "You'll see."

Then she turned around and fled into the darkness.

She'd made her choice.

No one went after her. We all knew that the real options weren't staying here or going there, but between a quick death at the hands of the gunslinger and a slow death at the hands of a likely hostile landscape.

I didn't care either way.

My heart had no room for the likes of Nettie Honeywell.

CHAPTER TWENTY-NINE

—✳—

THE CAVE CAT WOULDN'T GO THROUGH THE TEAR IN OUR
worlds, and its chance to go home was rapidly diminishing.
The edges of the portal were hazing, the line between the
cave and the wall softening.

I squatted before Chirp, though my body was fiercely complaining about the movement. It wasn't too long ago that I'd
almost died, after all. Giving in to my exhaustion, I sat, before
brushing my fingers along his face. "You could go, too, you
know?" I tipped my head toward the wall. "Go home." The
words rasped in my throat. Chirp leaving would make me
heartsore. I'd grown attached to having him around already.

But if that's what he wanted, I would help him. The grief
would be a small cost for his happiness.

Chirp stared at the opening for a long moment. Then he
let out a low whistle. He bumped his forehead against my
chin. A tentative emotion slipped through me. Chirp wanted
to stay, but it was my choice, too. He understood on some
level that him being here with me would make my life a bit
more complicated.

I scratched behind his ear. "I like complicated. It's never boring." He purred a rusty, grating sound, and I laughed.

Chirp glanced at the other cave cat, yowling plaintively.

It stared at the fading portal, an expression of naked longing in its eyes, but its feet didn't move. Tallis reached out, moving slowly so it wouldn't startle. He hummed the Rover song "Raina's Lament" in his soothing voice as he carefully undid the part of the tether that still hung from around the cave cat's neck.

Lost and sad, the cave cat turned to Tallis, who stroked along the creature's jaw with a thumb. "This world has treated you sorely. Maybe you're not ready to go home. Maybe you think you can't."

The cave cat chirped softly at him. Tallis sat so he could comfort it better.

"Why isn't it leaving?" I asked quietly.

"*She*," Tallis said absently, not looking away as he stroked a comforting hand over the feline face. "If that's what you want, you'll be welcome here. We'll do what we can to make up for the wrongs done against you." He dropped his hand. "But I don't know if we'll ever be able to reopen this door." He turned to Chirp. "This might be your last chance."

Chirp flopped into my lap, his weight nearly bowling me over. His choice appeared easily made.

The other cave cat took longer. But after a few long moments, she lay down, putting her head on Tallis's leg, and sighed, eyes closing. Tallis put his hand on her head.

Something in the air snapped, a weight, a heaviness to the atmosphere that I hadn't noticed until it left, evaporating in an instant. The symbols on the wall glowed with a powerful light, burning onto the backs of my eyelids, until they were too much to look at.

When my vision cleared, the symbols were gone, and Tallis was looking at the other cave cat with an expression I couldn't read. He reached a hand out toward me as far as he could, holding it in the air.

I didn't have to take his hand. I had a feeling that if I didn't, Tallis would accept it, but it would hurt him somehow. It wasn't a big thing, but there are moments in this world where it becomes a weighted action, that reaching out. The kind that can shift lifetimes, rattle the chains of existence, or fracture lives into so many pieces that they become irreconcilable.

A broken vase you cannot mend.

Or you can reach back, put your hand in theirs, and make right what had gone so terribly wrong.

This was one of those times. "Your people don't want me around."

Tallis made a tired sound. "You're my people, too."

My hand was bloodstained, my nails ragged. It was a hand that knew hard work, toil, and very little in the way of peace. It had been steeped in the blood of my enemies, which sounded a mite dramatic to my ear.

I reckoned I was a bit tired of blood.

And I'd lost so much already.

I ignored his offering, pushing myself up, wobbling slightly on my feet. Tallis dropped his hand, his jaw so tight that his scar stood out in relief. He watched with those fathomless eyes of his while I hobbled over, Chirp on my heels. Like a graceless puppet that had suddenly lost its strings, I collapsed next to him and slid an arm around his waist, careful not to jostle the other cave cat.

The faintest smile tugged at the corner of his mouth, his eyes lightening once again. He wrapped an arm around me, kissing my temple, before he heaved a sigh into my hair. "I knew if I was patient, you'd eventually come to me, Little Fox."

"It's only because I'm bone-weary," I mumbled, but we both knew I was lying. Tallis had worn me down—no, that wasn't right. That brought to mind the way a bird will peck away at a tree until the bark frays and its prize is revealed. An action that rewards one and destroys the other.

Tallis would never tear me apart like that. He'd worn me down like a long spring rain hitting parched dust, relentless and inevitable, but soaking into the dirt, bringing forth green and budding things. Something that rearranged the very configuration of the soil at your feet, sowing the promise of growth and good harvest. In a way that didn't diminish but expanded.

Exhaustion had made me poetic, it seemed.

Tallis sighed as if my response had been a blade he was expecting, which made me feel loutish.

I burrowed my head into his shoulder and grumbled, "Thank you." He didn't say anything in response, but his arm around me tightened.

We sat like that, the room quiet except for Obie's snuffling sobs, and watched the opening dissolve.

A few minutes later, the tear closed.

It was done.

—※—

The rest of the night was such a hazy mess that I stumbled through like I was half gone on my Pops's whiskey. I'm sure that, had I been left to my own devices, I would have slumped somewhere against a tree and left myself as carrion for the wild boars.

But I wasn't alone. I was herded by Jesse, scolded into movement by Dai Lo. Nudged by Chirp. Mocked into action by Will's dry comments. Half dragged by Tallis while the other cave cat watched us with solemn eyes. It was as if I were the smallest duckling in the brood and they were all harassing me into place.

I couldn't explain why, but it made me feel warm, like my heart had stretched until it filled every bit of space under my skin.

My eyes kept closing of their own accord. Before long, I was being tucked into blankets near a fire, the gentle murmur of a collection of people around me. Heat banked me at both sides, and it was a feeling that was instantly familiar, though I shouldn't be used to it already. Chirp was stretched along my front, Tallis at my back. His arm snaked around my waist, his hand splayed across my stomach.

I wasn't used to being held so close. I would have thought that I'd hate it. Akin to being smothered or trapped. But that wasn't how it felt. It felt like being held snug and tight. Like I was a cherished thing you wanted to clutch to you and not let go.

I had no idea what I mumbled, but Tallis's response was

clear as a newly minted bell, the words carved from the musical tones of the Rover tongue. "I will hold you as close as my own heart, always, if you'll let me, Little Fox."

I'm not sure what I would have said to that—what could you say to such a thing? I'm sure I didn't know. But I was asleep a moment later, lulled by Tallis's soft laugh in my ear and Chirp's warm purr against my chest.

I woke up in the last place I expected—Tallis and Zara's tent in the Rover camp. Zara sat across from me, a steaming tin mug in one hand, her posture loose, her gaze focused unapologetically on me.

From the slant of light gilding the tent flaps, the sun was well and truly up. My bones ached, my skin itched with the dry blood I'd been too tired to deal with—though I seemed to remember Tallis wiping off my face and hands at one point. My throat was a desert with no hope for rain. But since a Rover's favorite watch was a broken one, I didn't bother asking Zara what time it was.

I pushed myself up with a wince.

Zara snorted, set down her mug, and fetched the kettle that had been nestled above the coals. She poured the steaming water into a tin mug that had been hiding next to her on the floor. I took it carefully, everything in me aching and screaming out.

"You look like something that died, came back, and is thinking about dying again."

I blew on the mug, my hopes for coffee dashed. Tea. I liked tea normally, but I had a powerful thirst for coffee this morning. I also suspected this tea was one of Anna's creations, which meant it would be medicinal first, with flavor not a consideration whatsoever. And I was right.

"All of it," Zara said without an ounce of sympathy. "Keeping you alive seems like a full-time job."

"It's no one's job but my own," I said, bristling.

Her cup paused at her lips as she stared at me, her brows winging up. "Do you honestly think that?"

"Be very careful how you answer that question, Faolan Kelly," Dai Lo said as she stepped into the tent, her tone teacher-firm. Jesse stepped in behind her, a faintly amused expression on his face.

"Yes, ma'am," I said automatically, sipping my tea. Ugh. Vile.

Dai Lo eyed me carefully, shaking her head at what she saw. "Sometimes I wonder at how you're still alive with all your fingers and toes." She fluttered her hand at me. "Finish your tea. Jesse has some clothes for you."

"Before you ask, 'What's wrong with the clothes I have on?' I would like to remind you that you are covered in blood and reek of evil workings," Zara said dryly. "Your clothes need to be burned."

"How do you do it?" I asked.

Zara tilted her head, a movement that reminded me so much of her brother. "Do what?"

"Know what I'm going to say." I braced myself for another

sip of tea, knowing full well I wasn't leaving this tent until the cup was empty. "Your brother does it. I was starting to wonder if he could read minds."

Mischief lit Zara's eyes. "Wouldn't that be a lovely power?"

I did not think so, but I didn't say as much.

"Sadly," Zara said, "we don't have such a gift. You're just incredibly easy to read."

"Faolan?" Jesse asked, startled.

Zara waved a hand around her face. "Every thought, it's right here for her."

Jesse shook his head. "Maybe to you and yours, but the rest of us have a hell of a time."

"I'm very mysterious," I said, examining my shirt. "It's not that bad, surely."

"Remember when the skunk got you?" Zara asked.

"Yeah."

"This is worse." Zara never did mince words.

"I can't smell anything," I complained.

Zara motioned to my cup. "To the bottom, please. Then a bath."

I downed several gulps, trying to muscle past the taste. "Where's Chirp?"

Zara shrugged.

"Down by the river, I think," Dai Lo said, nudging Jesse forward. "Clothes, Jesse."

I traded my now-empty mug for the pile of clothes and fled the tent before Zara could make any more observations I didn't want to hear.

The sun was bright and high in the sky, like the day had woken up and decided suddenly to be spring. It wasn't hot, but the air lacked the frigid chill of winter that had been dogging my days.

A handful of people were down on the riverbank—folks fetching water and washing clothes, and a few youngins wading along under the watchful eyes of older children. I got several disinterested waves, despite the fact that I must have been a mite terrifying. I walked away from the busy shore, over to the place where Tallis had bathed the skunk off me.

As if my thoughts had summoned him, I spotted Tallis sprawled out on the grass. Both of the cave cats were spread out next to him, soaking up the sun. Chirp greeted me with a sleepy whistle, his tail flicking lazily among the clover.

Tallis gave me slitted eyes.

"I'm aware that I look a fright," I gritted, feeling twice as itchy as I'd been in the tent. "Your sister already gave me an earful on the topic."

Tallis shaded his eyes with one hand. "That wasn't what I was thinking at all." He levered himself to his feet, all easy grace and fluid movements. I could never figure out how Tallis made even the slightest gesture look like a dance.

"Oh," I said, holding my clothes awkwardly. "What were you thinking, then?"

He answered with a smile, tight-lipped and curled at the ends like spring fiddleheads. "Let's get you washed."

I felt the flush come up from my toes.

Delight lit Tallis's eyes. "Like a sunrise. I always wonder . . ." He stepped forward, hooked a finger into the waist of my trousers, and pulled until I was almost touching him. His next words hit my ears like a soft breath. "How far down that charming color goes."

I squeaked.

He laughed softly, and he was so close I could feel each exhalation. "Should we find out?"

I had no idea how he could say such things, even now, when I was such a wretched creature. He was a flirt, that was why. Came as natural as breathing. Probably didn't mean a single word. Just how he talked.

I didn't like to think that. Gave me an unmoored feeling I didn't care for. So it was with a stubborn chin that I looked up. Ready for a dustup if need be.

The naked wonder on his face made me freeze. How could anyone look at me like that—as if I was something worthy of a dragon's hoard?

"What a miracle you are, Little Fox." His arms slid around my waist, seemingly unaware that I was filthy.

"I am?" My brow furrowed. Couldn't make heads or tails of Tallis sometimes. "Zara said—" I cut the words off with my teeth. I didn't want to sound like I was setting my lure for sweet words.

He ducked down so our eyes were level. "What did my sister say?"

"Well," I said slowly. "She said it was amazing that I was

still kicking with all my toes, and she might have implied that I was a full-time job."

Tallis hummed thoughtfully. "You're a challenge. That's the honest truth."

I started to push away, but Tallis tightened his arms, keeping me in place with irritating ease.

"Quiet down, Little Fox. Be still." Quick as a wink, he dipped forward and bit my ear. Not hard, just enough to catch my attention. "I *like* a challenge."

"You do?" I couldn't keep the skepticism from my words.

He nodded seriously. "With you, Little Fox, life will always be interesting, I think. You're a gift. Trouble. I would like nothing more, I think, than for you to be *my* trouble."

I looked at him in amazement. "Some people," I said slowly, shaking my head, "have no sense."

He laughed with his whole body, burying his face in my neck. "As you say, Little Fox. How about we get you cleaned up now?"

"I do stink," I admitted.

"Like a gutted thing left out for the crows," he said gently. "But you carry my heart, anyway."

"Absolutely no sense."

CHAPTER THIRTY

·—✳—·

IT TOOK TWICE AS LONG AS IT SHOULD HAVE FOR ME TO get clean. Blood had crusted beneath my nails—I even had some in my hair. Tallis's hands liked to wander, which was fine by me, as it turns out I liked what he found. My hands had a bit of a mind of their own as well.

Tallis was ticklish in some surprising places.

After my bath, I sat by a fire with my friends—Anna, Zara, Jesse, Dai Lo, and Tallis—and ate anything handed to me. Sergio, Tallis's uncle, puffed on his pipe companionably. Chirp and the other cave cat were sniffing at the tobacco smoke curiously. No one seemed much bothered by their presence, which was perplexing. But my stomach was right wroth with me, and it had good reason. I'd abused it abominably. I focused on filling it and left my questions for later.

The Rover camp was fair to bursting. The entire Settlement, what was left of it, was inside its borders. Aside from Will, Miss Moon was the only adult left. They had a lot of littles between them to wrangle.

I'd never seen Miss Moon so happy, having all those children to manage. I'd also never seen her with her hair down. Miss Moon would never be a beautiful woman in a conventional sense, but seeing her now, how fiercely she loved the children in her care, her face relaxed, she wasn't plain, either. It was like she'd been coals and someone had blown on the embers, lighting her up inside.

It was a look that suited her so well that it made you realize she was handsome in her own way. From the way Will was gazing at her, I reckoned he'd figured it out miles before I did.

"What happens now?" Jesse asked, his arm around Dai Lo.

Sergio tapped his pipe over the fire, his expression grave. "No one is going back there." He paused like he expected us to argue, but no one did. I didn't think a soul among us wanted to return to the Settlement. He nodded, tucking his pipe away into his vest pocket. "We'll let the children gather their things, gather any animals, then we're burning it to the ground."

"It's a cursed place," Anna said. "We can't let someone go there and try again. We'll let the wild take it back."

I agreed wholeheartedly. No good could come from that place. None at all.

The Rovers didn't want to dally, so that afternoon I gathered up any of the older kids who could help, to pack up any goods we needed. Many Rovers came as well and aided us with horse and cart. Miss Moon took her apothecary. We packed up the foods in the cellar. We grabbed clothes, candles, dry goods, dishes. Anything we could use or sell.

I made sure Tallis got Dillard's trunk. Will would try and find the owners of the objects as best as he was able. The rest of the spoils we would divide and sell them for coin. Give some to the Rovers, some to Miss Moon to take care of the youngins. They'd have to start over, and that was a lot of mouths to feed.

The Rovers kept the smaller youngins at the camp while we worked. They didn't need to see more blood, more bodies.

They would have nightmares enough.

The moon had risen, the sunlight gone, by the time we were done. Once we were sure everyone was out and away, Tallis took the old blackout lantern and tossed it into the chapel. It shattered on the floor, flames blooming outward like water flowing to shore. All that gilt and pretty burned like any other wood. Dillard's dreams going up in smoke, a final gift to his god.

We dropped torches in the empty henhouse, the bunkhouses, the kitchen. Then fell back, far enough away for safety's sake, and watched the Settlement burn.

I sat there watching until the palisades fell, the light dimming the stars.

Tallis stood there with me, an arm around my shoulders. "What will you do now?"

"I don't rightly know," I said. I'd had a plan, and it had seemed a good one at the time, but it no longer had the same shine to it after everything I'd been through.

It was like I'd tried to put on my favorite pair of boots only to find them too tight and pinching. "I could . . ." The word drifted off, my gumption evaporating for a moment. The problem was I knew what I wanted, but I was terrified to ask for it. A scaredy-cat, that's what I was.

Kellys don't run. I sucked in a breath. "I could stay with you."

Tallis stilled. "Oh?"

I turned around in his arms to look up at him, examining his face. He didn't seem unhappy with my suggestion, more like he was waiting for something. And I realized that I was an absolute coward sometimes. Tallis had been very forthcoming in regard to how he felt about me.

I hadn't done the same.

Well. Never said a Kelly didn't give as good as they got.

"I want to stay with you," I said.

"How long?" Tallis said carefully.

"I was thinking," I said, my words just as careful, "that maybe, and this is just an estimate, mind, but maybe I'd stay until forever or as close to forever as we could get . . . if you want that." He let me stew like that for a moment, my own figurative hand extended for him to take.

He treated me to that slow, easy smile. His cat smile. "I think that estimate sounds very fine. Very fine indeed."

I nodded, then buried my face into his chest. "You have my whole heart, Tallis."

"I know, Little Fox," he murmured soothingly as he stroked my hair. "That was very difficult for you, wasn't it?"

"Like pulling actual teeth."

He laughed.

—*—

Having taken care of the immediate things, we had a grander conundrum to solve now. Or two, rather. First, I had to find out if Tallis's people would take us, what with us being abominations and all. Turns out, Tallis was as bound to the other cave cat as I was to Chirp. He considered calling her Raina, after the song, as she had so much in common with the hero, but decided she needed a fresh start. In the end he called her Hani, which meant "a restful place" in Rover.

So before I solved the other conundrum, I cornered Sergio and Zara and asked what they and their people thought about me and Chirp staying with them now.

Sergio shrugged. "You, we could banish, no problem. But Tallis?" Another shrug. "None of us want to do that. And if we have one, why not two?"

"What he's saying," Zara continued, in that dry way of hers, "is that you may be abominations now, but you're *our* abominations."

"Alright," I said with a sharp nod. I stuck my hand out. "I would be honored to be one of your abominations."

Zara patted my cheek, ignoring my hand. "Of course you would."

We couldn't all stay, of course. Or at least Miss Moon felt the youngins needed somewhere steady after all of the nightmares, and while I thought the Rovers were a solid folk, they were also a wandering folk.

And after much discussion with Jesse, Dai Lo, and Tallis, I came up with a solution.

"You're giving us your land?" Will said, tipping back his hat. "Faolan, it's yours. You've fought like hell for that land."

"I know," I said. "But here's how I see it. The land will go back to the Rovers eventually—it should be theirs anyhow.

And if you take it, the mayor and his underlings can't get their grubby little paws on it. Not now, not ever."

Miss Moon shook her head, bemused. "But, Faolan, where will you go?"

I grinned at her. "I'll travel with them. You'll take care of Pops's land until we decide to give it back to the Rovers. You'll need to build a bunkhouse for the children, but it's a nice piece of land. Enough there for you to raise the whole lot, Miss Moon."

She turned soft eyes on me. "You're a good soul, Mr. Kelly."

"I reckon it should be Miss Kelly, now that the danger has passed," I said thoughtfully. "Or Faolan. Unless I'm in trouble?"

"As you like, then, Miss Kelly. Faolan." She shook her head, her eyes full of tears. "Then I'd better be Esther, don't you think?" She wrapped me in a fierce hug. She smelled like lavender. "Oh, bless you, Faolan Kelly."

"And I figured," I said slyly as I stepped back, "you'll need help keeping the riffraff out. I don't trust that mayor any further than I could throw him." I handed them a bag of the treasures we'd gleaned from Dillard's hoard. "In that case, I suspect you'll need a gunslinger with you."

I rocked back on my heels. "Turns out, I know a pretty good one."

She looked at Will, a question in her eyes. "I'm not sure he'll want to stay put, Faolan," she said gently.

Will doffed his hat, holding it in front of him. "I think I'd like to stay a spell if you'd have me. I'd like to rest my feet by the same fire every night."

"You sure?" she asked.

He put his hat back on firmly. "Never more sure of anything in my entire life."

After a few days of rest, I borrowed a horse from the Rovers and rode alongside Tallis, Jesse, and Dai Lo. They'd be staying with us most of the time. The Rovers appreciated Jesse's drawing skills, and Dai Lo had managed to get Anna to agree to apprentice her. She was going to get to be a healer, just like she wanted.

We'd all visit Pops's farm to check up on everyone now and again, but otherwise we'd go with the Rovers for the foreseeable future. I reckoned I'd cobbled together this family, and I wasn't about to lose track of any of them.

We made quite a spectacle, riding back into New Retienne. We were a slow parade of children down the main street, a few carts, and a handful of Rovers along the edges. A few of the matrons came out, some with a hand placed over their throats or mouths, but all had wide eyes. It wasn't too long until the mayor himself was in the streets. His face turned red, and his eyes bugged at the sight of us.

"What is the meaning of this?" Mr. Clarke spluttered.

I leaned down in my saddle with a feline grin. "It's a fine day, isn't it, Mr. Clarke? Yes, very fine. I'm sure you'll be thrilled to know I found Pops's deed." Technically, I *had* found it in Dillard's trunk.

His face lit up. "Did you, now?"

"I did," I said, pulling out Pops's watch. "Can you believe it was in his pocket watch this whole time?" I shook my head slowly. "I would lose my own head if it weren't nailed on."

He puffed out his chest, about to jump into one of his endless speeches, but I plowed ahead like I hadn't noticed. "You were right. It was too much for my young mind."

"It was?" He straightened. "It was, yes. I'm glad you saw reason—"

"So I gave it back to the Rovers," I said easily. "It was their land, really." I waved at Esther and Will. "These two will be managing it, of course. New Retienne needs some new blood, I reckon, so here's a whole gaggle of it."

The mayor was speechless. It was a good look on him.

I sat high in my saddle. "Yes, sir, I think you'll agree it's a perfect solution." I looked at Tallis. "Ain't that right, Tallis?"

"That's right, Faolan." Now it was his turn to lean down in the saddle, his face set into menacing lines. "Naturally, we'll be here regular, my Rover clan. *All* of us. Just to make sure, you understand? That the children are doing okay. We take care of our children, we do."

The mayor spluttered again, making little sense, but sounding in the affirmative. We'd already stopped listening.

"You ready to see Pops's farm?"

Tallis clucked at Neev. "I can think of nothing I'd like more."

"Excellent." I tipped my hat at the folks of New Retienne. "You have a good day, now, you hear?" Then I clucked at my own horse, pulling up to Tallis's side. I left New Retienne behind me, as it always would be from now until forever, and rode into the future.

Not alone.

Never alone ever again.

I'd put down my roots, and no one, *no one*, would rip them out this time.

★ ACKNOWLEDGMENTS ★

THE JOURNEY FOR THIS BOOK WAS . . . ODD. WITH EVERY book, I'm always a little surprised they actually make it from thought to page to physical book, but this one especially so. *Red in Tooth and Claw* exists because I got mad at a movie. Specifically, a Western horror. Occasionally I watch a film where I see potential for a story that the film doesn't deliver, and because I am the way that I am, I end up having a hard time sleeping because my brain is trying to fix the plot. The Western horror was like that. I sat down to watch it with Man Friend (also known as my husband, but anyone on my socials knows I don't often call him that) because we both enjoy horror, Westerns, and have a deep and abiding love for the actor Clancy Brown, who plays the lead.

For the most part, I liked the movie, but the ending . . . I got mad at the ending. (I understand why they chose the one they did, but I don't like it.) So I kept thinking about it and complaining to Man Friend. And then I thought, *This kind of story would work pretty well as a YA book.*

The next day, a few of the opening lines popped into my head, Faolan's voice strong and ready, and so I started writing. The story in your hands is wildly different than the movie we watched, but that's where it all started. So I'd like to thank everyone who made that film, especially Clancy Brown, for inspiring me to write the story that gave me Faolan. (Seriously, no disrespect to Mr. Brown or his work. He's a gem.)

I would also like to thank my own Pops, James McBride, for lending me one of his many nicknames and making me watch so many Westerns as a kid. And of course, to my family, who do their best to support me in my many strange endeavors. Big thanks to everyone at Putnam for helping put this book together, and to Kristie Radwilowicz and Evangeline Gallagher for the stunning cover.

In some ways, this book was a book of transitions. It started with my editor Ari Lewin and my agent Jason Anthony at Massie & McQuilkin, and it ended with my editor Polo Orozco and my agent Cheyenne Faircloth at Handspun Literary. I've been very lucky to work with such amazing people who listen and support me when I say, "So, I've got kind of a weird story . . . What do you think?" And then tell them a mess of details that, frankly, don't sound like much of a story at all. That's trust, friend.

Massive and unwieldy thanks to Marissa Meyer, Kendare Blake, Rori Shay, Sajni Patel, Alison Kimble, Chelsea Mueller, Kristen Simmons, Molly Harper, Jeanette Battista, and Martha Brockenbrough for all of the writing dates, cookies, and, in Martha's case, constant grammar questions. To Team Bogwitch, Sarah Keliher, Anje Monte Calvo, and Haiden Lisenby, for answering many weird and random research questions. It's nice to have friends who won't blink twice when I say things like "Okay, but what does boneset smell like?"

I would like to offer thanks and gratitude to Keli O'Neill for lending her thoughtful and helpful comments, which made this a better, richer story. Any errors are of course my own. To all of my Patreon subscribers and editor Mel (Barnes) for the support, love, and helping me keep the lights on. To Vlad Verano, who I know will make me killer swag for this book because he always does. And finally, to all of the friends, family, readers, librarians, booksellers, and book bloggers out there who have helped make this happen. May fair winds greet you always.